# KISS OF ASH

## C.J. ARCHER

WWW.CJARCHER.COM

# CHAPTER 1

*1583 – Berkshire, England*

*S*he would kill him.

Pippa Ingleside crumpled the documents in her fist and slammed them down on the desk, rattling quills and ink horns and her own fragile nerves. The swine! The thieving scoundrel! She'd known he was a black-hearted cur but to steal on such a grand scale was low indeed. She wouldn't have believed her uncle capable of it if the evidence wasn't written on those pages. And from his own niece too.

She flattened out the documents and scanned the figures on the first one again, then the second and third just to be sure. Anger rose with each page so that by the time she read the last one, she was almost blinded by sheer rage and the frustrating hopelessness of it all. It had been five years since she'd felt the same spirit-crushing emotions. Five long years that had slowly and consistently worn her down, drip by drip, until all that was left was a hole where something solid had been.

Then, as now, there was nothing she could do. That realization crushed her more than anything else. As Simon's ward she was completely at his mercy. As his prisoner, even more so. She could do nothing about his theft. She couldn't go to the authorities, couldn't appeal to another family member even if there were any.

Not long after her arrival, he'd locked her inside the confines of The Grange with only old Widow Dawson for company during the afternoons. But even that had been denied her after Pippa's two unsuccessful escape attempts. Although she'd never stopped looking for a means to get away, never stopped cursing her predicament, she'd always longed to know *why*. What did he gain by her trapped presence? He couldn't have been saving her for marriage because he never presented any candidates to her.

But now she knew. The documents had given her the answer.

"What are you doing in here?"

She stood so fast the chair she'd been sitting on fell back with a soft thud onto the rushes. Her uncle, filling the doorway with his bulk, glared at her. She gathered her wits and courage and prepared to confront him.

But he strode into the study and snatched the documents from her hand before she found her voice. "I said, what are you doing?"

He towered over her, anger making him seem bigger. He seethed with it. She'd never seen him so furious and her own rage subsided beneath the unnatural ferocity of his glare. Normally he did everything in such a controlled, cold manner. On the rare occasions he spoke to her, he never so much as raised his voice. He shouted at the servants regularly, even beat them sometimes, but to Pippa he was a silent, morose figure who avoided interacting with her. If it had been different, if he had funneled his infamous rages onto her, she could never have endured the last five years.

"Well?" His ruddy complexion had turned a violent mottled red, a stark contrast to the snow-white of his hair and beard. "Answer me, you stupid girl! What are you doing in *my* study?" He emphasized the "my" by smacking the rolled up pages against the palm of his hand.

"I, I..." Fear made her tongue useless. She watched the pages as they thumped into Simon's hand over and over, like a club he would use to hit something.

Hit her.

No, he wouldn't do it. He'd never laid a finger on her, even when she'd railed at him for weeks after informing her that she could never leave The Grange. Never receive callers, never receive friends. Never receive potential suitors. He hadn't used violence then and he wouldn't use it now, she was sure of it. For some reason, he thought physical force perfectly acceptable with his servants, but not with his niece. She supposed she should be grateful for small mercies. If nothing else, that knowledge gave her the courage to speak now.

"I was looking for some parchment for sketching." It was the truth. Or close to it. She *had* run out of parchment, but she'd been looking for the steward to ask him to fetch more when she realized her ever present guard was asleep and her uncle away for the afternoon. Ordinarily Widow Dawson never let Pippa out of her sight but she'd not turned up thanks to a chest cough that kept her abed. The sudden taste of freedom, and the yearning to discover the reason for her imprisonment, led her to her uncle's study.

"I found those instead." She nodded at the papers in his hand.

"You should never come in here. Ever!" He stepped closer, only an arm's length away. "This is my private study and these are my private papers. Do you understand me?"

"Perfectly." He must think her too dull-witted to have understood what she'd read. But then he had never taken much interest in her, before her father's death and especially after it. How could he possibly have known that her father had ensured his only child received a good education? And with nothing else to do during her imprisonment at The Grange, she'd devoured every book in her uncle's library, even the obscurest Greek poets. Widow Dawson had asked her friends and relations for reading material, but books were difficult to come by in Shelton. Simon's ignorance of his niece's education would prove to be his folly. She had a head for numbers and accounts, something her father had put to good use as his health failed in the year before his death.

"I understand that you have been stealing from me, Uncle." She would not let him get away with it. He might be her uncle

3

and her guardian, but he was taking *her* money, her dowry. She might need it one day. She hadn't completely given up on being rescued by a knight in shining armor, although she had to admit knights, like books, were thin on the ground in Shelton.

"Stealing?" Simon snorted. With his round face and broad nose, the sound made him resemble a pig. "I'm merely taking what I am owed. Keeping you in the manner to which you have become accustomed is a costly business."

"Nonsense! It is clear from those figures that you are taking more than that. Much more. I demand an explanation. No, I demand every last penny be returned to me. With interest." Ha! Let him see what this stupid girl was capable of.

He stared at her. Then he burst into laughter. "Or you'll what?"

She flexed her fingers as an odd tingling sensation warmed them. It seemed to be emanating from deep within where her rage surged like a tide. She forced herself to remain calm. Anger would not solve this situation. It required clear thinking and calculated words. "I will get out of here one day, Uncle. And I can assure you, when I do, I will retrieve everything you owe me."

"With interest?" His laughter ended with snorts. "My girl, you know nothing of the world if you think you will ever get away from me. You seem to forget, you have nowhere to go. No family, no friends, not even the Widow Dawson would help you. She's too afraid of me. Everyone is too afraid of me in this county." He smacked his palm again with the papers.

"You are mistaken," she said with deliberate effort to keep her voice calm. "I have friends. You forget I had a full life before I came here. There are people who would gladly help me." But even as she said it, she could think of only one.

Georgiana. Sweet Georgiana Dale had never given up trying to contact her even though all Pippa's correspondence, in or out, had been confiscated. Nearly two years ago, a sympathetic servant had risked a great deal to smuggle in a letter from Pippa's elderly friend. But it was the only one. There had been nothing since.

"If you manage to get out of The Grange," he went on as if

she'd not spoken, "I can easily hunt you down and drag you back here. You will never leave. You and your land are mine."

The pool of rage surged again but this time she didn't check it. Couldn't. It was too fierce as it rushed through her body, along her arms and burst from her fingertips like bolts of lightning. She wasn't sure how it happened but suddenly the papers in her uncle's hand caught alight.

With a yelp, he dropped them onto the rushes and tried to stamp out the flames with his riding boots. But the pages scattered and Molly the house maid hadn't changed the rushes in too long. They were dry and the flames quickly spread across the floor.

"Fire!" her uncle shouted. "Fetch water! Fire!" He removed his cloak and swatted at the flames but it only served to fan them towards the curtains. "You witch," he yelled at her. "You did this. I'll see you hung for witchcraft, you filthy bitch." He returned to swatting the fire but fell back when the flames swallowed up the curtains.

Pippa watched in a kind of trance but her uncle's accusation was good as a slap to her face. Oh God. She *had* caused the fire. She knew it as clearly as she could feel its heat on her face and smell the smoke.

But how...?

There was no time to consider the answer. The fire was rapidly consuming the study. Servants handed pails of water through the door but their efforts did nothing to dampen the flames. Her uncle had given up trying to put it out and was frantically rummaging through one of his coffers, its edges already smoldering. He shouted orders, barely heard above the roar of the fire, for valuables to be rescued. Servants abandoned their buckets and ran to either do his bidding or save themselves.

The thick smoke stung Pippa's eyes and filled her nose and mouth. Her chest ached. She couldn't breathe. She had to get out.

The door was wide open. Some servants remained to help Simon with his papers and books but most had vanished. No one seemed to take notice of her.

She ran. Out of the study, down two flights of stairs, past scurrying, hysterical servants, to the front door. She would leave through the main entrance this time, no backstairs with her guard on her heels.

No one on her heels at all.

She fled to the stables where grooms led horses out and away from the rapidly spreading fire. She could probably take one in the confusion but she wasn't dressed for riding and she'd not ridden in five years anyway. No doubt one of the frightened creatures would throw her before she even left the estate.

She would have to flee on foot. She changed direction and ran towards the gatehouse, hampered by her skirts. She lifted them and kept running. The steep pitched roof of the gatehouse loomed closer. People from the village streamed past her, carrying buckets and blankets. They jostled her but didn't seem to see her. She was dressed plainly and most had never even met her—no doubt they thought her a frightened servant fleeing to safety.

"Stop her!" Simon's command rose above the confusion.

She looked back. He stood near the stables, his arms full of ledgers and papers, his white lace ruff and cuffs blackened by soot. He kicked one of the serving boys racing past but the lad was too scared or too occupied to stop. Simon swore at him then looked around for someone else but no one seemed aware that their master needed them. Behind him, black smoke billowed from the study windows and two of the adjoining rooms. Servants threw valuable tapestries and painted cloths out of the other windows, but most got trampled beneath frantic feet.

Pippa continued running towards the gatehouse and the arched entrance to the estate. Almost there. Even though she knew Simon could recapture her beyond the gates, she still desperately wanted to reach them, wanted to taste the air on the other side.

"Stop!" Simon again, his voice hoarse. "Get back here, Witch!" When she didn't stop, he shouted, "I'll send the Witch Hunter after you."

She stumbled and fell, tearing her hose and scraping her knee. Simon's threat lingered in the air with the ash and smoke. Despite the warmth of the day, she felt cold to the bone.

*Witch.*

No. Not her. Surely not.

Yet she had caused the fire. She'd felt the force of it gathering within, felt the heat and power flood her body and blast from her fingertips.

Her stomach lurched. She wanted to throw up. There was no doubt—she *was* a witch. But...how?

She had no time to consider the answer to that. Two fat hands clamped down on her shoulders and drew her roughly out of the dirt. She looked up at her uncle and shrank back from his crazed glare. His fingers dug into her skin where shoulders met throat. A little higher and he would strangle her.

Pippa fought down panic and tried to control her breathing. "Let me go!"

"Allow my dear niece to abandon me?" He sneered, as if that were amusing. "Foolish girl." Without warning, he slapped her.

She gasped at the sting but refused to rub her cheek or check if he'd drawn blood with his rings. She wouldn't show weakness. Not to Simon. He fed on it. He wanted it. Her fear only made him feel more powerful and she would rather die than give him what he wanted.

"That was for running off." He raised his hand, laughing like a madman when she flinched in anticipation of the pain. "And this is for burning my house down." His hand curled into a fist.

Instinctively, she lifted her arm to block his blow. But she did more than merely stop him hitting her. With an explosion of power that seemed to emanate from her core, her arm connected with his and he flew through the air, landing some distance away on his back.

Dusty, sooty and sprawled in the dirt like a beggar, he stared up at her, fear imprinted in every feature. He was afraid of her.

Good Lord, the giddiness of it. The sheer pleasure of knowing that *she* could make a man like Simon Rowe afraid. It was intoxicating, heady and thoroughly exhilarating, like riding extremely fast in rough terrain.

But also very, very dangerous.

Thankfully no one had seen but she needed to be more careful in the future. If she didn't learn to control these strange new powers, she would find herself at the end of a noose.

7

Simon pointed a finger at her. "You...you...!"

"Witch?" she offered after making sure no one was within earshot. "*Now* will you let me go?"

He licked cracked lips. "Go if you dare. But I will set the Witch Hunter onto you. He will find you no matter where you go, and when he does, I'll not stop him from doing his job."

She backed away from the sheer venom in his voice. The Witch Hunter's self-appointed job was to kill witches. Kill them and obliterate every trace of them as if they never existed. Legend said he knew how to negate a witch's powers, making it easier to capture them. No one knew how he did it and no one knew what he did to the women afterwards, but rumors were rife. Some said he tortured the accused before killing them, others said he took his perverse sexual desires out on their bodies first.

Pippa swallowed and backed away. Simon stood and dusted himself off, watching her all the while. Despite wobbling legs, she turned and ran.

"You'll never find peace again!" he shouted after her. "He will hunt you down. You can't hide, my girl. He'll find you and your kind. He always does."

The sound of his mad laugh dogged her heels. She had to get away, had to run far enough and hide somewhere that not even the Witch Hunter would find her. But where? The man was said to be omniscient. He could find witches anywhere in England.

She tried desperately to think of somewhere and of someone who could help her. But she knew of only one person—Georgiana Dale—and one place. With a silent prayer of thanks to Georgiana for her kindly offer in that final letter, Pippa ran through the gatehouse and didn't look back.

\* \* \*

2 Days Later

EVEN DRESSED IN BOYS' clothes and perched half way up a tree just outside London's ancient walls, Pippa didn't feel safe. She wouldn't until she reached Ashbourne House and Georgiana Dale. She needed some of her mother's friend's calm wisdom to help her get far away from Simon. And the Witch Hunter. Especially the Witch Hunter.

Now, if only she could climb down, she could complete her journey. Without stiff skirts and a bodice, climbing the tree had been easy. Getting down was a different matter entirely.

She tried stretching her foot to reach the lowest branch but it was a few inches beyond her toes. How had she managed to get up in the first place? She'd taken no notice of her progress, too intent on climbing high enough to see over the row of buildings lining the northern side of The Strand. Her tree stood in a large field behind those houses and gardens. Ashbourne House lay beyond them on the other side of the busy thoroughfare into London proper.

She looked down again and tried to determine the best route for a safe descent. With a sigh, she realized it was the one she'd already attempted.

*Curses.* No fifteen year-old boy would find himself stuck up a tree. That fact was of more concern than her current predicament because it meant she wasn't completely immersed in her disguise, even after two days in it. She could not let her concentration or her disguise slip, even at this late stage.

She blew out a breath. She could do it. Or more to the point, *Pip* could. She lowered herself again, this time holding onto the trunk for balance and—

*Crack!*

The branch snapped under her weight. Pippa grappled at leaves, twigs and then emptiness in vain. With a cry, she crashed to the ground, landing with a thud that bruised her rump and stole her breath. But any pain she felt was forgotten when an unearthly screech ripped through the air. She looked up to see a huge beast rise above her, its hooves threatening to smash her skull. She screamed, drowning out the creature's snorts.

The front legs descended. She rolled out of the way. Fear made her fast and she scrabbled backwards to the base of the tree. The creature, one of hell's beasts for sure, reared again. She gathered her strength around her, inside her, drawing on the well of heat at her core and feeling it surge down her arms to her fingers. In the two days since setting fire to The Grange, she'd grown accustomed to the new sensations building whenever her fear or anger rose. But in that time, she'd also learned to control it.

"Easy, Devil," a man's voice boomed over the snorts of the beast. Except the beast was nothing more than a horse. A very large horse, but still not the hellhound she'd thought it to be moments ago. "Easy now," he said again, his voice more soothing.

Pippa quickly stood and suppressed the magic until it was no more than a tingling warmth in her belly. The horse whinnied and shied away from her, its nostrils flaring, its big head jerking fiercely. The rider held the reins in one hand and leaned forward to stroke the horse's neck and murmur in its ear.

She stared at them and tried to control her galloping heart-beat. It took a moment of forcing herself to think rationally to realize horse and rider hadn't suddenly appeared from nowhere like some supernatural spirit. They must have emerged from around the small hill alongside her tree. She'd been so intent on getting down, she'd failed to notice their approach.

When the horse grew calm, the rider dismounted and fixed a glare on Pippa that made her wish she possessed the power to vanish as well.

"What kind of foolish prank was that?" he blasted. "You could have been killed!" He raised his hand and she put an arm up in defence, but instead of striking her, he merely pulled the hat off his head and wiped his brow.

"It was no prank," she said, hearing the tremor in her voice and not liking it. She had no reason to be afraid. Not here on the edge of London where no one knew her. She hadn't been followed—she'd made sure of that. She was safe.

Unless this horseman decided to thrash her.

He looked quite capable of doing it too, with his large hands and broad frame. He had the sort of shoulders used to hard work and breaking bones.

Yet she was quite capable of breaking bones too—something

she'd discovered when the highwayman tried to rob her only the day before. Still, it wouldn't do to draw attention to her...abilities. Her situation was precarious enough. It would be wiser simply to stay silent.

"Then what were you doing jumping in front of my horse?" His deep blue eyes brimmed with anger. "Well, lad?" he said when she didn't answer. When she still didn't answer, he growled low in his throat. "God's teeth, what a bloody foolish thing to do! You're lucky Devil didn't crush you to death."

Devil—how appropriate.

She stared up at him, a hundred retorts racing through her mind. She swallowed them all. *Easy, Pippa,* she told herself using the same tones the rider had with his horse. Best to let the man get his anger out of his system then she could be on her way. From her earlier vantage point in the tree, she guessed Lord Ashbourne's house to be at least another half hour away. It had been easy to spot amongst the other grand houses stretching from The Strand down to the riverfront, thanks to Georgiana Dale's detailed description.

The rider grunted again and turned his attention to the horse stamping at the ground with a hoof. He rubbed its neck and shoulder until the muscles stopped quivering and the horse quieted. When the man turned back to her, his face had lost some of its hardness and his eyes were more like deep, still lakes than stormy seas.

"Are you injured?" he asked.

"No." Except for the bruises. And her pride. She went to tuck her hair behind her ear only to remember it had been cropped short. She adjusted her cap instead.

The man swept her with a brisk gaze as if satisfying himself of her wellbeing. No, not *her* wellbeing, Pip's. The rider only saw a boy standing in front of him. She hoped.

"Well?" he asked, one eyebrow raised.

She frowned. "Well what?"

"Are you going to tell me why you thought it would be amusing to startle my horse?" Irritation threaded his words, even though his stance relaxed somewhat. He held the reins with one hand, the other clutching a piece of paper at his side which she hadn't noticed before. Had he been reading it when she dropped out of the tree? That would explain why he hadn't seen her fall.

"Amusing?" she said. "Am I laughing?"

His eyes locked on her mouth which suddenly went dry under his direct gaze.

"I didn't startle your horse on purpose," she continued. "And if you'd been watching where you were going, you'd have known that."

One corner of his mouth lifted, but not in humor. She had thought him quite handsome at first, not in a fashionably pretty way, but with unconventional roughness that couldn't be smoothed away by a mere improvement in his grooming. Now she thought him quite ugly. He was much too dark, too sharp of cheek, and too big. Far too big. Anyway, he looked to be well over thirty.

"You're quite forthright, aren't you?" he said, his voice low and dangerous. "Considering you don't know who I am or what I'm capable of."

She suspected he was capable of a lot of things, snapping her in half being one of them. However, she didn't think he would hurt her. There'd been genuine concern in his expression when he'd asked her if she was hurt. As to who he was, well, he dressed like any other traveler. Dirty boots, simple black cloak over black riding doublet and breeches. A rapier sat like an old friend at his hip, the hilt worn smooth as if he'd had it for years —and used it well. Not a shiny, gold-hilted weapon like her uncle's, but a real blade. How many people had he killed with it?

At least the dark rider didn't seem like anyone of importance, although he didn't have the same bearing as an artisan or simple villager either. He held himself erect, his broad back straight and his gaze shrewd. He didn't carry any bags so he was most likely a Londoner out for a ride, and London was no village. She'd seen it sprawling like a multi-legged beast across both sides of the river from her tree. She wondered if all Londoners were as arrogant as this one.

Again, he raised an eyebrow. Definitely arrogant. "So you just happened to jump out from behind a bush at the same time I passed?" He rolled his eyes. "Don't lie to me, lad. I'm an expert at detecting them."

"I am not lying! And furthermore, I don't like the accusation that I am."

There was a heavy pause in which Pippa's heart stopped beating. She really should have kept to her earlier decision not to say anything. But something about being in disguise so far from home made her feel safe. And adventurous. A dangerous notion that, and one she needed to suppress. She might be free but adventuring could end her freedom too soon.

"I see," was all he said. He studied her for a long time and she felt the familiar swell of fear overtaking her anger. Then the man blinked and began to chuckle. The chuckle turned to a laugh, crinkling his eyes and softening his features. "Then tell me your version of events."

She hesitated, not trusting his sudden change of mood. "I didn't jump, I fell." She pointed to the tree canopy above her. "From there."

He looked up then back at her, his gaze lingering like hot summer sunshine on her chest. Her cheeks reddened and she moved instinctively to cover her breasts but stopped herself when he looked at her face again.

"Are you sure you're not injured?" he said. "That's quite a fall."

Pippa shrugged then winced at the pain in her shoulders. "I'm perfectly fine. Thank you. I must be going." She picked up her satchel, still resting against the tree trunk where she'd left it, and walked off. Her hip felt a little sore but not enough to make her limp, something to be grateful for.

"Wait!" The rider joined her, leading his horse which followed meekly. "It seems I owe you an apology."

"Yes."

"Right." He coughed. "I'm sorry."

She inclined her head in acknowledgement.

"What's your name, lad?"

She glanced at him sideways. "Pip." It couldn't hurt to give him the false name she'd been using at inns between Shelton and London, and would continue to use at Ashbourne House.

"Where are you heading? Perhaps I could give you a ride. Devil can hold both—"

"No!" Good Lord, she couldn't sit behind this stranger! Her breasts may be small and easily hidden beneath her oversized cloak and the thick leather of her jerkin, but squashing them against his back was a little too risky. How could he fail not to notice them? He was a man after all.

He looked taken aback. "Are you sure? You've just had a fall. And a fright, if the expression on your face when Devil reared is anything to go by."

"I'm unharmed. And I've not far to go."

"You're going to The Strand?" He nodded in the direction they were heading.

She said nothing and kept her eyes on the worn dirt path.

"Very well," he said, tartly. "I can see you're not one to forgive easily."

"No, it's not—." She bit her lip to stop herself talking. Best to let him think her still annoyed.

He mounted and Devil began to prance as if sensing his master's urgency to be away. "You'll want to arrive at your destination before nightfall, lad," the rider said with a nod at the sinking sun. "London's not safe after dark." He urged Devil on and the horse charged off before Pippa could politely thank him for his advice.

She blew out a breath, relieved to see the back of him. If all Londoners were as unsettling as that man, she was in for a challenging time ahead.

* * *

Lord Ashbourne's steward regarded Pippa closely before turning away as if bored. The quick change in his manner made her uneasy and she held her breath waiting for him to speak, hoping he didn't see through her disguise.

"Would you care to sit?" he asked.

"No thank you, Sir." She preferred to stand near the door to make escape easier if necessary. A new habit, borne of two days fleeing in disguise.

"I understand you were enquiring after Mistress Dale?" he said, idly brushing his long fingers across the back of a chair. Checking for dust?

The chair was one of only two bracketing the fireplace in an otherwise bare chamber near the kitchens. Clean rushes covered the floor but the walls and chairs were unadorned. Not even a cushion offered comfort. The steward, Fallon, had directed her to the room after she asked to speak to him. The servant who'd let her in through the kitchen entrance hadn't been any help at all. He'd told her he'd never heard of Georgiana Dale. Thankfully Fallon didn't seem so ignorant.

"She was my mother's friend," Pippa explained. "She wrote telling me I would find her here."

"You won't," he said, rubbing his fingertips together to remove the dust. His attention seemed to be completely on his task. If he wasn't speaking to her, Pippa would have thought he didn't even see her. "She's gone," he went on. "She left Lord Ashbourne's service two years ago." His gaze met hers, direct and uncompromising. "As her *friend*, you would have known that."

Pippa swallowed around the lump in her throat. Gone? And soon after her last letter by the sound of it. "My mother died some time ago. Mistress Dale wrote to me saying that if I ever needed her, I was to come here."

Fallon's brown eyes grew softer as he took in ever inch of her from her newly cropped hair to her dirty boots. "I cannot help you. I'm sorry."

"Do you know where I can find her?" Please let it not be far. The sun was almost set and she needed somewhere to stay for the night. What little money she'd taken with her had run out after she'd paid for the previous night's room. If she left immediately, she could probably make it through the London gates before curfew.

"Haverford," he said.

"Is that nearby?"

"About half a day's ride from here."

"Ride?" she said weakly.

He nodded and glanced past her to the door, looking eager to be gone himself.

Pippa wished she'd taken up the offer of a chair. Her legs suddenly felt too weak to hold her. "Haverford," she said to no one in particular. "Oh."

His sad, bloodhound eyes regarded her again with cautious curiosity. "Mistress Dale was a friend of your mother's, you say?"

"Yes." She rallied under his sympathetic gaze. She had come this far and would not crumble at the final stage. All she needed was a bed for the night and then she would somehow complete her journey tomorrow. "Great friends but I believe it was mostly by correspondence. I've never met her." It was the truth. She had found during the years lived under her uncle's roof that it was best to keep to the truth where possible. It made it easier to keep track of the lies.

He nodded thoughtfully. "It'll be dark soon. Do you have somewhere to stay, lad?"

"No. I was hoping Mistress Dale would accommodate me here with the servants until she found me employment." Another lie, quickly formed and not very well thought through. She held her breath and watched the long, straight face of the imperial steward as he considered her words.

"Employment?" he said. "As what? A pageboy perhaps?"

"Yes." What did it matter now? Georgiana was gone and Pippa would say anything to get a room for the night.

"Good. Then you can start immediately."

"Pardon?" She blinked at him.

Fallon inclined his head. "Last week the page of the wardrobe received news of his father's illness and had to leave unexpectedly. You can take his position until he returns. I'm sure Geor...Mistress Dale would approve."

Pippa's fingers tightened around the strap of her satchel. "Page of the w, wardrobe?"

An almighty clatter from the kitchen made her jump. Fallon looked irritably past her. "It is a great honor," he said, distracted.

"B, but I simply want to find Mistress Dale. She will help me—"

"To find employment, yes? Well, you don't need to travel all the way to Haverford only to have her send you back here to be page of the wardrobe." He looked at her as if she was a dullard.

She snapped her mouth shut when she realized it was open. "Are you sure I am the most suitable person?"

The noise from the kitchens returned to the dull hum of earlier and his attention returned to Pippa. "And why wouldn't you be?"

Because she didn't want employment, she only wanted a night's shelter. And because she would have to see Lord Ashbourne naked! She would be required to help him dress and attend to his most personal needs. No, she couldn't possibly take the disguise that far.

"You require employment," he went on, not hiding his impatience, "Lord Asbhourne requires a page of the wardrobe."

"I've never been a page of the wardrobe before." Never served anyone in her life although she had been around servants since she was born and knew the duties each performed in a major household.

"You seem a well-bred boy, if a little travel-stained, and his lordship would dismiss me on the spot if I turned away a friend of Mistress Dale's." His eyes twinkled unexpectedly. The effect was rather delightful.

She longed to ask why his lordship would dismiss Fallon but refrained. She would ask Georgiana herself when she saw her. That's if she got through the night safely at Ashbourne House. But not as the page of the wardrobe. Certainly not.

"Is there some other service I could undertake, Sir? In the kitchens perhaps? It's just that I don't think I am suited to be page of the wardrobe."

"Nonsense! There's nothing to it. You simply do as his lordship requests. Besides, you're much too skinny to be of use anywhere else. Don't worry, Gertie will help you settle in. His lordship isn't expected to return until the morning anyway so you'll have all evening to familiarize yourself with your tasks."

Not expected until the morning? Perfect. She'd be gone by the time he returned. "Then I accept. Thank you, Sir."

"Good! I'll send Gertie to show you to the master's apartments." The steward moved past her, his stride brisk and purposeful.

"Just one question," she said and he stopped in the doorway. "Where will I sleep?" As a male servant, she would normally share a bed with one of the other male servants. It may be for only one night but that was long enough for her secret to be uncovered in the close proximity of a bed. However, her uncle's page had slept in a separate room within hearing of his master's shout. Hopefully the setup at Ashbourne House would be the same.

"You'll have a room adjoining the master's chamber," Fallon said. He gave her a brief nod of dismissal and left.

Pippa didn't let out her breath until the quick steps of the steward had disappeared. She drew in another and the delicious scent of cinnamon from the kitchen made her stomach rumble. She hadn't eaten since breaking her fast that morning.

She sat on one of the high-back chairs, clutched her satchel on her lap, and waited.

A few minutes later, a plump girl of about seventeen arrived and introduced herself as Gertie, one of the maids. She eyed Pippa from head to foot, lingering on the groin area. Pippa quickly stood and placed the satchel over herself before the maid found her lacking.

"You the Pip boy?" Gertie asked.

"Yes. I'm the new page—"

"Of the wardrobe. I know," the maid said cheerfully. "Come on, let's go." Gertie smiled and her entire face smiled too, from her brown eyes to her protruding front teeth.

"You new to London?" she asked, leading the way through the kitchen, two larders and a scullery.

"Is it that obvious?" Pippa wondered what had marked her as different. Her clothes? Her manner?

"You don't speak like one of us," Gertie said. "Where you from?"

"The west," Pippa said vaguely. "Tell me, what is Lord Ashbourne like?" She needed to keep the maid talking to stop her asking too many questions.

"He's a good master," Gertie said as she led the way up the

back stairs. "Never raised a hand to any of us, even though Ralphy deserved it when he pinched the countess's necklace. *She'd* have had Ralphy flogged but his lordship would hear nothin' of it. Dismissed the little dog turd with full wages, so I heard."

Pippa followed Gertie up the next flight of stairs to the second floor. "I'll get lost in this place."

"You get used to it. Just remember these stairs lead straight to the master's lodgings and you can't go wrong. Only the servants use them." She paused and waited for Pippa to join her. "And sometimes the master, so mind he doesn't knock you over if he passes you in a hurry. These stairs aren't wide and you bein' so slight and him bein' so big...well, you'll come off worse." She laughed and continued up.

"Why would his lordship come this way?" The backstairs were built to provide access for the servants between the master's lodgings and the kitchen, larders and cellars. Why would the earl want to traverse through such an undignified passage?

Gertie shrugged rounded shoulders. "Who knows why he does anythin'? He's...what's the word? Unperdickable. Yep, that's it."

"Unpredictable," Pippa corrected.

"That's what I said. Unperdickable. He comes and goes when he pleases, no matter the hour, and..." she lowered her voice, "his visitors sometimes come and go at strange hours too. Even in the middle of the night when they think we're all asleep."

Pippa's eyes widened. "What sort of visitors?"

"All sorts. Men, women—"

"Women!" She bit her lip when Gertie shushed her with a finger to her lips. "Oh, of course. Women," Pippa said simply. Why wouldn't the unwed earl have dalliances? It was only natural. Wasn't it? She really had no idea.

"His lordship's not in," Gertie said, opening a door at the top of the stairs. "This is the master's wardrobe." She swept her hand wide to encompass the daybed, large cupboard and coffers beside it and the fireplace surrounded by three stools. Although the room had none of the embellishments Pippa was used to in her own wardrobe—not a single embroidered cushion, Turkey carpet or wall hanging—it didn't feel cold or uninviting. The embers in the grate still glowed, effusing the room with warmth, and the last pale rays of daylight reached into even the furthest corner thanks to the large windows. She ran her hand along the top of one of the coffers, enjoying the feel of the cedar, worn smooth from years of use and polishing. The scent of cloves and something spicier lingered in the air.

"Is this where I am to sleep?" Pippa asked, wondering if she would be required to lie on a pallet on the floor. She was so tired she wouldn't mind curling up near the enormous fire as long as the straw mattress was clean.

"No, your room is through there." Gertie pointed to a door beside the stairwell entrance.

Pippa peeked inside. The room was tiny. A small trestle bed was pushed up against one wall and an oak chest squatted opposite. A single stool was situated to take in the view of the knot garden from the window.

"Peter's things are still here," Gertie said, opening the chest. She pulled out a garment in the Ashbourne colors of silver and green and held it up against Pippa. "He was about your height so his livery should fit. Everything'll be a bit big in the shoulders and legs but they'll do." She pulled it away but continued to scrutinize Pippa. "Get some of Cook's food into you and you'll soon be filling these out. His beef broth'll put hairs on your chest, mark my words."

"How...appetizing." Hairy chests notwithstanding, she'd been tall and slender ever since she'd reached womanhood and she didn't think she'd thicken out no matter what Cook concocted.

"Now," said Gertie, whisking Pippa out of her new room and back through the vast wardrobe, "through that door is the master's bedchamber."

Pippa nodded, growing curious about the earl even though she would never meet him. It must be the close proximity to all his things that made her wonder about their owner. "Can I ask you something?" she said.

"Of course." Gertie paused at the door to the master's chamber and crossed her arms in a way that pushed her large breasts up and out. Then she winked. "You can ask me anythin', Pip."

Pippa cleared her throat. Somehow she felt more in danger with this girl than she had in two days. "Is he feeble-minded? Or ugly? Or is he both perhaps?"

"Who?"

"The earl."

Gertie threw her head back and laughed, a high, nasally sound that ended with a snort. "He's very clever and one of the handsomest devils in London if you ask me. Why?"

Pippa shrugged. "Curiosity. He's not married and he's past the age that most men of noble birth are wed for the first time. Well past it, I believe."

"That is his lordship's business, not yours or mine, Pip," Gertie said with a wag of her finger. "Best not to wonder how your betters conduct their affairs. They're a mystery to me, especially this one." She stuck her thumb at the door leading to the backstairs.

At precisely that moment, it opened. Gertie gasped then quickly bobbed her head as she tucked her offending thumb into the folds of her apron. "My lord! You're not expected! I mean, I didn't know you were here."

Pippa froze as a man entered. Not just any man. *Him*. The rider. The one she'd angered in the field. And of all the cruel twists of Fate, it seemed he was the Earl of Ashbourne.

"My business finished earlier than expected," he said.

Pippa choked back her anguish. *Dear God, I promise to attend church twice every Sunday if you strike me dead now!*

Perhaps he wouldn't remember her. He was an earl after all, and she nothing but an ungainly youth. But when he looked at her, recognition flared.

"You again!" He made a sound—half grunt, half laugh, all humorless. "It seems our paths have crossed once more."

"So it would seem, my lord," she said, bowing low to hide her face which ran hot and cold.

"Are you going to fall in front of me again, lad?" he said. "Because you look quite ill."

21

"This here is Pip," Gertie said, nudging Pippa forward. "He's the new page of the wardrobe."

The earl cocked an eyebrow. "Really? Well, lad, I'm sorry."

"My lord?" Pippa dared to ask.

He smiled. "You'll see."

Pippa felt sick. Her stomach rolled, her skin felt cold and damp and she had to grip the back of a chair to steady herself. With any luck she was dying and her misery would soon be over.

But her luck had run out because Lord Ashbourne's smile broadened, leaving her with no doubt he was aware of her discomfort and enjoying it.

She had the distinct feeling her day was about to get a whole lot worse.

# CHAPTER 2

*L*ord Ashbourne dismissed Gertie with a nod and the maid left. Pippa was alone with someone who, as far as everyone in that house was concerned, was her new master. She kept her gaze diverted even when the silence stretched on. She could feel Ashbourne's own gaze on the top of her head but she couldn't bear to look at him. Even the tips of her ears and scalp burned with embarrassment.

"Cat got your tongue, lad? Or a nesting bird perhaps?"

She almost sank to the floor with relief when he spoke. Since her legs couldn't hold her up for much longer, she knelt before him, head still bowed. At least she would seem penitent. "I am deeply sorry if I spoke to you out of turn earlier, my lord. If you'd informed me of your name and rank I'd never have dared to say such things." Good grief, had she really chastised him for calling her a liar?

"So you'd not have spoken your mind?" he said.

She glanced up then quickly down again because he was looking at her with a sharpness that matched his voice.

Pippa said nothing. She couldn't. She'd forgotten how to speak. He was about to dismiss her and have her thrown out of his home. She knew it.

Where would she go? She hadn't enough money for supper let alone a room at an inn.

"Get up," he said. She stood. "Now tell me what you were doing on that path," he said. "You do know it would have been quicker on the main road." She knew. "The fields can be quite treacherous," he continued, "especially if you fall out of trees."

"I was lost," was all she said. In truth, avoiding the main road meant avoiding people. Or so she'd thought. Perhaps she would have been better to keep to the anonymity of the crowded thoroughfares. No one would notice an extra lad whereas on the muddy path, she stood out. Thanks to the broken branch, she couldn't have been more conspicuous if she'd waved her arms about and shouted, "I'm a fugitive!"

Lord Ashbourne didn't look particularly satisfied with her answer but he didn't question her further. He sat down on the day bed and stretched his long legs towards her. He leaned back and lifted one of the muddy boots.

She stared at it.

"I know it's unappealing," he said, "but I really think you need to touch it to remove it."

He wasn't dismissing her? Thank God. She didn't care how unappealing the task if it got her a free bed for the night.

She knelt before him, unlaced the leather boot and drew it off. Good Lord, what poor creature died in there? She held her breath but began to feel faint so she put a hand to her mouth and breathed behind it. Better.

He wriggled his hose-clad toes. "This is what I meant when I said you'd be sorry."

Her face heated. A good page would never have let it be known his master's foot smelled. Her uncle's page wouldn't dare.

Lord Ashbourne leaned forward and she saw the sparkle in his bright blue eyes and the lines bracketing his mouth. He was laughing at her!

She tried to stifle a giggle but wasn't entirely successful.

"That's better," he said, smiling openly. "Now, if you want us to get along, there is only one rule. You are to speak your mind to me when I ask it. I don't like people who say one thing and mean another. Understand?"

"Yes, my lord, but..." She trailed off. Did *he* mean what he was saying?

"Go on."

She took a deep breath. "You didn't appear to like it when I spoke my mind at our first meeting."

He waggled his other boot at her. "I was annoyed. It passed and now I admire you for being forthright. In my experience it goes hand in hand with honesty. And I like my servants to be honest, particularly those closest to me. And there'll be none closer to me than you, Pip."

Oh dear. Forthright? Her? Perhaps, since she discovered her uncle's theft of her money, but before that? Not a single resident at The Grange would have called her forthright. Mild certainly, and genteel too.

But those were womanly traits and she wasn't a woman at Ashbourne House, she was Pip the pageboy. She smiled to herself as she removed his other boot. Forthright. She liked it.

"My putrid feet amuse you?" Lord Ashbourne's eyes crinkled at the corners and his mouth quirked upwards in a rather wicked grin. He was definitely quite handsome when he smiled. However could she have thought him ugly? "Or is it their size you are laughing at? I'm told they're rather large."

She appreciated his attempts to relax her. It had certainly worked. "They are rather big, my lord." She turned her head to the side pretending to study them with as much earnestness as she would a Latin text.

He stood and began to unhook his cuff. "Well, you know what they say about men with big feet."

Pippa stepped forward and stayed his fingers with a touch of her own. It was the closest she'd ever been to a man and the event wasn't lost on her nerves. Tiny thrills raced along her fingertips, shot up her arm and radiated across every inch of her skin like ripples on a pond surface. Rather like when she used her powers, only in reverse.

"No," she said, inexplicably out of breath. Despite her fumbles, she managed to undo one of his cuffs and turned her attention to the other. "What do they say?"

He watched her, a frown creasing his brow. She flushed and concentrated on her task so he couldn't see her reddening face.

"Never mind," he said with a shake of his head. "Fill me a bath. I've been riding since first light and I'm expected at court tonight." He spoke as if it were a task as common and as tiresome as dressing every morning.

She only hoped it was interesting enough to keep him out for most of the night. Till dawn if possible. Perhaps by the time he returned, she'd even be gone.

With a little bob of her head as she'd seen Gertie do, Pippa left him and entered his bedchamber, relieved to be out of his presence. If a single touch of his fingers could make her behave like a foolish girl, what would she do when she had to undress him?

Oh dear. A bath meant he would have to be naked. And she would have to get him to that state. Oh dear, no. She couldn't possibly do it. Really, she *shouldn't*. Perhaps if she kept her eyes averted...

There was no point dwelling on it. She had work to do and a disguise to maintain—that must be her first priority, not wondering what the earl of Ashbourne looked like beneath his shirt and hose.

She raced downstairs where a cauldron was already warming in the huge fireplace for the master's bath. She tested the temperature then had the kitchen boys follow her up to the main bedchamber, the cauldron between them. They filled the bath then left at once.

She found a towel cloth in a coffer and arranged it over a stool beside the bath. The room felt a little cool so she placed another log in the grate but it didn't catch alight. She eyed the closed door to the wardrobe then turned back to the fire.

It was so very tempting...

No. She couldn't take the risk of using her powers to fuel the flames. Not in Lord Ashbourne's house. Not anywhere now that her uncle had set the Witch Hunter onto her like one of his prized hunting dogs. With a sigh, she knocked on the door to the adjoining wardrobe.

"There's no need to knock," Lord Ashbourne said, opening it.

Pippa stared. He was naked except for his trunk hose! "Uh." She stopped before she made a fool of herself.

"Is there something wrong?" he asked, straightening.

"No!" Absolutely nothing wrong at all. In fact, the sight was very right. His body was all sleek lines and athletic proportions, with smooth skin stretched taught over muscles. A lot of muscles. Pippa's knowledge of the male body extended only to the sketches of classical statues in her uncle's books but if they were considered the ideal male, then this man was masculine perfection. A sprinkling of black hair on his chest thinned to a fine line over his flat stomach and continued down to the top of his hose. She caught herself staring at the point of its disappearance and coughed to cover her embarrassment.

"No, but..." What were they talking about? He was staring at her with quizzical amusement and she couldn't think.

"Yes?" he prompted.

"Well, it's just that, er, I thought I was supposed to undress you."

He laughed. "I'm not completely inept. I can do it myself."

"Yes, but..." *I've been looking forward to it.* Her face was reddening again. She turned back to the bedchamber to hide her cheeks but the earl brushed past her to stand by the tub giving her a delightful view of his naked back. Who knew a bare back could be so...breath-taking. "But I'm the page of the wardrobe," she finished, somewhat pathetically.

"If it makes you feel better, I'll need your help later with my court attire." He began to draw down his hose and Pippa quickly turned her attention to the speck of dust on her sleeve that needed to be vigorously brushed off.

The earl moaned softly as water splashed. "You draw a good bath, Pip," he said. She risked a glance at him and saw that he was safely in the tub, leaning back with his arms resting on the rim. "Peter always made it too hot but this is perfect."

"I'll prepare your clothes," she said, moving quickly towards the wardrobe. "Do you have a preference?"

He closed his eyes and waved a hand in her direction. "Whatever you see fit for an audience with the queen."

The queen! What did a man wear when visiting Her Majesty?

She opened one of the coffers in the wardrobe and removed the top-most doublet. Too plain. The next was too black and the one below that too ostentatious. Finally, at the bottom, she found the perfect one to go with the earl's dark coloring. A pale blue satin doublet embroidered with silver thread and silver wrist-ruffs. The tailoring was superb, the embellishments intricate yet not elaborate. It must have cost a great deal of money. She chose a cambric shirt, black hose and a black velvet cloak to set it off. In another coffer she found gloves and hats but it seemed that none of the winter clothing had been put away yet. The late spring days could still be cool but there was no longer any need for the lambskins and furs. She might as well sort through his clothes later. It would be better than sitting around feeling sorry for herself.

She carried the clothing into the bedroom and laid everything carefully on the bed, flattening out each garment as she did so. The earl still lay in the tub, his eyes closed, his breathing heavy. He must have fallen asleep. She wondered if she should wake him but decided a few more minutes hopefully wouldn't make him late.

She moved quietly about the room, tidying up and becoming familiar with her new surroundings. A crumpled piece of paper lay partly obscured under the bed as if it had been tossed there and forgotten. She picked it up and placed it on the small table, ironing out the creases with her fingers. She didn't mean to read it but the awkward childish scrawl caught her attention and before she knew it, she'd seen the words:

*This is your last warning. Your secret will come out if you do not do as I asked.*

She gasped and dropped the note onto the table.

"What are you doing?" The sound of slopping water made her turn just in time to see the naked, dripping earl cross the floor in three long strides. He reached past her and snatched up the paper. "This is private!"

She backed away beneath the force of his anger. "I'm sorry, my lord. I was simply tidying up and..." She gulped and tried very hard to keep her eyes on his face, even though it was grim and rather terrifying as he loomed above her. Even though it hurt to keep her eyes from not wandering down.

He turned from her with an animal growl and strode into his adjoining study. Despite the crackle of his anger still lingering in the room, she couldn't help marveling at the delicious view of broad back, powerful thighs and buttocks glistening from the bathwater. How hard he looked. And how fascinating the way his muscles moved beneath his skin. Oh yes, quite...fascinating. Perhaps a little too fascinating. She fanned herself and remained in the bedchamber.

He threw the note onto his desk and leaned on the back of a chair, his head bowed. He stood without moving for a long time. Slowly his ragged breathing returned to normal and Pippa realized he would soon turn around. It was one thing to see his naked back but it was quite another to see his front. She certainly wasn't ready for it so she picked up the towel and advanced to the study, spreading the cloth out in front of her.

"My lord, you're wet," she said softly to be as unobtrusive as possible. She didn't want to disturb the calmness that had come over him in case his temper flared again.

She looked away as he stepped into the towel and took it from her. He moved back to the bedchamber where she could hear him dressing. After a few moments when she thought it would be safe, she peeked. He had his hose and nether hose on so she joined him to assist with his shirt and doublet.

"I take it from your reaction you can read," he said, allowing her to lace up his shirt.

"Yes, my lord."

"It doesn't surprise me. You speak well. Not like Peter. He could neither read nor write."

"My father taught me." She held up his doublet and he put it on. "He insisted I have a good education." Girls didn't attend school but her father had ensured she had the best tutor money could buy.

"An enlightened man."

She fastened the hooks of the doublet and arranged the cloak around his shoulders, all the while careful to touch only fabric, not skin. The silence was full and it wouldn't do to have it burst by girlish gasps of delight at the feel of him.

He sat on a stool and pulled on his own boots but allowed her to arrange his hat.

She stepped back and admired him. He looked every inch the nobleman. How could she ever have mistaken him for an ordinary Londoner? He looked like a man used to commanding armies with his formidable presence and his uncompromising gaze. He was extraordinarily handsome in a battle-hardened way. No wonder the queen desired his company. If Pippa was queen she would order him to her palace every evening just to admire him.

"About the note—" he began.

"My lord, I will never breathe a word about it to anyone. You can trust me."

He glared at her and she realized her mistake. She shouldn't have interrupted him. Servants do not speak over their masters.

"You sound honest enough when you say that," he said finally. A rush of air left her—it seemed her interruption didn't concern him after all. "But in my experience people may say one thing and mean it at the time, only to stop meaning it later."

She shook her head, confused. Was he admonishing her or not? "My lord?"

He sighed and waved her off. "Never mind, Pip. Go find yourself something to eat. I'll be leaving now."

She took one final look, devouring the sight of him in his court attire. It would be the last time she ever set eyes on the earl. If circumstances had been different, perhaps—.

No. She wouldn't allow herself to contemplate any Ifs. Circumstances *weren't* different. They never would be. Instead she should be thanking her good fortune he hadn't learned her dark secrets. Both of them—that she was a fugitive and a witch.

Pushing aside regrets, she left, feeling more disoriented and out of place than when she'd arrived. And yet her disguise had survived a very real test. All she had to do was make it through the rest of the night and another day on the road and she could be herself again with Georgiana Dale. She would know what to do.

She went down to the kitchen and found herself thinking about that awful note. What did it mean? Who'd written it?

But it was none of her business. The earl would sort it out. Hunger drove it from her mind.

She helped herself to a bowl of the delicious stew bubbling in a pot over one of the fires as she saw the other servants do, then found a corner in the large kitchen to eat. She was starving.

"How's it goin' with his lordship then?" Gertie asked, joining her. She tore a hunk of bread in half and handed a piece to Pippa.

"Thank you," Pippa said, taking it. "It goes well enough."

"Master just left. He seemed to be in one of his moods. Anythin' happen up there to set him off?"

Pippa shrugged. "No. He bathed, he dressed, that's it. Perhaps he was thinking of his evening ahead."

"P'haps. He don't much like goin' to court so that could be it."

"Why doesn't he like going?"

Gertie lifted one shoulder. "Too much fussin' I expect. He don't much like dressin' up and talkin' about nothin' in partic'lar. He likes to talk direct, not in riddles and rhymes like some in the queen's favor."

"I noticed," Pippa mumbled.

"That's what I hear, anyway."

"You hear a lot." Pippa gave her a friendly smile. She might only be a servant in Ashbourne House until the next day, but it wouldn't hurt to make friends with the girl.

Gertie grinned and leaned forward, revealing a lot of bosom. "I do. You can ask me anythin' anytime, Pip. It'll be my pleasure to teach you."

"Teach me?" The ruff at Pippa's throat suddenly felt too tight and she tugged at it. Maybe becoming friends with the maid wasn't a good idea.

"Of the ways around here," Gertie said with a snorting laugh.

"I see. Well, in that case..." She stopped, feeling foolish.

"Mmmm?"

Pippa waved her spoon in the air. "Oh, never mind," she said with a dismissive smile.

Gertie smiled too, as if she were about to hear a secret. "What is it?"

Pippa placed her spoon in her bowl and decided to ask anyway since her question was harmless enough. "What do people say about men with large feet?"

Gertie stared then burst out laughing until she choked on her bread. "You mean you don't know?" she said, dislodging the bread with her finger and flicking it into the fire.

Pippa was beginning to regret she'd asked. "No."

"They say a man with big feet has a big..." she looked around to see if anyone was close enough to hear then leaned even further forward, "a big cock," she said on a snigger which turned to another eruption of snorts.

Pippa sank lower. "Oh, I, uh...oh."

"So is it true?" Gertie asked, grinning broadly.

"What?"

"Well, you seen the master's feet and you've just been dressin' him." She winked. "Of all the people here, you would know if the sayin' is true or not."

"I, uh, didn't look."

"What? You didn't see his cock?"

"No, I didn't see his feet." She stood so fast her stool toppled over. "I'd best go. There's work to be done." She left before Gertie could ask any more questions.

* * *

ASH MANAGED to make it to his rooms via the backstairs without being coddled by Fallon or interrogated by his mother. It may be hours before dawn but that rarely mattered—neither his steward nor his mother ever seemed to sleep.

Like Ash himself.

He closed his door quietly so as not to wake Pip and entered the study where he settled into the chair at his desk. He stretched out his legs and took a moment to simply be still. After dealing with the politics of court then the grubby business of supervising one tentacle of Walsingham's spy network, it was nice to be alone, to let his mind be empty, even if only for a few moments.

With the evening's affairs shed like a second skin, he picked up an account book and ran his finger down the neat line of figures entered by the steward in charge of Dewbury Hall, Ash's Derbyshire estate.

"You must be tired, my lord." Ash looked up from the ledger to see the pageboy, Pip, standing in the doorway. The lad covered a yawn with one hand and held a candle in the other. "Let me help you undress."

Ash hadn't heard him enter, an indication that the boy was light on his feet or that Ash himself was weary. "That won't be necessary. I've got work to do. Go back to bed, Pip, you look exhausted."

"No, I'm not." The hand that had been rubbing his eye dropped to his side. "I'm wide awake, my lord. If you don't want me to help you undress, then perhaps you need some ale or wine?"

"No, thank you. I ate and drank in the kitchen before I came up."

The boy frowned as if considering that. No doubt he thought it odd that the master of the house should help himself to the servant's leftovers in the middle of the night.

"Something stronger perhaps?" Pip asked.

"A definite no." When the lad cocked his head to the side, Ash added, "I don't drink anything stronger than a little wine." *These days*, he almost added.

"Of course, my lord. I'll remember that in future." He still didn't move from the doorway where he stood blinking in the candlelight.

"It's late," he told Pip. "Go back to bed. I have no need of you now."

The boy seemed reluctant to go. The last page, Peter, would have happily returned to bed and snored the remainder of the night away, but this lad took his duties very seriously. His eagerness was another oddity to add to the tally Ash had already accumulated. So far he'd decided that Pip:

1. spoke like a highly educated boy not a country servant.

2. was mature enough to match wits with Ash even when he was in a fierce temper (Ash not the boy).

3. had an odd way of walking, with a sort of roll of his hips. And when his guard was down, as it was now, he stood with one hip thrust to the side.

4. didn't like looking at Ash without clothes on. In fact, he seemed quite uncomfortable about nudity.

5. had a good eye for clothing. Neither Ash nor Peter had been much good at choosing suitable court attire and it had often fallen to his mother or sister to tell him what to wear on important occasions.

But for all his strangeness, Ash liked him. He couldn't explain why. Perhaps it was the way Pip looked directly into Ash's eyes when he spoke. Ash knew of few people who did that. The boy was intelligent and sharp-tongued although he hid his wit beneath a servant's obedience once he discovered Ash was his master. Unfortunately. Ash could do with a sparring partner now that his friend and colleague, Merritt, spent more time with his wife.

However, as much as Ash liked his pageboy, there was something troubling about him. Something Ash couldn't put his finger on. Whatever it was, he intended to uncover it. There couldn't be any secrets in Ashbourne House. None that weren't his own, that is.

Secret. That was the word the blackmailer had used in the note. But what secret? And who had sent it? Everything about the note was odd.

"It is very late," the lad said. "Are you sure you don't want to go to bed now, my lord?"

"Not yet," Ash said, rifling through the missives cluttering his desk. Where had he left the note?

"If you don't mind me saying, my lord, you look a little...tired."

"Do I?" He waved the boy off. "I don't sleep much. But that's not your problem. Go to bed."

When he didn't hear the lad move away he looked up to check in case he simply hadn't heard Pip leave. "You're still here," he said when he saw Pip staring at him, wide awake now.

"Are you looking for something, my lord? Perhaps I can help?"

"You're entirely too helpful, Pip," he said, not bothering to hide his sarcasm.

"I'm sorry. But I...I thought perhaps you were looking for the blackm...the paper you had earlier."

Ash stopped scattering his correspondence about and fixed his page with a glare. "What have you done with it?"

"Nothing!" he said, wide-eyed. "I think the Countess may have taken it."

"My mother! God's blood, you let her in here?"

Ash half rose but instead of looking terrified, the lad simply raised his eyebrows in an "of course" gesture.

Ash conceded the point. The boy hadn't spoken but he didn't need to. His look said it all. How could a servant refuse the Countess access to a room in her own house? Pip would have been whipped if he'd tried.

"Are you certain she left with that note?" Ash asked.

"Yes, my lord."

He drummed his fingers on the desk. What was his mother up to? And how did she know he had a blackmailer's note in his possession anyway? Or had she? "Did she come specifically looking for it or was her presence a general one?"

"She didn't divulge her motivations to me, my lord."

Ash almost smiled at the boy's bluntness, but he was too tired and annoyed to be amused.

"However she did offer me money for my silence," Pip said.

Ash rubbed tired, gritty eyes. It seemed his mother had learned a thing or two from her spy master son. "Did you take it?"

Pip smiled and dug into his pocket. He produced a handful of coins which he dropped onto Ash's desk. "I thought it best to accept the money, my lord."

"Clever lad." Very clever. That way his mother thought she had the page in her pay and her son in the dark. The lad stifled another yawn. "Go to bed," Ash said. "I have work to do. Wake me for an early breakfast. And bring my suit of armor."

Pip blinked. "Armor, my lord?"

"Yes, I have a dragon to slay."

# CHAPTER 3

*A* creaking board awoke Ash with a start. "That you, Pip? What time is it?"

There was no answer from the direction of the sound and Ash thought he'd been mistaken. It wouldn't be the first time his dreams had seemed real.

"Yes, it's me, my lord," came Pip's light voice after a few moments. "It's very early. Perhaps you should go back to sleep."

Ash's eyelids felt like gravel against his eyeballs as he cracked them open. "Not possible now." He squinted at the silhouette of his pageboy near the door. He was fully dressed. "Is the sun up yet?"

"Just dawning now, my lord."

"Open the curtains then."

A hesitation before Pip did as ordered. Insipid morning light filtered into the room and revealed the boy's features. He looked worn out but on edge at the same time. His gaze kept flicking towards the wardrobe and back. He was fully dressed, right down to his boots, and was that a bag laying half obscured beside one of the chests?

Had Pip been about to leave? Ash suddenly regretted his outburst the night before when he'd discovered the boy reading that strange note. He should have held his tongue.

"Build up the fire please, Pip," he said and wondered how to make the boy feel more at ease. How to make him stay.

Again the lad hesitated before complying. Ash watched him as he carefully set log upon log and stoked the fire to life. He moved with small, efficient movements, reminding Ash of a bird fussing over its nest.

"Did you sleep well," Ash asked him when he stood.

"Yes. Did you, my lord?"

It was a ridiculously civil conversation. Even more strange, Pip seemed genuinely concerned about the answer. No doubt he'd heard all sorts of garbled noises coming from Ash's bed during the night and had wondered about his master's dreams.

"No," Ash said.

"Oh." The boy lowered his gaze.

"I never sleep well which I'm sure you discovered last night."

Pip quickly turned to tend to the fire again but not before Ash saw his blush.

Previous bed partners had told Ash he muttered or called out when he had nightmares. That's why he no longer kept bed partners. The last time he'd fallen asleep after spending a vigorous hour with Lady Wethinall, she'd awoken to Ash ranting and thrashing about. She'd screamed, waking her elderly husband who'd been asleep several rooms away. Ash had to climb out of her window and drop into the bushes below to avoid discovery. Although Lady Wethinall insisted her husband suspected nothing and suggested with a wicked smile that she and Ash resume their arrangement, he refused. Lord Wethinall must have suspected something because he'd moved his wife's rooms up to the second floor and the drop was somewhat deadlier. She wasn't worth the trouble.

"You'll get used to the noise, Pip," he said. "Just try to sleep through it."

"I will, my lord." Pip picked up the poker and stoked the fire. "Perhaps an apothecary could make up something to soothe your dreams. I could make enquiries for you."

Ash detected a ploy to be out of his presence. But he couldn't allow the boy to go, not over his previous night's outburst. It wasn't fair. Only how to make him stay? Perhaps if he kept Pip busy and offered kindness, he would simply change his mind. Yes, that might work.

"No. It's not necessary," he said, pushing back the covers and getting out of bed.

"But my lord, it might help." Pip straightened and turned. "Oh my!"

The boy swiveled back to the fire and stabbed at a burning log with the poker so hard he almost poked a hole right through the wood.

Ash frowned. "What's wrong?"

"Nothing, Sir." Pip's voice came out a squeak.

Ash was about to interrogate him further when he realized the problem. Nakedness. Or more to the point, Ash's nakedness. He grinned. There could be some fun to be had here. He stretched and went about performing his morning rituals, all the while watching the boy's back.

"Are my clothes ready?" Ash asked him.

"Set out in the wardrobe, my lord," Pip said without turning around. "I'll fetch them."

"Not necessary. I'll dress in the wardrobe. Follow me in."

The boy did as he was told but kept his head bowed.

"Where's my hose and shirt?" Ash said, regretting the severity of his voice. It still held a roughness that came with only a few hours restless sleep.

"Over there." Pip pointed to the articles in question, laid out on the daybed.

Ash had to admire the boy's efficiency. He'd been about to leave and yet he'd still performed his duty.

"Fetch them and then help me dress, please."

"B, but I thought perhaps you might want to do it yourself." The fine fingers of Pip's hands wound together. "Yesterday you said you weren't inept. My lord."

"Today I am. Hopelessly."

The boy flexed his fingers then fetched the hose and shirt and returned to Ash, all without looking up.

"How do you expect to dress me when you can't even look at me?" Ash could swear he saw the boy's scalp blush.

"I, uh..."

"Go on." Ash waggled his hips to make his cock swing. "We've both got one of these. I'm sure mine looks the same as yours."

The boy made a strangled sound in the back of his throat and Ash thought it best to let him off the hook before he expired from fright. Although whatever he had to be frightened about was a mystery. Ash's cock had been described as many things by the women who'd seen it but frightening wasn't one of them.

A knock at the study door beyond the bedchamber finally drew Pip's attention from the floor, but not in Ash's direction.

"I'll go see who it is, my lord." He rushed off before Ash could tell him not to bother because he knew his mother's knock and she always let herself in.

"Richard? Are you up yet?" She appeared at the door leading from the bedchamber to the study. Pip stopped dead in his tracks and gave her a low bow, lower than he'd ever bowed to Ash. The Countess's gaze swept right over the pageboy's head to Ash as he dressed himself in the wardrobe.

"Ah, you're up." She moved through the bedchamber towards the wardrobe, her stiff black skirts swishing about her. "I thought your night of *revels* might keep you abed today." She said the word as if it were the vilest crime.

"I was at court. The *revels* were all sanctioned by the queen."

"You left court three hours before you arrived home. It does not take that long to ride from Whitehall, Son."

Prickles of irritation crept down Ash's spine. "Mother, you have a spy network more extensive than Walsingham's and a character just as formidable. Heaven help our nation's enemies if you two ever decide to join forces."

"Sarcasm ill becomes you, Richard, as does the redness in your eyes. Have you been drinking again?"

Pip's mouth formed a soundless "O". Ash didn't think his mother had seen but Ash certainly had. Her gaze followed his and she appeared to notice the page for the first time. She raised her hand in dismissal and Pip bowed and turned to Ash.

"Shall I have some breakfast sent up, my lord?" he asked.

*So you can slip out while I'm occupied here?* No, Ash wouldn't let the lad out of his sight until he was certain he wasn't leaving.

He couldn't allow the lad to go off without having another position to go to. It would be irresponsible of him. However, if by the end of the day Pip still wanted to leave, Ash would arrange something at another house. But not before then.

"No. Stay here and...tidy up," he said.

Pip looked like he would argue but he nodded meekly and knelt at a chest to sort through its contents.

The countess crooked her finger for Ash to follow her. She led the way to the study and lowered herself onto one of the stools near the window, arranging her skirts about her. Ash sat where he could still see Pip.

"In answer to your question, no I haven't been drinking, Mother. Not that it's any of your business."

"It most certainly is. When you're too intoxicated to attend to the business of running the estates, or when you forget to pay your sister's creditors—"

He held up his hand for silence and for once, she obeyed. "I only forgot once. It won't happen again. I no longer drink to excess." It grated on his nerves to discuss his habits with his mother like a schoolboy, especially since she had never understood why he drank. It made the nightmares go away and made him forget that warm summer's night in Spain when the nightmares had started. Unfortunately it made him forget other things too.

Ash sat down and stretched out his leg. After the long ride yesterday, his old thigh injury ached a little. Perhaps he should've had Pip rub some ointment into it last night. He would ask him to do it later—that's if the boy was still around.

"I'm glad you came, Mother," he said, keeping his temper at bay. Getting angry at her never achieved anything. She simply ignored him. "You were here last night—"

She clicked her tongue and twisted the rings on her fingers. "I knew I couldn't trust that new pageboy!"

Pip must have heard but he didn't look up from the doublet he was inspecting.

"He didn't tell me," Ash said. "One of the other servants saw you." He couldn't be sure if she believed him. Her expression remained cool and impassive. Just to make sure she didn't suspect Pip, he added to the lie. "If my page knew and said nothing to me then I'll have a word with him."

"Words are never enough with servants, Richard. The sooner you discover that the sooner they'll stop hood-winking you."

He sighed and decided to ignore the on-going argument. Taking her to task would not change her mind and would only inflame the ire bubbling just beneath the surface of his skin.

"Don't change the subject," he said. "We were talking about your intrusion into my study."

"If you don't want anyone in here, you should lock the door."

"I shouldn't *have* to." He kept all the important documents and seals in locked coffers. Usually he didn't keep anything of importance lying about, but the blackmail letter had slipped his mind. "Why did you take the note, Mother?"

She turned to stare out the window. "What note?"

"Mother," he growled, "don't hinder me. That note—"

"Ah, yes." She turned back to him. "I remember it now." Her hazel eyes held no hint of duplicity but his mother was an expert at keeping her thoughts and emotions hidden. "Most unusual. It spoke of a secret. What secret is that do you think?"

Ash shrugged. "I have no idea. I thought you might know since you seemed interested enough to take it."

"Well, I don't. Then again, no one tells me anything." She even managed to look innocent as she said it.

"No one has to. You know everything before it even happens."

She smiled at that and the atmosphere in the study relaxed a little. "Richard, I don't know anything about that note. I took it because I didn't want that pageboy seeing it. I came looking for you and when I didn't find you I was about to leave a message on your desk. But then I saw him rifling through the coffers in your bedchamber."

"Like he is now?"

She lifted a shoulder without looking in Pip's direction.

"Mother, he was probably tidying up. He's very efficient. And he has every right to be rifling through those coffers."

"But what if he moved into the study next?" She leaned

forward. "He doesn't look all that trustworthy if you ask me." At least she had the decency to lower her voice.

"I'm not asking you."

Her only reaction was a lazy blink, a sign of her disappointment in him for talking back to her. She used to tell him to treat her with the deference a countess deserved but she'd stopped saying that years ago. She must have become accustomed to his bluntness.

"When I saw the note on your desk I thought it best to remove it to somewhere safer. Really, Richard," she shook her head, "you left it in full view for anyone to see."

Ash thought it best not to tell her Pip had already read it. "So you know nothing of the secret it mentions?"

She toyed with a large ruby ring. "Not a thing. But it did look quite sinister. That's why I burned it."

"Burned it! It was evidence!"

"Evidence of what? No crime has been committed."

"Blackmailing an earl isn't exactly innocent behavior, Mother."

Her nostrils flared. "You haven't paid anything to anyone have you?"

"No and nor will I if I don't know what the bloody secret is."

"Don't swear."

He grunted an apology and they both fell silent. For his part, Ash was wondering what secrets he had, apart from the obvious one of his position in Walsingham's network. It would be foolish to blackmail him over that since England's spymaster would simply have Ash removed from the position and then would seek out the blackmailer and remove his head from *its* position. But he couldn't think of anything else.

"So, Mother, why did you want to see me last night and now today? I'm sure it's not simply to tell me my eyes look bloodshot and my page can't be trusted."

"And your desk is a mess." But she softened her motherly chiding with a small smile. "I came to tell you that Mr. Briars is coming again today."

"Again! Good lord, he's persistent." His sister's latest suitor had visited every day for two weeks, sometimes to walk with

Annabel (when she had nothing better to do), sometimes to press his case with Ash or the countess. It was tiring and time consuming. Ash had more important things to think about than his sister's admirer, especially since she didn't seem overly interested in the youth.

"What will you tell him?" the countess asked.

"To come back tomorrow. I'm busy today."

"And tomorrow you'll tell him to come back the next day," she said. "You need to make a decision, Richard."

He sighed. It was too early to think about Briars. Dawn was only now baring its arse to the world, and he hadn't even broken his fast yet. "I didn't think Annabel liked him over-much," he said. "She called him a ham-fisted son of a merchant last week. I'm fairly sure she meant it as an insult."

His mother waved a hand and the weak daylight caught the reds, blues and greens of the gems set in her rings and sprayed the colors across the wall. "She'll grow used to the idea with time. I hear he's extraordinarily rich. His father owns more ships than the queen herself."

"We don't need his money. We have quite enough, despite my sister's extravagance."

"She must have the best clothing if she wants to attract the best suitor."

"And Briars is the best?"

Her hesitation was slight but it was there. "He would keep her in comfort for the rest of her life. And with our name and the Briars fortune, Annabel's children could be quite powerful in their time. And if *you* don't produce an heir," she said pointedly, "they may inherit two fortunes."

Ash sighed. Yet another topic of disagreement between them, one which didn't look like it would go away anytime soon. Not unless he found a wife and no one, not even his mother, thought that would happen in the near future. She had given up introducing him to all the eligible girls and widows in England. Of course, that may simply be because she'd run out of candidates.

The countess stood and her glossy black skirts fell perfectly into place. "Ever since the Montalbot heir died, I've been at my wits end over your sister's future."

Annabel had been betrothed to the heir to the earldom of Montalbot since they were both children but he died of a fever a year ago, just before the couple were to wed. With all the other young, eligible bachelors in the country already paired off with eligible girls, Annabel would have to wed an older widowed gentleman, something Ash didn't want to see his high-spirited sister do.

But giving her to Briars didn't sit well with him either. It felt a little too mercenary for his liking—exchanging the Savoy lineage for the Briars fortune. Not that Ash believed in love (not any more) but he did believe in happiness in marriage.

Which was precisely why he'd never contemplated marriage after returning from Spain three years ago. He couldn't see himself happy with any of the girls who paraded themselves in front of him at court. Or, perhaps more to the point, he couldn't see any of them being happy with him. He could be difficult and stubborn at times, and the nightmares would scare off all but the most resilient of women, not to mention the cause of those nightmares.

He resolved to speak to Annabel about the matter and find out once and for all her feelings. If she was completely against the marriage then his mother and Briars would have to accept her decision.

A knock at the door interrupted his thoughts. Fallon entered carrying a tray. He bowed and indicated a missive bearing Walsingham's seal resting on the tray.

"The messenger requires an answer, my lord," the steward said.

Ash took the missive and Fallon handed the tray to Pip who'd joined them. Ash broke the seal and read. When he was only half way through, his heart plunged to his stomach.

"What is it?" his mother asked.

He read to the end, not believing his eyes. Not *wanting* to believe them. He looked up at the faces now watching him expectantly. Even Pip had stopped before reaching the inner chamber where Ash took breakfast, the tray still in his hands.

"This is a request from Walsingham for my services," he told his mother. "He's asked me to investigate a suspicious death.

Since I knew the victim, he thought my investigation may be more expedient than someone with no interest—"

"Who?" his mother whispered. She sat forward on her stool, her head bent towards him, her face slowly draining of color. "Who is it?"

"Georgiana Dale."

"My God." It was Fallon, but his words were barely audible over the clatter of the tray and its contents falling to the floor.

"Oh!" Pip bent to pick up the trencher, cup and tray but it was too late to save the ale already seeping into the rushes. The maid would have to replace them, Ash thought dully.

"I'm sorry," Pip mumbled.

"It doesn't matter," Ash said. He turned to his mother who sat perfectly still on the edge of her stool, her face without expression. The only indication that she was disturbed by the news was her failure to chastise Pip.

"My lord." Fallon sounded distant, like he was speaking from another room. The poor man looked bereft.

"You knew her well, didn't you, Fallon?" Ash said.

"She was a...friend." His voice cracked. He coughed. "My lord, may I inform the others who knew her. Those of us who have been in service to your family for a long time recall her with great fondness. They will be shocked to hear of her death."

Her *suspicious* death. Ash passed a hand over his eyes, fighting back the urge to thump his fist clean through his desk. Now wasn't the time for anger, it was a time for control and reasoning. And sadness. So much sadness.

"By all means," he managed to say. "Give the day off to anyone you feel requires it." He dismissed Fallon and re-read the missive. Walsingham's words swirled on the page and he closed his eyes against the rising tide of nausea. But that only brought fond memories of Georgiana flooding back. Of the countless times she patched up his scraped knees, or when she comforted him or Annabel after they fell foul of their father's temper. She'd taught Ash to read and write before he went to school, she made him learn the lute even though he had a poor ear for music and she never let him get away with any of his pranks like the other servants did. Not that she was a servant, but neither was she a family member. Georgiana Dale fell somewhere in between. In her last few years of service, she became valued nurse to Annabel and companion to his mother. Was it already five years since she retired back to the village of her childhood?

He looked again at the missive. Haverford. That's where she'd died and where he now had to go.

"You'll need to make preparations to leave immediately," his mother said as if reading his mind. She stood and before he could say good-bye, she'd left, her skirts billowing about her like a dust cloud as she rushed out.

"Pip!" Ash called to the boy still in the inner chamber, presumably salvaging breakfast. "Start packing. If we leave right away we can get to Haverford by midday. We'll have to stay at least one night."

Pip emerged and Ash grew alarmed at the change in him. "Are you ill? You look much too pale. Come sit."

"No, I'm quite well." Pip's hands fidgeted, the fingers twining and untwining in constant movement. "It's just that...Fallon may not have told you who I expected to find here at Ashbourne House."

Ash frowned, failing to see the connection at first. But then he noticed the desolation in Pip's face and something in the depths of his eyes that Ash couldn't place. Not quite sadness or grief but...despair?

"It was Mistress Dale wasn't it?" he said. Pip nodded and bowed his head. "Did you know her well?"

"I never met her," the lad said. "She was a friend of my mother's and we sometimes corresponded after Mama's death. She offered to help me if ever I needed it. She was a friend. My only one." This last was spoken so softly, with the boy's chin almost at his chest, that Ash barely heard it. He had a sudden urge to go to the boy and comfort him.

But all he did was nod. "She was...valuable to us in her time here." He shook his head at the word. It simply wasn't the right one to describe what Georgiana meant to the household. To him.

"I'm sorry for your loss, my lord."

Ash's heart clenched. "Thank you. But I think your loss is just as great. Perhaps we can console each other." He coughed to clear the lump in his throat and held up Walsingham's orders. "Finding out how and why she died is the least we can do."

"*We,* my lord?"

"I need an attendant and you need to be away from my mother for a while." He tried to sound light when all he felt was a heavy weight pressing down on him. "It'll do us both some good."

The boy took a long time to answer, probably because he still wanted to leave but now he also wanted to help Ash investigate the death. Finally Pip nodded and Ash felt relieved. He suspected the boy might be alone in the world now that Georgiana was gone. Ash may not be in quite the same situation, but he certainly felt a deep hole in his heart at the death of someone so close to him.

And a very deep sense of responsibility to avenge her murder.

\* \* \*

Pippa was grateful for the easy chatter Lord Ashbourne and his groom, Lewis, kept up most of the way to Haverford. Silence would have given her time to think and she definitely didn't want to do that. Thinking would only allow her to contemplate the horror of what had happened.

Georgiana dead.

Pippa was now all alone.

Tears welled whenever she did allow herself to contemplate it but each time Lord Ashbourne engaged her in conversation. Usually a question about herself which she had so far managed to deflect without raising too much suspicion. She suspected he wasn't all that interested in the answers anyway, and was only attempting to raise her spirits. A noble gesture since he too was saddened by Georgiana's death if his reaction that morning was anything to go by.

His offer to take her to Haverford had been a surprise at first but one which she quickly decided to embrace. There was no longer any need to leave Ashbourne House. Where would she go now that Georgiana was dead? She had no money and no contacts. Her only real option was to stay in disguise as a servant until she could think of what to do in the longer term.

She shifted in her saddle and wished his lordship had chosen to travel by coach instead of horseback. Thankfully Haverford was an easy ride from London. She was out of practice and her thighs ached by the time they reached the village.

They went immediately to find the local justice of the peace who took them to Georgiana's cottage on the edge of the village. For one elderly lady, it was a sizeable two-storey house with a small but neat garden out front. Pippa supposed Mistress Dale had received a large settlement from the Savoy family after her many years of service to be able to afford it. Very large indeed.

The justice of the peace., Sir Francis Fordham, unlocked the door and went in. Lord Ashbourne followed but paused on the threshold when Pippa stayed out the front with the earl's groom and horses.

Although she desperately wanted to see where Georgiana had lived, wanted to touch her things and know more about the woman who'd dared befriend her, she stayed back. Her desperation to maintain her disguise as a serving boy was far greater and a servant stayed outside when his master conducted business.

But Lord Ashbourne surprised her. "You're coming, Pip," he said. She knew an order when she heard one so followed him inside.

She wanted to ask him why he needed her presence but didn't because he was already asking Fordham questions.

"Where was the body found?"

Sir Francis indicated a chair by the fireplace. "She was sitting there, slumped forward." He picked up the embroidery Georgiana must have been working on when she died. It was covered in dried blood. "This was on her knee."

"How did she die?" Lord Ashbourne asked.

"Knife wound to the chest." Sir Francis tapped his breast. "Straight through the heart."

"Only one stab wound?"

"Only one. Death must have been instant."

"Any other wounds? To her hands or arms perhaps?"

"Defensive wounds? No, my lord, none. Not even a bruise."

The earl bent to study the chair and its surroundings and Pippa looked about the room. It was a parlor situated to receive the morning sun and must have been used to entertain callers if its large size and the number of chairs was any indication. The clean rushes gave off the faint smell of lavender which failed to completely eradicate the lingering stench of death. A Turkey carpet covered a small table near the fireplace and embroidered cushions made the chair seats more comfortable. Tapestries and painted cloths hung on the walls. Pippa recognized the Biblical story of the prodigal son depicted in one and the court of Diana, the Roman goddess of the hunt, in another. She stepped closer for a better look. They were very fine.

Two framed pictures hanging near the mantelpiece caught her attention. One was of a young girl she didn't recognize, but the other made her gasp.

"What is it, Pip?" Lord Ashbourne asked from behind her. He stood so close she could smell him, a delicious mix of man, horse and something spicy.

"That's you, my lord."

Lord Ashbourne leaned forward. His chest brushed against Pippa's shoulder and his chin almost touched her head. She resisted the urge to step back into his strength and warmth, an irresistible combination in the unsettling atmosphere of the cottage.

"So it is," he said, a smile in his voice. "A lot younger and better looking, but it is me. And that's my sister, Annabel." He pointed at the other portrait.

"She looks very young," Pippa said.

"There's a sixteen year age difference between us. I recall sitting for my portrait about five or so years ago."

She turned to watch him and was startled to see sadness in his eyes. "This is hard for you, isn't it?"

"Aye," was all he said before looking away. "I knew Mistress Dale kept us in fond regard even after she left Ashbourne House but I didn't know these pictures were intended for her. Mother commissioned them I think."

They were beautifully framed. The detail in the silver was

superb with ivy climbing up each side, coming together at the top where the two vines twisted together.

Everywhere in the parlor were signs of Georgiana's good taste. She had surrounded herself with beautiful things like the frames and tapestries, but had not filled every corner with objects. Pippa liked the woman more for it. Her despair grew sharper, stabbing her in the chest.

It had been like this after she'd lost her father. One day Pippa had been enjoying a walk through the woods near the house and the next she'd become her uncle's ward. In those first few weeks, she'd blamed her father for abandoning her to a man who refused to let her out of the house without a guard and only then to walk in the garden. How could Father have been so selfish to leave her?

"Did she die alone?" she blurted out before she could stop herself. Lord Ashbourne and Sir Francis turned as one to look at her. "I'm sorry," she said, stepping back into the shadows.

"Don't be," Lord Ashbourne said. "She meant something to you and your family too. Ask as many questions as you want." He nodded in Sir Francis' direction. "Well?"

"She was alone when she died," he said.

It wasn't exactly what Pippa meant but she said nothing. She'd wanted to know if Georgiana had friends or relations who loved her. It was obvious Lord Ashbourne and perhaps Fallon had, but they were in London and would have seen her rarely once she moved back to Haverford.

"Who found her?" Lord Ashbourne asked.

"Bessie the maid comes every day. She has a key."

"The door was locked?"

"Yes. Didn't you know?" Sir Francis's bushy grey eyebrows rose. "That's what's so interesting. Both front and back doors and all windows were locked. Mistress Dale could have let the killer in but she couldn't have locked the door after they left. There's no bloodstains on the rushes," he said, indicating the floor. "I don't think she moved from that chair. There's simply no explanation as to how the killer got out and locked the door behind him."

"Unless he had a key," Lord Ashbourne reminded him.

"Bessie's the only one with a key and she swears she didn't kill her."

Lord Ashbourne didn't look like he believed Sir Francis or Bessie. "So how do you suppose someone came in and killed her then left, locking the door behind them?"

Sir Francis swallowed beneath the earl's bald glare. "I...uh, that is to say, I don't know."

"I think you have a supposition, Sir Francis. Well? What is it?"

The justice of the peace. looked like a cornered fox. "Witchcraft," he blurted out.

Lord Ashbourne rolled his eyes and crossed his arms over his chest. "Go on."

"I have two theories, my lord." He stretched his neck and scratched at the beard beneath his chin. "One is that a witch unlocked the door with her powers, killed Mistress Dale then locked it again after she left. The problem with that theory is *why* would she lock the door? There's no need. The other theory, more...controversial in nature—"

"This should be interesting."

Sir Francis swallowed but went on. "The other theory is that Mistress Dale was the witch. She was stabbed by a person whom she allowed into her house. After the killer left, as Mistress Dale sat here dying, she used her powers to lock the door so he couldn't return."

Blood rushed between Pippa's ears and the breath was sucked out of her.

Witchcraft. *Oh God oh God oh God.*

She put a hand out to clutch something, anything, to stop herself falling, and found the back of a chair.

Then Lord Ashbourne burst out laughing. It was a humorless, harsh sound and Pippa was grateful when it ended. "That is the most ludicrous thing I have ever heard," he said. "Mistress Dale was no witch. And if she was, why not use her powers to fight off her attacker? And you've missed the most important question of all. Why kill her in the first place? This doesn't appear to be a random attack. Nothing is disturbed or missing. Those picture frames alone are worth a lot of money. This was a deliberate act of violence against a well-liked woman." He seemed to be talking to himself now, unaware that he was speaking aloud. "Why kill sweet old Georgiana?"

Fordham said nothing as he watched Lord Ashbourne disappear into the adjoining room. Neither Sir Francis nor Pippa followed him.

"Is that what the villagers think?" she asked. "That Mistress Dale was a witch?"

Sir Francis hesitated before nodding. "Someone once said they saw her move a heavy log in the forest. It was in her path and she never touched it with her hands. Then there's the Simpson boy's broken leg which healed extraordinarily quickly after she laid her hands on the injury." He wrinkled his pointy nose as if he smelled something rotten. "And the fire in the Finley house was said to have been started by her after she and Mistress Finley argued two years back. No one was home at the time, but..." He shrugged and Pippa guessed how awful it had become for Georgiana. The villagers near her father's estate had been quick to blame someone already suspected of witchcraft for every unfavorable event—a poor harvest, an untimely death. After that it was a short step to a trial and execution.

All the more reason for Pippa to be afraid of her own new, untried abilities, and of her uncle. She had no doubt he'd already commissioned the Witch Hunter to find her. He could be looking for her right now.

"It doesn't make sense," she said, shaking her head to dislodge her fears over her own situation. "If she could heal as you say, then why not heal her own stab wound? And as Lord Ashbourne noted, why didn't she use her powers to defend herself? No, she couldn't possibly have been a witch." But doubt lingered like a thick fog.

She stared out a window at the pretty garden until Lord Ashbourne returned, looking even more dark and dangerous than when he left. "Have you spoken to the neighbors?" he asked.

"What for?" Sir Francis said.

The earl grunted. "Where's the body laid out? I'll need to see it."

Sir Francis's eyes widened. "But she was buried yesterday, my lord."

"What!" Lord Ashbourne looked like he wanted to put a fist through something, and Sir Francis looked like he suspected it would be his face. "How can that be? I only received my orders this morning."

"She died three days ago and the weather has been unseasonably warm. Nor was I told there would be an official investigation. There never has been before."

"The circumstances are suspicious in this case," Lord Ashbourne said without seeming to move his jaw. "And it so happens Mistress Dale was a friend of mine. I wanted to solve the puzzle of her death before she was laid to rest."

"Oh. I see." Sir Francis shrugged. "My humble apologies, but there was nothing else I could do."

Lord Ashbourne swore and stalked outside. "I want to speak to the neighbors." He stopped, turned and strode back inside the cottage. He emerged a moment later carrying the two framed portraits of himself and his sister. Without another word, he headed to the house next door.

The neighbor on one side was of little help. He claimed not to have seen anything out of the ordinary. He did, however, suspect witchcraft was involved because he'd regularly seen Mistress Dale feed a pigeon which *must* have been her familiar.

"A pigeon," Lord Ashbourne said with a derisive huff as they left to try the other neighbor. She also suspected witchcraft but added something more useful.

"Mistress Dale had a gentleman caller the day before her death," the woman said, shooing a little boy away with a swish of her apron. The child moved back a step but slowly crept forward again and peered up at the adults from behind his mother's skirts. "Late it was, after supper and growing dark. I'd lost Jimmy again." She ruffled the boy's hair. "So I was looking out the front window for him because he likes to play in the dirt. That's when I saw the man."

"Can you describe him?" Lord Ashbourne asked.

"The light was poor," she said, apologetically, "but I can tell you he was a big man like yourself. He had a lovely white horse too. That's where I found Jimmy, petting this great beast. He loves horses." She ruffled her son's hair again then shooed him off once more.

"Is there anything else you can tell us about this visitor?" Sir Francis asked.

"Why yes, his name. Mistress Dale called him Sir Guy."

"Thank you," Lord Ashbourne said. "You've been most helpful. If you think of anything else, I'll be staying at the Two Oaks."

Pippa followed Sir Francis and Lord Ashbourne to a small field across the road where the horses grazed idly in the late afternoon sunshine. Lewis the groom had fallen asleep under a tree and awoke with a start when they approached.

"We'll bid you good-day, Sir Francis," Lord Ashbourne said. "If I have any more questions I'll send Lewis for you."

Sir Francis looked like he'd just been slapped across the cheek. "But my wife and I were hoping you would join us for supper, my lord."

"Another time. My page has a headache."

Pippa bit her tongue as Sir Francis's lips pursed so tight they went white. To his credit, he extended the offer to dine with them to the following day.

"Fool," Lord Ashbourne muttered as Sir Francis rode off. He mounted his own horse with an athletic bound and waited while Lewis helped Pippa up into her saddle. Before this journey was through she decided she must at least learn to mount without assistance. It was embarrassing that a fifteen year-old youth needed help.

As the earl's servant, it would usually fall to her to make the accommodation arrangements at the inn but when they arrived, the earl took charge. Pippa thought it was simply because he liked to be in control of every situation but when the innkeeper greeted him like an old friend, she realized Lord Ashbourne had stayed many times at the Two Oaks and already knew what he wanted. He must have been a frequent visitor to Mistress Dale after all.

"My lord, I wondered if you would come," the innkeeper said with a sympathetic frown when he greeted them in the taproom. "You have my deepest sympathies. She was a good woman. A very good woman. Laid her out here, they did, and I was happy to do it too."

"I'm investigating her death. Tell me, Thomason, what have you heard?" Lord Ashbourne leaned against the bench looking like a man without a care in the world. Only Pippa, standing a little to the side, could see the tension in his stiff back and the sadness lurking in the corners of his eyes.

The innkeeper, standing opposite, leaned forward. "Did you hear the door was locked?"

The earl shot him a glare. "If I hear anything about witchcraft from you I'll make you regret it."

The innkeeper held up his hands. "I'm only repeating what I heard, my lord. But in my opinion, witchcraft must be involved. Why would the Witch Hunter be here if—"

"Witch Hunter?" Lord Ashbourne and Pippa said together.

Oh dear God! *He was here.*

Panic punched her in the gut and knocked the breath from her body. She swallowed the bile rising to her throat but that only made her feel more ill.

All was lost now. It was only a matter of time before he found her.

And the one person who could help her was dead.

# CHAPTER 4

"*S*ir Guy!" Lord Ashbourne thumped his fist on the table. "Of course! The gentleman leaving Mistress Dale's the day before her death was Sir Guy de St. Cyr." He turned to Pippa, his face alight. "Also known as the Witch Hunter. Good Lord, Pip, are you ill?"

Pippa scanned the taproom but none of the patrons looked like a gentleman intent on killing her. It didn't make her feel any easier. "Yes, my lord," she said weakly. "I have a headache."

"A real one?"

"I'm almost certain of it."

One corner of his mouth curved up then flattened again. "You must get to bed." He inclined his head at the innkeeper. "My usual room, Thomason."

A room. Yes. Somewhere she could hide.

Pippa waited for him to organize another room for her. He didn't. She followed him up the stairs on legs that wanted to run in the other direction, away from Haverford and the Witch Hunter. They entered a large bedchamber and her anxiety turned in another direction when she saw there was no adjoining chamber for her, not even a small closet. A single, albeit large, bed dominated the room and a pallet occupied a space near the hearth.

Lord Ashbourne put down the travel bags (he'd insisted on

carrying them because of Pippa's 'headache') and nodded in the direction of the pallet. "Rest awhile, Pip." He moved to the door. "It's been a long day."

"And you, my lord? Are you not going to rest too?"

"Not yet. I want to find out more about our Witch Hunter."

He left and Pippa sank onto the pallet and curled up into a ball. She was living in a nightmare. First Georgiana Dale murdered and now the Witch Hunter had turned up. Sir Guy must have discovered the connection between Georgiana and Pippa and come to Haverford to learn more. How long would it take him to find her? And what did he already know? Was he on his way to Ashbourne House in London right now?

Or was he still in Haverford? Waiting. Hoping to trap her.

She shivered beneath the woolen blanket even though the room wasn't cold. An even more sickening thought struck her. What if the Witch Hunter had killed Georgiana? What if Pippa had inadvertently led him to her and he'd discovered she too possessed unnatural powers?

It was too awful to contemplate and her mind froze, unable to think except to fuel her own fears. She wasn't sure how long she lay there before Lord Ashboune returned carrying a tray.

"Supper," he announced. "Hungry?"

"No." She sat up and automatically put a hand to her hair to smooth it only to remember it was now shorter. She flipped at the wisps barely covering her ears then looked up and caught the earl watching her with an odd expression. It was on the tip of her tongue to ask him why he stared but the servant in her thought best not to.

"Eat anyway," he said and she joined him at the small table where he set down the trenchers laden with bread, cheese and cold beef. "You need your strength to help me solve this puzzle."

Or to escape. With Georgiana gone and the Witch Hunter on her trail, she should leave. But where would she go?

"What of the Witch Hunter?" she asked with a serviceable attempt at keeping the tremble out of her voice. "Is he still in Haverford?"

"No." Lord Ashbourne sighed as he stacked cheese and beef between two slices of thick bread. "He's gone to places unknown." He lifted the lot to his mouth but stopped when he saw Pippa looking at him. "What?"

In her relief, she became a little light-headed which loosened her tongue. "I am curious if that will fit in your mouth, my lord."

"Some say my mouth is as big as other parts of me." She gasped and he threw his head back and laughed then bit down through his supper.

Pippa concentrated on her own supper while her blushes slowly receded. It seemed the earl was making a sport out of teasing her. Well, she would have to simply pretend not to be alarmed by his bawdy comments.

After supper, the earl lay on top of his bed without removing his boots. He clasped his hands behind his head and stared at the canopy above.

Pippa picked at her food, her thoughts only in one direction. "My lord, why do you suppose the Witch Hunter went to Mistress Dale's house?"

He didn't say anything or move for a long time. If his eyes hadn't been open she would have thought him asleep. Slowly he turned on his side and propped his head up with one hand. "I was hoping you could tell me."

Her supper rebelled in her stomach. Did he suspect her? "I...I..." She swallowed. "I couldn't possibly begin to suppose."

He sighed. "I have no idea either."

She blew out a long breath and some of the tension left her body. "Perhaps, sir, we should consider something which I think you will find rather disturbing."

"That Georgiana was a witch?"

She had expected him to snap at her as he had Sir Francis and Thomason but it seemed he'd grown accustomed to the idea. "It's something we must consider," she said again. "It appears the entire village thought she was one, and now the Witch Hunter's presence will be seen as confirmation."

"You think they are more than rumors don't you, Pip?"

She shrugged. "I truly don't know. But it's possible."

It was more than possible. And as she unraveled the tangled threads of her thoughts, she knew it must be true. Georgiana and her mother had been friends although no one could tell Pippa how the connection had begun. Not even her father when he had delivered Georgiana's first letter to Pippa after her mother's death all those years ago. In that letter, Georgiana had promised to write often and check on Pippa's wellbeing. At the end of each missive, she wrote that Pippa was to contact her if she needed help, no matter what difficulty she found herself in. It had always seemed an obscure thing to say.

Pippa had looked forward to the letters until her uncle had severed the acquaintance along with her freedom when she went to live with him.

"Georgiana must have been a witch," she finally said.

"Yes." Lord Ashbourne watched her from the bed. "It would seem she was."

It made sense, simply because only a witch would offer sanctuary to another, even one whose powers hadn't yet come in. Somehow she had known that Pippa's witchcraft would one day develop. Perhaps Georgiana had promised Pippa's dying mother to take care of her daughter when the time came, or perhaps it was a responsibility Georgiana wanted to take on anyway. Whatever the reason, Pippa was grateful. If Georgiana hadn't continued the friendship, Pippa may never have left The Grange —she would have been an easy target for the Witch Hunter.

But Georgiana's advanced knowledge of Pippa's powers did throw up one interesting point. "Witchcraft is an hereditary trait, is it not?" she asked him.

"I believe so. In the female line."

If Georgiana was a witch and she knew Pippa was one, that meant Pippa's mother must have been a witch too. It had been the connection between the two women, the one her father hadn't known about.

It was also the connection between Pippa and her mother, the woman she could barely remember. It was the one solid thing she had of her now, and the only thing her uncle could not take from her.

Tears prickled her eyes and she turned away so the earl couldn't see.

"Are you all right, Pip?" he asked, sitting up.

She dared not look at him in case the tears spilled. It was one thing to cry in front of the master, it was entirely another to be a *man* and cry in front of the master. Well, almost a man. Pip had some pride, as did Pippa.

"What else do you know of witchcraft, my lord?" she asked, hoping to distract him with theories. "Do they use familiars and cast spells on disgruntled neighbors?" She said it only half-joking —she truly had no idea what powers she was *supposed* to have. Her opinion was based solely on village gossip, and she knew *that* couldn't be trusted.

"Not in my experience."

The way he said it made her glance up suddenly. He was staring at her but he didn't seem to quite see her. "My lord? You have had an experience with a witch?"

One corner of his mouth crooked into something not quite a grin and his gaze re-focused on her. "I think I can trust you, Pip."

"Of course." She hardly breathed, wanting to hear what he had to say on the subject but wanting even more for him to honor her with his trust. She would cherish it. "Nothing you ever tell me in confidence would be repeated by my lips, my lord."

He watched her with a quizzical expression and she supposed he was warring with himself, trying to decide if he could trust her or not. Finally, he blinked, slowly. "I can, can't I?"

She nodded. A strange sort of air had descended around them, still and breathless and heavy. She didn't want to disturb it with words in case he revoked his decision.

"She is the wife of a very good friend," he said. "From her I know that witchcraft is inherited through the female line. I know that she uses her mind powers to heal, seek with the aid of a talisman and move objects about, sometimes with alarming effect." Again, the rueful smile.

Seeking? How intriguing. "And start fires," she added.

His gaze sharpened. "Really? Well, it seems we both know a witch then."

She held his gaze for fear she would appear guilty if she looked away. His friend's wife may be a witch but that did not mean the earl liked that fact. It simply meant he had not betrayed her to the authorities. Pippa would not risk telling him her secret. Not yet.

"So you think Sir Francis was right and Georgiana locked her door herself while she lay dying in her chair?" Pippa asked. The gruesome image made her shiver.

"You're cold." He stripped a blanket from his bed and tossed it to her then got up to stoke the dying fire to life. "I'm still not certain about Sir Francis' theory," he said, his broad back to her. "It needs more investigation. Tomorrow."

"Tomorrow." She rose from the table and lay the extra blanket on her pallet. "Are you going to bed, my lord?" she asked, moving up beside him to warm her hands by the fire.

He sighed. "I suppose I must. There aren't enough candles to read by."

"I can fetch some for you."

"No." He gave her a lazy smile. "I don't want to keep you awake. We have another long day ahead of us."

Pippa didn't think she'd get much sleep, not between her distressing thoughts and his nightmares. But she said nothing about either of those things.

She watched him surreptitiously beneath half-closed lids. The flames cast patterns of light and dark across his face, sharpening his cheeks and shadowing his eyes. The effect would have been devilish if he wasn't so handsome.

He must have sensed her scrutiny because he cocked his head to the side. A muscle in his jaw worked, as if he wanted to say something. But instead of talking, he strode to the bed and removed one of his boots.

She moved to help him but he held up his hand. "I'll undress myself." He dropped his other boot to the floor and she picked them up and tucked them under the bed. "I hope I don't keep you awake," he said without further explanation. There was no need of one.

"Is there anything I can do if you're troubled by dreams tonight, my lord?"

"Throw cold water over me."

She didn't laugh. Why did he not do something about his nightmares? "I could prepare a draught—"

She stopped when he rapidly undid his shirt buttons and cast a triumphant look in her direction. It seemed he had learned that his nakedness—even the threat of it—stopped her in her tracks. But why did he want to thwart her attempts to help him through his bad dreams? He was as much a mystery as the one they were investigating in Haverford.

She settled under the blankets on her pallet. When Lord Ashbourne blew out the candles and the fire had died to a dull glow in the grate, she removed her clothes and slept in her shirt. As long as she awoke before the earl, she would be able to quickly dress beneath the covers without raising suspicion.

Despite her raging fears and tumbled thoughts, she eventually drifted off to sleep, only to wake with a start some time later to shouting coming from the bed. It took a heartbeat to realize the earl was simply having one of his nightmares. No, not simply. There was nothing simple about them. From the moonlight streaming through the window, she could see him fling himself from one side to the other. He growled low in his chest like an animal and reached out for something that wasn't there.

"No," he mumbled, then louder: "No!"

She knelt by his bed, wanting to touch his sweat-soaked brow yet afraid of what he might do in his sleep. He thrashed about so violently, fisting his hands into the blanket and groaning as if in pain.

"No!" Suddenly his eyes opened and his face twisted into the grimace of a tortured man.

Pippa jerked back in horror but he grabbed her shirt and pulled her close.

He mumbled something unintelligible then his eyes closed and she realized he hadn't actually woken. But even in sleep he was strong. He hauled her up onto the bed by her shirt and flung his arm around her waist so that she had no choice but to lie beside him.

He nestled against her, his head on her shoulder, his face buried in her throat, and sighed deeply. The thrashing and mumblings stopped and his body relaxed. She didn't move, not daring to disturb him, partly for fear his nightmares would return but mostly because her breasts were pressed into him and if he awoke he would certainly know them for what they were.

She couldn't risk her identity being revealed, even now. Especially now.

She would have to lie still until he was in a deep sleep, then she could slip out from his grasp and return to the safety of her pallet and blankets. The earl would be none the wiser.

* * *

Ash woke up with a woman in his bed. Even half asleep, he knew it was a woman from her smell, her softness but mostly from the delicious mounds of her breasts. He lay still as the last remains of slumber were chased away by awakening desire. He grew hard. And with every breath he drew in her scent, sweet and tasty and vaguely familiar. He grew harder. He removed his arm from around her waist, slowly so as not to wake her.

Who was she? And why was she in his bed? He wasn't quite alert enough to let those questions jerk him into full wakefulness. First things first. He had some exploring to do. He found the opening of her shirt and allowed himself a touch. Just one fingertip. It was enough to know she was warm and smooth. She lay on her side, her long, lean body stretched out beside him. They fit together snugly, her curves molded to him, her chin resting on the top of his head.

He knew he should wake her, question her, but God help him, his cock overruled his head and he continued to explore the delights beneath her shirt. He gently palmed her breast, encasing its firm roundness. The nipple pebbled and he let out a ragged breath.

He had to taste her. He pressed his lips against her throat and a small shudder rippled through her body. A sigh escaped her lips and she pressed into his palm. Her fingers wound through his hair and she arched her neck to expose her throat to his kisses. He was only too willing to plant more there.

But the dream-like magic was broken too soon. She sat bolt upright with a yelp. Fumbling about, she pulled one of the blankets up to her chin and moved to get out of bed.

He caught her arm. "No you don't." He didn't want her to

leave. Not until he'd seen her face and questioned her. Who was she and what in God's name was she doing in his bed?

"Pip, are you awake?" he said softly. No sound came from the direction of the pallet. Ash would have to light the candles himself.

"Don't move," he said to the woman. He could feel her trembling as he let go of her to stoke the fire and light a candle in the glowing coals. He frowned when he noticed his page had abandoned his pallet. "I won't hurt you," he said to reassure the woman. She made no attempt to leave.

He returned to the bed with two lit candles and held one up to her face. "Pip!" He leapt off the bed, not believing his eyes. "What the devil is going on?"

Pip knelt on the bed, eyes closed. He (er, she) was breathing hard and shaking violently.

Ash's own hands began to tremble, but not from fear, and he put the candles down on the side table. He hurriedly dressed, keeping his eyes firmly on her the entire time. "Answer me!" The familiar ball of fire burst between his eyes and consumed him until he was shaking from anger and frustration. "I should thrash you," he growled.

Her eyes opened wide and she shifted as far back on the bed as she could to get away from him. "I'm sorry," she whispered. "I'm sorry, my lord, I never meant to deceive you."

"Never *meant* to deceive me," he repeated, a snarl making his voice low and harsh. "Swive, *woman*. What have you got to say for yourself?"

She clutched the blanket in front of her and climbed off the bed. She edged towards the door. He blocked her path and fixed her with a glare. "Well, Pip?" He swore. "What the bloody hell is your real name?"

"Pippa," she whispered. "Philippa. My lord, please don't hurt me."

His breathing came thick and fast. How could he have trusted her? He had told her about Isabel Merritt. He'd trusted her with a friend's secret. How could he have been so foolish?

Thank God he hadn't told her anything else.

Even so, he had been incredibly stupid not to see her for

what she was. Those big brown eyes, thick lashes and smooth skin. And her smell. Her scent would haunt many of his nights now, alongside his other dreams. How could he not have seen her as a woman when it was so obvious? He was a blind fool.

"Who do you work for?" he asked.

She blinked back at him and one tear spilled down her cheek. She swiped it away with the back of her hand. "Work for?"

"The Spanish? Scots? Or someone closer to home?"

"No one, my lord. I am no spy. I'm simply an innocent girl—"

"Innocent?" He snorted. "Ha! And I'm the queen of England."

She whimpered and pulled the blanket higher but it didn't hide her trembling. She was probably cold and frightened. Good. In his experience fear made interrogation easier, although he'd have expected his enemies to employ someone with a stronger constitution to infiltrate his household. His *home*.

Anger rose again, bittersweet. "Tell me who you work for and I might spare you the rack."

"No one," she whispered. "I work for no one. Please, my lord, may I dress?" Silent tears slid down her cheeks. He turned away, refusing to be moved. "Please, my lord, I'm so very sorry. Don't try to hurt me."

Try? He would do more than *try*. He hardened his heart against her pleas. A soft heart had got him into trouble in the past and he wasn't about to make the same mistake again.

"Do you have anything other than my livery?" he said, looking at her again. She shook her head. "Then use my cloak."

He reached for it and grabbed his sword at the same time. Couldn't have her lunging for it and using it on him. He threw her the cloak and she flung it about her shoulders but not before he saw the swelling of her breasts when she let go of the blanket.

He concentrated hard on his anger to dampen his desire. "Now, I repeat: who are you and who do you work for?"

"My lord, I already said—"

"Stop lying to me! Damn you, don't you know what will happen to you if you don't tell me?" He couldn't control the shudder that tore through him. He'd seen Walsingham's torture chamber once. It was no place for a lady, even if she was a spy.

"But you must hear my story," she pleaded.

"I don't want to hear fairytales.

"I'm telling the truth. I'm not a spy, my lord." She knelt before him and reached for his hand but he snatched it away before she could touch him. "Please." She raised tear-filled eyes. "You must believe me. Georgiana Dale—"

"Do not mention that good lady's name! I don't know how you dragged her into this dangerous game but I will see your head roll for it. Mark me, Pippa or whoever you are, if her death has anything to do with you, you will regret it."

Her gaze slid to the floor and her shoulders shook with silent crying. He looked to the fire, the bed, everywhere except at her. Kicking and screaming females he could handle. Weepy ones made him feel like his boat had run aground.

With a grunt of frustration at his weakness, he turned and fled from the room. He locked the door and expected to hear her fists pounding on the other side but there was only silence. Good. He would question her properly when he returned after a long walk to calm down. His interrogations were always more thorough when he was in control. He'd found (the hard way) that letting his emotions rule him never worked to his advantage.

It wasn't until he was outside that he realized he wore no jerkin or cloak and he still held his sword. The night air chilled his heated skin but had little effect on his temper. What was to be done with the girl? No, she was no girl. She was most definitely a woman. Probably in her early or mid-twenties. How could he have not noticed?

He cursed her, God, Fortune and himself again then reached for his flask. It was an old habit and of course he found nothing. The flask had been abandoned along with his hard drinking. It seemed he would have to calm himself some other way tonight.

He walked briskly from the inn to the other side of the village and back again but still his foul humor clung to him. As a result, his thoughts were a jumbled mess and all he could do was curse and blame and keep on walking. He'd almost completed a full circuit of the village when he heard footsteps behind him. He quickened his pace and the footsteps sped up too. More than one set of them if his hearing was correct.

He turned the corner and slipped into a narrow alley. The footsteps went past, stopped then returned.

"Where'd he go?" a man's voice carried on the crisp night air. Three shadowy figures stood at the alley entrance.

"Down there," another said.

"We got him then," the first man said with a self-satisfied sneer.

"How do we know it's him? Could be anyone."

"It's him," said the third man. "I seen him earlier in the Two Oaks. Thomason called him 'my lord Ashbourne'. It's him."

A sensible man would have remained hidden but Ash was in no mood to be sensible. Besides, three-to-one weren't bad odds. Not when he was in a murderous mood.

Although he was surrounded by buildings on three sides, the one on his left was only a single storey. Perfect. He kept to the shadows and jumped, catching the edge of the overhanging eave. He hauled himself up and onto the tiled roof then lay flat against the steep incline. Slowly he inched sideways until he was at the front of the building. He leapt to the ground, trapping the three men between him and the narrow alley.

"Looking for me?" he asked, flexing his fingers around his rapier's hilt.

As one, three men turned and drew their swords. Ash parried the blow from the closest man as he kicked the one on his left in the gut. The third came at him, sword raised and yelling like a madman. His blade slashed wildly through the air and Ash shook his head. Idiots. When the man charged, Ash side-stepped out of the way and the attacker flew right past him and careened into a stinking pile of refuse.

"Someone care to tell me why I've been set upon by three inept thugs."

The two remaining men ran into the fray together. Ash engaged both, parrying until he grew bored.

"No answer?" he said. "Perhaps I should kill one of you so the others see that I mean to find out who sent you?"

One of the men faltered and Ash saw the opening and stabbed. The opponent dropped his sword with a scream of pain, just as his friend from the refuse pile joined in. Ash smelled his approach before he saw him.

"Will someone please talk before we all lose our sense of smell." Ash held the upper hand against the two uninjured men but even so, one managed to tear the sleeve of Ash's shirt and cut his arm. "You shouldn't have done that," he said with a click of his tongue. He picked up the pace and took control of the fight. He disarmed one then the other and all three men stepped back out of his reach, nursing various minor cuts.

"Who employed you?" Ash snapped. "Come now, tell me before I get really mad and remove your heads."

"We don't know," said the one with the bleeding hand.

"Shut it!" snarled his stinking friend.

"He didn't pay us enough for this!"

"You're right," said the third.

Ash relaxed his grip on his sword but didn't sheath it. "You say you don't know who sent you?" he prompted.

"He wore a black cloak and kept his hood low over his head. Never saw his face."

"What about his voice? Anything unusual about it?"

The men shrugged. "Soft," one said, "so's we couldn't tell who was speakin'."

"Could it have been a woman?"

More shrugs. "Maybe."

The three men lingered, glancing uncertainly at each other. Clearly they were new to the business of hired killers.

"Thank you," Ash said, moving away.

"You're thanking us for attacking you?" one of the men asked.

"Yes, it's been most diverting. A little blood sport was just what I needed to ease my temper."

The men stared at him, mouths open.

"Women troubles," Ash explained.

All three nodded knowingly as they shuffled off, casting glances back in Ash's direction, probably to make sure he wasn't going to come after them while their backs were turned.

Ash headed in the direction of Two Oaks. He breathed deeply, filling his body with fresh air. He felt warmer after the fight at least, and his dark mood had vanished. His shirt might be torn and his arm bleeding but he could at least think clearly.

And one thought rose above the rest. Pip/Pippa/Phillippa/Whoever couldn't be a spy. Not if Georgiana had sent her as she claimed. Georgiana was like family, and although he didn't always get along the members of his family, he knew they would never betray him. Georgiana certainly wouldn't. Her sense of obligation was too strong. And according to Fallon, Pip hadn't sought employment at Ashbourne House, he'd sought Georgiana Dale. It was Fallon who'd talked him into the position of pageboy and by his steward's account, he (she!) had been reluctant.

Which meant Pippa was no spy.

And now he had to face her and admit his mistake.

He sighed heavily as he trudged back to Two Oaks. He at least owed her the chance to explain, especially after the liberties he'd taken in his semi-conscious state. God's blood, had he really touched her breast? He groaned. What had he been thinking?

Clearly his cock had taken control of his mind.

Well, there'd be no more of *that*. This woman had Trouble written all over her pretty face.

# CHAPTER 5

*P*ippa caressed the Ashbourne crest embroidered on the sleeve of her discarded livery. When she'd worn it, she'd been the earl's capable and efficient pageboy not the puddle of tears she was now, cowering beneath his cloak as if the sky might fall on her head if she so much as said the wrong thing. She didn't like that girl. Didn't want to *be* her anymore.

She needed to be Pip the pageboy again. As Pip, she had felt a measure of safety at Ashbourne House. She'd also felt more like herself—or at least the Pippa she *wanted* to be.

However, getting the earl to agree to keep her on as Pip might prove difficult if his dark rage when he left the inn was anything to go by. Hopefully when he returned he'd have calmed down enough to listen to reason. As a friend of Georgiana Dale's, surely he must see Pippa wasn't out to do him harm.

He did seem to be a reasonable man, and a good-natured one, when calm. If only he would stay calm long enough to hear her explanation. Or at least part of it. The part that didn't involve her being a witch.

Even leaving that piece of information out, it was not a simple thing to ask him to protect her within his home, and within his own lodgings at that. Not after what had just happened.

Good Lord, what *had* just happened?

Memories teased her mind and body, making her hot and confused all over again. A warm hand on her bare breast. Feathery kisses against her pulsing throat. Heat and desire spreading through her, driving out good sense and modesty. Wanting. Needing. Aching for more, for him.

With a deep sigh, she tried to shove the memories away. There was simply no point dwelling on what had happened in the bed. No good could come of it, particularly while she needed her wits about her. She tipped water from the ewer into the basin and splashed her face. It didn't help dampen her desire so she repeated the procedure twice more. Still she felt too hot, too weak in the head. She sighed again. It seemed she'd simply have to put up with the inconvenient sensations that crept over her whenever she thought of what Lord Ashbourne had done to her in bed.

She threw off the cloak and dressed in the Ashbourne livery, finishing just as the key rattled in the lock. The door swung open to reveal the earl looking like he'd been baiting wild animals. His hair stuck out at frightful angles, his clothes were in disarray and blood smeared the blade of his sword. Oh dear. If she'd been hoping for a good omen, she'd not been sent one.

Despite his appearance, the tension of earlier seemed to have left his body. He didn't stand like a tightly coiled rope ready to unravel and whip about the room wreaking havoc.

Then she saw his eyes and swallowed. They shone with a clear, wicked gleam. The sport he'd encountered on his walk may have helped him regain control but now he was sharper. And focused entirely on her.

Pippa clasped her fists at her sides and prepared for battle. She hoped he was including women when he said he liked people to be forthright, because she was about to be as forthright as she'd ever been with any man other than her father.

\* \* \*

THE PERSON STANDING before Ash was different to the one he had left. The shaking, frightened girl was replaced by a woman with a straight back and eyes that dared him to throw her out of the room. It only made him feel worse. Clearly this woman was of gentle breeding and he'd treated her like a traitor. He opened his mouth to eat humble pie but she spoke first.

"Say nothing until you hear my story," she said, crossing her arms. She wore the Ashbourne livery again. Ash allowed his gaze to rake over her body, looking for what he'd missed earlier when he thought her to be Pip. She was a tall woman, slim, with a narrow waist and a gentle flaring at hip and breast. Her shoulders were broader than the average woman's and he supposed she did look quite boyish with her cropped hair. But still, how could he not have seen through the disguise? Her long limbs moved with grace, and no boy he knew walked with a sway like that. Her large eyes, so dark they were nearly black, saw far too much and bore right into him, stripping back any last vestiges of anger he harbored.

He nodded for her to go on but she had already begun without his approval. "I am not a spy or a killer," she said. "I'm a friend to Georgiana Dale and if her memory means anything to you, then you will know I am not here to stab you in your bed."

Bed. She had to mention *that* word. Now all he could think about was her fingers twined in his hair, the softness of her breasts in his palm, and heat. A lot of heat.

Doing his best to ignore his stirring cock, he cleared his throat and said, "You're right. I know you won't harm me."

She looked surprised and some of the determination left her eyes. But just when he thought she might return to being the timid creature of earlier, she lifted her chin and clenched her fists and said, "You admit you're wrong?"

"Is that so hard to believe?"

"Well, yes. Clearly the walk cooled your temper, my lord."

"It was a vigorous walk."

She nodded at his torn sleeve, soaked with blood. "Trip over your conscience did you?"

He almost laughed out loud but checked himself. "I see you've taken my directive to speak plainly to heart. Are you sure that's entirely wise given the change in circumstances between us? You're my prisoner after all."

A flicker of alarm passed over her face before she schooled it. "I prefer to think that I have chosen to stay, my lord," she said with a rueful smile.

"Interesting," he said, half to himself.

"My lord?"

"It seems you are two people living in the one body."

She frowned. "I assure you I am a complete woman."

"That I can vouch for."

She flushed prettily in the dawn glow.

"I meant that you are afraid of me on the one hand," he said, "and yet quite brave to be confronting me like this. I find your duality intriguing."

"I, I..."

He held up his hand. "Never mind. Now, I want no lies and no appeals to my better nature. As you already know, I haven't got one." Anger prickled again as he remembered how this woman had taken him for a fool. And how he'd let her. Even after he'd vowed never to allow anyone, especially a woman, deceive him again. "Tell me—."

"My lord, you are dripping blood onto the rushes."

He looked down at his forearm in time to see a drop fall from the wound. "It's only a scratch."

"Even scratches fester. Let me dress it for you."

"No." He stepped back out of her reach.

She thrust a hand on one slender hip. "Stop behaving like a petulant child and let me tend to it."

"Petulant? Child? I am the Earl of Ashbourne." He cringed. He sounded like one of the queen's pompous favorites.

At least it stopped her coming closer. Her hands fell to her sides and she heaved a deep sigh. "Very well. Your health is not my concern now anyway since I am no longer your servant." She sat on a stool and fixed him with a questioning glare. "Unless you still wish me to be." She raised one eyebrow in question.

"I'll not be making any decisions until I've heard your story." He wrapped one of the inn's washing cloths around his wound then stood by the fire, putting as much distance between them as possible. Being near her did odd things to his brain and body—particularly his groin area. She stirred something basic and carnal within him. Something he thought he had under control.

She took a deep breath. "My father was Sir Henry Ingleside of Hampshire. He died just before my eighteenth birthday and I became the ward of my uncle. He's my mother's uncle, actually."

"And your mother?"

"She died in childbirth when I was eight. The babe died with her." Shadows clouded her eyes but she nudged them away with a shrug of her shoulder.

"Go on."

"My uncle kept me a prisoner in his home. From the day I arrived, he locked me in and never let me out again." She spoke matter-of-factly, as if relaying someone else's story. Ash marveled at the strength of a mind capable of staying detached under such circumstances.

"He put guards on my door at night and around the house during the day. My only companion was an elderly lady from the nearby village. And the servants of course. I wasn't allowed to ride anywhere or walk beyond the garden walls. A guard followed wherever I went. I never had visitors or letters, except for one from Georgiana which only reached me thanks to a kindly servant."

He shook his head. "I don't understand. Why keep you prisoner?"

"Money. I inherited some land from my father. As my guardian, it fell to Uncle to manage. He directed all the profits to himself instead of only what he was entitled to as my guardian." She told him about some papers she'd discovered that implicated the uncle. Ash wasn't surprised to find out this woman was capable of deciphering numbers in a ledger—she seemed capable of a great many things.

She went on to explain her theory that the uncle had kept her prisoner so that she would never meet any potential suitors. Pippa's marriage would have seen all her inheritance go to her husband. The uncle would be left with nothing.

"How many years did he keep you locked away?" he asked.

"I'm twenty-three now."

Five years! He swore. What sort of man could do that to his

own family? And for nothing more than a few sovereigns! "Was he ever violent?"

"Only to those who got close to me. He beat my maid after he caught her smuggling Georgiana's letter into the house. A groom once dared to take me for a ride. He nearly died from Uncle's thrashings. But he never touched me. Not directly."

"But indirectly?"

"My guard had orders to beat me if I tried to escape. I only tried twice."

*Swive.* Ash dragged a hand through his hair. How could someone hit a beautiful, vibrant young woman like Pippa? And to order another to do it too—what a black-hearted beast the uncle must be.

"But Uncle barely even looked at me," she went on. "He shouted and threw things a great deal, not specifically at anyone however. When he drank excessively, he was horrible to be near. No one escaped his wrath after a night of drunkenness. Not even his dogs."

Ash needed to sit. He managed to reach the bed. "I'm sorry," he muttered but Pippa didn't seem to hear him. She stared at the wall, lost in the horrors of her memories. He wanted to hold her, tell her he never meant to drink so much, but then he remembered his nightmares belonged to him. Pippa's were different ones altogether. It didn't make him feel any better.

"I learned how to become invisible," she went on. "When he entered a room I was in, I politely left. I never engaged him in conversation and I never gainsaid any of his orders although I wanted to on many occasions. God, how I wanted to," she said, bitterly. "I became so good at being unobtrusive that sometimes I think he forgot I was there."

Ash found that hard to believe. How could anyone not notice this woman? She was extraordinarily pretty, even with her hair cropped short. Her height and her slender figure set her apart from others of her age and sex, and her dark eyes were mesmerizing. Then there was her wit. He'd never met a woman like her. Not even with her eyes averted and her tongue controlled would she blend in.

75

"In Georgiana's letter," he said, pulling together the pieces of her story, "did she advise you to come to Ashbourne House?"

Pippa nodded. "It was two years ago now. She said if I ever needed her, I could find her at Ashbourne House on The Strand, or through someone there. The disguise was my idea—I thought a boy could travel easier than a woman."

"How did Georgiana propose to help you?"

Pippa's gaze slid to her hands clasped in her lap. The knuckles turned white. "I don't know. Through legal channels perhaps."

"Then why not inform me? Georgiana should have known I would help you if asked. And yet she told me nothing of your plight." His voice came out louder than he'd intended. It pained him that Georgiana hadn't trusted him. He would have trusted her if the positions had been reversed. She was almost family. These days family were the only ones he *could* trust.

A timely reminder that the woman standing before him was a stranger. He might like her, he might want to help her, but he wouldn't allow her to see more of him than she had already.

"We can't ask Georgiana her reasons now," she said softly.

"No," he said, equally soft. He frowned and tried sifting through the facts. He believed Pippa, and yet she was holding something back. Not a lie exactly, but not the complete truth. "Why didn't you tell me all this earlier?"

"I didn't know I could trust you. I thought you might send me back to him."

He drew in a deep breath and exhaled slowly. "Do you trust me now?"

"Yes." Her features lit up with the fire of her vehemence. Her eyes, so dull as she'd told her tale, brightened and her cheeks turned a gentle shade of pink.

Something inside Ash shifted, like a rock slipping off a cliff and crashing into the seas below. The force of it rattled him and he took several moments to grasp Pippa's story again.

"I'll confront him for you," he said, blurting out the words before he'd thought them through. He wasn't sure why he made the offer, all he knew was he had to help her. Her story tugged at something inside him.

She rolled her eyes, the unexpected impish gesture shattering the tension in the room. "You'd better do more than simply threaten him with the rack as you did me. I wasn't even remotely scared."

He laughed and the tightness across his shoulders eased. "You were shaking!"

"I was cold."

He grinned at her. She grinned back. "That's better," he said.

"What is?"

"You need as much strength of will as you can muster to fight your uncle. When we face him—"

"I'm not going back!" The laughter in her eyes died and she shrank into herself. "I told you I trusted you!"

He crossed the floor and knelt beside her, only stopping himself from grasping her hand at the last moment. "I'll not send you alone. I'll be there. Don't fear."

"I'm not afraid of him."

She said it in such an off-handed way that he believed her. So if she wasn't afraid of her uncle, who then? Or what? And what was she not telling him? He knew from years of interrogations that he'd never learn the answers if he asked directly. He'd need to use more subtle techniques.

He blew out a breath. Subtle was not his strong suit.

"How did you get away? It must have been difficult getting past the guards."

She lifted one shoulder casually. Too casually. "I created a diversion and slipped out during the commotion."

How like a woman to be evasive. "What kind of commotion?"

"A fire."

"And your uncle's name?"

She said nothing.

"I can find it out if I want to. You've given me sufficient information."

She crossed her arms, silent.

"I'll not return you to him." The promise slipped out before Ash could stop it. He got up and returned to the fire which seemed to be the safest place for him. When he was close to

Pippa, common sense fled. It had started the moment he'd found her in his bed.

The problem was, how did he know she spoke the truth? And if her uncle was indeed still her guardian, what legal right did anyone have to keep her from him? Not even Pippa herself could leave of her own free will. If her guardian wanted to keep her locked in a dungeon, he could. Ash certainly had no right to make promises he couldn't possibly keep.

"I won't hold you to that oath," she said, as if sensing his dilemma.

"I'll do everything in my power to help you," he said. "You must believe me on that score."

Pippa believed him. But she also believed that if he knew the truth, he wouldn't make such wild promises. As soon as her uncle told Lord Ashbourne about her witchcraft, the earl would conveniently forget that he'd made a vow to help her.

"You needn't feel obliged," she said.

"Obliged?" He stared at her. "Of course I'm obliged. You're Georgiana's friend. She gave many years good service to my family—that makes her concerns also *my* concern. If she suggested you come to my house, then I'll protect you to the best of my abilities. Besides, *you're* my servant too." He gave her a crooked smile. "And the earls of Ashbourne always take care of their own."

"I'll retain the disguise?" she asked, hope rising.

"Absolutely not!" He seemed disgusted by the very idea.

Her heart plunged. "But...what am I to do? Where am I to go?"

"You have no other family who could challenge him in the courts?"

"Would I have fled to Georgiana if I did?" Perhaps it was unfair of her to be so caustic but honestly, there was no legal avenues open to her. To a witch. She was not going back to The Grange and that was a certainty.

"I see." He sighed. "Then you can stay at Ashbourne House if you wish until I can speak to my lawyer and find a solution."

There was no legal solution to her most deadly problem—the Witch Hunter didn't believe in courts and lawyers. But she could see no way of dismissing Lord Ashbourne's suggestion without raising his suspicions, so she said nothing.

"But you must dispense with the boys' clothes—"

"No." If the Witch Hunter had linked her to Georgiana he would probably also discover the connection to Ashbourne House. If Pippa was to remain there then she had to be in disguise. "As Pip."

He threw his hands in the air. "You can't!"

"Then I'll leave"

"And go where?"

She shrugged and looked down at her hands. They'd begun to shake again so she linked her fingers to still them. "I'll not stay as myself. Uncle will find me."

He thumped his hand on the mantelpiece, making her jump. "If he does, I'll not let him remove you."

"You won't be able to stop him."

Their gazes locked and she knew he was coming around to her point of view. Reluctantly. Stubbornly.

"Very well," he said, rubbing his chin. "If you don't mind keeping up the disguise then I'll do what I can to protect you. But only until I think of a better option. However, there will be some adjustments. No more dressing me, bathing me or seeing my...nether regions."

"I never saw your nether regions." He raised both eyebrows and she lowered her gaze. "Well, only the once," she conceded. "But I erased the image from my memory immediately."

He scoffed. "I find that hard to believe."

He was right—the memory was etched into her brain. But she couldn't tell him that. "Shall I sleep with the servants?"

"Which ones? Male or female?"

Oh dear. He was right. "I'll stay in my room then."

"Yes. We'll muddle through the rest of the arrangements as we go along. Does that suit?"

She nodded. "Thank you." It felt like a great weight had been lifted from her shoulders.

"Now that I've made promises that go against my better judgment, will you tell me your uncle's name?"

"Simon Rowe. He's a Berkshire wool merchant. He owns The Grange, a manor house and estate outside the village of Shelton."

"Thank you," Lord Ashbourne said with a small nod.

"And you'll not try to contact him in any way?"

"Not unless you wish it."

Something about the earnestness of his voice, the way he leaned towards her as he said it, made her believe him. She wasn't entirely sure why he would agree to that particular term, however. Surely a man like Lord Ashbourne would want to know everything he could about the strange woman who'd turned up in his house dressed as a boy. Perhaps he believed her story. Perhaps she had convinced him there was nothing further to know.

But she didn't think the earl could be so easily fooled. He didn't seem like a man who would take everything he was told at face value. Not after the trickery she'd already performed.

"Thank you," she said and smiled at him.

He smiled back but it didn't reach his eyes.

* * *

AFTER BREAKING THEIR FAST, they visited Georgiana's grave at the old stone church. Lord Ashbourne knelt beside the freshly turned earth, his head bent, his dark hair falling over his forehead and shielding his eyes. Pippa looked away, feeling like an intruder.

Then he stood suddenly, glanced around and with a satisfied, "Ah," strode towards a bank of wildflowers growing outside the church gate. Pippa followed him. Together they picked the primroses and sweet williams and placed them against Georgiana's simple headstone.

"You were fond of her," Pippa said when they stepped back to admire their work.

"Fond?" He looked thoughtful, as if considering the suitability of the word. "Yes, I suppose I was. Fond," he said again, nodding.

They were about to leave when the vicar approached. He almost ran across the graveyard in his haste to reach them. "I'm sorry I wasn't here when you arrived, Lord Ashbourne," he said, puffing and bowing awkwardly. "But I see you've found Mistress Dale's resting place."

"I thank you, yes," Lord Ashbourne said. "Did you conduct the funeral service?"

"I did." He laid a hand on Georgiana's headstone as if touching the head of a penitent parishioner. "However, the service wasn't as I would have wished it."

"Oh?"

"Sir Francis Fordham wanted her buried quickly so I'm afraid I had no opportunity to contact her family, or your own good family, my lord. I know how much you would have wanted to be here."

Lord Ashbourne drew in a deep breath and nodded curtly. "Thank you. You did all you could." He signaled to Lewis the groom in the nearby paddock to prepare the horses. "Georgiana has no family, by the way," he told the vicar as they crossed the church yard. "There's no need to continue with your efforts in that direction."

The vicar's owlish eyes blinked up at Lord Ashbourne. "Oh? So the boys died? What a tragedy," he muttered.

The earl stopped, stared. "Boys? What boys?"

The vicar stopped too. "Her twin sons. I discovered an entry in the parish register while trying to find out more about her. She gave birth to twin boys thirty-five years ago."

Lord Ashbourne's mouth fell open. It appeared he hadn't known. Pippa certainly hadn't.

"But..." He drew breath to talk, let it out, then drew breath again. "But she never told us."

It was on the tip of Pippa's tongue to say that servants do not tell their masters everything but she didn't think it would be a particularly wise thing to point out at that moment.

"What are their names? And what happened to them?" Lord Ashbourne asked.

The vicar shook his head. "I'm very sorry, my lord, the entry in the register doesn't record the names, or if they survived."

"They must have died," Lord Ashbourne said with conviction. "Why else would their names not be recorded? Why else would she not have mentioned them?" he added thoughtfully.

"I'm sure you're right," the vicar said with far too much enthusiasm.

Pippa cleared her throat. "May I ask a question?"

"Of course," Lord Ashbourne said, absently.

The vicar looked at her for the first time, a mixture of surprise and disdain on his face. "Do you have something of *importance* to add, child?"

She would have puffed out her chest but she didn't want to emphasize that part of her body so she squared her shoulders instead. "Were you the serving vicar at the time?"

He sniffed. "Thirty-five years ago I was no older than you are now, lad."

"What about the mid-wife? Is she still alive?"

He tugged on his graying beard. "Try Mistress Kenilworth. She's a little doddery now, but she used to be the village mid-wife before her eyes failed her." He gave them directions to her house and it took only a few minutes for Pippa, the earl and Lewis to arrive at the small cottage.

After introductions, they followed Mistress Kenilworth into her kitchen.

"Gingerbread?" she asked, feeling her way across the table, touching spoons, bowls and other items in her path before moving on. Pippa pushed the trencher of breads closer. When Mistress Kenilworth's fingers found it, she smiled. "Ah, there they are. My neighbor brought them round fresh this morning. Care for one, my lord?" She picked one up and offered it to him.

"No, thank you. Mistress Kenilworth, I'm investigating Georgiana Dale's death."

"Ah." She placed the bread back on the trencher. "I see."

"I believe you delivered her twins thirty-five years ago. Correct?"

She hesitated then nodded. "I suppose since she's dead there's no need to keep the secret any longer."

"Secret?" Lord Ashbourne asked. "How could she keep her pregnancy a secret in a small village?"

"She arrived back only the day before the birth and kept to

her house. Her mother's house it was at the time. They told no one and she went nowhere. I was paid nicely for my silence too. Very nicely and I must say, I've kept my word till this day. Never told another living soul."

"You must be commended for your sense of honor, Mistress Kenilworth," the earl said with a wry smile that only Pippa could have seen.

The elderly mid-wife sat up straighter. "And of course, she delivered early so it took us by surprise. Or I should say *they* took everyone by surprise. All except me. I suspected twins from the moment I saw her." She tapped her temple with a gnarled finger. "These eyes used to work much better then."

"Did the twins live?"

"They were born alive but what happened to them afterwards I don't know. All I know is, one was sickly, the other bonny. They were kept in the house for weeks, no one allowed in or out, and me not allowed to talk of the birth. Very strange, but I never spoke a word in all these years. It was some months later when I went to visit I found mother and babes gone."

"Gone?" Lord Ashbourne and Pippa both said.

"Aye. Old Mary Dale, Georgiana's mother, told me she'd given them away. Of course, without a father to provide for them, it was the proper thing to do. Georgiana returned to London to serve your good family, I believe, my lord."

"How terribly sad," Pippa muttered.

"I think I'll have that gingerbread now." Lord Ashbourne took one from the trencher. "So you've kept the secret all this time? You've never told anyone?"

"I had to tell the old vicar so he could write it into the parish records. I would have been in all sorts of trouble if he'd found out I was keeping something like that from him. But I told no one else. Only Georgiana's mother and your own mother, the countess, knew."

Lord Ashbourne dropped the gingerbread. It broke in two when it hit the table. "My *mother*?"

"Oh yes. She came for the births."

# CHAPTER 6

"*I* think we should tell my mother that you're a woman," Lord Ashbourne said.

Pippa sighed. It was the fourth time he'd suggested confiding in the countess since leaving Haverford and the second since their arrival at Ashbourne House. And it was still early.

They'd spent most of the previous day questioning the Haverford locals and devising theories, not to mention sleeping. Pippa had been exhausted and yet still hadn't slept well. They'd woken early to leave for London that morning and had arrived in time for dinner at midday. Dining separately, he with his family and Pippa with the servants in the great hall, they'd met up again to discuss what to do about her situation. Pippa was quite content to do nothing. It seemed the earl had other ideas.

"No, don't tell her," she said firmly. "It will only cause complications. The fewer people who know I'm a woman, the better." Now that she'd had time to dwell on her predicament, she felt even more convinced of the necessity for secrecy. The Witch Hunter could already be in London. He might arrive at the house at any moment.

"She's bound to find out when this is all over anyway." Lord Ashbourne strode to the window in his study and peered down over the garden. Pippa wanted to join him. Partly for the simple sense of security she felt when near him but mostly because the window looked down onto the main approach to the house from the waterstairs. It would be the route any visitors traveling via the river would take. Sir Guy de St. Cyr for example.

"And when she does," he continued, "she'll be furious that I allowed a lady to act as my page of the wardrobe."

Pippa remained by the door, not sure what to do next. Pip the pageboy would offer to help him change out of his riding clothes. Pippa the gentlewoman refrained, even though the thought of seeing him naked again appealed to her. Very much.

She cleared her throat and pressed a cool hand to her heated cheeks. "I'm sure the countess will understand my need for secrecy when she learns the...circumstances."

He sighed. "When the time comes, I'll handle my mother."

She had no doubt he would. He looked capable of handling a great many things, although she was beginning to think he regretted his decision to keep Pippa on as his page. He seemed awkward now that they were back in London and the day was coming to a close. That meant undressing for bed, and sleeping in close proximity.

Pippa said nothing, simply waited for orders or a glance her way...*something* to suggest how she should act, what she should do next. But he gave no clue as to what he expected of her. She felt more uncomfortable now than she ever had as Pip. Something had changed between them since her revelations. He was stiff and formal towards her, as if meeting her for the first time. He'd even assisted her to get off her horse during the journey back to London. On the third attempt she'd reminded him a fifteen year-old boy could dismount by himself. His response to that had been a curt, "Very well," after which he'd unceremoniously let her go and she'd stumbled to the ground.

Since then he spoke only when necessary, rarely looked at her and certainly didn't go anywhere near enough to touch her.

It felt odd after what had transpired in the bed.

The bed. Oh, yes, *that*. Lord Ashbourne's breath against her throat, his lips brushing her tingling flesh, his big, gentle hands everywhere. Well, not quite *everywhere*. Not then anyway, only in her daydreams on the journey back to London. The ride had seemed to go fast and she wasn't in the least weary upon arriving at Ashbourne House. A little on edge and out of sorts perhaps. Even now. The thought of his hands exploring her body made her insides flop like a fish on a dry dock.

"What is it?" He was staring at her, an enquiring frown on his face. "You look strange."

She felt strange. Her skin was tight and hot, her heart drummed a loud and erratic beat against her ribs. It was terribly inconvenient when she was trying to behave calmly and rationally.

"Are you ill?" he asked.

"I'm quite sure I'm not," she said.

"Good." He moved away from the window towards the door that led to the main stairs. "Because we need to talk to my mother."

"Why?"

He pressed a hand up against the closed door and bowed his head, his back to her. "Firstly because she seems to know more about Georgiana than she's letting on, and secondly because this situation—you, here—is impossible." He spoke without turning around and his voice sounded muffled.

Oh. It seemed he wasn't sure how to treat their new circumstance either. Like her, he must have decided she was neither servant nor guest but some entirely new category. Or did he simply not like having a woman in his private apartments? Understandable. He was a bachelor, unused to having women in his rooms except his study. He must feel rather...violated.

She suddenly regretted her insistence on keeping up her disguise. She hadn't fully thought it through from his point of view. "Would you prefer if I slept in the servant quarters?" she offered.

"No!" He spun round. "Do you want to start a riot, Woman?"

She resisted the urge to roll her eyes. "Then let's compromise. I shall keep to my room at all times when you are here. If you require me for whatever reason, you can knock. It will all be quite civilized."

"Quite," he echoed, without much conviction.

"Can you think of an alternative?"

"Yes." The shadows on his face darkened, enhancing the blue flare in his eyes as they fixed on her. "But I doubt you'll agree to it."

She swallowed, suddenly feeling very thirsty. "Are you talking about telling your mother? Because I already told you—"

"No. Never mind." He jerked open the door. "Coming?"

She pressed her fingers to her temple, feeling like she'd missed something vital. "To see the countess?"

"Yes. I want to question her about Georgiana's twins."

"I think she'll find it a little unconventional for your page to accompany you, my lord."

"She's used to it." He blew out a breath. "In fact, she expects me to be unconventional."

"No. If I want to maintain this disguise then I must act like a servant." She crossed her arms. He was being ridiculous and he surely must know it.

He closed the door with a sigh. "Very well. I'll have her come here. You can listen in."

Fallon arrived with refreshments and a pile of correspondence which Lord Ashbourne tossed on his desk after a brief glance.

"Have my mother come here, Fallon," Lord Ashbourne said.

"Yes, my lord." The steward nodded.

"And make an appointment with my lawyer."

Another nod. "Anything else, my lord?"

"Yes." Lord Ashbourne studied his servant's long face. "You haven't asked me anything about Georgiana. How she died, who killed her...nothing. Aren't you curious about your friend's demise?"

Fallon blanched. "She's dead, Sir. That's all I need to know." He spoke with the same detached stiffness as he always did but seemed more stooped and somehow hollow, as if there was nothing inside holding him together. Pippa ached for him.

Lord Ashbourne cleared his throat. "Did you know she had children, Fallon?"

The steward's jaw dropped. "No, my lord, I...I..." He shook his head as if he couldn't think of any more words.

"She gave birth to twins thirty-five years ago in Haverford. April 1548. You never knew? Or suspected?"

"April?" He frowned in thought and shook his head slowly. "She didn't begin service here until some months later, my lord. She has not mentioned any children to me. Not ever."

Ash nodded. "I've asked Sir Francis Fordham to send Georgiana's things here when they arrive. You may choose something from them as a memento. If you know of any other particular friends who might also like something of Georgiana's, please let me know."

"Very well, my lord. You are most kind." He bowed and began to back out of the study but straightened again before he reached the door. "Forgive me, my lord, I forgot to mention that you had a visitor late yesterday. I've been a little distracted since..." He lowered his gaze to the floor rushes. "But that's no excuse. I'm sorry—"

"It's a very good excuse, Fallon," Lord Ashbourne said. "I know you were close to Georgiana. If you think you need time off—"

"No, my lord. I'd rather be here, especially now."

"I understand completely."

Pippa glanced from one to the other and shook her head. Neither man wanted to discuss their emotions regarding Georgiana's death. It seemed men, whether earl or servant, would rather smother their pain beneath an excess of activity. Her gaze wandered to Lord Ashbourne's desk. The piles of letters and documents threatened to topple over onto the floor and join the pieces of paper that had already found their way there. So what past pain made the earl bury himself in his work?

"Your visitor, my lord," Fallon said again, "was a Sir Guy de St. Cyr."

"Sir Guy!" Lord Ashbourne and Pippa said together.

"Good," Lord Ashbourne said.

*Oh God. It's all over. He has come.*

* * *

Ash TRIED NOT to look too long at Pippa in case she caught him staring, but he couldn't help it. He was worried about her. She looked pale and drawn and he wished she'd take his advice and sit down. She refused of course, just like he'd expected her to. If nothing else, she was a stubborn woman. Her determination to maintain her disguise was testament to that.

Perhaps he was overreacting about her health. Perhaps she was simply tired after the journey from Haverford. She wasn't an experienced rider and they had traveled quickly. Ash cursed himself for not considering her wellbeing when he'd done nothing but consider her ever since he'd learned she was a woman. He'd considered her from head to toe many times when she wasn't looking. He liked what he saw. His livery had never looked quite so good.

All the more reason to confess to his mother. The countess would see to it that Pippa was transferred to her own apartments or Annabel's. It was the only way to get Pippa out of his lodgings. Away from him. Not that he was such a rogue that he would seduce a young virgin who'd laid her trust in him, but he wasn't exactly a saint either. Definitely not. It would be torture having her in the next room and not be able to touch her the way he had at the Haverford inn.

He shook the disturbing thought from his mind when he heard his mother's light step approaching his study.

"In there, Pippa," he said, indicating the adjoining wardrobe. "Mother won't take any notice of you if you go about your duties while we talk."

Pippa entered the wardrobe just as his mother opened the study door. True to form, the countess's sweeping gaze never once rested on Pippa who began to unpack their travel bags.

"Did you put poor Georgiana's affairs in order, Richard?" the countess asked, breezing into the room like a winter wind. She settled herself on her usual stool near the window where she could see the entire room as well as the approach from the river.

"Not all of them," he said.

She lifted her face to him, one eyebrow arched. "Oh? Did you not learn who killed her?"

"No," he said. "I did not." He sat in his chair and rubbed his aching thigh. The old injury always gave him hell after long rides. "But I have learned something interesting. Georgiana gave birth to twin boys thirty-five years ago."

The fine lines above her top lip whitened but there was no other reaction. "I thought that information had been...suppressed."

"Not entirely. So you don't deny that you knew?"

"No. Why should I? Georgiana was the one who didn't want the village to know. I could hardly blame her. Unwed mothers weren't dealt with very kindly in places like Haverford. I simply went along with her wishes."

Ash watched her very closely but his mother showed no emotion of any kind. He wasn't sure why he thought this incident would elicit some kind of response when she rarely showed emotion towards anything. "Why were you there at all? She didn't even work for you thirty-five years ago."

"Georgiana was the nurse to Lady Duckworth's daughters when she became pregnant. She was eighteen, unwed and when Lady Duckworth learned of her plight, she wanted her removed from her household immediately. Georgiana's pregnancy was quite advanced by that time and I offered her a room here until the birth. I was already with child myself and I thought she would make a good nurse. She looked robust enough to take on an extra child."

"Who was the father?"

She shook her head. "Georgiana never told me. One of Lady Duckworth's servants I suspect. She had a rather handsome groom as I recall."

"Was she in love?"

"Love? Good lord, what strange notions you have, Richard!"

He shrugged one shoulder, not wanting to admit he agreed with her sentiment. "So why did she end up back in Haverford if you offered her a room here?"

"She wanted to be near her mother for the birth and I was heading to Dewbury Hall for my confinement so I offered to accompany her that far. By the time I was preparing to leave Haverford the next day, she'd already had the babies."

He frowned. "She went straight from here to Haverford?" He didn't know much about giving birth but he was reasonably sure heavily pregnant women shouldn't travel far, if at all. "She must have been near full term if the babies were born immediately upon arrival."

"They were early. That can happen with twins, I believe. If we'd known she was having two, I would have encouraged her to stay here."

He massaged his thigh harder. "So what happened to the boys? Did they survive?"

"As far as I know, although one was sickly and may have died." She shrugged. "Georgiana later told me she brought them to Christ's Hospital here in London." She spread her hands across her lustrous black skirt, the perfect backdrop to set off her colorful rings. "That's all I know."

Ash sat back and regarded his mother. She met his gaze without so much as a waver. "Poor Georgiana," he muttered.

She looked out the window. "She sinned."

He watched her hard profile, her eyes unblinking, her hands clasped loosely in her lap, and wondered if she was truly as cold inside as she appeared on the outside. Georgiana had been her closest female companion and yet her sad plight didn't seem to ruffle his mother in the least. "Yes, but she paid for it by losing her sons. That must have been difficult for her."

"I wouldn't know."

He sighed. No one would know now how Georgiana felt about that dark time of her life. She'd certainly shown no signs of it in her behavior with him. She'd always seemed happy and content. But then, some people hid their emotions well.

He should know.

He picked up the two framed pictures of himself and Annie which he'd taken from Georgiana's cottage. "She had our portraits painted some time ago." He handed them to his mother who studied them. "They're rather good," he said. "Do you want them?"

"I have two just like these in my rooms." She gave them back. "If you don't want them, give them to Annabel."

He walked over to the fireplace and placed them on the mantelpiece.

"Speaking of Annabel, she has expressed her wish that she be wed to Mr. Briars," his mother said.

"Really?" He looked at the portrait of his sister. Even in paint she looked imperial, as if she was turning up her nose at the artist. And yet he had managed to somehow capture the gleam in her eyes, the laughter and devilment that was never quite suppressed despite their mother's efforts to mould her into the perfect lady. "I had thought her rather cool on the idea."

"I think his latest gift to her sealed it. He gave her a magnificent ruby necklace. Not even Bess of Hardwick possesses anything like it."

Ash shook his head at the portrait. He knew his sister was fickle but he'd never thought her so easily bought. Perhaps she really did have feelings for the Briars fellow after all. How else to explain the unusual attatchment?

"He's coming here tomorrow to seek your consent," his mother said.

"If it's what she wants, I'm happy to give it."

"Lady Wethinall is also paying us a visit tomorrow. I do hope they don't arrive at the same time."

"Lady Wethinall?" Ash glanced at Pippa in the wardrobe. She fussed over one of his doublets, brushing it so hard not a scrap of dirt would dare cling to it. She remained intent on her task and didn't look up. Perhaps she wasn't listening. He lowered his voice anyway and said, "I didn't know you two moved in the same circles."

"We do now that she's become England's wealthiest widow."

His head jerked up. "The old fellow finally died, did he? Too bad. I liked him." Particularly because he was the only thing keeping Lady Wethinall's amorous attentions in check. Now that he was gone, she would be on the hunt and Ash suspected she had England's most eligible earl in her sights. It seemed she'd already got his mother on side.

"I'm busy tomorrow," he said. "All day," he added when she began to protest. "There's much to do to uncover Georgiana's murderer."

"Yes, of course, that's important." He thought he heard a note of sadness in her voice but couldn't be sure. "However, your future is also important. Lady Wethinall is wealthy in her own right and now controls a great deal of land, at least until her son is of an age. She'll need a husband to manage it all—"

"And I'm the perfect candidate? Mother, I do not *need* any more money or land. Or a wife for that matter."

"Of course you need a wife. How are you supposed to get heirs without one? And an earl can never have enough land. Bess of Hardwick—"

"Forget Bess of Hardwick! I will not marry Lady Wethinall, or anyone for that matter!"

Out of the corner of his eye he saw Pippa suddenly look up from her task. She seemed a little pale but then he remembered she was ill or tired or perhaps both.

"My apologies," he said to both women, "I didn't mean to shout." He turned to the fire, somewhere safe that didn't make his blood boil or his heart clench.

"I don't see what's wrong with Lady Wethinall," his mother said. "She's very attractive, still young and we know she can breed."

"She's avaricious, sly and has the morals of a snake." He should know. He'd taken advantage of those morals on many occasions when her husband was sleeping the sleep of the elderly only a few rooms away.

"A good husband can control her."

"That rules me out. I'd make a terrible husband." He dared to look at Pippa and was disturbed to see her staring at him with a mixture of surprise and something else. Concern? Disappointment?

No, it couldn't be that. Why would she be disappointed?

The memory of her soft moan as he palmed her breast returned unwanted and he clamped his teeth to grind it out of his mind. But it didn't work. All he could think about was kissing away the pout on her lips and replacing it with a smile.

Damnation, he needed to get away from her before he did something he regretted.

"I wonder who that is?" his mother said from her perch by the window.

Ash joined her, glad for the distraction. A man approached along the path from the waterstairs. He wore black, his cloak billowing out behind him. He strode towards the house with purpose.

"It's the gentleman from yesterday," his mother said, half rising. "He didn't want to speak to me so I didn't meet him but I'm sure it's the same one."

"What gentleman?"

"Sir Guy de St. Cyr," she said. "I believe he's called the Witch Hunter. I wonder what he wants with you."

Ash took his mother's arm and helped her up whether she wanted to stand or not. She took the hint, grudgingly, and left but not before she made him promise to be available the next day to see Lady Wethinall.

"Well, Pippa," he said as he crossed the study to the wardrobe, "it seems we don't have to go searching for our main suspect—." He stopped when he saw her face. Kneeling on the floor beside one of the coffers, she was deathly white. She stared into the distance and he doubted she even saw him. "Pippa? Are you going to faint?"

Her pale lips moved but she made no sound, and she began to shake. His heart galloped at the sight of her, so vulnerable and...afraid? He gripped her arms and looked into her eyes, trying to elicit some kind of confirmation that she was all right. He desperately needed to know that she was well, that she was simply fatigued.

"Pippa, talk to me!" He wanted to shake her out of her state but she seemed too fragile and he didn't want to break her.

"Hold me," she whispered.

He drew her close and she pressed her cheek to his chest, her fingers curling into his doublet at his waist. He held her slender frame as tightly as he dared and told her everything would be fine even though he didn't know what was wrong. Slowly her shuddering subsided but he didn't let her go. Didn't want to. She felt soft and warm and content like a cat in his arms, her head tucked beneath his chin where it fit perfectly. Her hair smelled like the countryside and he breathed deeply because he'd never smelled anything so glorious in his life.

She uncurled her fingers from his doublet but instead of moving away, she sighed and wrapped her arms around his waist. He closed his eyes and let the anxiety flow out of his body, but that allowed some other, unknown emotion to take its place. Whatever it was, it was more fulfilling, more joyful but equally disturbing. It scrambled his mind, made clear thought impossible but he didn't care. Holding her felt so...right.

"Pippa," he murmured. He traced a finger along the smooth skin of her jaw to her chin and up to her sweet, sensuous mouth.

She looked up, her dark brown eyes half-lidded, her lips pert and inviting. So very inviting. He bent his head and kissed her. Gently, exploring, giving her an opportunity to end it.

She didn't end it. Her mouth opened to him, her tongue darted out to meet his. She was unsure, inexperienced, but her eagerness was obvious in the way she pressed her body into his and dug her fingers through his hair. She tasted so sweet, so delicious and his hunger intensified then boiled over when her hand touched his thigh.

He groaned against her lips. "Pippa."

A loud knock at his study door made them spring apart. Pippa pressed her fingers to her lips as if checking they were still there. She smiled tentatively at him, and he was relieved to see her face flush, no longer the deathly pallor of earlier. He smiled back and touched one pink cheek.

"I must go," he said.

Suddenly her smile vanished and her gaze darted to the study. "Yes. As must I."

"Where to?" he asked, helping her to stand.

"Downstairs. The kitchens." She glanced towards his study again and he thought he saw panic flicker in her eyes but it was gone just as quickly as it had appeared. "My lord, may I ask you something?"

He rubbed a thumb across the back of her knuckles. "Of course."

"You must try to find out exactly what Georgiana told Sir Guy. Everything. Even if he avoids answering, you must...try."

She squeezed his hand between both of hers and looked up at him, imploring.

"Shall I beat it out of him?"

"If necessary."

Before he could determine if she was jesting, she fled down the backstairs and was gone.

# CHAPTER 7

$\mathcal{P}$ippa didn't stop for breath until she reached the kitchen. The delicious aromas of roasting meat and herbs welcomed her, teasing her nose and moistening her tongue. A serving boy struggling with a heavy sack of potatoes jostled her and mumbled an apology. His gaze darted to Cook but the enormous man was too busy shouting at another boy to notice. The large room was hot, noisy and chaotic. Perfect. At The Grange, she often went down to the kitchen simply to be near other people. The lower servants were mostly too afraid of her uncle to speak to her but that didn't matter. Their presence was comfort enough and the busy surroundings made her feel a part of something akin to a family.

"Countess can't 'ave her supper late," the boy told Pippa. He heaved the sack higher onto his shoulder, staggered, then went on his way.

Supper already! She felt a little dazed. Time had slipped past without her noticing. The sudden appearance of the Witch Hunter had scrambled her mind.

The Kiss had completely emptied it.

But she refused to think about it. She had enough to worry about without adding that to the mix.

She edged into the shadows and helped herself to a chunk of bread and a cup of ale. She leaned against the wall, out of the way, and watched as Cook shouted directions at the hapless kitchen hands.

"Th'onion should of bin put in already!" He grabbed an onion from one of the boys, slammed it down on the table and chopped it in half with such force it was amazing the blade didn't separate from the handle. If he'd missed by so much as a hair's width, he'd have removed a finger for sure.

The boy whose job it must have been to chop onions swallowed hard and scooped up the two halves then plopped them into a large pot. He looked relieved when Cook's sharp eye turned on someone else.

Fallon entered and the noise level dropped without anyone stopping what they were doing. Cook gave him a territorial glare but Fallon either didn't notice or pretended not to. He saw Pippa and made his way towards her. Servants who'd been going frantically about their business only moments before, made way for him. Moses himself couldn't have parted the sea with as much ease. Amazingly, not a single puff of flour landed on Fallon's meticulous livery.

"A word," he said to her.

"Sir?"

Lord Ashbourne must have sent for her. But she wouldn't go. Not until the Witch Hunter had left. She couldn't let Sir Guy see her, couldn't let him wonder why the new page of the wardrobe held an uncanny resemblance to his quarry. She shivered despite the warmth of the kitchen and the heat still pulsing through her after the Kiss.

Fallon glanced around to see if anyone was watching them. "I have something I must ask of you, Pip." Again he looked around.

"Yes?" she said when he didn't go on.

"Before I do, I require that you promise to tell no one of my interest in this matter." He spoke with complete authority, as if he expected no disagreement from her.

She sighed. More secrets. "You can trust me, Sir. I have no one to confide in anyway."

He seemed satisfied with that answer. "When you were at Mistress Dale's cottage with his lordship, did you...did you happen across anything...any correspondence, that is, with my name on it?"

Ah, she understood now. He was concerned that evidence of his lover's tryst with Georgiana would be discovered. "No, but I didn't have access to her personal effects." She shrugged. "Was there something in particular you wanted? Perhaps you could ask Lord Ashbourne if he found—"

"No! No need to trouble his lordship with such a minor matter." He raised his gaze to the ceiling, as if he could see through to Lord Ashbourne's study two floors up. "Thank you, Pip, you may go," he said, seeming to forget that *he* had approached *her*.

Despite his austerity, she quite liked the old steward and wanted to help him. He'd been close to Georgiana after all and she had some notion of how lost he must be feeling now his friend was gone.

"When her belongings arrive from Haverford, I'll set any correspondence of that nature aside for you," she said. "If I am allowed to see them at all," she added lest he think her impertinent for assuming such an honor.

His eyes brightened but the rest of his face remained dour. "If you could do it before...anyone else sees them, I would be *most* appreciative."

By 'anyone else' she assumed he meant Lord Ashbourne. "I shall remember you said that." She smiled.

He suddenly looked like a man who'd dug his own grave and she decided to put him out of his misery. "Don't worry, Sir, the debt will be canceled if you answer something for me."

"I will if I am able," he said, peering down his Roman nose at her.

"The man upstairs with Lord Ashbourne is known as the Witch Hunter."

"And?"

"And he was the last man to see Mistress Dale alive."

Fallon's lips parted and a little gasp escaped. "He killed her?"

"We...I mean, Lord Ashbourne doesn't know. But the Witch Hunter's appearance at her cottage does seem to suggest that he may have had a professional interest in Mistress Dale."

He frowned. "He thinks—*thought*—Georgiana was a witch?" He shook his head. "That's malicious gossip, Pip, and you shouldn't listen to it. Witches are evil, cruel creatures. Georgiana was a paragon of kindness. Her heart was gentle and pure. She was no more a witch than I am a king." He turned his face to the door with a look of revulsion. "If that man killed her because he thought she was a witch, I'll break every bone in his body."

Her blood ran cold at the undisguised menace in his voice. It would seem the steward's rake-thin body harbored a deadly hatred. Or perhaps an abundance of love. The two were remarkably similar emotions in many ways.

Fallon strode off, his fists clenched at his sides and his back stiffer than ever. He didn't seem to see the kitchen hands leaping out of his path, or hear Cook shouting at him to "Watch where yer going!"

Pippa blew out a long breath. The afternoon was becoming more and more alarming as it wore on. First the Witch Hunter appeared, then Lord Ashbourne kissed her (*kissed* her; kissed *her*!), and now Fallon was behaving like a cold-blooded killer. What oddities would visit her next?

"Finally!" Gertie sidled up to Pippa. "Thought the old fart'd never go. I been waitin' and waitin' to talk to you."

"About what?"

Gertie winked. "Come wiv me to the stables and I'll tell you. Lewis and the other stable lads'll leave us alone if I ask him."

Getting a jolly, buxom girl like Gertie alone was every fifteen year-old boy's dream. Pippa, however, went cold at the prospect. "I'm not sure—"

Gertie dug her elbow into Pippa's ribs, just below her breast. Pippa stepped back in alarm. "Come on," Gertie said, grabbing her by the arm and pulling her through the kitchen. "It's important."

Pippa allowed herself to be led. Gertie's news had better be important enough to drag her away from the sanctuary of the kitchen. She couldn't face the Witch Hunter or Lord Ashbourne yet, but for two very different reasons.

\* \* \*

"YOUR PRESENCE here at Ashbourne House is timely, Sir Guy," Ash said to his guest. They sat on opposing sides of the large desk and he was in no doubt the other man's direct gaze was assessing him, just as Ash assessed Sir Guy de St. Cyr.

His visitor was a tall man, dark haired with a straight nose and gray eyes that never seemed to blink. There was a haunted coldness about those eyes, as if they'd seen much and laughed little. "I must apologize for visiting unannounced, Lord Ashbourne," he said with a slight bow of his head. "I hope you'll forgive me."

Ash smiled in an attempt to lighten the mood and disarm the suspect. "Visitors are most welcome at Ashbourne House, Sir Guy, even the unexpected ones."

St. Cyr raised an eyebrow, the sudden movement out of place on the otherwise still man. "In that case, I hope you're able to help me. I believe you once retained Georgiana Dale in your service here at Ashbourne House."

Apparently St. Cyr didn't believe in polite chatter before getting to the heart of matters. Good. Neither did Ash. "She served my family for almost thirty years," he said. "That's why her death came as such a shock."

A muscle in St. Cyr's cheek pulsed and his nostrils flared slightly. Could it be possible that Ash's news was a surprise? "I'm sorry to hear it. When did she die? And how?"

"The day after you saw her. By foul means." Ash leaned forward in his chair. "In fact, you were the last one to see her alive."

"And that makes me the most likely to have killed her." It was a statement, not a question.

"You're a Justice of the Peace, Sir Guy, so I'm sure you know the last person to see the victim is usually the killer." Ash didn't care if his accusations made his guest uncomfortable. He wanted answers and he knew with a certainty he couldn't explain that the man sitting opposite was linked to Georgiana's demise.

St. Cyr didn't look the least uncomfortable. Where most people would vehemently express denial then storm off, he simply fixed his blank, unblinking gaze on his interrogator. "In my experience," he said, "the killer is usually a family member, often a spouse. Sometimes it's a disgruntled neighbor. It is rarely a stranger."

"Clearly we move in different circles." In his years abroad working for Her Majesty as an ambassadorial spy, Ash had found that most killers were strangers who'd never met their victims. But he mostly dealt with traitors and assassinators who wanted to overthrow kingdoms, not village murders. "What were you doing at Mistress Dale's that afternoon? I'm sure you weren't asking for directions. You don't look like a man who gets lost."

That elicited a small smile. "Only when necessary."

"I warn you, do not find it necessary to get lost any time soon. I've been charged with finding Georgiana's killer and I intend to succeed. I may need to speak to you again. Now, I repeat, what were you doing at her cottage?"

St. Cyr acknowledged the advice with a nod. "I was, in fact, asking for directions. Directions to the possible location of a woman I've been commissioned to find."

A cold sense of dread settled in Ash's stomach like a brick. "What woman?" But he knew.

He knew.

Pippa. It had to be. A missing woman, the connection to Georgiana...but why the Witch Hunter?

"Her name is Phillippa Ingleside, originally of Hampshire, lately of Shelton in Berkshire. Her uncle has commissioned me to find her."

Ash felt the familiar burn of anger rise within him but he was able to control it. Just. He chose his next words very carefully. "Commissioned? Are you a finder of people?"

A heartbeat lapsed before St. Cyr answered, "I think you know who I am."

"No," Ash lied. "Tell me."

St. Cyr's glare was uncompromising. "Do not play games with me, Lord Ashbourne. I know who you are just as well as you know who I am."

Ash respected his directness. He too disliked playing games. Very well, he would be equally direct. "You're called the Witch

Hunter because you hunt down women accused of witchcraft and see to it they are punished for their so-called crimes. But not by any legal means. You have not turned a single one of them over to the relevant authorities and so none have been tried by the courts. You gather the evidence yourself, judge them yourself and execute them yourself, none of which occurs in public view. Tell me, Sir Guy, how many women have you killed in this way?"

Still the man didn't blanch, didn't even move an eyelash. He did, however, take a long time to answer and when he spoke, the hardness of his voice matched that of his eyes. "It seems I am not the only judge and executioner in this room. But you are correct —I perform a service to our realm by removing witches."

Ash tried very hard to contain the urge to strangle the stone-faced man. "Why were you looking for this woman at Georgiana's house?"

"Phillippa Ingleside is the ward of her uncle, Simon Rowe. He informed me that Mistress Dale was her only friend outside Shelton. It seems the girl had a letter from her once."

Ash wondered what kind of persuasive techniques Pippa's uncle had used on the poor servants to discover that piece of information.

"As an investigator yourself," St. Cyr went on, "you will understand that I must follow up the connection. From my enquiries, I learned the Dale woman lived in Haverford."

"You expected to find the missing niece there? Haverford is a long way from Berkshire. Perhaps you should have started your search closer to home. The uncle's barn perhaps." Ash rubbed his chin, settling into his role. "I once knew the daughter of a viscount who ran away with a groom. They didn't get far before her father discovered them." He laughed. "Although it was far enough that she had to be promptly married off before the, er, side-effects of her adventure began to show."

St. Cyr was unmoved. "Phillippa Ingleside has not run off with a groom. She has left her uncle's care and could be in great danger traveling alone."

"Why did she leave?"

"That is not my business."

"Perhaps it should be."

St. Cyr said nothing.

"And this woman, this friend of Georgiana Dale's, you suspect she is a witch?" Ash asked, already knowing the answer. The sickening, horrible answer that struck him in the chest like the point of a blade. Someone had accused Pippa of witchcraft—that's why she left her uncle's.

St. Cyr's gray gaze focused on Ash. "There is evidence to suggest it."

"Evidence? Of what nature? Witnesses?" Please don't let there be witnesses.

St. Cyr nodded. "Her uncle has seen her use her powers."

Swive! "Anyone else?" The Witch Hunter shook his head. "A servant perhaps?" Another shake of his head. "What about a dog?" Ash asked, suddenly feeling light-headed with relief. Only one witness. He could deal with a single man.

"Simon Rowe is a highly respected gentleman. His word is enough for me to investigate the matter further."

Ash rubbed his aching thigh. "There are many people who think I am well respected too. And yet there are many others who would disagree with their assessment."

"Meaning?"

"Meaning you should not judge a man's character on his position, or on what you have been told."

St. Cyr crossed his arms and Ash could have sworn he saw the flicker of a smile cross the Witch Hunter's lips. "I assure you, Lord Ashbourne, I do not accept everything I am told. I fully intend to investigate this matter. In order to do that, I need to find the Ingleside woman."

Ash stretched out his leg and studied his opponent once more. It irritated him to admit, but he admired St. Cyr for his fortitude. But admiration was one thing. Trusting him with Pippa's life was entirely another.

"And what of Georgiana?" he asked. "Was she a witch too?"

Again the hesitation, as if St. Cyr didn't want to give away too much. "Would it surprise you to hear that she was?"

"No."

St. Cyr's brows rose.

"You thought I would deny it because she had been a loyal servant and friend to this family for many years?" Ash barked out a dry laugh. "I am prepared to admit she may have had powers no ordinary person possesses, but they do not make her a witch. She had a good heart and she never hurt anyone."

"Forgive me, Lord Ashbourne, I didn't think you had the clarity of mind in this matter to see her for what she truly was. I cannot say what was in her heart, but you are wrong in one respect. She did hurt people. She set fire to a house—"

"A rumor only."

"And she picked a man up bodily and threw him against a wall. She also killed two people by making them fall ill."

Ash scoffed. "Witches cannot *make* people ill."

Again St. Cyr's brows rose. "You are an expert on witchcraft?"

"I am an expert at determining fact from fiction. A skill you would do well to cultivate, Sir Guy."

The other man remained very still, but Ash was beginning to think it was done with conscious effort on St. Cyr's part. Perhaps he was trying as hard as Ash to control his temper. "I came to you today because I thought perhaps you might be able to help me locate the Ingleside woman. With your connection to Mistress Dale—"

"Did she tell you anything about the fugitive?" Ash had heard enough. He wanted St. Cyr gone, out of his home, far away from Pippa. "Did she even admit to knowing her? Did she say where the Ingleside woman might be?"

"No."

"And yet you thought I could help you because of my connection to Georgiana." Ash leaned forward, resting his elbows on the desk. "It sounds to me like you are clutching at half-truths in the hope you will grasp something firm."

St. Cyr's gaze became wary, watchful, a fox sizing up its prey. "You said yourself she worked for your family for many years. It was a logical conclusion that you may have become unwittingly involved in the Ingleside woman's concealment. Perhaps Mistress Dale requested some funds from you that she couldn't account for, or perhaps you offered a position to a serving girl on her recommendation."

Ash's breath caught. The Witch Hunter had struck too close to the truth. It was time to rid himself of the man. "I have neither wittingly nor unwittingly helped Georgiana conceal anyone." He stood. "But I'm beginning to wish I had."

"I see." St. Cyr also stood. "I must apologize for taking up your valuable time, Lord Ashbourne." With a bow, he left.

Ash sat down in his chair and the air left his body in a rush. He felt drained, like he'd fought bare-knuckled in the ring against the country's champion.

He had interrogated traitors before, faced down cold-blooded killers and battled wits with the best spies in the world, but none of that compared to this. This was different. It was real. It was close to his home and his heart.

Nevertheless, the meeting had been most enlightening. And most disturbing.

He rose to find Pippa. She had a lot of explaining to do.

* * *

GERTIE SAT on a bale of straw near the entrance to the stables. "Sit," she said, patting the spot next to her.

Pippa shook her head. "I prefer to stand." That way she could get away faster if the Witch Hunter suddenly appeared. The stables were off to the side of the main house, out of the way for someone going directly to the river, but she wanted to be alert to any eventuality.

But Gertie pulled hard on Pippa's arm and forced her to sit. "Can't talk to you if you're all the way up there," she said.

Pippa scowled at her and rubbed her shoulder.

"Did I hurt you?" Gertie nudged Pippa's hand away and began to rub, or rather squeeze, the sore joint. "Poor love. You're a delicate one, aren't you?"

"I am not!" Pippa moved to the edge of the straw bail but Gertie only followed her, shuffling her ample bottom across until her apron half covered Pippa's leg.

She looked around for someone, anyone. She'd even welcome the countess. But, as Gertie had cheerfully informed her, Lewis and the stable boys had taken most of the horses out for exercise.

The two remaining mares in the nearby stalls weren't enough to protect her from the amorous maid.

Gertie crinkled her nose. "Sorry about the stink but I couldna think of anywhere else to meet. The house is too busy and the garden is too open."

Too open for what? Pippa had the distinct feeling the girl hadn't lured her out to the stables for an informative chat. "The smell doesn't bother me." She yawned theatrically, stretching her arms, careful not to touch Gertie. "I'm tired. What do you want to tell—?"

"Poor poppet." Gertie clicked her tongue and gave her a sympathetic look. "What with all this ridin' round the countryside and his lordship's nightmares, you're prob'ly not gettin' much sleep. Poor pet," she said, taking Pippa's hand and cradling it in her rough one.

Pippa didn't pull away. This could be her only opportunity to learn more about Lord Ashbourne. "Do you know why he has the nightmares? What's the downstairs gossip?"

Gertie chewed her lower lip. "I shouldna talk out o' turn. But," she leaned closer, "I hear it's somethin' to do wiv a woman."

Pippa blinked. "Oh." She hadn't expected that at all. But of course she should have. Lord Ashbourne was a handsome man, and although she couldn't call him charming, he had a rather powerful presence. "Who?"

Gertie shrugged broad shoulders. "Dunno. Some foreigner I 'spect. His lordship used to travel to the Continent a lot on official business, but not so much since he got a hackbut ball in his leg."

"Is the injury connected to the woman?"

"How should I know?" When she saw Pippa's disappointment, she added, "All I knows is, his lordship went off to some foreign place and came back with a sore leg and nightmares. I hear it's because of a woman." She shrugged. "He don't travel so much now. Too many responsibilities here he says but most of us think her ladyship asked the queen to change his duties and keep him on good ol' English soil."

"The countess intervened?"

Gertie puffed out her chest, relishing the role of storyteller.

"So I heard. She wanted him home, safe. But his lordship *hates* bein' stuck in the big house all the time. Drives him mad some days. He used to be happy. I was only a little scrap but I remember him always laughin' in the ol' days. When he came home after bein' away for a few years, the nightmares started. He stopped sleepin', stopped laughin' and started mopin' about. And drinkin'. He was horrible when he was drunk. Not hard on any of us, mind. No, it was like he was bein' hard on himself. Anyway he don't drink no more."

Pippa nodded, enthralled. She knew about the nightmares and the drinking but now she was a step closer to finding out what had caused them. What exactly *had* happened on the Continent? What had changed him from happy youth to someone dogged by nightmares?

Good Lord, she'd turned into a gossiping snoop! She'd been hanging on Gertie's every word. But she had an insatiable desire to know everything about Lord Ashbourne. Not just that he kept an untidy desk, had large feet and a large, er, appendage, or that his kisses had the power to turn her body to water. She wanted to know more about the man.

Her interest in the earl was solely so she could understand him better and therefore determine if he was a person she could trust. Nothing else. Simply a matter of trust. Yes. That was most definitely the reason for her interest.

Gertie placed a hand on Pippa's knee, making her jump. "You were miles away just now," the maid said. Her eyes narrowed and she peered into Pippa's face. Pippa leaned back. "Quite a pretty lad, aren't you?"

"Pardon?"

"High cheeks and a nice mouth. And big eyes. I like big, brown eyes on a lad."

Pippa gulped. "They're more black than brown," she said quickly, "and they're not that big. And some say I'm a little too pretty for a boy. I need to be more...manly."

"I like you the way you are. Maybe a mite skinny." She squeezed Pippa's thigh. "But you'll do."

"Do? Do for what?"

"Don't look so scared, Pip. I'm not goin' to hurt you." She

cocked her head to the side and a look of earnestness crossed her round face. "I'm goin' to kiss you."

Pippa stood up so fast Gertie kissed nothing but air and nearly toppled to the mucky floor. "Now, Pip," she said, standing and brushing off her apron, "I know a first kiss can scare a skittish lad like yourself but I promise I'll be gentle. I won't bite. Unless you want me to—"

"Bite! I haven't kissed too many girls before, Gertie, but I'm fairly certain there's not meant to be any biting involved." There certainly hadn't been when Lord Ashbourne had kissed her. No, no biting. Only soft lips, a gently insistent tongue and a lot of heat everywhere.

"Now," Pippa said, "you lured me out here to tell me something."

Gertie pouted. "If I tell you, can I kiss you?"

Pippa crossed her arms. "Depends if the information is good enough."

Gertie considered that then nodded. "That old fart, Fallon, and Mistress Dale was lovers."

Pippa waited but Gertie said nothing else. "That's it? I already know that."

Gertie shrugged. "So do I get a kiss?"

"No!"

"I'll let you feel my titties." Gertie cupped her breasts and pushed them higher in offering.

"No!"

"What if I told you they were lovers for years and years, right up until Mistress Dale left Ashbourne House?"

Pippa lifted one shoulder. "I knew that too."

"Did you know he's had a wife the whole time?" Gertie added.

"I do. Do you know when they started the affair?"

Gertie let go of her breasts. "Well, let's see." She chewed her lip again. "It was already goin' on when I came here some ten years ago. One of the old maids told me it started about ten years before that."

"Twenty years," Pippa said in amazement. "Where does Mistress Fallon live?"

"Wiv her old mother in town somewhere." She indicated the general direction of the city of London to the east. "She comes here sometimes but not often."

"Any children?"

"Not as I knows of." Gertie brightened. "That's two things you didna know already. So how's about that kiss?" Her lips puckered and she closed her eyes.

"Gertie, you really shouldn't go about kissing all the serving lads."

The maid's eyes opened. "I don't!" She stamped her hands on her hips. "What kinda girl do you think I am? I only kiss the pretty ones. And it's just a kiss, mind you. And sometimes a feel. Nothin' more. My virtue's intact," she said with a sniff.

Footsteps crunched on the gravel outside. Pippa glanced at the entrance and her blood froze. A man wearing a long black cloak strode towards the stables, his hat pulled low over his eyes.

The Witch Hunter.

Her limbs tightened, ready to run. But there was nowhere to go. The only way out was past him. She could climb the ladder and hide in the loft but he was already too close. He would be inside the stables before she was half way up.

"What is it?" Gertie asked. She rose but Pippa pushed her back down onto the straw bail.

"I'll take that kiss now." She cupped the maid's face in both hands, closed her eyes and plunged.

# CHAPTER 8

*G*ertie gave a little muffled gasp then her body relaxed. She wrapped her arms around Pippa and pulled her roughly onto her lap, cushioning her against her considerable bosom. The kiss was nothing like the other one Pippa had experienced that day—the only other kiss she'd *ever* experienced. This one was awkward and fierce, like a battle, and teeth were involved.

Nevertheless, she didn't want it to end. She could hear the Witch Hunter's footsteps on the floor of the stables behind her. Too close.

Gertie gasped against Pippa's lips and broke off the kiss. She looked past Pippa and flushed scarlet. "I, er, I best get back to the house." She scrambled off the bail of straw and ran from the stables.

Pippa didn't move, didn't turn around. The hair on the back of her neck stood on end as she waited for what felt like forever for the man to speak.

"Sorry to have disturbed you," the Witch Hunter finally said, a smile in his voice.

"I best be off too," she said. If she kept her face down she might just be able to get past him without being recognized. She had never met Sir Guy but she had no doubt her uncle had given him a detailed description of her.

"I want to ask you something first." He waited, perhaps expecting her to look up. When she didn't, he went on. "I'm searching for a new maid for my London residence. Lord Ashbourne said I'm welcome to any of his newer ones but to leave his most faithful, older servants alone." He laughed. "Very generous of him."

Pippa didn't laugh.

"Can you tell me," he said, "are there any girls who've started service here at Ashbourne House in, say, the past week?"

Pippa shivered. He was so close to the truth, chillingly close. But he was looking for a woman, not a boy. Her identity was safe. The assurance didn't make her heart beat any slower or make the trembling stop.

"None that I know of, Sir. Please, I must go."

More footsteps crunched on the gravel outside and Pippa wondered if Gertie had returned or one of the grooms. *Please God.*

"I thought I told you to leave." The deep, booming voice of Lord Ashbourne made her heart pound even faster.

"As you wish," Sir Guy said. Pippa heard him take two steps and she finally dared to look up. The two men stood toe to toe, eye to eye, squaring off.

Pippa was struck by the similarities between them. Both were dark, the same height and strongly built although Sir Guy was slightly leaner but no less formidable because of it.

"Last time I looked, the stables weren't on the way to the waterstairs," Lord Asbhourne said.

"I got lost."

The earl bared his teeth in a snarl. The air crackled with tension and Pippa half expected them to draw swords. She marveled that Lord Ashbourne hadn't punched the other man in the nose yet. He looked like he ached to do it, his fists clenching and unclenching by his sides.

But Sir Guy proved that Pippa didn't know much about men after all. He backed down with a brief bow to the earl and left in the direction of the waterstairs. He didn't look back.

Once the Witch Hunter was out of sight, Lord Ashbourne

turned to Pippa and all his thwarted anger washed over her like a torrent. "Upstairs," he growled. "Now."

Her legs wouldn't move. Only the determination not to make a fool of herself in front of him kept them from collapsing under her.

"*Now*, Pip!" He turned and marched towards the house.

Tears welled in her eyes at his abrupt tone but she told herself he was merely maintaining the ruse of master and servant in case someone was watching.

But in her heart she knew it was because the Witch Hunter had told him everything.

Suddenly her legs wanted to run. She was torn between going in the opposite direction or running after him. She wanted to be far away from him and the accusations, but she also wanted to beat her fists against his chest and tell him not to listen to Sir Guy de St. Cyr. She was *not* a witch!

Yet she was. She was she was she was. And now Lord Ashbourne knew it too.

She didn't run anywhere. Like a trained animal, she followed a few steps behind her master all the way to his apartments. Once in his study, he shut the door and leaned back against it. He closed his eyes and sighed deeply. His body seemed to deflate as if some of the anger had flowed out of him along with his breath.

"What did he say?" she asked, her voice small and distant.

He opened his eyes. They were flat, calm. She hadn't a clue what was going through his mind. He opened his mouth to say something but closed it again. With another sigh, he pinched the bridge of his nose and screwed up his face.

"I think you already know," he said.

"Perhaps." The word nearly choked her.

His gaze leveled with hers, sucking her into its depths with the force of a whirlpool. "He told me he's looking for you, that your uncle commissioned him."

A droplet of sweat trickled down her spine and her mouth went dry. "Is that all?"

"He told me you're a witch."

There. The bald, brutal word was out. It lingered between

them like a foul stench that would dog her for the rest of her life. That one word described power beyond imagining. It also condemned her to death.

But what did the man standing before her think? Still she couldn't read him.

"He's wrong," she said. Denial was the only course open to her now. "I'm not a witch."

"Pippa," he said with obvious effort, "don't be afraid of me. I don't care what you are. If you're a witch—"

"I'm not!"

He sighed deeply again and she thought he would move closer but he stayed near the door. To block her escape?

"It's all right," he said with calm strength. "You're secret will be safe with me. Do you recall the friend's wife I told you about? The witch? I can take you to her if you like and she'll tell you I can be trusted."

He looked so earnest, so desperate for her to believe him that her heart flapped wildly, breaking down the cage she'd erected around it. Suddenly she wanted to tell him everything. It seemed vital that he know it all.

"I should have told you," she said. "I'm sorry, I didn't."

"Pippa—"

"No, let me speak." She took a step towards him but stopped herself getting any closer. He still had an odd look about him, like a man who'd wandered into the wrong room and couldn't find the door to get back out. "In her letter, Georgiana said that if I was ever in any kind of trouble, I was to go to her and only her."

"But—"

"And when she died," she went on, "I wasn't sure who I could trust."

He looked wounded. "You could have trusted me."

"Could I? You threatened to have me racked when you thought I was spying on you."

He winced. "I was angry then."

"Were you angry afterwards?"

"What do you mean?"

"You've been acting oddly towards me ever since Haverford.

Not angry but...awkward. That's how it feels between us. You stopped speaking to me in the easy manner of those first two days."

"I thought you were a boy then!" He threw up his hands and pushed off from the door but maintained his distance. "Suddenly I find I've had a young woman undressing me, bathing me, sleeping near me...of course I feel awkward!"

"You're right. I'm sorry," she mumbled. She couldn't quite place her finger on what had changed but it was more than mere awkwardness. It was everything—but it was mostly the Kiss. "Georgiana had never *said* I could trust you, only that I should come here until she could help me."

"Well *I'm* telling you that you can trust me!" He strode across the room to his desk where he promptly turned around and strode back again. She stood her ground when he waggled a finger at her then walked off again.

"Please don't be angry with me, my lord."

He stopped pacing. "Angry?" He blinked and half shook his head in confusion. "With you? No, Pippa," he said softly, "I'm not. I'm..." He sighed again and rubbed a hand through his hair. "It doesn't matter. But I'm certainly not angry. Not with you anyway. Only with that snake, St. Cyr," he snarled. "Believe it or not, I do understand why you felt you couldn't trust me yet. We're virtually strangers. I'd have done the same thing."

Not angry with her? Not even a little bit annoyed? Well, she certainly hadn't learned how to read him. She tried to hide her relief behind a cough. "What did Sir Guy say exactly about my...witchcraft?"

He sat on the edge of his desk and crossed his ankles. "He said that your uncle witnessed your...powers."

"I told you, I set his study alight."

"Yes, but you didn't say how. I thought an errant candle perhaps."

"Errant documents actually. I set them on fire and he dropped them onto the rushes."

He chuckled. "So he burned his own house down."

"It's not funny," she said, smirking. "It was quite awful. I had no idea I could start fires until that moment."

"I'll wager your surprise was nothing compared to his."

She couldn't stop grinning with relief and the release of emotions. "He did look rather alarmed." She quickly sobered, remembering the choking black smoke, the speed with which the flames swallowed up the curtains, the panicked servants and horses. It hadn't been funny, it had been terrifying.

"Someone could have been badly hurt," she said, quietly.

"But you may have to do something like that again," he said.

"What do you mean?"

"If the Witch Hunter comes back and recognizes you, you may have to use your powers on him."

"Oh." She had thought of it of course. Down in the stables, she'd badly wanted to be rid of him. What would she have done if Lord Ashbourne hadn't shown up? "Wouldn't that reveal my hand? At the moment, only my uncle and a footpad have witnessed my...unnatural abilities."

He cocked an eyebrow. "A footpad? Sounds like an interesting story."

She half smiled. "He tried to take my satchel. I managed to push him and he ended up slamming into a tree on the other side of the road. It was quite a surprise, and a rather thrilling experience."

"Not for the footpad, I suspect."

"I didn't wait to find out."

He watched her with wonder in his eyes. She blushed and tried not to grin like a foolish girl.

"You're right," he said, turning serious. "You shouldn't reveal your powers to anyone, especially a man like Sir Guy de St. Cyr...*unless* it's absolutely vital to your wellbeing."

Or someone else's, she wanted to say but didn't.

He placed his hands on the desk beside his thighs and leaned forward. "Do you understand me, Pippa? It's vital you use whatever powers you can to save yourself."

"But only when necessary," she added.

"Yes. We don't want the Witch Hunter to have any more evidence against you. As it is, your uncle may not be enough. We might be able to convince a jury that he made it up to benefit himself."

It was a good plan. With only one flaw. "But the Witch Hunter doesn't wait for a trial," she said, her voice small and high. She folded her arms to keep out the cold that breezed through her body.

Lord Ashbourne suddenly appeared in front of her. He took her shoulders and bent his head to look into her eyes. His dark blue gaze held hers and she fed off the strength in them. "I will protect you from St. Cyr, Pippa. I promise you. I just haven't worked out how yet. Until I do, you will keep up your disguise here with me.

She blinked back hot tears. He seemed so earnest, so determined. Not since her father was alive had she felt so confident in someone's abilities to fulfill such a promise. She knew without a doubt that Lord Ashbourne meant what he said.

"But why?" she said. "I barely know you."

He let go of her, straightened, frowned. "Why?" He looked as confused by the question as she was. Then he shrugged. "Because you are my responsibility now. Georgiana led you here and you were her friend. I won't let her down. Not only was she a loyal servant for many years but I owe so much to her. Taking care of you is the least I can do."

"Oh. I see. You are doing your duty."

He nodded. "I take my responsibilities very seriously."

"I'm sure you do."

"But?"

She shrugged, not really sure she could explain how she felt when she couldn't quite identify the emotions spinning inside her. All she did know was that she didn't like being somebody's *duty*. It made her sound so...helpless. "But you've already done so much," she said instead. "You've given me safety, you've engaged your lawyer on my behalf—."

He waved a hand to stop her. "Those are nothing."

"They're not to me. I will repay you."

"I don't want repayment." He shook his head at her in disbelief.

"But I must." If she didn't pay him then she would be allowing herself to become his responsibility. And she'd had enough of being a burden. Her uncle had ensured she always knew how much her upkeep cost him. Every meal, every scrap of ribbon, was accounted for. As it turned out, he took his payment and then some.

"If it's not money you want, then what?"

"I want..." He raised his gaze to the ceiling as if searching for the answer there and her heart skid to a halt as her mind raced back to the Kiss. Was he thinking of it now? "I want you to believe that I will do everything in my power to help you," he said.

Oh. Not the Kiss then.

"So," he said, "will you?"

"Will I what?"

Lord Ashbourne's stare caught hers, trapping her in its blue depths. "Trust me?"

"Yes," she whispered. "Yes, I will."

* * *

WHEN ASH AWOKE after a late night out, the sun was already hanging brightly in a perfect blue sky and Pippa hovered nearby with a tray.

"Good morning," she said, cheerfully. "I'm sorry to wake you but your mother is expecting you in the south parlor soon to greet your guests."

He groaned. "Can't I just pretend I slept through their visit?"

She smiled. "I think your mother might notice. She seems the observant sort."

"Observant is an understatement." He pushed the covers off and rose.

Pippa yelped and spun on her heel. "My lord! You're naked!" She sounded cross.

He grinned. He liked her when she was cross. In truth, he liked her all the time, but she was exceptionally pretty when she was irritated with him. Her brow furrowed, her cheeks flushed and those very kissable lips pouted. She was quite an alluring young woman. And she didn't even suspect it.

Not that he should be thinking of her as alluring, or pretty. But still, teasing her was an enjoyable way to pass the morning.

A little nakedness on his part couldn't do any harm, even though he'd said to her in Haverford that she couldn't do all the services of a pageboy now—which meant no nakedness. But back then he'd been in a sour mood. This morning, he wanted a little fun with her, to see her smile.

"Sorry," he said, "I forgot."

"You did not. You did that deliberately."

He laughed. "You're right, I did. But I do always sleep naked," he said innocently, "and you do know that."

She marched from the room, still carrying the tray. "I forgot," she said, repeating his lie. He laughed again. Yes, definitely alluring.

"Your breakfast will be in the breakfast room when you're ready," she said huffily. "I'm going downstairs to the kitchen. I assume you can dress yourself."

"I can but it's more fun when you do it."

"You are incorrigible."

He pulled on his hose. "Don't you mean charming?"

She snorted, still out of sight. "That highwayman had more charm than you and look what happened to him."

He laughed again, enjoying the banter as he put on the clean shirt she had set out for him.

"Are you dressed?" She peeked round the door. "Good." She stood fully in the entrance, her head bowed, and tugged at the short strands of her glossy black hair. "I want to apologize for saying you're not charming."

"Oh? Why?"

"Because you, er, are a reasonably charming man."

"Reasonably?"

She cleared her throat. "Yes. I'm sure many women find you quite charming. More or less. Perhaps."

He laughed. "Pippa, no one finds me charming. Even you, I see."

She blushed to the roots of her hair.

"Don't worry yourself, I won't hold it against you if you think I'm as subtle as a blunt axe."

She looked up, relief obvious in her face.

He chucked her under the chin. "Forthright remember?"

"I remember."

But she still looked uncomfortable. Not afraid, just embarrassed. He wanted more than anything to set her mind at ease. There were to be no awkward barriers between them. Not now. He'd kissed her for God's sake!

"Just because I'm an earl doesn't mean I don't have a sense of humor."

"Yes, of course. But you *are* the only earl I've ever met and I..." She trailed off and looked down at her feet again.

"Yes? Go on."

"I forget your station sometimes. And mine."

"Good. I want you to forget. I think we've been through enough together in the last few days to dispense with formalities."

"Yes, my lord."

"Starting with that. 'My lord' is much too formal. My mother calls me Richard but most of my friends call me Ash. Which do you prefer?"

"I prefer to call you my lord."

He laughed. "Ash then."

She sighed and gave a small nod as if he'd just asked her to muck out the stables. "If it's what you wish."

"It is. And I want you to always speak your mind to me."

Her gaze shifted to one side, then the other and finally met his. "Very well, I shall. Starting with your nightmares. Why won't you let me have something made up to ease them?"

He returned to dressing, picking up a plain black doublet with hooks and eyes down the front which made it easier for him to do up himself. Pippa didn't look like she wanted to go anywhere near him. He tried to recall if she'd been like this before they kissed but he couldn't. He hoped that hadn't added to her awkwardness around him. Because he'd liked it. So very, very much.

He wanted to do it again.

"I've created a monster," he muttered, not wanting to think about the kiss and get all hot and hard again. He'd spent half the night that way, he didn't want to spend half the day with an ache in his groin as well.

"I could do it today," she went on, completely unaware of the effect she had on him. It was as if the kiss hadn't meant anything to her. So much for his prowess with women. He couldn't even raise the passions of a virgin with one of the best kisses he'd ever bestowed.

"Very well," he said to appease her. He had no intention of using any potions. He was well content with his nightmares. He deserved them. "Try the apothecary under the sign of the rose in Bucklersbury Street. The proprietor, Isabel, is the witch I've told you about. Mention my name and she'll take care of you. But do not mention that the potion is for me." The last thing he needed was Isabel Merritt fussing over him.

He picked up a purse of coins and handed them to her. "Take this."

"Thank you." She pocketed it. "And I'll stop at Christ's Hospital to see what I can learn about Georgiana's twins."

"Good idea. I wish I could come with you but a letter of introduction will have to suffice. It should open doors for you without too many questions asked." He went to the desk in the study and wrote. He sealed the letter and handed it to her then gave her directions.

"I'll leave you then," she said.

He grunted. "Leave me to face the dragon and the wolves you mean. Very cruel of you."

"I don't think the page of the wardrobe would be welcomed into the parlor along with your guests."

He humphed. "This disguise is proving very limiting." As he said it, it struck him that he had come to enjoy her constant presence. Expect it even. So much so that he really did wish she could join him in the parlor. Between his mother pushing him in the Merry Widow's direction and Briars attempting to convince him he was worthy of Annabel, he'd not get a moment's peace.

\* \* \*

"Are you absolutely sure you want to marry that man?" Ash asked his sister. They stood near the window, pretending to admire the garden in its full splendor. Ash glanced across the room to where his mother was engaged in conversation with Ralph Briars, only son of John Briars and heir to his vast fortune. They seemed to be discussing something in earnest. Or rather, Briars was talking in earnest, the countess merely nodded occasionally when he paused for breath.

"Absolutely is perhaps too strong a word," Annabel said, still looking out the window. "Let's just say quite sure and be done with it."

"Annie," Ash said, "don't do this if you don't want to. If it's Mother, then I can confront her for you."

"It's not Mother. It's not anything." She touched his sleeve with her white gloved hand and gave him a reassuring smile. "As I said, I'm quite sure. As sure as I've been about any of them."

She meant her other suitors. And there had been many since the death of her betrothed. Briars was the first she'd shown any interest in at all.

"But...why?" Ash had spent the last half hour determining if Briars was worthy of his sister's hand. He could see a certain appeal —Briars was tall, handsome and extraordinarily wealthy. But he was a dullard. If he wasn't talking about himself, he was talking about the family business of merchant adventuring. Which would have been fascinating if Briars had been on one of the company's ships and not desk-bound in London. Ash could discuss finances as well as any man but that didn't mean he found it interesting.

Annabel turned from the window and studied her intended. "He dresses fashionably," she said without a hint of sarcasm.

"You like the way he dresses?" Ash barked out a laugh which drew his mother's attention. She scowled at him. Briars' rhythm didn't falter.

"Yes," Annabel said decisively. "A man who likes to dress well will want his wife to be fashionable too. That suits me perfectly. I think I can look forward to an extravagant and indulgent husband in the future."

Ash rolled his eyes. She couldn't possibly be serious. He never was quite sure with his sister. She certainly liked to buy things. He should know, he paid all her accounts. But was she really only interested in wealth and comfort? Or was she teasing him? Ash sighed. He never would understand women, not even the ones closest to him.

"Don't look at me like that, Brother," she said, tapping his shoulder lightly. "I'm perfectly content with my choice. As should you be. Just think of all the money my marriage will save you," she said brightly

"I'm not concerned with money, Annie, it's your happiness I want."

"I will be happy," she said with the certainty of a nineteen year-old girl who'd never experienced hardship beyond choosing the right dress to wear to a ball. "As Mother said, Briars is a remarkably boring man. And as everyone knows, boring men treat their wives with great fondness. Especially wives they count themselves fortunate to have."

"You think he'd be fortunate to have a self-centered, greedy, snobbish girl like you?" Ash was partly serious but his sister chose to ignore that and laughed.

"Of course!" She took her brother's arm and rested her head on his shoulder. "I'm pretty, well connected and have an indulgent brother who'll see that my husband's business interests aren't affected by any Privy Council decisions."

"I'll do no such thing! And you, dear sister," he tweaked her nose, "better stay out of his business affairs if that's how you think. Heaven help this country if you take over the management of The Cathay Trading Company."

"Oh, and I forgot to mention clever."

He couldn't help laughing. "I think my concern is misplaced," he said. "I should be counseling Briars. The poor man doesn't know what he's in for."

"What would you tell him?"

"Beware of the Savoy women. They're dangerous."

She grinned up at him. "Speaking of Savoy women, present and future, where is Lady Wethinall?"

"What?" he choked out.

"Is everything all right, Richard?" his mother asked.

"I've been better," he said. Lowering his voice so only

Annabel could hear, he said, "Lady Wethinall will not be the future Countess of Ashbourne."

"Oh *really*, Ash." She clicked her tongue. "*Everyone* knows she will be. There're even wagering on it at court."

"Her husband hasn't been dead a week!"

"Then you have quite a bit of time in which to get used to the idea." She winked at him. "Unless the situation becomes...urgent, if you understand my meaning."

He looked at her aghast. He thought back to all the nights he'd spent in Lady Wethinall's bed. He was quite certain they'd been careful.

He regarded his sister again. She was the picture of innocence in her white dress and gloves, her small, slender frame barely reaching his shoulder. When did she turn into this cynical know-all? Somehow when his back was turned, she'd changed into a younger version of their mother. He'd been so busy with affairs of state he hadn't noticed.

Speaking of affairs... "The Merry Widow and I are not going to get married, sooner or later. You can spread that rumor about court if you like."

"It's not just court you need worry about," she said in her sweet, sing-song voice that he no longer trusted. "It's Mother and the Merry Widow herself that are the ones spreading the rumors."

He groaned. He needed to have some very unpleasant discussions with those two. "Why does everyone expect me to marry Lady Wethinall anyway?" It's not like anyone else knew about their affair. He'd not told a soul and he was certain Lady Wethinall had kept it quiet. At least, she had while her husband was alive.

Annabel lifted one slender finger. "She's wealthy," another gloved finger joined its mate, "she's fertile," a third finger rose, "and she's absolutely ravishing. The first two are important for a man in your position, the third is vital for a man like you."

"She's not ravishing," he said, thinking about a pair of soft brown eyes, pouting lips and a slim figure that he wanted to explore again. "At least, not to me."

His perfectly graceful and composed little sister snorted. "Oh,

*Brother*, I'm not stupid. You must find her somewhat ravishing or you wouldn't have risked your handsome neck climbing into her bedchamber every night for a month."

His jaw dropped. How did the women in his household become better spies than him? "How do you know?"

She gave him a sly grin. "I didn't. You just gave yourself away now. Although I was fairly sure when you called her the Merry Widow."

He stared at her. "You're scaring me, Annie. Between you and Mother, I no longer have any secrets." Except he did. One very big, very important secret. And she was all his. Er, her *secret* was all his, that is.

"I'm pleased you've been having trysts, Ash, and I don't care who they're with," she said.

"You are? Why?"

"You need a pastime. Lord knows you've been rather agitated lately. I know dear old Georgiana's death has come as a shock to you—to all of us—but it was going on well before that."

"What was?"

"Your moodiness!" she said as if he should have known. "You've been an irritable bear. The servants are walking on eggshells in fear of you."

He gave a short, humorless laugh. "The servants aren't afraid of me."

"Well, Mother and I then."

A harder laugh.

"Oh, very well," she said crossly, "no one is walking on eggshells. But you certainly haven't been yourself of late, although you have improved since you gave up the excessive drinking."

He sighed. "Only a little sister could point that out and get away with it."

"Why don't you visit your friend Merritt more often?" she suggested. "He's such a charming fellow."

"I see him less because that's what happens when a man gets married, he loses his friends."

"*He* hasn't lost anyone."

"I have."

"You can be such a child sometimes, Ash." She wiggled her fingers in a wave at Briars when he glanced her way. Briars stumbled over his words, blushed, and turned back to the countess.

"Thank you, my very grown-up eighteen year-old sister."

"I'm nineteen. And at least I act my age."

"I act my age."

"You're thirty-five, Ash, not twenty-five. It was quite all right for you to avoid marriage then, but it's not all right now."

He cocked his head to the side. "You've been around Mother far too much lately. You're turning into her. Is that gray hairs and wrinkles I see? Even your nose has become more austere," he said tweaking it.

She swatted his hand away. "There is nothing wrong with my nose. It's small and perfect. Nor do I have wrinkles. Anyway, what I said is true. For someone so concerned with doing his duty and taking care of his responsibilities, you've neglected your biggest duty of all. Getting married and having heirs."

He crossed his arms. "I will not marry the Merry Widow to please you and Mother," he said.

"Then why agree to meet her this morning?"

"Mother can be persuasive when she wants to be," he muttered.

Annabel sighed. "She certainly can."

Fallon entered the parlor and announced Lady Wethinall. The widow breezed into the room, her black silk mourning shimmering in the sunlight, an apologetic smile on her face. She held out both hands to greet the countess who smiled back at her like a cat that had stumbled across a crate full of fish.

Ash tried to think up an excuse for leaving early. All he wanted to do was find Pippa and laugh about this strange, ridiculous morning.

# CHAPTER 9

"I'm so sorry for keeping you, Lady Ashbourne," Lady Wethinall said. "I do hope I haven't missed all the fun."

"No," the countess said before anyone else could mention the proposal. "You haven't missed a thing."

Dismissed, Briars retreated to the fireplace where he unsuccessfully tried to hide a deep blush.

Ash felt sorry for him. Briars wanted to announce his betrothal to Annabel to the world. He might not have known that protocol meant noble marriages had to be sanctioned by the queen first. Her Majesty rarely objected but it was customary to honor her with the information before anyone else. And his mother was a stickler for custom.

"Nothing of importance," she went on. "We've been entertaining my son's friend, Mr. Briars. He's a most delightful conversationalist."

"Indeed?" Lady Wethinall's eyes lit up as they skimmed over Briars. Her sharp gaze missed nothing. Not the expensive doublet, the golden hair or the smooth hands. "I shall look forward to hearing you converse, Mr. Briars."

Briars opened his mouth, no doubt to give her a sample of his delightful conversation, but Lady Wethinall turned away from him and he spluttered something that no one heard.

"Ah, Lord Ashbourne, how charming to see you again." She crossed the room, her skirts gliding over the rushes. He took her black gloved hand, bowed over it then dropped it quickly when she squeezed his fingers. The sentiment didn't go unnoticed by Annabel who raised one impish eyebrow at him behind Lady Wethinall's back.

"I'm deeply sorry for your loss," Ash said. "Lord Wethinall was a good man. His wit and honesty will be missed at court."

She thanked him and pressed a wisp of fine black lace to her dry eye. "I'm still in mourning but of course an invitation from Lady Ashbourne cannot be dismissed."

His mother's invitation had come very soon after the death but of course she would want to show her cards before all the other mothers of eligible gentlemen. If she'd waited a more appropriate length of time, Lady Wethinall could already be off the marriage market.

Annabel offered her condolences too in a soft voice, her head lowered, the picture of sincerity.

"Dear sweet girl," Lady Wethinall said. "Lord Ashbourne, I think I should warn you that all the young men at court are finding your sister's charms quite appealing. It won't be long before one of them snaps her up."

Briars made a strangled sort of sound and stared determinedly into the fireplace.

"I think you'll find the young men at court are already married or betrothed, Lady Wethinall," Ash said. "It's only us old farts left now." He practically *heard* his mother roll her eyes. "And I wouldn't wish any of them on my sister. Would you?"

It was perhaps a low blow for someone who'd been married to a man old enough to be her father and he regretted his bluntness as soon as the words were out.

But Lady Wethinall tipped her head back and laughed her lilting laugh, exposing a great deal of white throat above her oversized ruff. "Marrying an old fart like you would be horrid for any woman. Unless she was marrying you for your fortune or your position at court."

Her bold truths stung. He may not know Lady Wethinall very well outside of her bed, but she had gone straight to the core of him. She had precisely stated the reasons why he'd never married.

He'd had many offers from eager parents over the years, and several from the young ladies themselves, but none of them proved to be interested in him beyond the value of his lands or his title. As a nobleman, he knew he *must* marry well and produce heirs to secure the line, but he wasn't ready. Before his inheritance of the Ashbourne title, he'd never felt any urgency to take a wife. There was time.

But even after he inherited, and especially after he returned from Spain, he'd put it off, much to his mother's chagrin. He couldn't make such an important, far-reaching decision when he wasn't in the right frame of mind. Drinking to excess hadn't helped.

Once he gave up drinking, however, he'd become more open to the idea of marriage. If only he could find someone he liked enough. Liked, not loved. Definitely not that. He simply wanted comfort and companionship, the sort that lasted a lifetime. He wanted someone who made him laugh, someone to hold onto in the darker times and someone he could trust. Above all, he wanted that. None of those characteristics would appear in a wife who only married him because of what he could do for *her*. And so far, those were the only women he'd met.

His gaze wandered to the door. "I have to go," he announced.

"Already?" Lady Wethinall pouted but not in the way Pippa pouted with her full lips.

"Richard," his mother said, managing to sound stern and gracious at the same time, "our guest has just arrived. And you can't leave poor Mr. Briars in the company of us women. We'll eat him alive." She cast a smile at the hapless fellow. He gulped and cast a pleading look first to his intended then to Ash.

"You're not going anywhere," Annabel announced. She looped her arm through Ash's as if to anchor him. "What could possibly be so urgent that you can't spend another five minutes with us?"

Ash assessed his sister. She was small—he could drag her out with him if he had to. "Business," he said. Pippa was business. Of sorts. And she might still be frightened after her encounter with the Witch Hunter. He should go to her. It was the decent thing to do.

"Come sit with me," Lady Wethinall said, taking his other arm. "You can tell me all about your country estate. I've never been to Derbyshire."

Ash found himself being marched to the nearest bench seat by his sister and the Merry Widow.

"It's very pretty this time of year," Annabel said, sitting down on one side of him.

"We had hoped to be there now," the countess said, settling back down in her seat, "but matters here have kept us in London." She raised her brows triumphantly at Ash, knowing his escape had been foiled.

He sighed. It was no good. He was surrounded on three sides and his ally—Briars—was ill prepared for battle. Ash either had to surrender or find a more devious way to retreat without alerting the opposing forces.

The opportunity arose in the form of Fallon a few minutes later, carrying a tray of sweetmeats. Ash caught his gaze and tried to convey his dilemma with sideways glances at the enemy. With a nod of understanding, Fallon straightened and cleared his throat. The chatter ceased.

"Lord Ashbourne, an urgent correspondence has arrived for you. It awaits you in your study."

Ash stood and bowed to his visitors. "My apologies. It seems I must leave you after all." He pretended not to see his mother's glare or Briars' expression of alarm, and left.

"Thank you, Fallon," he whispered as he closed the door to the parlor. "Remind me to give you a fat bonus this month."

"If you insist, my lord," Fallon said flatly.

"Pip told me he was going out," Ash said. "Do you know if he's returned?"

"Not yet. Do you need assistance with your wardrobe, my lord? Perhaps I can be of service."

"No, thank you. I think I'll go for a ride."

He headed up to his lodgings, changed into his riding clothes and left the house, ensuring he kept well away from the south parlor window.

\* \* \*

PIPPA WAITED for the clerk to finish reading Lord Ashbourne's letter of introduction. She stayed near the door while the clerk, barely older than herself, sat at his desk, his unwashed hair spilling over his forehead as he read.

"You're fortunate to have found service with Lord Ashbourne," he said, handing the letter back to her. "His lordship is a kind gentleman and a generous benefactor of Christ's Hospital."

"He is?"

"Most certainly." He rifled through a small coffer on his desk and pulled out an enormous key. "As was his father before him. It's somewhat of a family tradition of the Savoys I believe, ever since the old monastery was turned into a hospital for unwanted babes."

"I didn't know that."

"I'm not surprised." The clerk smiled as he fiddled the key into the enormous lock on the chest hunkering on the floor near his desk. "I've met your master several times," he said, cheerfully, "and he doesn't strike me as the type to blow his own trumpet."

No, no trumpet blowing from Lord Ashbourne. Ash.

The clerk knelt and rummaged through the coffer, pulling out large ledgers and reading the spine before setting them aside. "Ah, here we are. The year of our lord, 1548." He flipped through the pages then ran his finger down the left column. "No, nothing from Haverford in April of that year. Only a baby girl found in the common privy at Queenhithe down near the river."

Pippa screwed up her nose. Poor child. What an unfortunate way to start life. At least she had been taken to the hospital where she would have been fed, clothed and kept warm.

"She was sent to the country," the clerk went on. His finger continued down the page. "We don't keep babies here, you see. They're nursed in the country then they come back to us weaned. Better for the child's constitution, we find. Must be the country air. Ah, here we are." He tapped his finger on an entry. "February 1549, a ten month-old baby boy is returned. Thomas

Haverford. We name them as best we can," he said with an apologetic shrug.

"Only one boy?"

The clerk checked the next page, shrugged, and said, "Only the one."

"What happened to him?"

He slammed the book shut. "Nothing."

"Nothing?"

He returned the ledger to the coffer and locked it. "Nothing I can tell you at least. Sorry," he said with a shrug. "It's marked Confidential. Not even Lord Ashbourne has access to it."

Pippa wanted to stamp her foot in frustration. "Confidential? Why would it be confidential?"

The clerk shrugged again. "I cannot say. Perhaps the rightful father doesn't want anyone to know he's got an illegitimate son, or perhaps the adopting family don't want it known they get their servants from the Hospital. Or the boy might be someone important now and not want his unsatisfactory origins known. Could be all sorts of reasons. But I can't tell you as I don't have access to that information."

"Oh? It's not in there?" She pointed to the coffer with its annual ledgers.

"No, the confidential records are kept in the storage room." He indicated a heavy wooden door off the corridor. "It's locked and only the master has a key."

Pippa sat on a stool. This wasn't happening the way she envisaged. She'd thought Ash's letter would open any door she'd chosen to unlock. To have a setback so soon into her investigation was so *infuriating*.

"Are you feeling ill, boy? You've gone quite red in the face."

Pippa pressed the back of her hand to her hot cheek. "Ah, no I don't feel all that well. Could I prevail upon you for a drink please Sir."

The clerk looked like he wanted her out of his office where she would no longer be his responsibility if she fell ill. "Of course," he said. "I'll be right back. Don't...you know." He waved a hand in the air which Pippa took to mean anything from "faint" to "die". He left, leaving the door open.

She watched him until he was out of sight then rushed out of the office and tried the door to the storage room. Locked, as he'd said. She glanced up and down the corridor, took a deep breath and focused her mind. If she could move a man then surely she could tumble a lock.

Tingling warmth spread across her fingers and the resounding click proved her right. She wanted to squeal with delight but instead opened the door and slipped inside. Light filtered through the single high window, revealing a small room stacked with dusty filing boxes of all sizes, each labeled with a letter of the alphabet. She quickly located the ones labeled H and glanced at the main door. No sound came from beyond but she probably only had precious seconds before the clerk returned.

She rifled through the first box, the second then the third until she finally found a parchment with Thomas Haverford's name on it. Below that was written:

*Born April 1548.*

*Returned to Christ's Hospital February 1549.*

*Mother: Georgiana Dale of Haverford, Middlesex.*

*Father: Richard Savoy, London.*

Richard Savoy! No, that couldn't be right. Ash was only a baby himself at the time.

Which meant this Richard Savoy must have been his father.

Pippa sat back on her haunches and stared at the yellowing parchment in her hand. If Ash's father was this baby's father, then what was his mother the countess doing at the child's birth?

She must have known about her husband's dalliance with Georgiana. Poor woman. What an awful discovery to make. And yet she'd helped Georgiana return home to Haverford, even been there for the births. It was a remarkably unselfish thing to do for someone who had wronged her in such a dreadful way.

Pippa rifled through the box but there were no records of any other Haverfords. No sign of the other twin. Why had only one come to Christ's Hospital? What had happened to the other?

Pippa studied the parchment again. The bottom right corner had been torn off. Prior to the tear were the words:

*Adopted July 1550 by*

She flipped the parchment over but there was nothing

written on the other side. Hog's breath! Of all the ill luck. The tear had removed the name of the adopting man.

There was no time to lament her misfortune. She replaced the parchment and returned the box to its position in the stack. She opened the storage room door a little, peered out and when she saw no one along the corridor, slipped out and closed the door behind her. She focused on the lock to turn it but froze at the sound of footsteps on the stone floor.

They drew closer. She turned back to the lock but her racing heart distracted her from her task and the lock simply wouldn't budge. Abandoning her efforts, she crossed the corridor just as the clerk emerged round the corner.

"Ah, you're standing at least," he said, sounding relieved. He offered her a cup. "Wine? It's the strongest we have."

"No, thank you, I'm feeling much better. I was just about to leave. Thank you for your help." She bobbed her head and sidled past him.

She almost ran out to the courtyard, so eager was she to get away before the clerk discovered the storeroom door was unlocked. If she was lucky and the room was used as rarely as the undisturbed dust on the boxes indicated, it might not be discovered for a long time. The thought didn't give her much comfort.

She crossed the courtyard, shivering in the cool shadows cast by the old stone buildings surrounding her. The breeze rustled her hair at her ears and whispered through the cloisters as if the ghosts of the Greyfriars monks who'd once inhabited the monastery-turned-orphanage were displeased with her sleuthing.

Once out on Newgate Street, she walked quickly to put distance between her and Christ's Hospital. It wasn't until she reached St. Paul's Cross that she felt she could slow her pace. She asked a boy dressed in the dark blue clothing of apprentices for directions to Bucklersbury Street and followed his pointed finger along Cheapside.

As she walked, Pippa's anxiety melted away, replaced by awe and wonder at the magnificent thoroughfare. Lining each side were the tallest buildings she'd ever seen, some five levels high, their signs swaying in the gentle spring breeze that had so alarmed her back at Christ's Hospital. She marveled at the width of the street, nearly three times as wide as anything in Shelton. It had to be broad enough to carry the vast number of coaches, carts and drays that jostled each other, and the livestock being herded to market.

Women of all classes kept to the edges out of the way and nearer the shops. Shop keepers shouted over the top of one another so it was almost impossible to determine who was selling what. There were goldsmiths, jewelers, mercers, drapers, and every kind of food in the world seemed to be sold there.

It was noisy and dusty and chaotic and Pippa drank it in. Life pulsed here like a vein. It flowed around her, through her, filling her like a surging tide. It was a feeling only equaled when she used her powers. And when Ash had kissed her.

This was life. People here didn't just exist, they *lived.* They laughed, they shouted, they drove too fast, they struggled under the weight of their purchases, and they laughed some more.

Because they were free.

As *she* was free now too.

She was far away from her uncle and not even the Witch Hunter had recognized her at Ashbourne House. On her journey to London, she'd been too busy looking over her shoulder to have felt truly free. But now, as an anonymous boy in a vibrant city, she was freer than she'd ever been in her life. Even as a child with her father, she'd never had this much liberty. A gentleman's young daughter couldn't simply wander into the village whenever she wanted to. But here in London, she could go anywhere, do anything, be anybody. It was intoxicating and she drank her fill.

She lifted her face to the sunshine and let its warmth soak into her skin, replenishing the well that had run dry for so long. One thought rose above all others like a floating bubble——she would do anything to keep her freedom, even use her powers if necessary. She would never give it up again. Not to anyone.

With a smile she couldn't control, she turned into Bucklersbury Street and breathed in the exotic scents from the dozens of apothecary shops along it. She spotted the sign of the one she wanted and headed towards it, her heart still singing and her head awash with new and powerful thoughts.

* * *

I⊤ WASN'T until Pippa began the long walk back to The Strand, a package of herbs tucked under her arm, that she began to ponder what she'd learned at Christ's Hospital. Questions and potential answers jumbled about untidily in her head so that by the time she reached Ashbourne House, she had no solutions. All she knew was, she had to tell Ash about his father and Georgiana. It was only fair.

She made her way up to his lodgings via the kitchen and the backstairs, nodding at the servants she recognized. They nodded back or smiled in greeting and she felt a sense of acceptance, belonging. She was one of them.

And yet she wasn't.

As soon as she opened the door to Ash's wardrobe, the first room near the stairs, she knew he wasn't there. She couldn't feel his presence. But *someone* was. Something rustled in the master bedchamber.

Perhaps Gertie was changing the rushes or the linen. Pippa wasn't sure she wanted to see the maid after their adventure in the stable, but the air had to be cleared some time so she might as well do it while Ash was absent.

She drew in two deep breaths and strode towards the bedchamber door, an explanation on her lips. She stopped in the doorway. And stared.

Lying on the bed was a fair-haired woman dressed in black, her eyes closed, a smile on her lips.

"Aren't you going to kiss me, darling?" she said seductively.

Pippa stared. Then she coughed. "I think there's been a mistake."

The woman's eyes flew open. Shock registered for a fleeting moment but she quickly regained her composure and smiled instead. She sat up on the edge of the bed and beckoned Pippa over with a crook of her finger.

"Well, well," she said, voice low and thick. "Aren't you a pretty boy."

"Not that pretty," Pippa said for want of anything better to say. Not a boy either, but she kept that to herself.

The woman patted the bed beside her and Pippa silently groaned. She'd been in this position before and it had *not* gone well. This time she would stay far away.

"I have to go and...do something in the kitchen," she said.

"Nonsense. You can stay awhile. I need some company until Ash returns."

"Ash?" Pippa hadn't meant to say it out loud but the informality of this stranger surprised her, both towards Pippa and her 'master'.

"Lord Ashbourne," the woman clarified. "We're good friends."

Very good by the look of it. *Too good,* a small voice said. "He could be quite a while," Pippa said out loud. "If you'd like to wait for him, you can do so in his study...er, Mistress..."

"*Lady* Wethinall," the woman said with a distinct emphasis on the 'Lady'.

Well that explained a great deal. This was the woman the countess wanted Ash to marry. She appeared to already be his lover. How convenient. To already know a marriage prospect was fortunate, to desire them carnally was a most advantageous way to start life together.

Yet Ash had refused her to his mother's face. Refused to marry anyone. Why? Lady Wethinall was beautiful, noble and wealthy according to the countess, and now she was a widow too. Why would he refuse?

Even as she thought it, relief made her feel light and silly. Which was ridiculous because she was *not* jealous of this woman. She had no right. Ash didn't belong to Pippa. Their kiss had not branded him.

But the hard lump of jealousy remained lodged in her chest and no amount of denial would remove it.

"If you insist on staying," Pippa said, "I'll run down to the kitchen for refreshments."

"I don't want refreshments." Lady Wethinall stood and

prowled across the rushes to Pippa, licking her lips with a flick of her tongue.

Pippa backed away. "I, er, really have to be elsewhere."

"Not yet." Lady Wethinall kept coming and Pippa stepped back until she was up against the wall. "*So* pretty," she said, throatily. She traced a fingernail down Pippa's cheek.

Pippa gulped and jerked away from her touch. But Lady Wethinall would not be distracted. "If I kiss you, will you leave me alone?" Pippa asked, hoping to bargain her way out of the peculiar predicament.

"No." Lady Wethinall blew on Pippa's throat.

Pippa yelped and rubbed the spot vigorously.

"You've never done this before, have you? Don't be scared. I'll be gentle."

"I'm not scared." Pippa placed her hands on Lady Wethinall's shoulders and pushed her gently away. She didn't use her powers, didn't need to. The widow was much smaller than Pippa, except in the chest. "I just don't want to incur Lord Ashbourne's wrath. He has a strict policy about his staff having dalliances with his...friends."

Lady Wethinall frowned. "He does? His last page never mentioned it."

"In that case," came Lord Ashbourne's hard voice from the doorway, "I'll be having a word to Peter when he returns."

# CHAPTER 10

*B*oth women jumped. Neither had seen Lord Ashbourne arrive. He must have come up via the backstairs and slipped quietly into the room.

"Lady Wethinall," he said with amusement, "what are you doing with my page?"

The widow's tongue slid across her top lip. "Just filling in time." She left Pippa and flung her arms around Ash's neck. "I grew so bored waiting for you, my darling."

He looked over her head at Pippa. "Are you all right, Pip?" he asked, a grin playing at the corners of his mouth. "You seem a little hot."

Pippa cleared her throat, annoyed at him for finding her predicament humorous. "No," she said casually. "This sort of thing happens to me all the time lately."

That wiped the smile off his face. "It does?" He set Lady Wethinall aside and came to Pippa. The discarded woman thrust her hands onto her hips and glared after him. "Who else has been seducing you *lately*?"

"Oh, you'd be surprised, my lord."

"Ash!" Lady Wethinall said, stomping her foot.

Ash ignored her. "It seems I have to keep a closer eye on you," he said to Pippa. "Can't have all and sundry seducing an innocent lad like yourself."

"I came here to seduce you!" Lady Wethinall said.

"But my page got here first, is that it?" he asked her without turning round. He sounded neither angry nor hurt, simply tired.

Lady Wethinall made a huffing sound. "If you hadn't been gone so long, I wouldn't have grown so bored. You can't deny me a little pleasure while I wait, can you?"

"I can." He finally turned to her. "And my servants are off limits to you. Now leave."

She sniffed and headed for the backstairs.

"Use the main stairs," Ash said.

"But your mother thinks I've already left. She'll know where I've been." She looked horrified.

"Believe me, there's no keeping secrets from her anyway." He held the door open for her. "Go."

She sidled up to him and placed a hand on his arm. "You're behaving rather strangely, Ash. He's only a servant. A boy. I'm not interested in him."

He removed her hand. With a tilt of her chin, she stepped out of the study but stopped on the landing at the top step. She turned back and instead of looking hurt, she looked pleased, almost triumphant.

"It just struck me," she said in wonder. "You're jealous. You're jealous of your page! Oh, Ash, that's so sweet." She began to move back towards him.

He slammed the door in her face. "So," he said and Pippa realized he must be speaking to her, "what do you mean this sort of thing is happening all the time?"

"Nevermind." She waved her hand. He looked like he would protest so she headed him off. "Lady Wethinall seems rather...eager to please."

He raised an eyebrow. "That's putting it mildly. I must apologize, Pippa—"

"Don't." She held up her hand. "It's not your fault. It seems I make quite a pretty boy, something many women find appealing if today is anything to go by."

Ash's amused smile withered and he regarded her levelly. "I do want to apologize. She was here for me. She's under the mistaken belief I want to marry her."

"And you don't?" She couldn't help asking. She wanted very much to hear what he had to say on the matter.

He strode past her to the wardrobe. "You know I don't. My denial yesterday when Mother confronted me over the matter could have been heard in Scotland let alone the next room." He stopped long enough to wink at her. "Perhaps now you can see why I don't want her as my wife."

"Actually, no," she said, mischievously. "She looked very much like a woman a normal man would want to marry."

He gave her a boyish grin. "I'm not often thought of as normal."

She grinned back. "I think I'm beginning to learn that."

He continued into the master bedroom. "I told Fallon I'd be dining up here with you today. I'm going to change," he said, heading through to the wardrobe. "And no, I don't need your assistance."

"I wasn't going to offer it," she called after him.

"No? And here I thought all women wanted to get me out of my clothes."

She smiled. He was bold and funny and she couldn't help but like him for it. He also brought out the mischievous side in her too. She was still smiling when Fallon arrived. He placed a tray in the adjoining breakfast room then returned to the study. He narrowed his eyes at Pippa, scrutinizing her as hard as he had the first day they met. She wondered if he saw anything different now. A woman perhaps.

"You do realize it is an honor to dine with the master," he said, pulling himself up to his full height.

"Of course," she said deferentially.

He peered down his nose at her. "And a highly unorthodox one. His lordship usually dines with the family or with all the servants in the great hall, not with his page in the breakfast chamber."

"It is a privilege to be asked," Pippa agreed.

"A *great* privilege. You have obviously made an impression on him." He cocked his head to the side as if waiting for an answer to his unspoken question of: "Why you?"

"Oh," she said with a wave of her hand, "it's nothing. I believe he wants to ask me what I can recall of our visit to Georgiana's cottage in Haverford. He was a little too...distressed at the time to notice all of the details."

He seemed satisfied with that explanation. "I see. Carry on, Pip."

\* \* \*

ASH CONCENTRATED on his beef and tried to forget the incident with Lady Wethinall. At first he'd been amused but then something inside him had switched. By the time he threw Lady Wethinall out, he was livid. Pippa was his. Or rather, she was in his care and no one could take advantage of her, even mistakenly.

Sitting opposite her now as they ate, something else stirred at the thought of Pippa being taken advantage of. Something far baser. It took all his self-control not to wonder what she would look like out of her boy's clothes. He'd had a taste at Haverford, but he hungered for more. To see all of her, from the rosy tips of her breasts to the V between her thighs, to feel her quivering beneath him, to hear her whisper his name—

"I can't hold it in any longer."

He swallowed when he should have chewed and ended up choking. He reached for his ale and saw Pippa watching him, her face troubled, her food uneaten.

"What is it?" he asked, touching her hand. The gesture had been an impulsive one and he had the impression the closing of her fingers over his was equally spontaneous. She certainly didn't seem too perturbed by the contact. For his part, his skin was on fire. "Is it the incident with Lady Wethinall?"

"What?" She withdrew her hand. "No, nothing like that. It's what I learned at Christ's Hospital."

"You learned something of importance there?" He'd doubted she would, simply because in his experience, places like the orphanage rarely kept sufficient records. "Why didn't you tell me earlier?"

Her gaze dropped to her trencher. "I was avoiding it."

"Avoiding it? Why would you do that?"

She sighed and slumped back in her chair. "Very well. It must be said. I learned that only one of Georgiana's boys turned up at Christ's Hospital. There's no record of the other."

He had the distinct feeling from her lack of eye contact that there was more. "And?"

She drew in a deep breath and her eyes slowly lifted to engage his. What he saw in them set him on edge—she felt sorry for him.

"Tell me, Pippa, what is it?"

"The boy's father was...your father."

He blinked at her, began to laugh then stopped. She was neither lying nor joking. She was too kind to be so cruel, of that he was sure.

It was about the only thing he was sure of. It suddenly felt like the floor was shifting beneath him.

"I see." He placed his hands flat on the table on either side of his trencher. They were his father's hands, his mother often said. Broad, strong. A laborer's hands. Or a farmer's hands, according to Georgiana.

Sweet, gentle Georgiana. He could understand his father keeping the secret of the twins from him but how could she have not told him? He'd thought he knew everything about her. And yet here was something so enormous, so important.

How had she felt bearing her master's babies? Had they been in love? Or had his father forced himself...

He recoiled at the thought, shoved it from his mind. He wouldn't think on it. *Wouldn't.*

But what of his mother? What did she know of it all? More importantly, how did she feel when she discovered the truth? *If* she had. She might believe Georgiana's twins were fathered by someone else, Lady Duckworth's groom perhaps.

"Some gentlemen openly acknowledge their illegitimate offspring," Pippa said in that quiet, calm manner of hers. "Why didn't he?" It was her turn to touch his hand and he held onto her fingers tightly. He would not allow her to withdraw this time.

"Not because he didn't want to, I'm sure of that. If nothing else, Father could be a possessive man. I'd say it was more for

Georgiana's and Mother's sakes. He held them both in high regard and he wouldn't want to embarrass either of them."

"But the children." She shook her head. "To have them sent to Christ's Hospital when their father was not only alive but was the Earl of Ashbourne. It seems so..." She shook her head.

"Cold."

She looked away.

"He was proud," Ash said, "but not cold. Not to that extent anyway. He would have acknowledged a child of his own blood if he could. I'm certain of it."

Ash had seen little of his father when he was a child. Not because his father didn't like him, more because he didn't know what to do with him. It wasn't until Ash was much older and his father could take an active role in molding him into the next earl that Ash began to understand him. It was then that he learned his father was more than the austere, fiery-tempered man he'd seen only on formal occasions when Georgiana marched Ash out for assessment.

He could be generous, with both his money and his time, considerate towards his servants, and loyal to his monarch. He taught Ash to ride when the groom could have done it adequately, and to fight with both sword and fists. He also tried to teach Ash the nuances of politics and the subtlety of diplomacy. It wasn't his father's fault that Ash had no liking for those arts, however he probably shouldn't have recommended Ash for diplomatic posts on the Continent when he clearly hadn't the temperament for it. But it was family tradition for the next earl to wet his feet in the courts of Europe before returning to further the family's vast interests in England.

Sometimes Ash found it difficult to forgive his father for his blind following of tradition. But what had happened in Spain wasn't his father's fault. It wasn't anyone's fault except Ash's own. The old earl simply couldn't see that his son wasn't the perfect diplomat.

"He wasn't a bad man," Ash told Pippa. He wanted her to understand that no matter what his father was, he would never have forced himself on Georgiana. Never have hurt any woman.

She squeezed his hand. He squeezed back. "But if his name

was on Thomas Haverford's records," she said, "he must have known of that son's existence *and* that he ended up at Christ's Hospital."

"He probably knew about both boys. Mother does." Mother. She would have to be questioned again sooner or later. "But what happened to Thomas? Did the records say?"

"He was adopted. The parchment was torn so I couldn't read by whom. Perhaps your father arranged an adoption to a suitable family."

Ash nodded. It was possible.

To think, he had a half brother. Perhaps two if the other child survived. It was an astonishing thing to discover and he hadn't fully digested the information yet. "I wonder what happened to the other twin?" he said.

She rubbed his thumb with her own and the sensation soothed him. "One of the twins was sickly at birth," she said. "Perhaps he didn't survive beyond infancy. He may never have made it to Christ's Hospital."

Ash nodded numbly. He should feel something for the lost child. He was his brother, after all. But he felt nothing except a vague sense of sympathy for the boy buried somewhere unknown to his real family.

"Do you think your mother would know?" Pippa asked quietly.

"And not have told me in the hope I would never discover I had half brothers?" He grunted. "Perhaps. I will ask her as soon as possible."

More rubbing and he got the feeling another, even more direct question, was coming his way. He braced himself. Pippa was nothing if not direct, something he only had himself to blame for since he'd encouraged it.

"Ash, when exactly were you born?"

"By that I suppose you mean is it possible I'm Thomas Haverford or the other twin?" It was a logical conclusion and he wasn't surprised Pippa had thought of it. Not only was she quite resourceful, but she was entirely too clever.

She broke the contact between them. "It was a silly notion. Forget I asked."

"No, it's a question I would have asked if I were in your position. I was born at Dewbury Hall five months after Georgiana's twins. And no, I have no proof of that except Mother's word. The local church may have a record." He shrugged, wishing he could assuage Pippa's reservations.

For his part, he knew he wasn't Thomas Haverford. If he was, his mother wouldn't have accepted him into her home let alone treat him as the rightful earl. She was nothing if not a stickler for protocol. His father may have been a proud man, but she was ten times prouder.

"We shall simply accept the countess's word then." But Pippa didn't look convinced.

He wanted to change the subject. "You did well, Pip," he said, using her page's name. "You're quite the investigator. The clerks at Christ's Hospital like their rules and their rules are strict. How *did* you come by the link between my father and Thomas Haverford? I'd have thought something like that would be confidential information."

She picked up her knife and attacked her beef. "I simply asked the right questions of the right people."

He snorted. "No you didn't." He leaned forward. "You either used your feminine wiles to charm someone or you used your powers." He leaned back and watched her eat and avoid his gaze. "Please tell me I'm mistaken because I'd hate to think it was either of those." When she said nothing, he said, "Let me guess then. Since you were dressed as a boy, you probably didn't use your feminine wiles. That leaves your witchcraft. Did you hit someone over the head with a heavy object?"

"No! I distracted him then tumbled a few locks. It was simple and harmless."

"Harmless." He shook his head, annoyed at the ease with which she'd used her magic. "Nothing is harmless when it comes to your powers. Do *not* use them in public. What if you were seen? Do you understand the implications?"

A muscle pulsed in her jaw. "Yes, I do. And don't treat me like a child, Ash. I am perfectly able to determine when I am safe and when I'm not. Do *you* understand?"

He stared at her, dumbfounded. Was this really his Pippa? Had she really just admonished him?

He crossed his arms and stared at her some more. She matched him, glare for glare. "I was simply advising you—"

"No, you were simply *ordering* me. I am not yours to be ordered. I'm not your wife, daughter, sister, not even your servant."

He opened his mouth to protest but closed it because she was right. And yet she wasn't. By sending Pippa to Ashbourne House, Georgiana had entrusted her to his care, that made her his responsibility now Georgiana was gone. But he didn't think he should say that to Pippa right now. She didn't look like she wanted to hear it. What had happened to her while she was out?

"Do not tell me what to do," she said again.

"Very well," he said. "I don't think you'll listen even if I do."

She smiled at that and the room suddenly seemed brighter. "Let's not argue."

He smiled back. "No. Now, at the risk of being hit over the head with your trencher, I'm going to tell you to finish your meal. My lawyer is coming this afternoon."

* * *

"I WAS LUCKY," Bartholomew Umberfield said, his bleak manner of speaking matching his long face and sad eyes. "A copy of Sir Henry Ingleside's last will and testament was lodged here in London at the office of Montague and Portman. They have connections to Hampshire so it was elementary that they should have it in their possession."

"Well?" prompted Ash, leaning forward at his desk. "What does it say?"

Pippa wasn't sure why he was so eager to know the contents of her father's will. It couldn't make a difference to her situation —she would still have to hide from the Witch Hunter, even if her uncle had no legal claim to her anymore.

Umberfield pointed his finger at a place half way down his notes. "It states that his issue, that's your friend, is to inherit all his property."

To avoid detection, Ash had told his lawyer that his pageboy was interested in the law and wished to sit in on the meeting. The 'friend' in question was conveniently absent.

"What else does it say?" Ash asked.

Umberfield cleared his throat and studied his notes. "As per the directives of the will, her wardship was to be purchased by Simon Rowe under an agreement reached by both men." He paused and Pippa could feel Ash vibrating with frustration. Fortunately Umberfield continued on before Ash could shake the information out of him.

"As payment for his care of Mistress Ingleside, Simon Rowe was to receive half the income from her inherited lands."

"That's an excessive amount," Ash said.

"It's not unheard of," the lawyer said. "Sometimes an incentive is required for a family member to agree to take on the guardianship."

"It doesn't surprise me," Pippa said. Catching Umberfield's querying gaze, she added, "Perhaps her uncle is not the sort of man to do anything out of the goodness of his heart. If no financial benefit could be gained, he wouldn't have taken her in."

"And the wardship would have been sold to someone else," Ash said. "Someone outside the family."

"A stranger," Pippa said.

"Better the devil you know," Ash muttered.

For a fleeting moment she thought he was going to reach for her. She sat on a stool to one side of the desk, close enough for him to touch her if he chose. He chose not to and instead returned his attention to Umberfield.

"There's more," he said to the lawyer. "There must be. She's twenty-three and still living with him. Why?" He watched the lawyer with his sharp blue eyes, his attention entirely on the man sitting across from him. "Can she leave without marrying?"

Umberfield's sagging jowls wobbled as his mouth opened and shut twice before he said, "In short, no. The will states that Simon Rowe is to arrange a marriage with a man of good character at a time he sees fit."

"But once married, all the income from her lands would go to her husband," Pippa said.

"Plus the extra the uncle was taking illegally," Ash added bitterly. "But surely this is a lot of trouble for one man to go to over a few fields."

Pippa swallowed. It was more than a few fields. Much more.

Umberfield removed his page of notes to reveal another page beneath with a list of place names. Nine in total. She recognized them all. "These are the properties now owned by your..." He coughed. "...friend."

Ash took the page from him and stared at it. "But some of these are enormous." He flicked the middle of the paper with his finger. "And are located in the most lucrative areas in England. Look at this. Northumberland is rich in coal. And the best fleece in the country grows on the backs of Buckinghamshire sheep. If these properties are managed well, then my friend is a very wealthy woman." He stared at Pippa. "Far wealthier than most peers of the realm."

She shrugged and attempted a smile. "No wonder the uncle wanted her to remain as his ward," she said. "She was probably his sole source of income. That's why he locked her away. He didn't want her to leave, or wed."

"I wonder if she knows how wealthy she is," he said to no one in particular.

"Depends how clever she is," Umberfield said.

"Oh, she's wickedly clever."

Pippa flushed. He thought her clever?

"No wonder the uncle kept her away from the presence of eligible young men." Ash rubbed his thigh beneath the desk and stared down at the list of properties. "He must have realized then how a girl with Phillippa's charms would easily attract suitors."

First she was clever and now she had charms? "It doesn't matter anyway," Pippa said quickly. She looked to Umberfield then back to Ash. "We've learned nothing that could help your friend, considering her unique circumstances." Her hands were tied now just as much as they had been when she still lived in Simon's house. If she alerted her uncle to her whereabouts through a lawyer, he would send the Witch Hunter to her door. She was trapped. This had all been for naught.

Ash studied the page again then folded it precisely, running his fingernail along the edge to sharpen the crease. "Thank you, Mr. Umberfield. It was enlightening but there is nothing further to be done."

"But there is," he protested. "The law—."

"No, thank you. There are other circumstances as my page said. A letter demanding her release and that of her properties will not be enough, I'm afraid.

Umberfield's sagging jowls twitched. "What if Mistress Ingleside got married."

"Married!" Ash and Pippa said together.

Umberfield grew taller in his seat, relishing his role. "It's the only way to be free of the uncle."

Pippa shook her head. "Not even that would help her. She—"

Ash laid a hand on her arm to stop her. "Thank you, Umberfield. I'll be in touch."

The lawyer left without instruction to continue with the matter. There was nothing to be done. Pippa was rich, she had the means to be independent, yet she could not claim her inheritance. The very thing that had freed her from her uncle would keep her in hiding, and in poverty.

Witchcraft.

"Well," Ash said, closing the door behind the lawyer, "it's obvious what we have to do. Let's get married."

# CHAPTER 11

"*A*ren't you forgetting one thing?" Pippa said once she recovered from her shock.

"Sir Guy de St. Cyr? No, I haven't forgotten him." Ash crossed the floor and took her hands in both of his. His blue eyes flared brightly as he fixed her with an intense stare that stirred something deep within her. Something basic and fierce and uncontrollable. It terrified her, yet thrilled her at the same time.

"Listen," he said, massaging her fingers, "marrying me will not only end your uncle's guardianship and give you back your inheritance, it will also offer you the sanctuary of my name."

Tempting. So very tempting, but... "No," she said, looking away before she got sucked into his whirlpool.

"Why not? St. Cyr wouldn't dare accuse the new Countess of Ashbourne of witchcraft. The Savoy name is a powerful one and I have friends in the Privy Council. You'll be perfectly safe. It *will* work, Pippa. Trust me."

His childlike enthusiasm made her want to weep , but she bit back the tears and withdrew her hands from his. "That is precisely why I can't marry you. The Savoy name will be linked to a witch. Whether the Witch Hunter proves it or not, he or my uncle or perhaps both will spread rumors against me. I'll never be completely vindicated. Your good name will be damaged and your family along with it. Your mother and sister will be ostra-cized by everyone at court. Your sister's marriage prospects will be in ruins."

"Forget about them! I'll take care of Mother and Annabel when the need arises. This is about saving you, Pippa!" He drew in a ragged breath and let it out slowly. "Don't give me an answer now. Think on it."

"I have and I can't allow it. You've been much too kind already. That kindness doesn't need to extend to marriage."

He threw up his hands. "I'm not doing this out of kindness."

"Duty then. Towards Georgiana. Whatever your reasons, I know you don't want to marry me."

"I'm offering, aren't I?"

"You are, but out of a sense of obligation."

He said nothing and she knew she'd guessed correctly. She wished she hadn't. She turned to the window and looked up at the grey sky that seemed to go on forever. Tears threatened to spill but she held them in check through sheer force of will. "I cannot accept your offer. You've been much to kind already."

She felt his heat as he came up behind her. He didn't touch her but he affected her just as much as if he did. Her skin tingled and her thoughts centered around what he could do to her if they were married. What she *wanted* him to do to her.

"You're mine," he whispered hoarsely. Her heart thudded but before she could clarify if she'd heard correctly, he said, "Yes, you are my responsibility and I take that very seriously."

Her breathing became loud in her ears. "We cannot marry," she said to the sky. "You are the Earl of Ashbourne. You have a duty to marry nobility, not the daughter of a humble country gentleman."

"Damn duty!" he shouted. She turned sharply to face him. The only time she'd seen him look so grim was when he heard about Georgiana's death. "When it comes to marriage," he said, "I have a duty to no one but myself and my wife."

"But you said yourself that you would never marry. I heard you tell the countess."

He looked to the ceiling and shook his head. She knew he

was recalling his own words spoken angrily to his mother only the day before.

"I cannot allow you to sacrifice yourself for me," she said. "I simply can't."

She spoke truthfully, but there was more to it. *She* couldn't sacrifice *her*self either. Marriage was for a lifetime. They would one day be rid of her uncle and even the Witch Hunter if Ash's scheme worked, but they would always be legally bound even when the reason for their hasty marriage no longer existed. Divorce wasn't so easily come by, despite old King Henry's precedent. They would be together forever, and forever was much too long to be trapped in an artificial marriage. Besides, she'd only just freed herself from her uncle, she didn't want to jump into a situation where she must obey another.

"It would not be a sacrifice," he said but his voice sounded thin. He moved away, cleared his throat and looked anywhere but at her. He didn't really believe his own words.

Suddenly being near him felt awkward. The air had grown fuller and breathing became difficult. Would it always be like this now? Would his proposal always hang between them like a heavy load dangling on the end of a frayed rope, threatening to snap?

"You really have done enough," she said to the sky. "More than necessary." She drew in a breath and courage, and turned to him. "It's time I leave."

"Leave?" He looked at her, incredulous. "You mean this room, don't you?"

"I mean this house. You. I cannot stay here any longer, accepting your charity—"

"It is not charity! Saints, Pippa, you *cannot* leave."

"Ash," she said as calmly as possible to placate the beast raging before her, "I know you feel bound by your connection to Georgiana, but really it is not necessary to help me any more."

"It most certainly is!" He bent down to her level and the tide of his anger forced her to take a step back. "You have no money, no friends or relations and no skills."

"I have skills," she said, trying to think of one that didn't include embroidery or starting fires.

He humphed. "Even if you maintain your disguise as a boy, what will you do?"

"I could go into service at one of the other big houses. As a household groom perhaps."

"Not without a letter of recommendation. And I refuse to give you one."

His smugness irritated her and her own anger swelled. She dampened it, knowing what it could unleash if she wasn't careful.

As her temper eased, her clarity returned. He was right. She couldn't leave. It was not only imprudent it was unnecessary. But it would be hard to stay, with his proposal pressing down on them both, suffocating.

"If you go I will find you," he said.

She thrust her hands on her hips. "You wouldn't dare!"

"I would. For your own safety." Ash caught her shoulders and shook her lightly. "Stop being so stubborn, Pippa. You can't go anywhere. It's much too dangerous."

She felt so tired, so worn out from running and hiding and being scared. She liked Ashbourne House. She felt safe within its solid walls and countless rooms. And she liked Ash. Very much. She wouldn't deny that she had feelings for him.

Which is why it would be awkward to stay. She couldn't allow her feelings to develop into something more. Not towards an earl who'd vowed not to marry anyone, and who didn't deserve to be shackled to a witch.

But stay she must. For now.

"I'll remain here until the mystery of Georgiana's death is solved," she said. "But I'll not marry you. It's not necessary. Sir Guy looked me directly in the face and didn't recognize me. I'm perfectly safe as your pageboy. When her killer is discovered, I'll decide what to do about my future then."

"With any luck, we'll prove Sir Guy is the killer," Ash said. "That'll solve your most pressing problem."

As long as her uncle could be silenced.

"It's settled then," Ash said, warily watching her. "You'll stay?"

"I'll stay."

The quirk of his lips was too fleeting to be called a smile. "Good. Right." He cleared his throat. "I must pay Mother a visit and find out once and for all everything she knows about Georgiana's twins. Perhaps you'll reconsider my offer of marriage while I'm gone."

She sighed and would have refused again but he was already striding out the door. She didn't understand him at all. For someone so against marriage, why did he continue to offer that lifeline to her? Was his sense of responsibility really so great that he was prepared to sacrifice his freedom for her security?

* * *

ASH WAS PREPARED to sacrifice his freedom.

That thought shocked him into stopping mid-stride as he passed through the empty great hall. Had his desire for Pippa and his sense of duty conspired together to undo him?

He had acted rashly up in his lodgings, on impulse and instinct rather than rational, clear thought. Marriage. What had he been thinking! He blamed his cock. It had a habit of getting him into trouble.

But at least he had stopped all foolish talk of her leaving. God's blood, it was the most dangerous, most irrational, most...selfish thing to do. Selfish because she had not considered how her departure would affect him. He couldn't allow her to walk out of his life! What kind of gentleman would that make him?

A lonely one.

He allowed himself a rueful smile. At least now he had the pleasure of her company until they found Georgiana's killer, and even beyond that if he could convince her it was in her best interests to stay. He would take one day at a time and enjoy every one of them spent in her company.

He continued on to the small parlor but his mother wasn't there either. She must have retreated to her rooms or gone out for the afternoon.

Fallon appeared as Ash was about to ascend the main stairs. "My lord," he said, "several crates have arrived for you. From Sir Francis Fordham in Haverford."

Ash nodded. "Good. Send them up to my study. Ask Pip to start cataloguing the contents." She would want something to do. It wasn't in her nature to be idle. "Have supper sent up for us both shortly," he added, mindful of the time. "I won't be long."

Fallon bowed and left. Ash continued up and knocked on the door to his mother's withdrawing chamber. At her command, he entered and strode to where she sat by the fire with her embroidery.

"You haven't been telling me the entire truth," he said.

"Sit down, Richard, this ruff is too stiff for me to look up at you if you insist on standing so close."

He rolled his eyes but took the chair opposite her. The fire blazed in the grate, throwing heat into the chamber. It reflected off the lush swathes of crimson curtains and was absorbed by the cloth of gold cushions and Turkey carpets adorning the furniture. The room sweltered. The scent of spices, used to freshen the rushes, clung to air and skin. Ash felt like he was back in Constantinople again, in one of the Sultan's luxurious private chambers. His mother would have liked that city. It was filled with color and opulence, an assault on all the senses.

"Now," she said, not laying down her embroidery, "what haven't I been telling you?"

"My father was the father of Georgiana's twin boys."

She completed her stitch before laying the frame carefully on her knee. "That information was supposed to be private. How did you come across it?"

"Very little escapes me, Mother. So am I to assume you knew all along? And that it's true?"

"It is true. And of course I knew." She made it sound like he shouldn't have doubted her. "It was a mistake."

"The pregnancy?" He scoffed. "I do know something of how babies are made and I'm quite certain the act is never a mistake. Is that what Father told you?"

The look she gave him could have pierced flesh and bone. "You know nothing of it, Richard, so do not mock. When I found out, it was horrid. My world fell apart in that instant. I'd thought my husband faithful, the most outstanding of men. He'd never shown an interest in other women, including Georgiana."

"So why did he do it?"

She traced the gold thread of her embroidery with a finger, her focus completely on its swirling movement. "For a long time, I blamed her. I thought Georgiana entrapped him. She was very pretty, voluptuous too—an enticing combination in a young girl. Men used to look at her with hunger in their eyes. I worried for her at Lady Duckworth's. The countess enjoyed surrounding herself with beautiful young men who hardly possessed a moral fiber between them. But Georgiana wasn't my responsibility. Not then."

"Anyway," she said to her embroidery, "I don't think she entrapped him. You see, she was quite the innocent. It wasn't until much later, when she had been working here for some time, that I came to know her better. I realized she was completely without guile. She wasn't a seductress. She didn't have the cunning for it, nor the inclination. Georgiana was quite simply the nicest person one could hope to meet. So you see, the blame rests entirely with your father. He seduced her. He must have."

Ash rubbed his injured thigh. "You never spoke to him about it?"

"Of course not." She wrinkled her nose. "One evening he summoned me to his study and said his mistress was having his baby. When he told me who his mistress was, I couldn't speak from the shock."

A very great shock indeed to have achieved that. But the thought was unkind given the circumstances. His mother did have heart, although she preferred to keep it locked away.

"It wasn't until I took Georgiana to her home in Haverford that she told me he'd only ever lain with her the once. So...she wasn't really his mistress." Shining eyes turned to Ash. "Was she?"

He swallowed, unable to give her an answer. He was too shaken to speak properly. Not because of what his mother had told him, but by the effect those memories seemed to have on *her.* For her to want his reassurance on the matter, she must be more disturbed by the situation than she cared to admit.

But Ash couldn't give her the reassurance she needed to hear. His father wasn't faithful. One dalliance was enough to shatter his honor and the image of the upright gentleman Ash thought him to be.

"Did Georgiana tell you anything else?" At her blank look he cleared his throat and continued. "He didn't harm her, did he?"

"No!" She pressed the back of her hand to her glistening forehead. "For all his faults, unkindness towards women wasn't one of them."

"Then...love?"

Her hand dropped to her lap. "Don't be absurd. He wanted her carnally, that is all. You of all people should understand that."

"I am not like Father!" He rubbed his thigh harder. "If I marry, I will not be unfaithful to my wife."

"Ah, so that is the reason you haven't wed?" She appeared to have returned to her usual shrewd self, something Ash never thought he'd be grateful for.

"How did Father meet her?" he said. "As nurse to the Duckworth girls, they certainly wouldn't have moved in the same circles."

She picked up her embroidery and began unpicking the last stitch. "You must remember that Lord Duckworth was a friend of your father's. They probably met during one of his frequent visits to Duckworth House."

"But...why did Father never acknowledge the boys as his own?"

The countess's back stiffened but she continued to embroider. "I asked him not to."

"But to send them to Christ's Hospital? It seems so unlike Father. And Georgiana. Did she agree?"

"Of course. She wanted them to be adopted and brought up as regular children. It was the best thing that could be done for them under the circumstances. And her dearest wish. I made sure of that."

Ash stopped rubbing. Unease settled into his stomach but

he couldn't put his finger on the exact cause. His mother's obvious distress over the matter? His father's dishonorable actions or Georgiana's apparent complicity with the arrangements? None of it made any sense whatsoever. He wished Pippa was there to offer her unbiased opinion. She had no interest in these events and would perhaps see clearly what he could not.

"Do you know who adopted them?" he asked.

"No."

"Did Father know?"

"I have no idea. If he did, he never told me. Now, if your questions are finished, I'm tired. I wish to lie down."

"Not quite finished, Mother. One more. Why ask Georgiana to work here if you believed she'd seduced your husband?"

She picked up a fan sitting on the nearby table and flapped it wildly in front of her face. "Mary always makes the fire much too hot. I must speak with her."

"Mother, I know this is difficult but it's important. I have brothers I never knew existed. Do not avoid the question."

"I wasn't avoiding it, Richard, I was merely commenting on the heat. As to an answer, all I can say is, I liked Georgiana. And I felt we owed her."

"Owed her?"

"Of course. The earl had...inconvenienced her by begetting children on her. She could not go back to the Duckworths and no other respectable family in London would have her once the rumor spread. All my friends advised me against it and none of them even knew who had fathered her children. They told me she was a whore and could not be trusted. But I'm not one to be easily persuaded when I've made up my mind. Of course I told her there were to be no more dalliances with the earl or she would be cast out."

Ash stared at his mother, seeing her in a new light. It was an incredibly kind thing to shelter the woman who'd borne her husband's children. Quite unexpected too.

"That was very good of you, Mother."

She shrugged. Her maid entered with a tray and the countess waved her into the inner chamber. "My supper is here."

He took the hint and stood. He leaned down and kissed her hot forehead. "You're not such an old dragon after all, are you?"

"If I seem like a dragon on occasion, it is simply because you and your sister vex me greatly. At least she has now agreed to marry that Briars boy. However *you* could have been a little more charming to Lady Wethinall."

"Lady Wethinall is not someone you would wish me to marry, Mother. Trust me on that score."

She clicked her tongue. "Very well. I'll bow to you this time. But I will see you married before I meet my maker, Richard. Trust *me* on that score." The twinkle in her eye made him smile and he leaned down again so she could kiss his cheek. "Now go and leave me be," she said.

"Oh, I nearly forgot. There's one other thing. Can anyone confirm my birth date?"

She looked like he'd just struck her across the face and he regretted his bluntness. Yet again he spoke before thinking. He began to apologize when she held up her hand for him to stop.

"Despite your impertinence, I understand what you're asking, and why. You want to know if you are one of Georgiana's twins."

He really should have left without opening his mouth. "Er, yes. I know I'm not, but..." Hell, how could he get out of this?

"But you want to be sure?" She lifted her chin, defiant. "Any of my friends who were in London at the time could vouch for your birth dates. And Fallon of course."

"Fallon? I don't understand. I thought I was born at Dewbury Hall."

"You were but I returned to London when you were not yet two months old. Fallon may not have children of his own but anyone can tell a near-newborn babe from one that would be..." she counted on her fingers, "seven or eight months. Ask him." It sounded more like an order than a suggestion. "It will ease your mind if nothing else."

"Thank you. I meant no disrespect."

She disappeared into her adjoining chamber without saying anything. Ash let himself out and almost bumped into Fallon lurking on the landing.

"My lord," the steward said, blocking Ash's way, "I have an urgent message for you."

"Who from?"

"Sir Nicholas Merritt. He requests your presence for supper at the Four Feathers immediately."

"Thank you." He was about to step past his steward but stopped. "Fallon, do you recall when I was first brought to Ashbourne House as a babe?" Ash felt a little ridiculous asking but it would ease Pippa's mind. And his own, if he was being completely honest.

Fallon looked askance. "It was a long time ago, my lord."

"Try to recall. Was I considered a large babe?"

"Large? Ah, well...that is to say, I don't think so. About right I'd say, my lord. You were quite a small thing, really. Quite...fragile. No bigger than my forearm." He stretched out his arm for Ash to see. "Although I am hardly an authority on babies."

Ash clapped him on the shoulder. "Thank you." He moved off.

"My lord, the meeting with Sir Nicholas."

"I'll go directly after I've changed into riding clothes," Ash assured him.

"The message did say it was urgent," Fallon said, "so I had the coach prepared. That way you don't need to change and with the way Jolly drives, you'll be there in no time."

"I hate the coach," Ash grumbled. He sighed and conceded that Fallon was right. Changing would take too long. If Merritt needed him urgently, then he must leave without delay. "Tell Pip I'll return as soon as I can to help him with the cataloguing of Georgiana's things."

"I'll go see him directly," Fallon said.

* * *

PIPPA WELCOMED the distraction the arrival of Georgiana's belongings provided. She sat cross-legged on the floor of Ash's study, paper, pen and ink at her side, and wrote a detailed account of each crate. She was half way through the third when

Fallon returned. His face was red and his breathing irregular as if he'd hurried up the stairs.

"His lordship has gone out for supper," he said. "Have you discovered anything...of interest?"

"To you?" She smiled as she handed him a small wooden box. "I think so."

He knelt beside her and opened the lid to reveal a dozen letters bound together with a red ribbon. He fingered it gently and caressed the yellowing paper as if it would crumble.

"Thank you." He stood. "I'll leave you to your duty."

He left and she picked out a box from the crate similar to the one that held Fallon's letters. She unlocked it using one of the several keys Sir Francis had found at Georgiana's cottage and included with her belongings. Inside was a small parcel tied with another ribbon, white this time. She hesitated before removing it. The package, so carefully wrapped, obviously contained a personal item. She really shouldn't open it. She barely knew Georgiana Dale. It would feel like an invasion. But Ash had specifically instructed her to catalogue *all* the contents of Georgiana's crates. Besides, the tiny parcel practically unwrapped itself in her palm. She only had to help it a little.

Inside was a woolen baby's cap. It was white, or nearly so, and made from such finely spun wool that it was impossibly soft against her skin.

She knew beyond doubt that it had belonged to one of the twins. Why else would Georgiana wrap it so carefully and keep it locked away in a keepsake box?

She turned it over, hoping to find a name stitched onto the wool but found none. She checked inside the box. Nothing. No false base, nothing under the lid, no identifying features of any kind. Just a plain box.

She sighed and folded the paper around the cap again. She was retying the ribbon when she remembered something. Ash had told her witches could find people using an object that had belonged to them as a talisman.

She unwrapped the cap once more and stared at it. Nothing happened. She picked it up and held it to her heart. Still nothing. She held it in front of her eyes and willed it to lead her somewhere, anywhere. No path cleared, no map appeared before her. What was she supposed to do to make it work? She'd never divined for anything before, never even knew she could until Ash mentioned it.

Another witch would know, one with more experience. And the only other witch she knew was Isabel Merritt, apothecary and the wife of Ash's good friend.

Pippa ran to get her coat and pocketed the cap. She just hoped Mistress Merritt would be willing to help her.

# CHAPTER 12

*T*he Bucklersbury Street shop had been closed when Pippa arrived but the apprentice who lived above it had recognized her from the earlier visit and directed her to the Merritt's house near Bishopsgate Street. Isabel had welcomed her heartily and the two women talked for some time before Isabel taught her the seeking incantation. When Pippa had repeated the words while holding the baby's cap, the colors and images around her blended, swirling together then separating, revealing a clear direction to the cap's original owner. So easy! She couldn't wait to get started.

"It's almost dark," Isabel warned. "Perhaps you should wait for Ash and find this person together."

But Ashbourne House was in the opposite direction to where the cap led, and Ash himself may not return there for hours. Besides, no harm could come to her with the cap tucked safely in her pocket and the incantation already invoked. There was no need to do it again, no need for anyone to know she'd used supernatural abilities to find the baby. Or the man, as he would be now. And as to going about London in near-darkness, well she could protect herself on that score too. So she thanked Isabel and left.

To Pippa's surprise, she didn't have far to go. The seeking magic took her to a nearby inn on Bishopsgate Street bearing the sign of four black feathers. Uncertainty made her hesitate but she shrugged if off and entered. Inside, the inn was clean and well lit with a mixed crowd of men, women, young apprentices and tradesmen enjoying their supper.

And Ash.

She slipped into a shadowy corner and pulled her hat down low. After a moment, she ventured another peek. It was definitely him. He would have seen her too if his attention wasn't drawn to the serving woman and the two tankards of ale she deposited on his table. He sat with another man, dark haired and handsome with dimples studding each cheek when he laughed.

Pippa ran out of the inn before he saw her. She hurried back along Bishopsgate Street, down to Three Needle Street and past the Merchant Taylors Hall and the imposing Royal Exchange, the many shops it housed closed for the day. She slowed and glanced over her shoulder but no one followed her. Ash mustn't have seen her.

She started breathing again and drew out the baby's cap from her coat pocket. It was his. Without a doubt. The seeking incantation had led directly to Ash. *He* was Georgiana's child. The countess wasn't his mother.

He was illegitimate.

She felt sick even though she wasn't completely surprised. The pieces had all been there, she'd just been slow putting them together. Denial can do that.

The odd thing about it all was the countess's role. She had perpetuated the secret all these years, even lied to him recently. But why? Why would any woman take on another's child as her own?

Someone jostled her, apologized, and she pocketed the cap again for safekeeping. Night had finally shrouded the city in darkness. The streets were almost empty of life and it occurred to Pippa that she was walking alone in a strange city. As a woman, she was in a perilous position. As a boy dressed as a servant she would probably be left alone by any ruffians out to earn quick money from their victims. Her disguise, combined with her witchcraft, would keep her safe. She pulled her coat closer and bent her head into the stiff breeze. It smelled of rain, the sweat of the city and something fouler.

She tried to keep her wits about her as she hurried back to Ashbourne House but her thoughts continued to wander to what she'd just learned. Two things became clear: firstly that Ash was most likely the twin adopted from Christ's Hospital—by his own father—and secondly that the other, weaker twin had probably died in infancy which explained why there was no record of him at the orphanage.

It all made sense. The heirless earl begets a child on a young woman, perhaps intentionally, perhaps not, then brings him up as his legitimate one. It also explained the countess's continuing compliance in the scheme. Now that the mystery was solved, Pippa felt like an immense burden had been lifted from her shoulders.

But another replaced it. What should she tell Ash? The news of his illegitimacy could destroy such a proud man so sure of his place in the world. Being illegitimate, he should not be the rightful earl, he should not be wealthy, he should not have power and influence. Ash would feel the weight of these should nots on his very soul. If nothing else, his sense of responsibility was too great *not* to acknowledge them. He would not want to remain the earl if the title wasn't rightfully his. It simply wasn't in his nature to be so deceitful.

But then what would happen to Ash and his family? He was a good man with a kind heart, despite his tempestuous moments. Pippa cared for him, cared what happened to him. She didn't want to see him unhappy, especially not by her actions.

It became obvious what she must do. She would simply pretend she had not used her divination skills. She would hide the cap altogether.

Footsteps tapping on the road behind her drew her attention to the present. She was already on The Strand and hadn't passed anyone for some time. The houses of the nobility rose like cliffs on her left and the homes to her right, although smaller, were still more grand than anything else in the city. She was almost at Ashbourne House.

"Boy!" shouted someone behind her. "'Lo! Stop a moment! I wish to speak with you."

She knew that voice. Knew the deep cadence, the steely edge to the command. Sir Guy de St. Cyr. For one instant, she froze. Then she ran.

"Wait!" he shouted. "I won't harm you."

She ran faster. Blood rushed between her ears and pumped in her chest but she felt sluggish, like she was running through water. Why oh why didn't her powers extend to speed?

She was slow. Too slow. He caught her within sight of the torches lighting the entrance to Ashbourne House. He pulled her to a stop, not roughly but not kindly either.

"Why did you run?" Sir Guy asked. His breathing was even and regular whereas she couldn't seem to catch enough air. "I am not a stranger. We met yesterday, remember?"

"It's dark," she said, jerking her arm out of his hold. "I thought you were a vagabond."

"Do vagabonds usually hail you?" She couldn't tell in the darkness if he was angry but he didn't sound it.

"My fears got the better of me. I'm sorry, Sir."

"There's no need to be afraid of me. I'll not harm you. What is your name, lad?"

"Pip."

He hesitated before saying, "Pip? What is your full name?"

"That is not your business." She surprised herself by sounding brave when all she felt was slack with fear.

He said nothing for some time and she wondered if he was trying to see through the veil of night to her face. Did he suspect her true identity?

Did he already know it?

"Very well," he said, quietly. "You are probably wondering why I stopped you, *Pip*." Something in the way he spoke her name, with a hint of disbelief, made her heart race. "You see, it occurred to me after I left you yesterday that I had asked you if a *female* servant had started at Ashbourne House in the last week. However the woman I'm looking for could have disguised herself as a boy. What say you? Do you think that is a viable possibility?"

He knew! Oh God. He was simply toying with her, teasing the fear out of her. She braced herself, against what would come and tried not to throw up over his boots.

"It would be difficult for a girl to go unnoticed in the men's sleeping quarters," she said.

"But not impossible."

"If you say so. Sir, I am expected at Ashbourne House. I must go."

She didn't see his hand reach out to grab her until he'd already caught her arm, anchoring her. "But first I want to talk some more," he said.

"I haven't the time." She tried to pull away but his grip tightened. Not bruising, but hard enough that she couldn't easily pull free. Not without using her supernatural abilities.

And that would be foolish beyond reason. The last thing she should do was reveal her powers to the Witch Hunter. He wanted proof of her identity and of her witchcraft. Best not to hand it to him on a silver platter.

"Let go of me, Sir Guy," she said calmly, "or I shall scream so loudly it will bring out every servant up and down The Strand."

His head dropped back and he sighed up at the starless sky. Thunder rumbled in the distance, seeming to go on and on. "Are you Phillippa Ingleside?" he said. "From the description I have, you are a close match." He shook her arm when she didn't answer. "Just tell me!"

"Let. Me. Go." The thunder grew louder, closer, unstoppable.

"Damn you, it will be so much easier if you just admit it to me! I have to be sure—"

Pippa screamed.

A coach crashed through the darkness like a spectral warrior. It hadn't been thunder she'd heard but the rumble of hooves and wheels traveling at high speed.

She screamed and screamed and screamed.

Sir Guy clapped a hand across her mouth. "For God's sake, be quiet."

She struggled against him, tried to pull his hand free. It was useless. He was too strong. She had to use her powers, unless she could solicit aid from the passing coach. It was almost upon them, grinding to a resounding halt. Thank Heaven.

Someone leapt out of the coach while it was still moving. Driver and passenger shouted, their words running together, not making sense.

A whip cracked, the horses shied but the driver kept them under control. Sir Guy dropped his hand and squared up to the passenger, an impossibly big silhouette storming towards them with his cloak billowing about him.

Pippa remembered to breathe. She was at least free. She could run to Ashbourne House now and Sir Guy would not chase her there. Not with this gentleman as witness.

"What is this?" the newcomer shouted. Good lord, it sounded like...Ash? "What is going on here? Why are you handling that boy—? Sir Guy?"

She almost sobbed with relief. "Lord Ashbourne!" She ran to his side, wanted desperately to curl into his solid body and feel his arms surrounding her. But she simply stood before him, hands at her sides and looked up at him with what she knew were wild eyes.

"Pip!" He stared but she couldn't quite see his expression in the darkness. "Are you all right?" he asked but didn't wait for her answer. He stepped past her and the sleek sound of a sword withdrawing from its sheath cut through the night. "Draw," he growled at Sir Guy.

"There's been a mistake." Sir Guy's hand hovered at his sword hilt. "I was simply having a conversation—"

"Draw!"

Sir Guy drew out his rapier, slowly, reluctantly. "I do not want to fight you, Lord Ashbourne."

"Then you shouldn't have assaulted my page."

"I wasn't assaulting her."

*Her.* He said it so naturally, without even a small hesitation, that Pippa almost missed its significance. Then it hit her with the force of a raging storm, smacking her fully in the chest.

Ash must have heard it too. He immediately attacked but his blade struck the steel of Sir Guy's sword. He thrust again and again but Sir Guy parried every blow. For every strike, Ash took one step forward and Sir Guy took one back.

"Lord Ashbourne," he said, ducking under his adversary's blade as it attempted to separate his head from his body, "we don't need to fight."

"I do," Ash snarled.

Sir Guy grunted and Pippa wondered if he had been injured. They were too far away for her to see clearly in the poor light. Two shadows performing a deadly dance, one advancing, the other retreating. The clank of steel and grunted curses peppered the night.

It soon became clear that if Sir Guy continued to defend only, he would soon find himself missing a limb or perhaps a head. Ash seemed intent on removing some part of his opponent's body. Sir Guy must have been aware of the situation for he switched tactics and went on the offensive.

The moon emerged from behind a cloud and the blades, wielded with speed and precision, flashed like the underbellies of fish in the river. To Pippa's untrained eye, the two men were a match in skill and both possessed the swordsman's instinct—that intangible element that often determined the outcome of a fight. It would go on like this, blow met by blow, until one of them was mortally wounded.

It was all her fault. They were now trying to kill each other because of her.

"Stop!" she shouted. "Stop at once!" The moon hid again but neither man slowed. "No blood should be shed tonight," she told them. "Not because of me."

"No closer!" Ash ordered her.

She stopped and watched, horrified, as Ash's sleeve was ripped the length of his arm. He grunted but easily parried the next strike.

"You mustn't do this!" she cried. "One of you will be harmed and then what?" She wanted to butt their heads together, make them see sense. Nothing good could come of this. "There are witnesses." People, servants probably, had emerged from some of the nearby houses to see what the noise was about. No doubt the coach with the Ashbourne coat of arms on it had alerted them to the identity of one of the swordsmen. If he killed Sir Guy, the news would be all over the city by morning. How far would the queen's favor go if he took the life of a knight of the realm?

"If Lord Ashbourne will put down his weapon," Sir Guy said, parrying, "then I shall not harm him."

Ash kept fighting. "You'll not have her," he growled. He thrust wildly and Sir Guy parried the rushed attempt easily. The pace of the fight slowed somewhat but still their blades met and parted over and over in their dangerous dance.

"She belongs with her uncle," Sir Guy said. "It's best if I take her home."

"Is it? And who decides what is *best*?" Ash's sword whipped through the air, barely missing Sir Guy's ear.

"*I* decide," Pippa said. Still they fought and her fear turned to irritation. She was not a piece in a game of chess to be moved here and there at someone's whim. She made her own moves now. The taste of freedom had given her that determination. "Lay down your weapons." When her command went unheeded, she used a more feminine approach. "Ash, please, I want to go home. To Ashbourne House," she amended in case he thought she meant to her uncle's.

His step faltered, his blade missed its mark and Sir Guy's sword had a clear run, straight through Ash's chest. No doubt he expected it to be parried as all the others had been.

But not this time. Ash stumbled but kept swinging his blade, even though the thrusts weakened. He fell to his knees, clutching his chest.

Pippa screamed and ran to him. She cradled him in her arms and covered the wound with her hand. So much blood! She had to stop it. Had to keep it inside him.

But his life seeped out between her fingers, dripped down her arm onto her lap.

Sir Guy knelt at her side, a cloth in his hand. He went to press it against the wound but Pippa took it. "Fetch a surgeon," she said. "Take the coach. Go!"

He nodded and melted into the night.

"Ash," she whispered, "don't leave me." She pressed her lips to his forehead. Damp, cool. Too cool. His life force was slipping away. She held him tight and prayed.

"Heal me," he whispered.

"Heal you?"

His eyelids fluttered closed but he gave a small nod.

Yes! Yes, she could heal. Apparently Georgiana had done it in Haverford. Pippa had no idea how but there was no time to experiment or take him to Isabel. She ripped open his clothing and placed both hands over the wound in his chest. There was blood everywhere. She closed her eyes, breathed deeply to still her wild heartbeat and focused on the injury.

When she started fires she imagined flames, when she moved objects she saw it happen in her mind first. Hopefully healing was the same. She pictured the flesh closed, the blood flowing through his body, the wound gone.

Nothing happened. Precious seconds ebbed. Ash became still in her arms and heavy as his life poured out through her fingers. His head lolled against her shoulder and she wanted to scream. This wasn't supposed to happen! She wasn't supposed to lose him!

Then something stirred within her, from a deep place at her core. Power surged beneath her skin, along her arms to the tips of her fingers and out to Ash's chest.

His flesh heated beneath her hands. Pain seared her palms. She was on fire. She'd used the wrong magic!

But there was no fire, only immense heat. She kept her hands on his chest for as long as possible but it simply became too hot. She could stand it no longer and let go.

Then she waited, listening and watching.

He breathed. She could hear it in the darkness. It sounded...normal. A little ragged from exertion but not rattling or gurgling. Not the sound of a dying man.

"Ash?" She touched his chest, felt through the slippery blood for the wound. It was gone. His skin was sealed where before it had been torn. "Ash?" she said, squinting at the dark shadows of his face.

His hand met hers. He squeezed her fingers. "I'm fine."

She squeezed back. And burst into tears.

He drew her head down to his shoulder, away from the blood, and cradled her until her sobs eased. "You did it," he said, brushing her hair. "Thank you." Then his hand stilled. "Did anyone see you?"

She shook her head, still buried in his shoulder. She didn't want to move away. Not yet. Not until she'd had her fill of being close to him, of feeling his life force gathering its strength. "It's too dark and no one is near."

As if on cue, a man approached. She hadn't heard the coach return so it couldn't be Sir Guy. "The villain'll pay for this," he said, kneeling beside Pippa. "The murder of Lord Ashbourne is a terrible thing. A terrible thing."

"I'm not dead." Ash sat up, dislodging Pippa.

The man fell back and gasped. "You're alive! Hogs in Heaven! I coulda sworn you was dead, my lord. The way your page was carrying on and all, I thought you'd breathed your last. But...thank the good Lord you're alive!"

"Quite." Ash stood and Pippa picked herself up too, gathering her wits about her once more. "Pip was crying with relief, weren't you?"

She nodded and wiped her nose. "It was overwhelming. I, like you, thought he was dead. You see, he's a reasonably fair master and I didn't want to lose him. Not until he'd paid me at least."

"Right," the man muttered. "Well, uh, do you need help getting to the house, my lord?"

"No, Pip will see me there. The wound isn't as bad as it must have seemed to you all." He looked around at the gathering faces, about a dozen in all. "Thank you for your concern," he said. "Come, Pip, let's go."

The crowd dispersed and Pippa walked by Ash's side, half expecting him to topple over at any moment. When they were out of earshot of everyone, she said, "Are you sure you are well?"

"Yes. There's no pain. Although I feel a little cold."

She removed her coat and handed it to him. "Take it," she said when he refused. He thanked her and swung it about his shoulders.

They entered Ashbourne House through the servants' entrance and Fallon met them inside.

"My lord! You're not dead!"

"A solid observation, Fallon," Ash said.

The steward blinked rapidly. "But a...a boy from Lord Croxley's was here and he said he saw you run through with a blade. He was quite certain you were dead, my lord. I was on my way to find out for myself. Might I add that I'm pleased to find you are not."

"Good of you, Fallon." Ash pulled Pippa's coat closer and hunched into the too-small garment as best he could.

"Are you quite well, my lord?"

"A little tired, Fallon, that is all." His body shuddered. "And cold."

"I'll put an extra log on the fire in your bedchamber."

"I'll do it," Pippa said. Her powers would bring instant flame and heat instead of waiting for a new log to catch alight. "Perhaps a warm bath could be organized for his lordship," she ventured.

She thought Fallon would bristle at her order but he simply gave a curt nod and said, "A good idea."

"And if my coach brings a surgeon, tell him he isn't needed," Ash said.

"Is that wise?" Pippa said. It couldn't hurt to have a medical man check his other wounds.

"I'm all right, Pip. Don't fuss."

Fallon bowed and headed in the direction of the kitchen. Pippa and Ash made their way up the stairs. Half way up, she placed her arm around his waist on the pretense of helping him. He no longer looked like he would fall but she felt compelled to touch him for some reason. He smiled down at her and rested his arm across her shoulders.

"Thank you, Pip," he said, using her moniker despite their solitude.

"You're welcome, my lord."

Inside his rooms, he lay down on the bed with his eyes closed while she used her magic to build up the fire. The flames quickly engulfed a new log and the bedchamber soon warmed.

She watched him from the hearth. Some of his color had returned to his cheeks and he no longer huddled into the coat, but he wasn't himself yet. He just lay there in his bloodied and torn clothes, not moving.

Blood covered her own hands and caked under her fingernails. It would take some scrubbing to remove it all. "Are you sure you're well?" she asked, sitting on the edge of the bed.

Ash opened his eyes and rolled to one side, facing her. He propped his head up with his hand and gave her a smile. "I'm sure." He parted his doublet and shirt to reveal his chest. "See? Not a mark on me."

"But...inside?"

He tapped his chest where the injury had been. "All feels fine. You did it, Pippa. Don't worry, I'm all right. Although I do enjoy your fussing. Feel free to do it more often."

She giggled like a girl with relief. "You must be well if you've resorted to teasing me again."

His smile faded and he sat up. "Thank you," he said, catching her hands in his.

"Don't thank me." She swallowed around the lump in her throat. "If this is part of being a witch, then I am glad I am one." She meant it. Imagine the good she could do! She could heal all sorts of injuries, save so many lives.

"You must be careful about using your powers, including this one," he said, reading her mind. "Someone you heal today could be used as a witness against you tomorrow."

She nodded, hating that he was right. "Oh! But Sir Guy...he'll know now that I am a witch. This is proof."

"It was dark. We'll tell him he only slightly wounded me. As far as he's concerned there's still a flesh wound here." He tapped his chest again. "You're safe from him, Pippa. For now. But for how much longer, I cannot say."

Cold fingers of fear squeezed her heart and a kind of fog clouded her mind. She nodded, numb. "He knows who I am." She stood suddenly. "I must leave. Tonight. Now!"

He caught her before she could run to her room and gather her belongings. "You're not going anywhere."

"But Ash...he *knows*. I cannot hide here anymore." For his

sake, and his family's, as well as her own, she had to leave before Sir Guy returned. She pressed a hand to her temple, trying to think through the haze but not reaching any other conclusion except that she had to get away.

"I agree. You cannot hide anymore." He took her other hand and turned her so she was fully facing him. "Pippa—"

"Then I'll leave immediately." She attempted to extricate herself but his grip was too firm.

"No. You won't."

"But you said—"

"Listen to me!" His booming command blew away the fog and she blinked at him. His eyes gleamed like hard steel. "You will not leave," he said. "You'll stay here at Ashbourne House...as my wife."

Her heart gave a single, resounding thud. "Ash, we've been through this—."

"It's different this time. Sir Guy has seen through your disguise. We can no longer deny who you are. Unless you want to keep running, taking my name is your only option. Trust me, Pippa, he cannot touch you if you are my wife."

As Lady Ashbourne, perhaps not, but Ash was not legally Lord Ashbourne. If anyone found out he was illegitimate, then he would be hounded out of society and his name would be no good to anyone.

She shook her head, slowly. Regardless of his illegitimacy, she could not accept him. She would be too great a burden. He would one day come to regret making her such an offer. "I cannot allow you to do this for me," she said.

"It's not just for you. I will benefit as well."

"How?"

His smile was completely, utterly wicked. "Need I tell you?"

Pippa's knees went weak. No, he needn't. She knew enough of the world to guess that he wanted a wife in every sense of the word.

# CHAPTER 13

*A* knock at the door made Ash drop his hands. Fallon entered and behind him followed men carrying cauldrons of steaming water. Pippa watched them fill the tub, her back to Ash as he undressed. When the servants left, she didn't go with them as he thought she might. That was the first positive sign.

"So...you agree?" he ventured.

"Are you quite certain this is what you want?" she said. "I mean," she looked down at her hands, "this is not something we'll easily be able to end."

"I have no notion of ending it."

"Oh. I see."

His heart, so recently emptied of life, now felt full of it. She had not said no. Another good sign. "Then you consent?"

She didn't answer for a long time. "Put a cloth around yourself," she finally said, pointing to one of his coffers. "There'll be a fresh one in there."

How had she known he was naked? "I know where they are."

"Of course, I forgot, you're not inept." Her soft laugh gave him hope. Humor was another positive sign. Perhaps. Hopefully.

He found a cloth and wrapped it around his lower body. "You may turn around now." She did and immediately appraised his bare chest, still bloodied but no longer bearing the mark of St. Cyr's blade. "There's no need to be so sensitive to my naked-ness," he said. "Now that we are engaged, it is perfectly accept-able to see me like this."

"I have not said yes!"

"You have not said no."

Their gazes locked. Doubt still lingered in her eyes, those deep, dark pools that could swallow a man whole.

"Perhaps I should shed this covering. To get you used to the sight."

He had wanted to tease her, relax her, take her mind off the decision she must make. But she surprised him yet again. "Very well. I should get used to your...manly...bits being on display. Take the towel off."

He blushed. He, not her. This wasn't going the way he'd planned. However... "So that's a yes to my proposal of marriage?"

She crossed the short distance between them and tugged the cloth off. He was completely naked and she didn't avert her eyes. On the contrary, she drank her fill of his...manly bits.

"Yes," she breathed. "I think marriage to you will be...a good idea."

"I think so too. For both of us."

She put her head to one side, still studying his cock. Did she think it would look better from a different angle? Bigger perhaps? It wasn't like he'd had any complaints before.

"It will certainly alleviate certain...problems," she said.

"Alleviate?" He swiped at a drop of sweat trickling down his temple. Where before he'd felt so cold, like his insides had turned to ice, now he sweltered. The room was far too hot. "Oh yes, it will definitely alleviate my problems." And if she didn't stop staring at him like she wanted to, uh, devour him, he would be alleviating his problems before he'd had a bath.

"And mine." She looked up at him through long, dark lashes which barely hid the wicked gleam in her eyes.

He couldn't stand it any longer. She may be a virgin but she was a wanton one. He cupped her face in his hands and kissed her. He'd wanted it to be gentle and encouraging but as with the last time, madness took over. He couldn't get enough of her delicious, soft lips.

It seemed she couldn't get enough of him either. She deepened the kiss, explored with her tongue, dug her fingers through his hair. All the tentativeness of the last time was gone. She kissed like a woman sure of herself and eager for more.

Her hands moved from his head to his hips, caressing his bare skin. He groaned into her mouth. "Unless you want your first time to be with a man covered in blood," he murmured against her lips, "we'd best stop now."

She stepped back and nodded. "Yes, you're right," she said, looking everywhere but at him. "You'd best take your bath." She placed a hand to her chest and blew out a loud breath. "And perhaps the physical side of our marriage should wait until the marriage has actually begun."

Damnation, he shouldn't have broken the kiss. "I see no reason to wait."

"No, of course you wouldn't. You're a man."

"Thanks for noticing," he said wryly.

She studied her fingernails as she picked the dried blood out of them. "It's just that...it's not a certainty, our marriage. And I wouldn't want to start something we cannot stop."

"Stop?" He glared at her but it had no effect because she avoided his gaze. "Not a certainty? Of course it is. I agree, you agree, what more is there except to have it sealed by the church?"

"Your mother has to agree. And doesn't the queen need to know?"

"My mother," he ground out, "will not get a choice in the matter. I suspect she will be relieved I'm finally going to marry. As to the queen, I'm not so much a favorite that she'll care one way or another."

"In that case, I'm relieved," she said, not sounding in the least relieved.

He shook his head as he stepped into the warm bath. Damn women. He would never understand them. Hot one minute, cold the next. Wait—ha! What good would waiting do? It certainly wouldn't do *him* any good. He ached enough for her as it was, did she want to torture him too?

Damn women.

He washed away the blood covering his chest and inspected his healed wound. A thin stripe of new pink skin was the only evidence that his life had nearly ended out in The Strand. He looked over at Pippa, pouring water into the basin from the ewer Fallon had brought up. She had saved his life. Now, with this marriage, he had a chance to save hers.

The memory of another woman whose life he couldn't save flashed through his mind. Whose life he played a part in ending. A significant part. He shivered despite the warm water.

The parallels between Sofia and Pippa struck him too. Both had come into his life mysteriously. Both had driven him wild with desire. Both had accepted his marriage proposal.

But one difference was that Sofia had become his lover before their wedding day. Pippa refused.

He was beginning to think it a wise decision.

He leaned back in the tub and let the hot water soak into his remaining cuts. He closed his eyes against the sting and the memories and breathed in the lavender scented steam. He would not think of Sofia anymore. He would not allow her to ruin his future the way she had ruined a great deal of his past.

He smiled to himself. To think, he'd been on death's door only an hour ago and now he was engaged to be married to a woman he desired more than he thought possible. Someone gentle and witty and good-natured. Someone who put up with his temper and made him want to be a better man.

He opened his eyes a little and watched her through his lashes. She stood at the basin, scrubbing her hands so furiously, water sloshed over the sides and soaked into the rushes.

"Pippa, are you all right?"

She nodded but scrubbed harder.

"You'll remove skin if you continue like that."

A muscle in her jaw pulsed but she didn't stop, didn't acknowledge him. So intent was she on scrubbing off the blood that she didn't even look up when he got out of the tub. He quickly dried himself and wrapped the cloth around his hips.

"Pippa," he said gently, "no more." He took her wrists, forcing her hands to be still. "What is it?" he whispered. "What's the matter?"

She stared unblinking down at the red water and said nothing.

"If it's the marriage..." *God, don't let it be that.*

"There's so much blood," she said, sounding distant. "I have to remove it all."

"You have." He held her hands up so she could see. "It's all gone."

"No, there's more." She tried to pull her hands free but he held them tightly. "Let go, Ash, I have to clean them."

"It's all right, Pippa, they're clean. It's all right."

A shudder rippled through her and she burst into tears. He pulled her to him, cradled her head against the wound she'd healed. He held her, just as he'd held her on The Strand after she'd used her healing magic on him. Now, like then, she sobbed and he could do nothing but comfort her until her distress eased.

When her crying had reduced to the occasional gasp for air, he said, "What has upset you so?"

"You...you nearly died, Ash."

He kissed the top of her head. "But I didn't."

She tilted her chin and peered at him through watery eyes. "But you might have. If I hadn't been there."

"Don't think of it." Her lips were swollen from her crying. Crying for him. He wanted to take her tears away, make her happy again.

He bent his head and kissed her. This time it was soft and sweet and everything it should be. He knew in that instant that his resolution not to make love to her before their marriage wouldn't last. He simply didn't have enough willpower.

It seemed Pippa didn't either. She pressed her body into his and suddenly the cloth at his waist slipped off. His cock sprang up and rubbed against her doublet. He much preferred bare skin. Without breaking the kiss, he removed the doublet and unfastened the points of her boy's hose. They slipped down her legs to the floor and puddled at her feet.

She stepped out of them and broke the kiss to remove her shirt herself. Standing before him, naked except for her hose, he couldn't help but stare. She was more magnificent than he'd imagined. And he'd imagined what she'd look like naked a lot since that night in Haverford when he'd *felt* her.

Her skin was soft and pale, her hips and thighs slender but not boyishly so, her breasts high and firm and topped with the most ripe nipples he'd ever seen. He had to taste them.

He bent to suck one and she gasped, arching her body into him. Lord, she tasted good. Any lingering doubts about making love to her quickly fled as he gave into his desire.

Maybe he should almost die more often if this was the response he'd get from her.

PIPPA HAD BEEN DETERMINED to resist Ash. But every time he kissed her, she lost her senses. Waiting until they were married would have been best—what would happen if it didn't eventuate despite his assurances? She would be ruined, that's what. But Ash was simply irresistible. The force of his presence made her forget common sense and propriety. She wanted him. Every part of her ached to feel his touch.

When he sucked her nipple, she thought she'd shatter. Prickles of heat fled across her skin, from head to toe, arrowing into her sex.

"Oh," she murmured when he changed to her other nipple and the sensations rocked her all over again. "Oh yesssss..."

She felt him smile around her breast. She'd always thought them too small but he didn't seem to mind if his devotion to them both was anything to go by.

He picked her up and carried her to the bed, gently laying her on the covers. Then he stood back and his gaze roamed over every inch of her. Instead of feeling humiliated by the overt attention, she felt beautiful, desirable. He wanted her. She could see it in his eyes and in his impossibly hard...oh my! *That* was going inside *her*?

But before she had time to worry about proportions, he lay down beside her. "So perfect," he murmured. He caressed her shoulder with the back of his hand then slowly brushed the swell of her breast, her ribs and down to her waist and thigh. "So soft."

She'd never seen his eyes filled with such wonder, as if he'd never seen a female body before. Yet that was ridiculous. Every move he made, every touch was expert. He knew what he was doing. And yet he marveled.

She felt her body blooming beneath his fingers, opening for him. He kissed her again and moved his hand down to her sex. He cupped her and she thought she'd never known anything so thrilling. She couldn't wait to feel him inside her, filling her. It would be the most delicious thing.

Thanks to an overly talkative maid in her father's service, Pippa knew what was supposed to happen between a man and a woman, although she was beginning to suspect theory was very different to reality.

"Oh!" she cried when one of Ash's fingers caressed her moist nether lips. No, the maid hadn't told her it could be this good.

"You're so wet," he murmured into her throat. "So ready."

His words shocked her but she supposed this was how lovers spoke and she should get used to it if she was to be his wife. She would have analyzed her thoughts further but he was doing something amazing with his fingers and she didn't care about anything else. She felt hot and tingly all over and so very very good that she couldn't believe it could get any better.

Then it did. His fingers ignited something inside her, something fierce and unstoppable that spread to the very limits of her body. She arched into his hand and pulled his head up to kiss him hard and deep.

Then she exploded. Sensations shot from her inner thighs to her very extremities, much like the gathering of her magic but more powerful. Her body, no longer in her control, bucked against him, wanting more of him. When the crest of the wave broke, she became loose and languid in his arms.

"Well," she said between deep breaths and tiny aftershocks, "I thought you were supposed to use this." She circled her fingers around his hard length, enjoying the network of ridges and veins, the smooth cap beneath the sheath of skin.

His lashes fluttered closed and he groaned low in his throat.

"Don't worry," he said, "I'll use it." He positioned himself above her, his thick penis pulsing, but he didn't enter her. A shadow passed across his face, brief but intense.

"What is it?" she said. She stroked the hair from his forehead. "Is your thigh bothering you?"

"No. It's...I don't want to hurt you."

"Oh." She knew there would probably be some pain the first time. The maid had told her about that. "It'll be all right." She stroked his big, smooth back. "And next time will be better."

He smiled. "I think that's supposed to be my line."

She grinned. "Now, if you don't enter me soon I'll have to take control myself."

His smile turned lop-sided. "Now that sounds like fun."

She cocked a brow and was about to make a retort but forgot it as soon as he pushed inside her. So far so good. So very good. They rocked together in a gentle, slow rhythm as he pushed a little further in.

Oh. Oh! OH!

It hurt when he broke through her barrier. But he held her for a moment, let her get used to him, and murmured endearments in her ear. She nodded when she was ready and after that it wasn't so bad. She even enjoyed it. The closeness of their bodies, the warmth of his skin, the taste of him. Every sense thirsted for more. She'd never wanted anything so much in her life and couldn't imagine being anywhere else, with anyone else. He filled her so completely.

She felt the tremble of his muscles, heard his breathing hitch and then quicken, felt him swell inside her.

He grunted an apology and drove into her faster, harder. Instinctively she lifted her knees to give him deeper access and he cried out, or perhaps she did. Abruptly, he tipped his head back and let out a primal growl. His body shuddered once, twice, then he collapsed on the bed, half on her and half off.

His breathing slowly returned to normal and he eventually opened his eyes. Her smile quickly vanished. Instead of seeing her own fulfilled happiness reflected back at her, she saw...guilt.

"I'm sorry," he said, fingers drawing little circles on her hip over and over. "I wanted to be gentle—"

"You were."

"I wasn't. Not at the end." He shook his head. "My...urgency got the better of me. Pippa, I so very much wanted your first time to be good."

She cupped his cheeks and kissed him gently. "It was. Better than good. I can't describe it. Amazing. Beautiful. Wonderful. Addictive." She laughed. "It seems I can describe it after all."

"Addictive? Does this mean you want to do it again?"

"Yes. But not yet, lover."

"Husband," he said, sounding hurt.

"Almost husband," she corrected. "We'll do whatever you want after a nap. Besides," she looked down at his sated member, "you look like you need some time."

He licked her nipple and the fire kindled low in her belly again. "I won't need time if you give it a little bit of care. Just a touch will suffice. He'll be standing to attention awaiting your command before long."

She grinned into his hair. "You are unbelievable."

"Thank you."

She smacked his shoulder lightly. "As I said, after a nap. I'm so tired."

He moved up so they were eye to eye. "I know." He kissed the top of her head. "Good night, Wife."

"Almost wife," she said around a yawn.

* * *

THERE WAS a mad scramble for clothing in the morning when they heard Fallon moving through the study beyond.

"He must have brought up breakfast," Ash whispered, pulling on his hose.

Pippa climbed out of bed and he had to stop what he was doing to stare at her lusciousness. She reminded him of a cat, all slender lines stretching with graceful, languid movements. How had he ever thought she was a boy?

"Stay here until he's gone then join me. Fallon usually brings up too much for one person to eat." He leaned over her and kissed her thoroughly. His body stirred when she kissed him back with equal fervor. He might get used to having a wife if he could wake up to this every day of his life.

She grinned when he broke off the kiss and he allowed himself to hope she felt the same way.

The knock at his bedchamber door drew him reluctantly away from his bed and the woman in it. "Good morning, Fallon," he said upon opening the door only wide enough so he could slip through to the study. "I must have overslept."

"Your schedule is on your desk, my lord," Fallon said. "I trust you are well today?" He looked directly at Ash's chest.

"Perfectly. Only a few minor cuts and bruises. Nothing to concern yourself. Or anyone else," he stressed. No point alarming his mother or sister unduly.

"Very well, my lord. If there's nothing else..." He backed away towards the door.

"Actually, there is. You lied to me, Fallon."

The steward's eyes widened and his usually flat face became pinched. "I, I'm not sure I know what you mean, my lord."

"Yesterday afternoon you said Merritt wanted to see me."

"He did!"

"But you also said it was urgent. It was not. Merritt told me he never expressed expediency in his message." In the events of the evening, he'd entirely forgotten his steward's deception until now. Coming from an otherwise completely loyal member of his household, the lie was like a strike of lightning—unexpected and shocking. "What have you got to say for yourself?"

Fallon blinked rapidly. "I, I..."

"It's my fault," Pippa said.

Ash turned. She had emerged silently from the bedchamber dressed as a pageboy. He raised an eyebrow. "Yours?" he said, holding himself very still to stop reaching for her.

"Yes, my lord. I had asked Fallon to ensure you didn't return to your lodgings after you spoke with the countess. He was simply doing me a favor."

"And why would you ask him to do that?" There was something going on here and he didn't like it.

"Because I wished to see if there was something in Georgiana's belongings that might implicate someone from this house. I thought perhaps you might not want to know about it and so I asked him to...divert you."

"And did you find something to implicate anyone in this house?" He thought she hesitated but he couldn't be sure.

"No," she said.

"No," he repeated. He didn't want to shout at her, not after their night together, but damned if he would allow her to lie to him now they were on intimate terms. She had to know he would not countenance it. "I fail to see why a long-time servant of the Savoys would assist a pageboy of barely a week's service to dupe his master."

She gave him a look that pleaded with him not to continue. He decided to let it be and question her further over breakfast. "Very well," he said to Fallon. "It seems you are not to blame. You may go. No, wait, one more thing. Have Lady Annabel's maid bring one of her mistress's dresses here, and various other feminine garments to go with it. If my sister enquires as to why, tell the maid to inform her that all will be revealed this morning. Then have the countess and Lady Annabel await me in the summer parlor. I have news."

When he was gone, Ash strode into the breakfast parlor and Pippa followed. She handed him his shirt.

"I don't need to put this on to eat my breakfast," he said petulantly.

"No, but I need you to. I can't eat when I'm distracted." She offered him a smile, a peace-offering. He sighed and put the shirt on.

"What in God's name was all that about, Pippa?" Anger simmered but he found he couldn't shout at her despite her deception. Their all-night love-making had lulled him but that didn't mean he was prepared to drop the subject altogether.

"You do realize I was covering up for Fallon?" she said, sitting down at the breakfast table as if nothing was amiss.

"I do? Yes." He sighed and sat down heavily. "Actually, no, I haven't a clue what just happened." Ten years of courtly diplomacy and three years of heading up an arm of Walsingham's intelligence network hadn't prepared him for the guilelessness of women. History told him that. "Pippa, what is going on?" Anger gave way to foolishness. He got the distinct feeling he owed her an apology.

"I had no idea Fallon had sent you away under a false terms," she said, spreading jam over her bread.

"It wasn't entirely false. Merritt did want to see me. I would have ridden out but Fallon said it would be quicker to take the coach he'd readied for my use. I take it *he* didn't want me up here? It had nothing to do with you?"

"Not directly. When Georgiana's things arrived, he asked me to look for anything concerning himself. They'd been having a...relationship for some years and I suspect he didn't want you finding any evidence of it."

He sat back and regarded her. She spoke so coolly, as if she did this sort of thing all the time. He on the other hand never possessed half as much composure under interrogation. He marveled at how far his little Pip had come since they met. But then she must have been like this before fear of her uncle changed her. Did that mean she felt safe with Ash? He hoped so.

"So you were covering up for him in there?" He pointed his knife towards the study.

"Yes. I thought it the best thing to do. He would hate to disappoint you, Ash. You and your family are his entire life. For him to think he was lowered in your eyes would be devastating."

"What about me? I'm devastated that my steward lied to me!"

"You'll recover. Just don't let on that you know." She took a bite and he watched her chew. She had the most sensual lips, kissable lips.

He leaned over and kissed her mid-chew. He couldn't stay mad at her for long. "And did you find anything of Fallon's?" he asked, sitting back and enjoying the way her cheeks flushed.

"Some letters. I gave them back to him. I didn't think there would be anything in them pointing to her killer."

"Not likely. Fallon didn't do it. He was here with me." He ate in thoughtful silence, wishing the sweetness of the morning wasn't overshadowed by Georgiana's death. "Let's talk about pleasanter things for now."

Her tongue darted and moistened her top lip. He gulped down half a cup of ale and tried not to think of that tongue moistening parts of his body. "I slept soundly last night, after you eventually allowed me to," she said playfully.

"I seem to recall *you* were the one not letting *me* sleep." He grinned at her and she grinned back. God's teeth she was beautiful. "I too slept peacefully."

"No nightmares?"

"None." He studied her over the top of a chunk of bread he'd been about to eat. "Did you somehow use Isabel's potion on me without my knowledge?"

"I didn't get the opportunity. Perhaps I can throw it out if you sleep like that again tonight."

"If you lie with me then perhaps I will. It seems your presence in my bed is potion enough."

She tilted her chin in the most adorably obstinate way. "We really should wait." She frowned. "Although waiting for the banns to be read will take an awfully long time."

"I'll purchase a special license this afternoon and have a word with the Bishop of London. We can be married as soon as arrangements can be made."

"Your mother won't like it," she said, doubtful. "Even if she agrees to the marriage, she'll want more time to prepare."

"My mother will have to make do with what time she has. We must be wed as soon as possible. Besides," he reached across the table and covered her hand with his own, "she'll adore you. Anyone who could get me to the altar is an angel in her book." He smiled to reassure her. "It'll be fine, Pippa. The meeting will go well. You'll see."

She didn't look in the least like she believed him.

\* \* \*

LADY ANNABEL'S GREEN GOWN, matching bodice and skirts fit Pippa well enough but were two inches too short and a little too big in the bosom. Ash tightened the laces as much as possible but nothing could be done about the length.

"It'll have to do," she said. It was a simple dress of deep green with white sleeves and white underskirt. Teamed with a matching French hood which did a serviceable job of hiding her cropped hair, it wasn't quite elegant enough for a lady to formally meet a countess who was to be her mother-in-law.

With a sigh, she twirled for him. "Do I look well enough in lady's clothes?"

His gaze took in every inch of her. "You look beautiful in either lady's or men's clothing but I prefer you in neither." His grin was wickedly sensual.

For once, it didn't affect her. She was too nervous. She flounced onto the daybed. "I can't do this," she said, burying her head in her hands. The countess would faint or fly into a rage when she saw her son's intended dressed in an ill-fitting borrowed gown. Yet another thing to worry about on top of all the secrets she knew and the lies she'd told to keep them.

"The color suits you," he said, sitting beside her. "With your dark hair and eyes, you look ravishing."

"I don't want to look ravishing," she wailed, "I want to look elegant and composed and...suitable."

He drew her to him and kissed the top of her head. "Stop caring about what my mother thinks. I'm the head of this family and I want to marry you. She can turn her nose up all she likes, it won't make a difference. Not that she will," he added too quickly for Pippa's liking.

"Thank you," she said. He was trying at least. And the next few hours were going to be hard on him too, perhaps more so.

"But there is one more thing that I think will set off this gown beautifully." He pulled a ring from his smallest finger and took her hand. Gently, he tried it on her middle finger. It was a little big but would not slip off if she was careful. "Well?" he said, when she didn't say anything.

"I...Are you sure you want me to have this?"

"Of course! I'm only sorry I haven't had time to buy something prettier. This will have to do for now as a betrothal ring."

She twisted the thick band of gold set with a ruby. It was smooth and warm from his skin. It would be a comfort to have something of his close to her all the time. "Thank you."

He stood and offered his hand. "Ready?"

She drew in a deep breath and placed her beringed hand in his. "Ready."

They passed only two servants on the way to the summer parlor and Pippa studiously avoided looking at either of them. Perhaps they wouldn't recognize her with her head down. If they did, the news would be all over the house soon that the master was going to marry his pageboy. She stifled a nervous giggle and it came out as an unladylike snort.

"Glad your spirits have lifted, Pip." He patted her hand, opened the door and ushered her inside before she had a chance to change her mind.

The summer parlor lived up to its name. Sunlight streamed through the large windows and reflected off the yellow walls. Up until now, Pippa had been restricted to the servants' areas and Ash's rooms, but she was beginning to see that the rest of the house was decorated quite differently. Where Ash kept his lodgings free of bold color and clutter, the rooms they'd walked through to get to the summer parlor were awash with crimson and jade, purple and gold, emerald and silver. The summer parlor itself was more golden than vivid. Cushions and Turkey carpets threaded with gold adorned every seat, paintings of grave looking men and women hung on the walls in ornate gilded frames. Even the candlesticks were golden.

The colors were at odds with the two women standing in the middle of the room. Lady Ashbourne wore black and a stern expression and the other, a young girl, wore cream and white.

"Mother, Annie, meet the woman I intend to marry," Ash said. Both women gasped. "May I present to you Phillippa Ingleside."

Ash's sister recovered from the shock first. She grinned at her brother then at Pippa. Pippa tried to smile back but her attention was drawn to the countess. She lifted one severe brow and the simple gesture made Pippa's heart plunge.

This was going to be an arduous morning.

# CHAPTER 14

*L*ady Annabel took Pippa's hands in her own. "Very happy to meet you, Phillippa."

"And I am happy to meet you, Lady Annabel. Please call me Pippa."

"Then you shall call me Annie." She was younger than Pippa, probably only nineteen or twenty, with the same blue eyes as her brother. That's where the resemblance ended, however. Where he was dark, she was light. Fair skin, hair of pale gold and the most delicate, sweetly arranged features. When she smiled, as she did now, her whole face smiled with her. "That gown suits you much better than it ever did me. But if I'd known my brother wanted to give something of mine to his intended, I would have chosen a prettier one." This last she said pointedly to Ash.

"Thank you for the loan, Annie," he said. "You'll have it back as soon as possible."

Annie glanced between them both and it was probably only politeness that stopped her from asking her brother why his future wife had no clothes of her own.

His mother, however, appeared to have no such reservations. Her narrowed eyes scrutinized Pippa and it took all her strength of will not to shrink into Ash's side. "Well, Richard," Lady Ashbourne said, "your jests have reached a new low."

"Jests? I assure you, Mother, this is no jest. I am marrying Pippa."

"Yes," she said after a moment, "I'm sure you will." Her mouth stretched into a firm line, her gaze sharpened. Pippa shivered but Ash's solid presence reassured her. He didn't move, merely met his mother's stare with one of his own equally formidable ones. "Nothing I say will change your mind, as usual," she said. "However, was it necessary to hide her in your rooms as your pageboy?"

"Pageboy!" Annie laughed. Her mother gave her a cool look but the girl merely laughed harder.

"I'm surprised you recognized Pippa, Mother," Ash said. "You hardly noticed her before now even when speaking to her."

"Nothing escapes my notice."

So it seemed.

"Then we have your approval?" he ventured.

"Do you need it?"

"No, but I'd like it nonetheless."

"As would I, Lady Ashbourne," Pippa said, smiling tentatively.

The countess didn't return it. "I don't know any Inglesides." With a snap of her skirts, she sat on a cushioned chair near the window. She half turned to look out at the gardens and Pippa noted how youthful she appeared for her age. Only faint lines marked her face and her features had none of the slackness of other women beyond their middle years. Her figure was remarkably trim and her hair, although streaked with gray, appeared soft beneath the cap.

"Phillippa's father was Sir Henry Ingleside of Hampshire," Ash said. "Her mother was a friend of Georgiana's before her own death some years ago."

The countess turned away from the window, a spark of interest in her dark eyes. "Georgiana Dale?"

"Yes," Ash said. "It was on her advice that Pippa came to Ashbourne House in disguise as my pageboy. Her uncle and guardian is a tyrant. She needed to escape him and Georgiana offered help."

"How awful," Annie said, sitting beside Pippa and taking her hand. "We're so glad you came here. We'll take care of you, won't we, Mother?"

"We'll do our best," the countess said, stiffly. "Your father was a knight of the realm, Phillippa?"

"Yes," Pippa said, glad to have something useful to say. "And quite a wealthy man." She didn't know why she blurted out that piece of information but she felt she had to bring *something* to the marriage. Whether the countess cared or not was irrelevant—it made Pippa feel better. The heiress of a rich knight was an acceptable match, more so if it was true Ash had refused all the eligible women his mother presented.

"I do wish you had come to me immediately, Richard," the countess said. "It's quite inappropriate to stow her away in your lodgings and fool the entire household into thinking she was a serving boy. If the story gets out—"

"I shall be forced to marry her?"

She scowled at him. "Sarcasm ill becomes you, Son."

"As you so often remind me, Mother. The subterfuge was necessary, and no harm's been done. I'm going to arrange a special license this afternoon. The sooner we wed the better. I don't want her uncle taking her away from me. Er, us, here." He coughed. "Pippa's security is my main priority."

The countess raised her eyebrow again and regarded first her son then Pippa. "I see," she said, and Pippa wondered how much she really did see. Did she know it was essentially an arranged marriage? Even so, did she detect the passion simmering between them? Or did she wonder if Pippa had trapped her son into a union that clearly favored her more than him?

"I hope you'll give me sufficient time to organize a suitable wedding feast," the countess said.

"We want something small," Ash said.

"Lord Ashbourne is getting married. It will be a grand affair."

Ash sighed. "Fallon and Cook are competent enough for a surprise such as this."

Her nostrils flared and she inclined her head in agreement. "I'll have the guest list made up for approval upon your return." She turned to Pippa. "I assume we won't be inviting your uncle."

"Absolutely not!" Ash said before Pippa could.

"He'll be informed after we are married," Pippa said.

"If he doesn't like the match, he can answer to me."

"And to Her Majesty," the countess added. "She will not abide having the marriage of one her nobles questioned."

Pippa couldn't believe what she was hearing. Not only was Lady Ashbourne agreeing to the marriage, she was actually ensuring it would survive.

"And I suggest we find you something appropriate to wear, Phillippa," the countess continued. "Lady Annabel's old dresses really aren't appropriate for a bride on her wedding day."

Pippa would have smiled if she'd been sure the countess was attempting humor. Instead she thanked her and looked to Annie. The girl winked and Pippa felt a little less ill.

"And while we're talking about happy occasions," the countess said, "I see you're not dead, Richard."

Ash said, "Ah."

"Why would he be dead?" Annie asked.

Pippa wished she was somewhere else. How much did the wily old woman know? Her scalp prickled and the tiny hairs on the back of her neck rose.

"I was told you'd died last night and came back to life," Lady Ashbourne said, idly smoothing down her skirts. "I see it is true."

"Only in that I am alive, yes. I can assure you I didn't die." He laughed. "Not even close. Only a few cuts. I can show you if you like."

"Spare us." Lady Ashbourne fingered the froth of lace at her cuff. "You really shouldn't be out dueling, Richard. It's not...becoming of an earl."

"Not to mention dangerous." Annie glowered at her brother. "Ash, you really must stop being so foolish. Especially now you'll have a wife to care for. Pippa, you tell him. Perhaps he'll listen to you."

"I...I'm sure he wasn't in any real danger." Pippa wanted to reassure the women but it wasn't easy when she felt no reassurance herself. The way he had carelessly challenged Sir Guy, with little regard for his own safety, she had the feeling violent confrontations weren't rare for Ash. "But I would feel happier if you refrained from dueling in future," she said to him.

He frowned at her then muttered something under his breath which sounded like "Women."

Pippa was granted a small nod of approval from his mother. "Hopefully my son will come to appreciate your feelings on this matter more than he does that of his mother and sister." Perhaps the countess wasn't an old dragon after all. She clearly only wanted what was best for her son, as any mother would.

No, not *her* son. She was not his mother.

That knowledge pulled at Pippa. She lowered her gaze, unable to look at either Ash or the countess lest she give herself away. She studied her hands and only half-listened to Annie chatter about the style of wedding gown that would suit Pippa's figure.

During her pause for breath, Lady Ashbourne said, "I'm fortunate to have both of *my* children betrothed. It's a mother's dearest wish." The way she said it, with an emphasis on the *my*, made Pippa look up. "Don't you think, Phillippa?"

Pippa's heart stopped beating. The cool, penetrating regard of the countess froze her to the bone. *She knew.* Pippa had no idea how she did, but the countess *knew* that Pippa was aware of the secret of Ash's birth. It was there in her eyes, in the set of her jaw, challenging and almost daring Pippa to say something. But then Lady Ashbourne blinked rapidly and the challenge was gone, replaced by a questioning raise of her brows.

Pippa glanced up to Ash to see if he'd noticed the exchange but he was busy watching his sister. Annie had stood up and turned her back to the room as she stared out the window.

"Annie?" he said. "What is it?"

"May I speak with you, Ash? Regarding my creditors of course," she said with forced lightness that didn't fool Pippa and assuredly wouldn't fool the countess either.

"Now?" Ash said.

"Now." She sailed past him and waited by the door.

Pippa willed him to stay but her powers unfortunately didn't extend to controlling minds.

"I won't be long," he said and left with his sister.

Beads of sweat broke out along Pippa's brow and breathing

suddenly became difficult. Was this what the condemned felt like as they were transported to Tyburn Gallows?

"Shall we use this unexpected opportunity to get to know one another better?" Lady Ashbourne said.

Pippa smiled warily. She doubted very much that the countess wanted to get to know her at all.

"So..." Lady Ashbourne spread long, be-ringed fingers over her black silken skirts. "How did you find out?"

Pippa bit the inside of her cheek. The bitter taste of blood filled her mouth. It was possible the countess was talking about something entirely different, nothing to do with Ash's parentage at all. Possible, but not likely. "Find out what?"

"Don't play me for a fool, child." A sharp edge underlay the calmness of her voice. No one would think this woman a fool. "I've known all along you were a woman. I've known you were a friend of Georgiana's and I know you found out something about my family."

"No, I—"

"Do not lie to me. I *know*. You may have an exceptional talent for discovering information but you are a poor liar. It's written all over your face. Now, tell me exactly how you learned that Ash's real mother is Georgiana because as far as I am aware very few people alive are privilege to the knowledge."

Pippa had no intention of telling the countess about her witchcraft. Matters were already balanced precariously enough. "I bribed the clerk at Christ's Hospital to show me the records." It was a leap but it was the only answer she could think of under pressure.

"I don't believe you."

"No?" Pippa leaned forward conspiratorially. "Then you shall go mad with wondering because it's the only explanation you'll get as it's the truth."

The countess's lips pursed and her fingers curled in her lap. "Not such a meek girl after all, are you?"

Pippa said nothing. What could she say? She hadn't meant to speak so boldly but the words had tumbled out before she could check them. It was too late to take them back. Nor did she want to. It felt liberating to speak her mind to this woman.

"How you got the information is irrelevant," Lady Ashbourne said with a tilt of her chin. "For now. What I do want to know is, what do you want in exchange for your secrecy?"

"Exchange?" Pippa shook her head. "Nothing. Why would I want something?"

A muscle in Lady Ashbourne's cheek twitched. "I find it...highly coincidental that you have arrived in this house, lured my son into marriage and that you know this rather...personal information about him. Those are an interesting set of circumstances, are they not?"

Pippa suddenly remembered a note with a hasty scrawl that mentioned a secret. Was this the secret it referred to? Ash's parentage? It seemed likely that it was, and that it had also been meant for the countess all along, not Ash. *She* knew the family secret, *he* did not. Lady Ashbourne must be the one being blackmailed.

If that were the case, and she didn't know who had sent the note, then it seemed logical that the countess might think Pippa had written it—to trap Ash into marriage.

Pippa gathered her outrage and her courage. She would not allow this woman to turn her into a gold-digging blackmailer. "I have not lured him. I've not even told him who his real mother is."

"Of that I am sure. He would have been demanding the truth from me if you had." She nodded and Pippa wondered if that was meant as thanks.

"Nor will I," Pippa added.

Lady Ashbourne's face remained perfectly still but her gaze was brutal as it bored into her future daughter-in-law.

"As you have probably already guessed," Pippa said, "this marriage is not a love match."

A rather inelegant huff came unexpectedly out of her ladyship's mouth. "Of that, I am certain. My son doesn't believe in love. He's not a fool."

But he most certainly believed in passion and lust. Of *that*, Pippa was certain. She refrained from gloating to his mother.

"You say you won't tell him of his parentage," the countess said, "but I trust you will not mention it to anyone else either. I think you're intelligent enough to see it is not in your best interests to divulge the secret."

"Thank you for the compliment," Pippa said through a tight jaw. "However I'd like you to understand my silence on the matter has nothing to do with my own *best interests*. It would hurt Ash very deeply to learn that he's not the true earl of Ashbourne and I don't want to be the author of his pain. He's been very good to me. In fact, I want nothing from him except the sanctuary he's offered through marriage. His title and money don't concern me."

"And yet his title and fortune go hand in hand with your security, do they not?"

Pippa's gaze faltered. "They do," she admitted. "I am perfectly aware of it." More than the countess knew. If knowledge of Ash's illegitimacy became public, he would be stripped of his title and his influence. Without those, Ash could not stop Sir Guy from accusing her of witchcraft. Accusing her, judging her and punishing her.

"Good," the countess said. "Then we are of like mind. I see no reason for this matter to be discussed any further." And with a turn of her head, the conversation ended.

\* \* \*

"I CAN'T MARRY HIM." Annie paced from one side of the great hall to the other, pausing only to turn a pleading eye on Ash. "You do understand, don't you?"

Understand? Yesterday his sister had been eager to marry Briars. Today she wanted to cancel the arrangement. No, he didn't understand. Why did women always change their minds?

"You don't love Briars?" he asked.

"No. I don't think I ever did." The high pitch of her voice was the closest thing to distress he'd ever heard from her. She was usually so confident and composed.

"I can't say I'm surprised," he said. "You didn't seem to particularly like him."

She stopped pacing and looked thoughtful. "I like him. I just found him difficult to tolerate."

"Not a good start to a marriage," he muttered, his gaze wandering to the door leading to the summer parlor. He really should be in there helping organize his own wedding feast. It was his duty. But his sister was also his duty and she needed him more than Pippa right now. Besides, she was probably deep in conversation with his mother about wedding dresses and feasts. He would only be in the way. "At least you're ending it before it's too late," he said, placing an arm around Annie's shoulders and hugging her.

"But what about Mother? She had her heart set on me marrying him."

"Marrying his fortune, you mean."

She moaned into his shoulder. "Are we so desperate for money?"

"Not at all! We're not quite as well off as Briars but we're hardly poor either."

"Then...I don't understand it. Why did she want me to marry him?"

He sighed. He hadn't understood it either. Then again, who understood anything his mother did? She was a force unto herself. "I don't know. Briars is one of the most foolish men I've ever met."

She bit her lip but couldn't hide her smile. "I'm quite sure I've never heard anyone talk about so many dull things in one day." The smile faded. "But he *was* kind to me. His gifts were very generous...and numerous. Oh Ash, what should I do? I don't want to hurt his feelings, or mother's if she truly desired the match, but I'm not sure I can live with him for the rest of my life."

"I'm quite certain you can't." He took her hands in both of his. "You can't marry someone simply because he gives you a few trinkets."

"His last gift was a ruby ring."

Ash raised an eyebrow. "A few expensive trinkets then. But jewels are not enough for someone like you, Annie. You need someone interesting and intelligent, as well as someone kind. Nothing less would be good enough for my little sister."

She sighed theatrically. "There's not a man alive who meets all those criteria."

He crossed his arms. "What about me?"

She rolled her eyes. "Brothers don't count. Besides, you're much too temperamental. Fortunately your bride doesn't seem to be as discerning as I am."

He almost told her that Pippa couldn't be all that discerning because she was only marrying him for the security his name offered. He wanted to tell her. Annie had always been his confidante, the one person he could turn to. But this secret wasn't his to tell, it was Pippa's. It was *her* life at stake.

"Do you want me to tell Briars?" he said.

She sighed again. "No. I'd best tell him in person as soon as possible. Today. As to Mother...you can tell her if you like."

"No, you're not getting out of that one. We'll do it together, now."

She looked to the door. "At least it will take her attention off poor Pippa."

"Poor Pippa? Attention? What do you mean?"

"Oh, nothing, except you know how protective Mother can be, especially of you."

"Do I?" He frowned. "No, you've got it wrong. She's certainly not protective of *me*. Not in the least."

"No?" She touched a fingertip to the side of her mouth in mock thought. "Hmmm, let's see. Oh yes, does working behind a desk in London instead of being posted overseas mean anything to you?"

"I was needed here," he said ungraciously. "By Walsingham and the queen, and by you and Mother."

"Mother and I were perfectly fine on our own. As for Walsingham and the queen, wouldn't your knowledge of languages be more useful to them in the courts of foreign kings?"

"I, uh..." He was struck dumb. Not needed at Ashbourne House? But he was the earl of Ashbourne! Surely they needed him in some capacity. They must have.

"After that business in Spain," Annie said, "Mother had Walsingham keep you here."

He knew it. He'd known it all along, he simply didn't like

acknowledging it. "Because I was needed here." There, his point was proven. "Anyway, that has nothing to do with Pippa."

"It certainly does. Mother simply wants you to form a suitable alliance with a girl who's...worthy of you."

"I'm the one who's not worthy of Pippa," he said quietly. "She's the most gentle-natured woman I've ever met."

"She must be to put up with you." It was teasingly said but it struck Ash close to the bone.

"I resent that," he said, heading for the door leading to the summer parlor. "However, despite your unsisterly conduct, I'll support you with regard to Briars. I only want you to be happy, Annie. As does Mother, I'm sure."

"Thank you, Ash." She gave him a wan smile. "Now, let's go before I change my mind again."

Ash raised his eyes to the ceiling. *Amen.*

* * *

PIPPA WAS RELIEVED to have the awkward silences broken by the return of Ash and his sister. But a few moments later, she would have preferred any sort of silence to the raging storm they unleashed in the summer parlor by announcing Annie's broken betrothal.

"You *must* marry him!" the countess said, rising from her seat. Her mouth twisted and her face, always so composed, turned an unhealthy shade of scarlet. "It has all been arranged! You...you cannot break it off now, Annabel."

Annie looked like she either wanted to burst into tears or run from the room or perhaps both. Pippa admired her for not only staying but for standing up to her mother. "I'm sorry, Mother. I am. I know how much trouble you've gone to—"

"No, Annabel you have NO idea."

"But I don't love him."

"What's love got to do with marriage?" The countess pulled herself up to her full height, considerably taller than her diminutive daughter. "You. Are. An. Ashbourne. You canNOT afford to marry for love." The last word came out as a sneer.

"Mother," Ash said in a placating tone that Pippa had never

heard from him before. "She wouldn't be happy with Briars. You know it."

"I do not! No." Lady Ashbourne sliced her hand through the air in a move so violent, so out of character, that Pippa jumped. It was to her children's credit that they both remained unmoved. Perhaps these rages weren't such an uncommon occurrence after all. "No, I won't allow it. She doesn't know what she's doing."

"I most certainly do!" Annie said.

Pippa wanted to cheer for the girl. It couldn't be easy to defy the countess in full flight, but Annie must possess as much of the Savoy courage and determination as her brother. Even as her mother approached her she did not move back, not even an inch. She merely tipped her chin to look up at her. "I do not love him. Worse, I cannot abide him. He is a foolish bore—"

"He is much less of a fool than you," the countess hissed. She turned on Ash. "I suppose you support her?"

"I do. It's for the best. You'll see." He stood as still as an island battered by tumultuous seas.

"For the *best*! The BEST!" his mother echoed. "You have no idea what is *best* for this family! You, who weds the first girl to come along and dazzle you with her cow eyes."

Cow eyes?

Ash bristled, straightened, but his mother didn't give him a chance to speak.

"I do hope you chose your bride with more care this time, Richard," the countess went on, "or this family will be ruined and not even Briars will want to marry Annabel then." Like a dark cloud, she blew out of the room, slamming the door behind her.

"Well," Ash said when the furniture stopped rattling, "that went better than expected."

Annie plopped down on the settle beside Pippa. She was shaking. "Do you think she'll ever forgive me?"

Pippa put an arm around the girl and hugged her. "Of course she will. She's your mother. It'll all be forgotten soon enough."

Annie sighed then kissed Pippa on the cheek. "Thank goodness you and Ash are going to marry. At least all Mother's hopes weren't pinned on me."

Pippa glanced up at Ash and caught him staring at her. He quickly looked away. Perhaps he was thinking of the remark his mother so casually cast away as if it meant nothing.

*I do hope you chose your bride with more care this time.*

This time.

That meant he'd had another wife once. Pippa swallowed past the lump in her throat. She shouldn't feel annoyed that he hadn't mentioned being married before. She had no right. Their marriage was an arranged one, he didn't have to tell her anything.

And yet she felt hurt that he hadn't. And if she was being brutally honest with herself, she was quite devastated that another woman had gone before her. Perhaps his first wife was the reason he no longer believed in love or perhaps he had loved her so completely, he couldn't possibly love another. She desperately wanted to know, and yet didn't. Either way, it was not Pippa's place to ask him.

She cast aside her questions and the emotions gnawing at her heart, even though they were growing fiercer and rawer every day, particularly after their love making. Which was exactly why she couldn't allow it to happen again. She was fragile enough. Another night of passion and she might do something foolish like declare her feelings for him.

"Will you be all right, Annie?" Ash said, suddenly kneeling in front of his sister. "Do you want me to accompany you to see Briars?"

"No," she said with a toss of her head. "When Mother is calmer, I'm sure she'll want to come with me. Besides, you've got your own affairs to see to." She leaned forward and kissed his cheek.

He chucked her under the chin and stood, holding his hand out to Pippa. She took it since it was more of a command than an offer.

Tension crackled between them on the long walk back to his rooms and Pippa got the distinct impression he wanted to say something. Not able to stand it any longer, she broke the silence on the landing outside his rooms.

"Poor Annie," she said, taking the safest course of conversation. "Will she be all right?"

"Don't worry about her," he said, sounding relieved at the diversion. "She's remarkably resilient. I was more surprised by Mother's reaction. I don't understand why she's taking the broken betrothal so hard. It's almost as if it's a blow to her personally."

She entered his study first and he followed behind, closing the door softly. "Perhaps she feels a little embarrassed now after pushing his suit so strongly," Pippa said. "She'll have a lot of explaining to do to Briars, his father and of course her friends." She moved to stand by the large window near the desk, her back to Ash. "Especially since there have been a few false starts in the Savoy marital sagas." She turned round quickly to see his reaction.

He winced. "Ah. About that..." He vigorously scratched the side of his head and looked at her left shoulder instead of her face. "Perhaps I should have told you I was once betrothed, but it had nothing to do with us, this." He shrugged. "So I simply didn't think it worth mentioning. Which it wasn't. Worth mentioning, that is. It didn't go ahead, the marriage I mean, so there's nothing to discuss." His gaze fleetingly met hers but settled once more on her left shoulder. "It isn't important now. Not to this, to what we're about to do. If I thought it was important—"

"Ash." She couldn't let him ramble on even if he was saying all the right things. "You're right. It's not important to our own circumstances. We have other things that need discussing right now."

"We do?" He looked bemused but at least he was no longer fixated with her left shoulder.

"Yes. Such as what are you going to tell the servants. I think they need to be told soon. They're going to be most put out at having to prepare for your sudden wedding as it is, but to learn that you're marrying me..." It was going to be awkward. Fallon would act as stoic as ever but would the others be as professional? And what of Gertie? Pippa closed her eyes. Poor Gertie. She was in for quite a shock.

Ash sighed. "I'll have Fallon assemble them in the great hall." But something on his desk caught his eye and he moved away from the door instead of towards it. He picked up a letter and broke the seal. "It's from Sir Francis Fordham, Haverford's justice of the peace."

Pippa was at his side in an instant. "Does he have anything useful to say?" In all the turmoil of the previous day's discoveries, the investigation into Georgiana's death had slipped from her mind somewhat. She wanted to right that wrong as best she could and as soon as possible.

"He says another witness has come forward. A vagrant known around the village as Old Tom. According to Fordham, Old Tom saw someone leave Georgiana's cottage on the night of her death."

"Sir Guy?"

"Probably not." He pointed to a line half way down the page. "Old Tom says *the moonlight shone on a tall man with fair hair as he left Mistress Dale's home.*"

"Fair? Not Sir Guy then."

"Unlikely. According to my own enquiries, Sir Guy left Haverford almost immediately after he met with Georgiana. He was easily traceable all the way to London. He didn't try to cover his tracks which suggests he had nothing to hide." Ash gave her an apologetic smile. "I had Merritt trace St. Cyr's movements and he reported to me last night. Sorry I didn't inform you earlier but I was...waylaid."

"By Sir Guy or me?" she put in wickedly.

"Both." He put down the letter and caught her round the waist. "Any chance of being waylaid again tonight?"

She shrugged, feigning nonchalance—not an easy task when desire curled through her body at his touch and rippled across her skin. "I don't know what Sir Guy's schedule is like."

He grinned and picked up the letter again. "Stop distracting me. I'm trying to think."

She cleared her throat and dampened the fire smoldering within. "You're right, this is serious. Please continue. What else does the letter say?"

Ash read the rest then looked up at her, his brow deeply

creased. "It says that Old Tom saw the door close after this fair-haired stranger left. But he saw no one close it."

"Perhaps he wasn't standing at the right angle to see her close it from the inside." But she didn't really believe it. Sir Francis Fordham had put the idea into her head and the more she thought about it, the more she was convinced Georgiana had used her powers to close the door from her chair by the hearth. The same chair in which she'd bled to death from a stab wound to the heart.

"Perhaps," was all Ash said. He folded the letter and put it aside. "So Sir Guy is not our killer."

Pippa wasn't prepared to give up on him as a suspect just yet. "Unless," she said, "he has been very cunning and deceived us all."

# CHAPTER 15

$\mathcal{I}$n the end, Pippa convinced Ash to tell Fallon the news of their betrothal alone and have the steward inform the rest of the household. It wasn't his preferred method but she seemed agitated at the prospect of facing all the servants together so he agreed. He didn't want her agitated. It would only make it more difficult to get her back into his bed later.

And he most certainly wanted her in his bed again. His body ached for her. The female clothing only made it worse, not better. He'd thought all those skirts and material would dampen his desire by hiding her womanly figure but the tight bodice only enhanced it and he found himself anticipating the thrill of removing all that clothing.

The wait for Fallon was excruciating. Ash kept imagining taking Pippa on his desk, in the chair, across the stool... The room had endless possibilities. Then there were all the adjoining rooms...

"What is it?" she said, frowning at him from her position by the window. The late morning sun bathed her face in light and highlighted the lustrous depths to her dark hair. He wanted to run his fingers through it, feel its silky strands. "Why are you staring at me like that?"

"I, er—." A fortuitous knock at the door interrupted him. "Fallon!"

The steward entered, bowed. "My lord? Is there something you require?"

"No. Yes." *Concentrate!* "Ah, Fallon, I'd like you to meet my future wife. We are to be wed as soon as possible."

Fallon's eyes widened so much Ash thought the steward would do himself an injury.

"What his lordship is trying to say," Pippa said, coming up beside Ash, "is that I am a woman, as you can see, and have agreed to be married. That is, he has offered, and I have accepted."

A feather could have dropped in the silence and it would have sounded like an explosion. Fallon stared, mouth agape.

"Perhaps we haven't explained it very well," Ash said.

"I require no explanation, my lord." His face cleared and he suddenly seemed completely recovered from the shock. It was more than could be said for Ash. He was still wondering how to explain the situation.

"My lord, my lady," Fallon said with a bow to them both, "may I congratulate you on your impending nuptials."

"Thank you, Fallon," Ash and Pippa said together.

"We can explain the ruse," Pippa began.

"No, we can't," Ash said, resting a hand on her shoulder. He didn't want to elaborate at this point. "Fallon, please inform the other servants. Ensure everyone is given extra helpings at dinner in celebration."

"Very well, my lord."

"As to the wedding feast, it will take place as soon as possible. Consult with Mother on the arrangements."

Fallon nodded. To his credit, he showed neither alarm at the sudden increase in his work load nor questioned why the lord was marrying his page of the wardrobe.

"Good man," Ash said. "There'll be a bonus for you after the feast."

With a nod at Ash and an expressionless bow to Pippa, he was gone.

Pippa's breath came out in a burst as if she'd been holding it for some time. "Thank goodness that's over."

"It wasn't so bad, was it?"

"No, but he's a man who takes his service very seriously. He hides his emotions well." She rubbed her temple. "Imagine the downstairs gossip when he tells the other servants. Their reactions will not be so calm as Fallon's, I'll wager."

He caught her round the waist and kissed her. "You don't have to worry about what the servants are saying, Lady Ashbourne."

She swatted his arm. "Don't call me that yet. And, as a word of advice, one should always worry about what the servants are saying. They tend to know a great deal about the comings and goings of their master's household."

As one who'd interrogated servants to ensnare the masters, he agreed with her wholeheartedly. "I bow to your wisdom, my lady."

"Don't call me that." Where before she'd been lighthearted, now she seemed irritated. She removed his hands from her waist and moved back to her position by the window. "Not until after the ceremony," she said to the pane of glass.

She must still have doubts about marrying him. He didn't like it. All he wanted to do was hold her, make love to her, but he couldn't do that if she changed her mind and ended their betrothal. He couldn't face not making love to her ever again, not having her in his bed every night, soothing his aches and nightmares. No, the prospect of a future without her was a bleak one.

The sooner they married the better.

She gasped and her hand flew to her heart as if it hurt. "Oh, no," she said, panic thinning her voice. "Sir Guy is here!"

\* \* \*

"I SEE YOU'RE NOT DEAD," Sir Guy said when he entered Ash's study. His smile didn't reach his eyes.

"Give me one good reason not to kill you where you stand," Ash snarled. He held himself like a tightly wound coil—hands at his sides, body rigid but with a slight shudder as if he were about to unravel. Pippa wanted to go to him and soothe away his tautness, but she held her position by the window. She simply couldn't take one step closer to the Witch Hunter.

"Because I don't think even you could kill in cold-blood," Sir Guy said.

A muscle pulsed in Ash's jaw. "Then you don't know me very well."

"Oh, I think I do. There is a lot I know about you. Things that I'll wager you haven't told your...pageboy." Sir Guy turned his gaze on her for the first time. He showed no surprise to see her in women's clothing. She shivered despite the warmth of the sun at her back. "I see Mistress Ingleside has decided to dispense with her disguise."

"State your business then remove yourself from my premises," Ash said. He took a step towards Sir Guy, not seeming to care that he was unarmed and the Witch Hunter had a rapier strapped to his hip.

"I simply wanted to find out for myself if the rumor was correct. It seems that it is. You are quite alive."

"Does that disappoint you?"

"It surprises me," Sir Guy said. "I was covered in your blood when I left to fetch the surgeon. There was also a great deal of it all over The Strand when I returned to the spot this morning. Mistress Ingleside there, dressed as your servant, was much closer than I—she must have been covered in it too. I've seen death many times, Lord Ashbourne."

"I do not doubt that," Ash said, menacing.

Sir Guy flexed his gloved fingers. "And yet I have not seen anyone lose so much blood and live. No, not only live, but be in the fullness of health as you appear before me now."

Ash's own fingers clenched and unclenched at his sides. Pippa wondered how much provocation it would take for him to use them. "Then perhaps you have not seen as much death as you say," he said.

"Perhaps." The Witch Hunter's gaze settled on Pippa. "Are you quite well, Mistress Ingleside?" An innocent bystander would have thought it a well-meaning question for her regard. It was not.

"I am," she said.

"Now that you have established we are in good health," Ash said before Sir Guy could speak again, "you may leave. Leave

Ashbourne House and leave London. Get far away from Pippa and from me before I rip your heart out. If I can find it."

Sir Guy was unmoved. "I will leave when my business here is complete. I have a commission to fulfill—"

"You can thrust that commission up your—"

"What Lord Ashbourne is trying to say," Pippa said quickly, "is that we would like you to take a message to my uncle. Circumstances have changed, and it may be that your commission will be canceled in light of those changes."

She had not wanted to reveal their plan to Sir Guy yet. She'd wanted to wait until the marriage was formalized and the feast over, but he was here, now, and must be dealt with. It was the only way to stop him from exercising his legal right to take her and return her to her uncle. Her reservations about the marriage were irrelevant. She could not let this man see that she was having second thoughts about embroiling Ash in her problem. Her very dangerous problem.

"What changes?" Sir Guy said.

"We are betrothed," Ash said, triumphant. "Pippa will soon be the new countess of Ashbourne."

A hint of surprise passed across Sir Guy's face before being banished by his usual somber mask. Moments passed before he spoke and Pippa wondered if he was digesting the full implications of the announcement. "You need permission from her uncle before she can be legally wed."

"I need permission from no one," Ash growled, "especially from a man who kept her prisoner. Do I need to remind you that the Ashbourne title is an old and respected one? That I have some influence at court?"

The air in the study grew thick with silence. Pippa's blood rushed between her ears, her breath came short and fast. The two men glared at each other, inches apart, their hands bunched into matching fists at their sides, ready to use at a moment's notice.

"I think we both know," Sir Guy said, speaking carefully, "that *some* influence is an understatement." Again the heavy pause. And then he did something completely unexpected. He bowed. "My congratulations to you both on your impending nuptials."

Ash seemed to recover from his surprise faster than Pippa, if he had been surprised at all. He certainly didn't appear to be, but then he appeared to be nothing except an angry man barely containing a violent outburst. "You will take the news of our marriage to Simon Rowe," he said. "By the time you reach him, we shall be wed. Tell him he can do nothing. That he is to leave Pippa alone. Forever. And if he doesn't, I will personally introduce him to Sir Francis Walsingham's interrogation equipment. Do you understand me?"

Sir Guy's fingers flexed again. "I will deliver your message, Lord Ashbourne. As you say, it's likely my commission will be...forgotten."

"If it is not, if Rowe orders you to—"

"No one orders me."

Ash inclined his head in acknowledgement. "If you *decide* to take matters into your own hands, then be assured that the same fate will await you. I will not allow my wife to be hunted like an animal. Is that clear?"

"Perfectly." Sir Guy glanced at Pippa and although he didn't exactly smile at her, his expression changed to one of lightness. Then he returned to Ash and once more he became dark, formidable, a wall of impenetrable stone. "I do hope, my lord, that you are fully aware of what you are getting yourself into. You and your family."

Ash raised his hand to strike. Pippa shouted, "No!" and his hand moved past Sir Guy and reached for the door.

He jerked it open. "Get out of here," Ash said, so low she barely heard him. "Fallon!" he yelled and the steward appeared. He must have been hovering.

With a nod at each of them, Sir Guy strode off, Fallon almost running after him in an attempt to keep up.

Ash closed the door and leaned one arm against it, his head bowed, his back to Pippa and the room. "Next time I see him," he said, "I'm going to kill him."

She didn't doubt it. "We won't see him again," she said, coming up behind him. "I'm sure of it." Almost sure. She pressed her palm to his back and felt him shudder.

"Pippa," he said on a groan, tipping his head back.

She wanted to ease his tension, take away some of the anger in his system. She pressed her body against him and circled her arms around his waist, holding him. With her ear to his back, she could hear the rapid thud of his heart, matching her own. The tension seeped out of his body and he relaxed into her with a satisfied groan.

They stood for some time, melded together like two figures carved from the same block of wood. Interminably joined. After a while, he turned and brushed her cheeks with his knuckles. "I mean it Pippa. I'll protect you in any way I can. If I have to kill him in order to do that—"

"Don't," she said, heart and eyes brimming. "Don't say it. Just kiss me."

He did. Thoroughly, completely and oh so softly it made her melt. Made her want him inside her again, filling her, possessing her. She'd never felt so protected, so safe in all her life, despite the ever-present danger of the Witch Hunter and her uncle. Ash had given her that and it was a gift she would cherish.

She wanted to tell him how much he meant to her, how much his protection meant to her, but she could not. He had made it clear their marriage was for convenience only, that he was simply doing his duty. In return he gained a woman in his bed and a wife to satisfy his family obligations. But not love. Certainly not love. He'd always been clear on that score. His scalding kisses may make her forget sometimes, but she could not afford to, or she might find herself in danger of losing her heart instead of her life.

A knock at the door forced them apart. Gertie entered. She appraised Pippa with the interest of someone studying a fascinating painting but blushed when their gazes connected. She quickly looked away but not before Pippa saw the hurt in her eyes.

"Lady Ashbourne asked me to prepare your new rooms and see you settled in them before dinner," the maid said stiffly.

"Rooms?" Ash said.

"In the west wing."

"But that's on the other side of the house!"

"Is that not suitable, my lord? I only did what her ladyship told me."

He sighed. "I suppose it is for the best."

"Mistress Sutherland is waiting to see you too, er...Mistress Ingleside."

"Who?" Pippa asked.

"Our family tailor's daughter," Ash said. "She is the best in London, or so Mother tells me. She should be, for what I pay her." He winked at Pippa. "Go have some beautiful clothes made up. Whatever you want." His fingers brushed against hers. "I'll see you at dinner."

Pippa turned to Gertie. The maid spun on her heel. "Follow me," she said.

Pippa was glad she didn't have to find her way on her own. She would have got lost by herself. They seemed to walk for an age, traipsing down stairs and then up again on the other side of the house, along a gallery and through rooms of varying sizes, some with obvious uses, others not so obvious. None were devoid of furniture and most were decorated in a manner similar to the summer parlor. Lots of gold and color, and a great deal of pattern in the plasterwork ceilings, wallpaper and tapestries. Most pieces of furniture were decorated with embroidery or Turkey carpets and the floors were covered with scented rushes or matting. Everything had the countess's excessive touch, not Ash's sparse one. Lady Ashbourne was a woman who knew her place in the world and what was expected of her. Pippa could almost hear her saying "the London residence of the Savoys must be suitably furnished."

She giggled and Gertie half-turned without breaking her stride. She said nothing and continued on to a door which she opened with a key attached to her girdle.

"Here you go, m'lady," she said, stepping aside.

"There's no need to call me that yet," Pippa said in as friendly manner as she could. "We are not to be wed for a few more days."

"What am I to call you then?"

"Mistress Ingleside will suffice."

"Very well," she said without looking directly at Pippa. "This room is your sitting chamber, through there is the bedchamber and beyond that is the wardrobe and a small breakfast room."

Pippa poked her head into the bedchamber. It was a smaller version of Ash's with a bed in the center of the room and a fire already burning in the grate. Despite the warm spring air outside, the rooms smelled damp and in need of air. "It's quite large."

"It was built spercifically for the lady of the house."

"Specifically," Pippa corrected. "But why so far away from the master of the house?"

Gertie shrugged. "Some say distance makes for a happy marriage."

Pippa smiled. "I'm not sure that expression is referring to the distance between bedchambers."

Gertie huffed. "I wouldn't know. Me a humble maid and all."

"Gertie, there is nothing humble about you." Pippa stopped in front of her but the maid refused to look in her direction, preferring to stare at the wall. "Are you going to remain angry with me forever or are you going to acknowledge that our kiss was something...unique."

Gertie's mouth opened in a silent gasp and finally she looked at Pippa. "Unique?"

"Special. Something you and I shared that no one can take from us."

"Oh. Right. Unique." She thought about that for a moment. "'Twas wasn't it? Special. Can't say I've ever kissed a girl before."

Pippa grinned, relieved the ice had been broken. "Me either."

"But you could've told me you were goin' to be the lady of the house one day."

"I wasn't planning on being the lady of the house. Not until Lord Ashbourne asked me yesterday."

Gertie's flushed face turned redder and she sucked on her lip.

"Go on," Pippa said, "ask me anything you like. I think I owe you an explanation."

"Well, did, uh, did his lordship know you was a woman the whole time? Or did he just find out yesterday?"

Pippa tried not to smile. "He found out when we went to Haverford."

"And you've been sleeping in his rooms all this time!" She stared wide-eyed at Pippa then suddenly coughed. "Not that it's my business."

Pippa refrained from agreeing with her. "Do you have another question?"

"Yes. Why did you dress as a serving boy?"

"To escape my uncle. It's a complicated story but you can be assured I did not come here to lure his lordship into marriage."

"I never said!"

"I know." Pippa patted the girl's arm. "But I wanted to put your mind at rest. I did not intend to deceive anyone. Circumstances changed and the ruse had to be maintained for longer than expected. I'm sorry you and I..." She searched for the right term but couldn't think of one.

"Became friendly?"

Pippa smiled. She had always enjoyed the company of the servants in her uncle's household. Indeed, they'd been her only friends for five years, her only link to the outside world. After a while, they'd come to accept her as not being so different to them. In fact, they probably considered themselves more fortunate. They at least had a day off once a week and could go where they pleased. She wanted to have that sort of relationship with Gertie and the other servants at Ashbourne House if at all possible. The countess's authoritative way did not suit Pippa in the least.

"I am certainly not sorry we became friends," she said to Gertie. "And I hope you will not be sorry either."

The maid gave her a tentative smile. "No, I'm not."

"Good."

Gertie cleared her throat and looked away again. It seemed the awkwardness between them could not be put aside anytime soon. Not for the maid at least, and Pippa needed to respect that. Hopefully time would heal any humiliation Gertie felt.

"Mistress Sutherland's waitin' downstairs," Gertie said. "I'll show her up."

Pippa thanked her and watched Gertie bob her head and leave. She waited, alone, with not a single thing in the room of her own. Not even the clothing she wore. She sat on one of the chairs by the fire and looked down at her hands folded in her lap. The nails were cut short, like her hair. It made her fingers look stubbier, not like her fingers at all.

The fire cracked, drawing her attention. The flames licked the wood and threw out heat into the room, something Pippa was grateful for. There was no need to use her powers to fuel it. She wondered if the countess had ensured a fire was lit for Pippa's arrival in the lodgings, or whether it had been Gertie's doing. The warmth lulled her and she closed her eyes, fighting sleep. But the alternative was to think about how her situation had changed so dramatically in such a short space of time and she didn't want to do that. Didn't want to think about the Witch Hunter returning to her uncle and Simon's angry reaction to the marriage. Didn't want to think about the pending marriage at all. Didn't want to think about the Savoy family secret, and certainly didn't want to think about poor Georgiana, the woman who'd set all this in motion for a girl she'd never met. An action that might have got her killed.

No, Pippa didn't want to think at all.

* * *

SHE AWOKE with a start when someone knocked on the door. "Come in," she said, rubbing her eyes.

Gertie entered, followed by a short, barrel-shaped woman who moved with an awkward rolling gait. She introduced herself as Mistress Sutherland, the daughter of the Savoys' tailor.

"Lady Ashbourne has requested I make the gown you are wearing more serviceable," she said. Everyone looked down at the hem of the skirt which brushed Pippa's legs above the ankles. The tailoress clicked her tongue. "Yes, yes. A panel in a contrasting color will suffice. Black. Now, take it off."

Gertie helped Pippa remove the gown and offered her a cloak to wear while the tailoress's nimble fingers stitched on a panel of black velvet to the hem of the dress. When she'd finished, Gertie helped Pippa dress again.

"Let's measure you for the new clothes," Mistress Sutherland said, rummaging through her bag. "Do you have any ideas what you want?"

"My tastes are quite simple," Pippa said. "Nothing too elaborate."

"Yes, yes, some simple but elegant skirts, bodices and gowns will look very nice. You'll be wanting more shifts, hose and underskirts no doubt." Mistress Sutherland measured Pippa's waist. "As to your wedding gown, Lady Ashbourne has directed me to create something appropriate for the bride of Lord Ashbourne."

"But there's no time!"

"Do not concern yourself. I have a large team working with me. Yes, yes, you'll have something befitting your new station."

She finished measuring Pippa then produced some fabric samples from her bag. Many, many samples.

An hour later, Pippa's head was spinning and she couldn't decide between the deep indigo or the white satin for her wedding gown. She'd already chosen less expensive fabrics and colors for her day clothing but Mistress Sutherland had insisted she choose something finer for her wedding dress. Pippa had agreed only because she would need one good set of clothes if she was to attend court.

Court. Good Lord, what was she getting herself into?

When Annie tentatively poked her head round the door, Pippa leapt up and dragged her into the room.

"Thank goodness you're here!" she said. "Which of these do you prefer?"

Annie studied the fabrics laid out on the daybed. "The white. Worn with a farthingale under the skirt for fullest effect. And embroider the sleeves with gold and perhaps a stomacher too. I think a ruff and cuffs of lawn, edged with lace will set it off beautifully."

"Exquisite!" the tailoress exclaimed.

"But there isn't time for all that," Pippa said.

Annie caught her hand. "Mistress Sutherland is a miracle worker. She'll have something ready."

"Yes, yes." the woman in question said, gathering up her

samples. "I'll have them sent to you within days, Mistress Ingleside. Days!" She left with her arms full and a smile on her face.

"I think you've made her very happy," Annie said. "She loves creating fine clothes. It's her passion. Her father has the business sense but she has all the ideas and skill."

"A fine arrangement for her then." Pippa took Annie's hands and turned the girl to see her fully. She looked worn out. "Do you want to talk?"

Annie gave her a tired nod. "Thank the lord he sent you to me. My brother tries to understand but I think the female mind is beyond him." She sat down on the daybed and drew Pippa down with her.

"Was it really awful?" Pippa asked.

A deep frown wrinkled Annie's brow. "I saw a completely different side to Briars today. He was angry. So angry. He's always been amenable and gentle, but today he shouted at me. Told me I was foolish, that I was not good enough for him anyway. He called me a spoiled princess, no use to a merchant like him. He said he'd wanted to marry me despite my drawbacks—my *drawbacks*!—and against his father's wishes. Can you believe it!" She threw up her hands and let them fall on her lap. "Me, a spoiled princess! I thought him rude and I told him so."

Pippa cringed. "You did?"

Annie nodded. "And I told him I was glad I wasn't marrying him now I knew what he was really like. That only made him angrier."

"I'm not surprised."

"He threw a candlestick at the wall. It made an awful noise."

"What did your mother say?"

"She remained out of sight in another room and wouldn't speak to me on the way home. She's been quite unreasonable." Annie sniffed.

Pippa thought it a little unfair that her mother should abandon her daughter when she needed her most but didn't say so. She hugged Annie. "At least it's over now."

Annie drew in a deep breath. "Yes, and now I never have to think of him again. I can concentrate on pleasanter things like your wedding." She clapped her hands. "That dress will look so beautiful. And after the wedding, we can sew some pearls onto it and it'll be suitable for an evening of entertainment at court."

Pippa tried to smile but couldn't. Fortunately Annie didn't seem to notice her hesitation. She sprang up and held out her hand to Pippa.

"Let's go down to dinner. We don't want to keep Mother waiting."

\* \* \*

THE FOUR OF them sat at the family's table at one end of the spacious great hall, overlooking the servants seated at two tables running the length of the room. They ate in stilted silence peppered with occasional conversation about the wedding. The servants seemed to sense the unease and their chatter barely rose above a hum. Annie began to tell her brother about her visit to see Briars but the countess put her hand up.

"That is not appropriate dinner talk," she said.

"Come see me later," Ash said to Annie. He then turned the conversation to food and guest lists and all the other minute wedding details. Despite having assured his mother she had a free hand with the preparations, she continued to involve him. Pippa thought he made a good show of feigning interest.

She, however, couldn't even pretend to concentrate. She tried at first, she really did. But she didn't know who Lord Whathisname or Lady Whoever were and didn't particularly care.

She was grateful when the meal was over. All she wanted to do was find a quiet corner and escape all the wedding talk and the stares of the servants.

"Come along, Phillippa," Lady Ashbourne said, rising. "There is much to be done."

"I thought I would go through the remainder of Georgiana's belongings," Pippa said.

"Georgiana's death no longer concerns you. That is Richard's business."

"Mother," Ash said, "Pippa has been helping me and I will continue to require her assistance."

Lady Ashbourne's eyes narrowed. "*I* require her assistance with this wedding."

Pippa doubted that very much but she agreed before battle lines were drawn. Ash looked like he was prepared to argue with the countess all afternoon.

"I'll have Fallon finish the cataloguing of Georgiana's belongings," he said. He stood very close to Pippa, not touching her. She wanted to reach for him, feel his arms around her, feel his skin against hers. And yet she didn't move. She didn't want to start something she couldn't stop.

And she may have to stop all of it—the wedding, the lovemaking, Ash's involvement in her life.

"Are you all right?" he asked, peering at her.

"Yes, of course." She wanted to reassure him. More than anything, she didn't want him to think something was wrong.

"Then try to enjoy the afternoon. I'll be back as soon as possible." He pecked her dryly on the cheek, gave her a small smile and left.

The countess led the two younger women to the summer parlor where they sat and embroidered for the afternoon. Pippa pricked her finger three times and bled all over her fabric, but it didn't really matter because she would never use the cushion cover anyway.

She was leaving.

Leaving Ashbourne House, leaving London, leaving Ash.

The decision had crept up on her slowly as she worked and listened to mother and daughter chat. But like all weighty things, it gathered momentum so when the full force of it finally slammed into her she was left battered and bruised.

She would never see Ash again. Never see his crooked smile, never hear the deep timber of his voice or feel his solidness pressed against her. It was too much. Her stomach rolled, rebelled at the very idea and she nearly threw up all over her bloodied embroidery.

But her heart and her head knew it was the right thing to do.

She could not marry Ash. She could not endanger him or his family. She had embroiled Georgiana in her troubles and possibly got her killed, she would not see the same thing happen to Ash, Annie or the countess. Pippa could not risk life again, not anyone's.

She must take action, on her own, and face the consequences. The consequences would probably be dire but at least *her* life would be the only one endangered.

Ash would not agree. He would use every weapon he possessed to get her to change her mind, from argument to reason to seduction. Not particularly in that order.

Which is why he must not learn of her plan. Tomorrow, first thing, she would leave.

Which meant there was only one more night in which to say goodbye.

# CHAPTER 16

*A*sh couldn't wait to tell Pippa the news—they would wed in two days. She would be safe. She would be his. He paused on the steps leading to her rooms.

*His.* His wife. His lover. Always his. He grinned and tightened his grip on the balustrade to steady himself. Very soon he would have secured the woman he wanted more than any other. The woman he adored. The woman he...

Oh, Lord. He'd best keep moving or his legs might betray him if he even thought *that* word.

He knocked on Pippa's door but when he received no answer, he tried the handle. Unlocked. He entered but there was no one in the sitting room so he peered into the bedchamber. His bride-to-be lay on the bed, fully clothed, snoring softly. He smiled and moved up beside her, placing his candle on the table near her bed.

She was so peaceful, so beautiful. He knelt beside the bed and dared to brush a lock of dark hair from her forehead. Her long lashes fluttered briefly but stayed shut, her breathing remained even and deep. On each exhalation, her lips parted slightly in the most adorable pout. He wanted to kiss them, taste them, taste her.

But he didn't want to wake her so he moved away. The rushes scrunched under his feet and perhaps that's what woke her, or perhaps it was an innate sense that came with being a woman, or a witch.

"Ash?" she murmured.

He sat on the edge of the bed. "I'm here."

She smothered a yawn with the back of her hand. "How long have you been there?"

"Not long. I came to tell you we shall be married in two days."

"Oh." She sat up. "So soon?"

He frowned at her tone. "Isn't that what we want? What you want?"

She laughed but it sounded forced. "Oh, I simply meant that it's such a short time to get everything in order. There's so much still to be done."

He laughed too, relieved. "Let Mother and Fallon take care of it."

"Yes, of course."

He touched the crease at her brow. "You look tired. You should be in bed."

"I am."

"I mean in your night shirt. Why are you still dressed?"

"I can't undress myself and I didn't want to disturb Gertie."

He laughed. "Being a servant has gone to your head. It's her duty to be disturbed."

"Yes, but...never mind." She sighed.

Something in her tone tugged at him. Perhaps she'd been in disguise too long, become too close to the servants. It was all very well for the future Lady Ashbourne to be on good terms with the people who worked for her but it was entirely another for her to be on the same level as them.

"Allow me to help you." He used his candle to light others then took her hand and gently pulled her up to stand before him. He unpinned her sleeves and carefully placed all the pins on the table and draped the sleeves over a nearby chair. She'd already removed her ruff so he concentrated on the small eyelets fastening the gown but it wasn't easy with her breath warming his cheek as he bent to the task. His fingers brushed the hollow of her throat and her breathing paused then started again, faster than before.

He put the gown and her girdle aside and unlaced the points joining the stiff bodice to the skirt. It fell away, freeing her breasts beneath the shift. He bent to lick one through the fine linen then the other and was rewarded with a groan. He placed his hands at the small of her back and pulled her closer and drew one nipple, fabric and all, into his mouth.

"Yessss," she hissed, arching into him. "Make love to me, Ash."

"Not yet." He removed her skirt then her padded underskirt so that she stood before him in nothing but her shift and nether hose. Her shoes already lay tucked under the end of the bed.

He dropped to his knees and breathed in the scent of musk and lavender and woman. All woman. *His* woman.

Slowly, deliberately, he slid his hands up one of her legs, caressing the curve of her calf to the knee. He drew down both garter and hose and marveled at the long, lean lines and the impossibly smooth skin. So much skin. He wanted to savor every inch.

"I love your legs," he said, hooking his fingers inside the other garter and hose. He followed the garments down with kisses, all the way to her toes, leaving behind a trail of goosebumps.

She stood before him in her shift, the only item of clothing she owned. When she was his wife, he would buy her hundreds of clothes. The finest silks, the richest colors and the most intricately embroidered pieces. She would outshine everyone at court, even the queen.

But that was for later. Right now, he only wanted her out of the shift. He unlaced it at the collar and she raised her arms so he could remove it. Finally, gloriously, she was naked. Perfect.

"Are you cold?" he said, voice thick. "I'll build up the fire." But he didn't move, couldn't. The sight of her was much too powerful.

Without saying anything, she lifted a hand and pointed it at the fire. Flames suddenly ignited with a whoosh as if the wind had caught them.

He smiled. She smiled back. "I think you have an unfair advantage, my lord. Allow me to undress you."

He laughed. "When you were my pageboy you couldn't bear to see me naked now you can't wait to relieve me of my clothing."

"Pip was such a sensitive boy," she said, a twinkle brightening her eyes. "However Pippa is neither sensitive nor a boy." She unfastened the buttons down the front of his jerkin and slipped it off his shoulders. "And she wants to see you naked." There was none of the careful placing of clothes on a stool or table for Pippa, she simply threw the jerkin into a corner of the room.

"She can see me naked all the time, now that we are to be husband and wife."

Her nimble fingers suddenly paused then resumed unbuttoning his doublet, fumbling with the fastenings all the way down to his waist.

He caught her wrist. "What is it, Pippa? What's wrong?" He became very still, waiting breathlessly for her answer. Even his heart stopped beating.

She pressed her palms to his chest and smiled up at him. "It's nothing. A bride's nerves, that is all. I've never married an earl before."

He pushed the hair off her forehead with his fingertips to better see her eyes. There was no guile in them, only uncertainty and fear. She was such an innocent and his heart began to beat again, faster than ever. She needed him. He had to protect her. But *he* needed *her* just as much.

"I've never married an earl either," he said, to put her at ease. "Perhaps we can learn together."

She lightly thumped his chest in that familiar, friendly way that he liked. It was even better when she did it naked because her breasts jiggled. Yes, he definitely liked that.

"No need to stop," he said, forcing his hands to remain at his sides with great willpower. The longer he refrained from touching her, the better it would be when he finally allowed himself to caress her.

She unlaced the points joining doublet to breeches and

removed the doublet. Then she dropped to her knees and drew down his breeches. Her knuckles brushed against his legs and he sucked in air between his teeth, willing himself to stand still and savor the touch. One part of him refused to be still although it did stand, almost flat against his stomach. Lord, she drove him mad. His whole body was aware of her, ached to touch her and drive into her.

But this time he wanted to go slow, be gentle. He would treat her with tenderness and make it a night she would not soon forget.

He kicked off his shoes so she could remove his garters and hose then helped her to stand. Her gaze locked with his and he became lost in the dark depths of her eyes, a man drowning in a lake at midnight. His very own lady of the lake.

She touched the scar slicing through his eyebrow with her fingertip and blazed a trail down to his chin, his throat and over his Adam's apple. He closed his eyes against the exquisite agony of her touch. She unlaced his shirt and tugged it up.

"Off," she ordered. He quickly obliged, throwing it into the corner with as little regard as she had shown his other clothes. "Better."

She was so tall she could kiss the hollow where his shoulder met his throat without standing on her toes. He loved that about her. The long, sleek lines, the small waist and breasts with their big, ripe nipples.

He tipped his head back and moaned. She felt so good. So right. So perfect. Especially when she touched him like that, her hands roaming over his chest, teasing the nipples between her fingers and heading down, down...

"Not yet," he said, catching her hand before she could take him to the point of no return.

He picked her up and carried her to the bed, laying her gently down on top of the covers. "Tonight is for seduction. Your seduction."

"Sounds promising. But I can assure you," she said with a wicked smile, "the seduction won't be one-sided."

He grew harder just thinking about it. God's blood, but she had more power over him than anyone ever had. Thankfully she didn't know it or he'd be in Trouble. On second thought, that kind of trouble suited him perfectly, it was the reason he was marrying her.

Wasn't it?

He cast all serious thought aside. Tonight was for desire and satisfying a burning, aching need.

He kissed her, or she kissed him, and he forgot what he had been thinking anyway. Her fingers rifled through his hair and she arched her body up to his. Her nipples brushed against his chest, peaking into hard points. He shifted so he could kiss them and took one into his mouth then the other, savoring their taste, savoring her.

"Ash," she murmured. "Enter me now."

But he kissed her ribs, her stomach and moved down to the triangle of hair between her thighs. She parted her legs and he breathed in the heady scent of her. Then he tasted her. She gasped on the first flick of his tongue. On the second, she cried out "Oh!" On the third, she began to pant and on the fourth she bunched the bedcover into her fists.

Her hips rose to meet each lick and a tremor rippled through her body. "I. Can't. Stand. It," she said between heaving breaths.

But he wasn't finished yet. He played with her opening, slipping a finger in and out and was gratified to hear a low moan escape her lips. She squirmed, pushing his finger further inside, and flung her arms above her head. She scrabbled for the bed rail, found it and held on as her body erupted.

Wave after wave of shudders swamped her. She called out his name, over and over. When she finally stopped quivering, she stretched beneath him, her eyes half-closed. Her skin felt hot and he couldn't resist licking one plump nipple. She was magnificent, all soft and languid and flushed. He loved her.

A jolt hit him between the chest, made his heart skip erratically.

Love. Well...huh.

He watched her as the aftershocks of her climax continued to pulse through her body. She was perfect. Everything about her balanced him. Where he was rough, she was smooth. Where he boiled over, she remained cool. Where he was all brash action, she was all rational thought. She made him whole. With her at his side, he was a better person, worthy of an earldom.

Love. It must be.

He closed his eyes against the word but it hammered inside his brain and echoed in his heart until he had to open them. Had to tell her.

"Your turn," she said, before he could speak. She pushed him over onto his back and all words dissolved. What she did next blew away all sensible thought.

* * *

PIPPA WANTED TO FEEL IT, hold it, explore it. She cupped his balls in her hand, measuring the weight of them, amazed at how they filled her palm. Her thumb rubbed along the ridges of his shaft and circled the smooth tip, spreading the droplet she found there.

But it wasn't enough. She wanted to do to him what he'd done to her.

She knelt between his knees and licked his hard length, slowly so as to savor him. He moaned, deep in his chest, and pushed his fingers through her hair.

"That feels incredible," he muttered. "You're incredible."

She responded with another lick. He sucked in air between his teeth and his body went rigid beneath her.

"Enough," he said, "or I'll explode in your mouth."

"I don't mind," she said, curious to see what it would taste like.

"I do." He pulled her up to lie on top of him. "I want to be inside you." He kissed her hungrily but then softened it as if he'd remembered that tonight he'd promised her slow seduction.

But she'd also promised him something and she wasn't about to let him take over. When he tried to roll her off, she resisted.

"Not yet," she said. "I want to experience it from up here."

He gave her a lopsided grin that made her knees weak and her stomach flip. With his tousled hair and flushed cheeks, he was extraordinarily handsome. How he'd managed to remain unwed for so long was a miracle. He must have had women beating a path to his door. Somehow, he'd resisted them. But not her. Amazing. Extraordinary. She was nobody. A naïve country girl who was too thin, too tall, too dark, too dangerous thanks to her witchcraft.

His sense of honor must be very strong indeed to play the noble knight to her tainted princess. But she didn't want to dwell on that. Not tonight. Tonight, as he said, was for seduction. It was also for savoring. She wanted to remember everything about making love to him—his taste, his smell, the way he filled her and made her feel feminine and beautiful—so that she had something for the lonely nights ahead.

Regrets would come later.

She rose above him on her knees and guided his erection into her. Just the tip at first, rubbing it against the sensitive nub. They both groaned. Tiny pulses throbbed down her legs, across her belly and between her thighs. A little more and he was half way in, feeling impossibly big inside her.

"If you want to stop," he said but didn't get a chance to continue. She pushed down and he slipped all the way in. He grunted and screwed his eyes shut. "Don't stop," he said, sounding drunk. "Don't ever stop."

She eased herself up again and slowly, so slowly, pushed down his shaft once more. His long, low groan melded with hers and his hands flew to her hips, massaging her flesh.

"Like that?" she managed to say between short, sharp breaths.

"Mmmmm."

She moved her hips back and forth, riding him, but it didn't have the same effect as up and down so she switched back and was rewarded with a primal growl. She wasn't sure who it came from. To get better leverage, she leaned forward and pressed her hands on his shoulders, all the while maintaining a steady, slow rhythm. He opened his eyes and gazed up at her but the intensity in their depths frightened her and she had to shut her own eyes.

His hands moved from her hips along her spine and around to her breasts. He cupped them, gently kneading with his palms, teasing out the nipples. Heat shot through her body, her skin tightened and tingled and she felt like she was on fire. Just when she thought she couldn't stand it any longer, he stopped and licked each one then drew her down and kissed her fiercely on the lips.

It was a possessive I'm-yours-and-you're-mine kiss. She pumped him harder, not breaking the kiss, not wanting to. If only it could go on forever. If only the night could last an eternity.

He moaned into her mouth and his hips bucked beneath her, driving his length in deeper. She gasped as the spiral of heat burst inside her and surged along every nerve. With a final thrust, he shuddered, tensed and shuddered again.

He pulled her against his chest and held her while the shocks eased. His heart beat furiously alongside her full one. Neither spoke. She couldn't. Her mouth was too dry, her throat too tight. She simply wanted to feel his heat seep into her skin, drink in his scent and commit everything about him to memory.

"That was amazing, Pippa," he whispered into her hair. He kissed her forehead and held her cheeks so that she had no choice but to look at him. "I love you."

No. No, no, no. She hadn't expected it. Hadn't been prepared for those three devastating little words. They hit her with all the force of a house tumbling down around her. Indeed, she felt like the sky was falling, the earth shifting, and everything had been turned upside down and shaken loose.

"I...I love you too," she said. The words came naturally, from her heart, but they were too late. She'd hesitated too long. That small moment she'd taken to sift through her shock and confusion had registered with him. His mouth sagged, his eyes lost their intensity, and a mask descended.

What should she say? What should she do? Her heart told her one thing and her head something entirely different.

He sat up, dislodging her, and swung his legs over the side of the bed. "I'd best return to my own rooms tonight," he said, picking up his clothing. "I'll see you at breakfast."

"Ash." She stood on shaky legs and watched him put on his nether hose, not bothering with the garters, and pull his shirt over his head. She wanted to say so much, tell him she really did love him, but she didn't. Once she was gone, it might help him to think that she had never loved him. It might make the pain easier to bear. "Let me help you with that." She buttoned up his doublet then stood back and watched as he slipped on his shoes.

"Until the morning," he said with a nod in her general direction.

She couldn't let him leave like this, with the weight of her hesitation hanging between them. Not after the magic they'd just shared. She stood in front of the door, placed her hands on his cheeks and drew him down for one last kiss. His lips were hard, unyielding but soon softened and he kissed her back, gently, sweetly. He broke the kiss and held her gaze with his own.

With a crooked smile that captured everything she adored about Ash, he said, "I love you anyway." And then he was gone.

She had no idea how long she stared at the closed door. It wasn't until she began to shiver that she realized it must have been several minutes. She pulled on her shift and returned to bed but couldn't sleep. Her heart ached beneath the weight of the decision she had made.

She had to leave, had to protect Ash from herself. Making love had been a glorious farewell that she'd wanted despite its complications.

But now she must think about leaving. It was only a matter of choosing the right moment. She rolled over and sobbed into her pillow, allowing misery to seep into her and take control.

He loved her. She loved him. It was hopeless.

Ash balanced the breakfast tray with one hand and one knee as he knocked on Pippa's door. He was in a surprisingly good mood considering his future wife didn't love him. Her brief hesitation had said more than her actual words. She didn't love him—yet.

But she would. She was half-way there. Even he could see that, and his knowledge was feeble at best where women were concerned. She wanted him in her bed, her body responded like a blazing fire every time he was near. He could feel the desire simmering within her, waiting for release. It wouldn't be long before that intensity turned to love. All he had to do was wait, and he could do that quite easily if he was already married to her.

It was a situation with no losers.

He knocked again and she opened the door, rubbing her eyes with the back of her hand. Clearly she'd expected a maid and when she saw it was him, she smiled. Smiled. What more evidence did he need that she was in the early stages of love?

"Breakfast for two, m'lady," he said.

She stepped aside to let him through and closed the door behind him. "I'm glad you came," she said. "I thought perhaps after last night..." She looked down at her hands, twisted together in front of her.

"Let's eat." He didn't want to discuss last night. That hesitation was best left forgotten. One day they would laugh about it, but not yet. It was too raw.

"I am starving," she conceded, sitting at the table.

"The broth is getting cold, I'm afraid. Your rooms are so far from the kitchen, it's impossible for anything to stay warm. After we are wed, you can have the suite near mine." She'd need her own wardrobe for her clothes but he planned to have her share his bed every night and his breakfast every morning. "It'll be easier."

They ate in agreeable silence, although she spent more time pulling apart her bread than eating it and she avoided his gaze. She must still be apprehensive about the wedding plans. There was much to be done before she was safe.

He recognized a knock on the door as Fallon's. His steward entered on Ash's order and said, "Lady Wethinall is in the south parlor, my lord."

"What in God's name does that witch want?" He turned to Pippa in horror at the word he'd let slip but she merely smiled gently at him.

"It's all right," she said, sounding relieved. "Go."

He leaned over the table and kissed her forehead then left. He strode ahead of Fallon to the south parlor, cursing all the way. This had better be good. The woman he loved was waiting for him dressed in only her night shift and a loose gown. He'd planned on taking advantage of that before the morning grew old.

"Lady Wethinall," he said upon opening the door.

She stood near the window, a fan held loosely at her side. "Lord Ashbourne. Lovely to see you again."

"Do not pretend we are friends," he said. "What do you want? I have urgent business to attend to regarding my up coming nuptials."

"Ah, yes, I must congratulate you. The lucky woman is your pageboy I hear." Her laughter tinkled from her long, white throat. "Oh, Ash, if only you could hear the jokes at court."

"Is that what you've come to tell me? Because if it is, then I can assure you I care nothing about it."

"No? But you should, Ash. Even the queen laughs at them. And Walsingham. Well, he smirks."

He shrugged. "It will be gossip for a few weeks and then somebody else will do something even more scandalous and my wife and I will be forgotten." He held the door open for her. "If that is all you came to say, Lady Wethinall, then please oblige me with a view of your back."

The back in question stiffened and the fan snapped shut. "It is not all. Not by any means." He didn't like her smug tone. "Close the door, Ash. You won't wish the servants to hear what I have to say."

Reluctantly, he closed it. "Well? Is it something else to do with my bride or my wedding?"

"No. This is to do with you. It is quite shocking." She looked pleased with herself. "Perhaps you should sit."

"Tell me!"

She cleared her throat. "A rumor came to me late yesterday which I found quite intriguing. It concerns you. And your mother."

"Mother? What about her?"

"She is not who you think she is."

"Don't talk in riddles," he snapped. He wasn't' in the mood for her antics.

She sat on a stool near the window and arranged her skirts

before continuing. "Thirty-five years ago, the woman who later became your nurse, a Mistress Dale I believe, gave birth to twin boys. One of them was you."

A cold chill settled into his bones. What game was she playing? "You're mistaken."

"I can assure you I am not. I have seen proof."

"What proof?" He took three long strides to reach her but stopped himself from striking her. Just.

"A letter from the countess to Mistress Dale arranging the birth and the adoption. It was all in the letter written in Lady Ashbourne's hand."

Despite the anger surging through him, he wanted to hear more. Had to hear more. "Arranging what exactly?"

"Let's see." She turned to the rain-splattered window. "They were to travel to Dewbury Hall together where Mistress Dale would give birth. Upon the baby's safe arrival, she would be paid handsomely. She would then remain as the babe's nurse for as long as needed after which a large sum would be settled upon her. A neat arrangement for both parties it would seem, especially since it was clear from the letter that Lord Ashbourne was the father."

"But the twins weren't born at Dewbury Hall."

"No. According to the rumor, twins weren't expected and the birth was early. The traveling party which consisted of your mother and Mistress Dale barely reached Haverford in time. A rather convenient place to have them as it turned out."

Ash didn't like how she had an answer for everything. It was much too neat. He sat in a chair near the hearth but his thigh ached so he stood and walked about the room. "And what of the adoption?"

"Of you?" She shrugged as if this were merely the latest piece of court gossip to spread. As if it couldn't bring down Ash, his family, his entire world. He wanted to strip that smugness off her face. "Well, one twin was chosen by Lady Ashbourne as the next earl and the other was taken to Christ's Hospital after he was weaned I believe. What happened to him then is not important."

"It is to me."

She shrugged again. "Perhaps Lady Ashbourne knows more. You should ask her." She rose. "I do hope for your sake that this is simply a rumor and that the letter is a malicious joke." She headed for the door but he caught her wrist and spun her round to face him.

"Who showed you the letter? Who started this rumor?"

She opened the fan and held it in front of her lips. "A lady never tells—"

His hand flew to her throat. God help him he wanted to squeeze, wanted to stop her taunting smiles and her casual shrugs. But he knew he couldn't. He'd only harmed a woman once and he could never do it again, no matter how much the world would be a better place without Lady Wethinall. "Tell me or I'll snap your neck," he said.

Her face turned scarlet, her eyes widened and genuine fear made her tremble. She nodded and he let go.

"No lies," he said.

She rubbed her throat and fluttered her fan furiously in front of her face. When her color returned to normal, she said, "Who do you think?" When he didn't answer, she went on. "Someone who is new to you or this wouldn't be occurring now after all these years. Someone who knew Mistress Dale, who could have had easy access to this information."

He could only think of one person.

Ash's heart plunged. His leg throbbed and he had to sit down. Somewhere in the distance he heard Lady Wethinall leave and the door close, but that seemed far away, another room, another time. Here, now, a name hammered over and over in his head, a bell clanging inside his brain. He pressed the heel of his hand into his eye to stop the noise but it kept slamming into his skull. The name wouldn't go away.

Pippa.

# CHAPTER 17

$\mathcal{P}$ippa dismissed Gertie after the maid finished helping her to dress and sat in the window seat to await Ash's return. She wondered what Lady Wethinall could want but didn't really care. It was too hard to think of anything except her own problem. She'd lain awake most of the night planning what to do and today she was tired and irritable and heart-sore.

Near dawn she had made up her mind to leave after the midday dinner. She would plead a headache and retire to her rooms. She wouldn't be missed for the remainder of the day, perhaps not even until the following morning, and by then she would be long gone. Dressed in boys' clothes, it would be easy to go to one of the inns and secure a ride on a departing coach. She would be far away by the time Ash began looking for her.

But until the afternoon, she had a role to play, a mask to keep securely in place. Ash had to believe she would marry him. She practiced a smile at her reflection in the window but it was weak and would convince no one of her happiness. It was hard to smile when all she wanted to do was cry until the tears were spent.

A lone figure strode down to the waterstairs and she recognized Lady Wethinall's saunter. Pippa tried to rally her wits and courage. Ash would return soon.

Even before the thought had fully formed, the door crashed

back. She jumped and stood when Ash entered, looking like he wanted to strike someone. Strike her.

He strode across the room and caught her arms in a bruising grip. "You little...! How could you?" He shook her, his fingers digging into her flesh. She winced and his grip lessened somewhat. "Answer me, damn you! How could you do this!"

She stared at the man she loved but didn't recognize. He was hidden beneath this raging beast, boiling over with hatred—for her. "A...Ash," she managed to splutter, "you're hurting me."

He pushed her roughly onto the window seat and strode away. She hugged her arms to stave off the sudden coldness enveloping her but it was useless.

"Wh...what are you accusing me of? What have I done?"

"You know," he said, his back to her. "You *know!*"

Tears spilled down her cheeks and she swiped at them angrily. Now was not the time for crying. She would not be condemned without knowing her crime. "No, I do not. Is it my witchcraft?"

He barked out a laugh. "You are a witch all right. A heartless, cunning witch, but not in the way you say."

She shook her head, confused, terrified, but determined to have answers. "I don't understand. Tell me what is wrong?"

He swung round and she blanched. He hated her. It was evident in his cruel glare, his hard face. She hadn't thought it possible after last night but she saw it now. She'd seen his temper of course, but had never thought she would be the target of his wrath. "You have ruined me!" he shouted. "My family. Everything!"

"Ruined you? What are you talking about?" An awful thought struck her. "Has Sir Guy told someone about me? Has the rumor spread that I am a witch and you—"

"No! Damn you, Pippa, this is not about your witchcraft, this is about the Savoys." He took a step towards her but instead of striking her, he rubbed his hands over his eyes and groaned. "Why?" he said, pleading. "For money? Marriage? Tell me why you did this? What could I have possibly done to make you hate me so?"

"Hate you?" She stood on shaking legs but was determined to

meet him on his own level. "What I feel for you is very far from hate, Ash. Although right now I am afraid of you. Is that what you want?"

"Yes," he said on a hiss. "You should be afraid." He stretched out a hand, palm up. It shook. "Hand over the letter."

"What letter? What is going on?" She wanted to pummel her fists into his chest but with her emotions wrung out as they were, she wasn't sure what would happen. She didn't want to slam him against the wall. Not unless there was real danger. And despite his rage, she didn't think he would harm her. He loved her. She was sure of it, and not even the ferocious Earl of Ashbourne in full rage could harm the women he loved.

"Do not deny that you went to Lady Wethinall with my mother's letter to Georgiana. I know it, Pippa." He tapped his chest. "I feel it in here like a knife to my heart. Who else could have found it?"

"What letter? What are you talking about?"

He scoffed. "The letter that proves my illegitimacy. Did you find it in Georgiana's belongings? Or when you murdered her?"

"Wh, what!" She stared at him in horror. How could he think that of her? She bit her lip to stop its wobble. "You don't know me at all, Ash, if you believe me capable of murdering Georgiana."

His gaze faltered. He looked away. It was the only thing that stopped her from walking out the door right then and using her powers to ensure he didn't follow her.

His Adam's apple bobbed. "Perhaps not that," he conceded. "But the other."

"Of spreading the rumor of your illegitimacy? What possible motive could I have to do it?"

"That's what I want to know," he growled. He paced the room like a caged lion. Every now and again he rubbed his old thigh injury as if it troubled him or perhaps out of habit. Although he still looked angry, some of the edge was gone. He no longer looked like he wanted to shake her but he didn't seem to want to believe her either.

"I can assure you, I had nothing to do with any of this," she said. "I have not seen Lady Wethinall since she was here two days ago."

He stopped pacing and narrowed his eyes at her. "You say that, and yet I noticed you weren't surprised to hear of my illegitimacy."

She felt sick. He had her there. "You're right. I already knew about it."

With a roar of pure rage, he picked up a book from the table and threw it into the grate. "Damn you, Pippa! I trusted you! I took care of you! I even offered you marriage." His chest heaved with each ragged breath. "I told you I loved you." His voice cracked and he lowered his head so she couldn't see his face. He was hurting. She wanted to go to him but she stayed back. Not out of fear of what he might do to her but because it was for the best.

As much as she didn't want him to hate her and think she had betrayed him, it made it easier to leave. It was better that way. Better for him.

Silent tears slipped down her cheeks for the love she had briefly held close to her heart and which now lay shattered like glass at her feet.

With a shake of his head and still without looking at her, he strode to the door. "I'll deal with you later," he said, voice rough. He slammed the door and she heard a key tumble the lock.

He'd locked her in!

She ran to the door and hammered her fists against the oak. "Ash! Ash, no! Please!"

But it was useless. He was probably already gone. She slumped against the door and slipped down it to sit in a heap on the floor, all the breath gone out of her, all the courage, all the hope. All the love.

He had locked her in. Just like her uncle.

She pulled her knees up and sobbed into her skirt. How could he do this? Could she have been wrong and he didn't love her? She lay on the floor and let the tears flow until even those failed her and she couldn't cry anymore. Some time after, sensible thought finally returned.

She wasn't locked in. No one could keep her prisoner ever again.

She stood and concentrated on the lock. Nothing happened. She delved into a deeper place and summoned more power. The lock clicked open on the second attempt. She slipped out and locked the door again.

"Goodbye," she whispered to Ash and to the life she almost had.

Then she ran.

* * *

ASH'S CHEST felt like it had the night St. Cyr rammed it through with his blade. He rubbed the wound but the pain didn't go away. It hurt. God, it hurt.

He stopped because he couldn't breathe, couldn't see through the razor-sharp rage that clawed at him. How could she! How could she!

He'd trusted her with his heart, his soul, with everything of value and she'd betrayed him. For the second time, he'd allowed his feelings for a woman to blind him to her true nature. It didn't matter that he'd thought Pippa different, thought her incapable of maliciousness or deception. He'd been wrong. Foolishly, damnably wrong.

He'd once seen a woman killed for betraying him.

He groaned. He couldn't harm a hair on Pippa's head let alone kill her. Beyond that he couldn't think what to do with her. There would be time for thinking later. Now he must clear his mind and concentrate. There was one more confrontation to make. He pushed on. He didn't know if he had it in him to face his mother with the awful truths but he needed answers. Needed to make sense of something in his life because the one beautiful, wonderful thing in it had been sliced out like a canker.

He met his mother and sister on the stairs. Annie rushed forward and flung her arms about him. He enveloped her in a hug, held her to him, the one person in his life he could trust. The only one.

"Oh, Ash, *everyone* knows. I heard the servants talking about

it and then Lady Fortnum sent a note asking if it were true and
—." She sniffed and rested her chin on his chest to peer up at
him. "Lord, you look like the Devil. Are you all right?"

He nodded and looked over her head at his mother. She
stood like a sentinel, her pallor unnaturally white. She signaled
him to follow and she turned and opened the door leading to her
own private sitting room.

Inside, she sat near the unlit fire. She indicated they should
sit too. Annie did but Ash did not.

"It's true, isn't it?" He didn't need to raise his voice. He
couldn't anyway, he was bone-weary. He felt empty, as if he'd
left behind half of himself in Pippa's room.

His mother's gaze slid away and she lowered her eyes. Her
head barely moved in a nod.

Annie gasped. "But...there must be some mistake! Some maliciousness afoot." She glanced from one to the other, no doubt
wanting assurances. He could give her none. Not when he had
nothing left in him to give.

"There is," his mother said, her face stoic but pinched as if she
were holding the pieces of herself together by sheer willpower.
"A very great maliciousness to this family." She paused and held
her son's gaze with a steady one of her own. "But the rumor is
quite true. Richard is not of my body but Georgiana's."

"And Father?" Annie asked, leaning forward. "Is he...?"

"He is Richard's father, yes." She folded her hands in her lap,
one on top of the other, but the knuckles were as white as her
face.

"Then...he is a Savoy at least," Annie said.

"I am." Ash didn't take his eyes off his mother. "But I should
not have inherited."

"No," the countess said quietly. "You should not."

"But what will happen if the rumor can be proved?" Annie
said.

"The Ashbourne title will be revoked," he said.

"Revoked?"

"We'll become nothing," their mother said. She twisted the
rings on her fingers, causing the gems to flash in the light. The
surrounding skin reddened.

"Nothing?" Annie stared at her. "That cannot be. The Savoys are an old family. We've been part of the English nobility for generations. We've held the Ashbourne title for...ages."

"I am not legitimate," Ash said, trying to sound matter-of-fact for his sister's sake. And trying to keep his mind off Pippa for his own. "So therefore it will be taken from me. From us. We'll simply be the Savoys."

"B, but...we are the children of the last Earl of Ashbourne." Panic made her voice high. "You are the current earl. It's too late to take that away from you."

"No, it's not." He knelt in front of her and drew her hand to his cheek. "It'll be all right, Annie. I'll take care of it. And you and Mother. We might lose the title and Dewbury Hall but everything else belongs to us. Father built up a good fortune. We will be all right." If only he believed it.

"But it won't be!" she cried. "We'll be banished from court. Our friends will shun us. Who of any consequence will marry me now? And what of Pippa? You promised her that your position would keep her safe from her uncle."

"Do not talk of Pippa!" He stood and flung his arms in the air.

"Why?" She frowned. "Has something happened between you? Is the marriage off?"

"The marriage is on," he said. "It is definitely on." Until he said it, he hadn't given the wedding a thought. He'd been too ensconced in Pippa's betrayal. But now he was determined that it would go ahead. Pippa was his. He had promised her he would keep her safe and he never broke his promise. Whether he was still the earl or not, he would never allow anyone to harm her.

Because he loved her.

He loved her still and he would forever, no matter what she did. *This* was love he realized with a jolt. Not the half-hearted childish feelings he'd had for his Spanish traitor, but this mindless insanity that stripped him raw and left him bleeding all over the rushes. In happier times it had also lifted him up to be a better person, made him fuller, stronger, whole. Nothing could destroy it. Not even Pippa's betrayal.

"Tell me," he said to his mother, emotions grinding. "Tell me everything you should have told me years ago." He had to get to the bottom of this. Everything depended on it. His title, his position at court and his bride's safety.

Her gaze sharpened. "I never told you because what would be the point?"

"She was my mother!" He smashed his fist into the back of a chair, splintering the wood. It hurt but the pain felt good, reassuring. "*That* is the point."

She turned to look out the window but he saw her blink rapidly before turning back to regard him with her usual coolness.

"And I have a brother," he added.

"Yes. We weren't expecting twins. We only got as far as Haverford when Georgiana felt pains. The midwife came and the babies were born. Two boys. One was sickly and both were small.

"It was some time before she was well enough to travel but that worked out perfectly. She joined me at Dewbury Hall when I was due to have my baby a few months later. The house is so large and no one else was allowed near us, not even the most valued servants, so it was easy to keep the twins hidden and to...give birth. When the time came, I produced a healthy male child. No one knew he was hers and that my pregnancy was false."

"But you only had one," Annie said. "What did you do with the other twin?"

"We kept him in Georgiana's adjoining room and Richard stayed with me. But it didn't really matter since no one visited us. The benefits of an estate so far from London," she said with a stiff smile.

"And once weaned, you gave the sickly child to Christ's Hospital in the hope it would die and be forgotten," Ash said, a bitter taste in his mouth.

"No. *You* were the sickly one."

"Me?"

"Yes. It was easier to pass off the smaller child as my own. Some months had already passed since your actual birth and you still hadn't grown as much as the other."

"Christ's Hospital?" Annie looked from her mother to her brother. "But why not take him too?"

Lady Ashbourne looked down at her rings, twisting them roughly. "One was enough."

"But what became of him?"

"He was adopted," Ash said. "But no one knows by whom. Father must have arranged it."

A few heartbeats passed before Lady Ashbourne said, "He did."

"Who to? I would like to meet my brother." Finding a brother would be one positive to come out of this hateful story.

"I, I cannot say."

"You cannot say? Or will not?" he snapped.

"Mother," Annie said, touching the countess's hand, "tell us."

The countess squared her shoulders. "I suppose it must all come out now."

"What must come out?" Ash said, wary. He had a sick feeling in his stomach that the day was about to get worse. "Who is it?"

"Briars."

Silence. And then Annie gasped for breath as if she couldn't get enough air.

Ash stared at his mother, numb with horror. "Briars?"

"I almost married my brother!" Annie bent over, her fingers tangled in her hair. "God's blood, that's revolting!"

Ash rubbed her back but kept his eyes on his mother.

"I wouldn't have allowed you to marry him," the countess said. "But I had to make it appear as if you would."

"Why?" Annie shouted at her. "Why in God's name?"

"Do not raise your voice. The servants will hear."

"I don't care about the bloody servants!"

Ash pulled her to his chest and she buried her face in his doublet. "Answer her," he ordered his mother.

The countess licked her lips. "I received a letter a few weeks ago. It said the author was in possession of some information that was harmful to myself and my family. Naturally I ignored it. Then I received another which revealed the information." She unclasped her hands and spread them, palms up on her lap. "Your illegitimacy, Richard. Then I had a third letter which spelled out the terms of payment and revealed the author's identity. It was Briars. The payment was you, Annie."

"But he knew his parentage," she said, whimpering, "knew I was his half-sister and he still wanted to marry me."

The countess spread her hands in her lap. "Only he can explain his actions."

Annie buried her face in Ash's chest and moaned.

"How did he come into this information?" Ash asked his mother. Something gnawed at him. Something vital he couldn't put his finger on.

"He must have learned that he was adopted from Christ's Hospital and went there to view their records."

Ash heard the words but his mind was elsewhere. He skipped ahead, putting the pieces of the puzzle into place. The more he thought, the sicker he felt. "He killed Georgiana, didn't he? My own brother. Her child."

Annie mewled like a hungry cat. "And to think I let him kiss me!"

"When he came to me, I told him he had no proof." The countess's fingers fidgeted with her rings, twisting them back and forth, round and round. "Especially since I'd had the vital piece of information destroyed from the hospital's records when I received his first blackmail note."

So she had been the one to tear the records Pippa had seen at Christ's Hospital. Pippa. "Go on," he said, forcing himself to concentrate and not picture Pippa's face when he had accused her of betraying him.

"He went to see Georgiana to find the proof." Her eyes filled with tears and for the first time, Ash realized his mother cared. It shook him and he held his sister closer. "I suppose he found it," she said, barely loud enough to be heard.

"Yes," he said, just as quietly.

Oh. Oh, no. Pippa...

Briars had been the one blackmailing his mother. *He* had been in possession of the secret and the letter, not Pippa.

Not Pippa.

Now that he could see clearly, Ash couldn't think why he had ever suspected her. Why would she reveal his illegitimacy to anyone? It would not serve her purpose. Indeed, she would want very much to keep it secret as her own safety depended on his position and good favor at court.

Blunt realization slammed into his gut like an axe, knocking the wind out of him. What had he done? What in God's name had he gone and done?

He pushed Annie back and jumped up, knocking over a nearby table in his haste. "I must go."

His mother caught his arm. "Not yet. There is something we can do to stop the rumor."

"Yes," Annie whispered. "It's my fault. Briars broke his silence yesterday after I broke our engagement. I'll go to him now and tell him I'll marry him." She wiped her cheeks and patted her hair. "Perhaps the rumor can be stopped if I do this. Has the queen heard?"

"You can be certain she has," the countess said wryly. "Lady Wethinall would have made sure of it."

"Stay, Annie," Ash ordered. "You'll not be going to Briars. I'll not allow my sister to marry a murderer, not under any circumstances." He wrenched free. "I must see Pippa."

But the countess stepped in front of the door, blocking him. "We must find the letter and burn it," she said as if he hadn't spoken. "Without proof, the rumor will go away eventually."

"But Lady Wethinall has seen it," Annie said.

"Forget Lady Wethinall. I have enough information about her *activities* to ensure her silence."

"I will get the letter from Briars," Ash said. "But first I have to see Pippa." He pushed her aside and wrenched the door open. He ran through the house, his mother's protests fading behind him.

He reached Pippa's door and tried the handle but it was locked. Memory flooded back. He wanted to throw up. He'd locked her in! What had he been thinking? He'd locked in a woman who'd been held prisoner by her uncle for five years.

He deserved to be hung, drawn and quartered.

"Pippa," he said, unlocking the door and opening it. She wasn't inside. "Pippa!" He ran to the bedchamber, the wardrobe, the closet. Empty. "Pippa!" He heard the panic in his voice but didn't care. She was gone. She must have used her powers on the lock. He sat on the bed and buried his head in his hands.

Violent shudders wracked him and he suddenly felt raw, as if a layer of skin had been stripped from his body and he lay exposed to the elements. He welcomed the sharp sting of pain, like a thousand needles piercing his flesh. He deserved every bite of agony for what he had done to Pippa.

"Where is she?" It was Annie's voice, coming from the direction of the door. "Ash? Are you all right?"

He said nothing. Didn't look up. Couldn't.

"What did you expect?" asked his mother.

"What do you mean?" Annie asked.

"She obviously was only marrying him for his position. Now that she believes Richard's title will be stripped from him, she has shown her true colors and left."

At least Ash's speed had not diminished. It only took a heartbeat for him to reach his mother. He could have snapped her neck or strangled her. Instead, it took a very great effort to keep his hands at his sides. "Do not accuse her! She is innocent. I will find her and make everything right. I have to." He turned away so they couldn't see his face. "I have to."

Two small hands he recognized as Annie's gripped his arms as if she were holding him up.

"Don't worry," she said, quietly. "We'll find her."

"After we have paid Briars a visit," the countess said with all the authority of someone used to having her way.

"No," Ash managed to choke out. "Pippa first."

Annie's fingers squeezed. "Mother is right. We must go to Briars now, before this scandal spreads."

He lowered his head. He knew they were right but his heart was on fire with the desperate need to find Pippa.

"Send some men out looking for her," Annie said. "I'm sure they'll convince her to return—"

"I'll not have her hunted like an animal."

"I am going to see Briars," his mother said. "If you do not come with me, I'll go alone." The swish of skirts signaled her departure.

He closed his eyes.

"Please," Annie pleaded. "Send your men out looking for Pippa while you go with Mother. She shouldn't do it alone. You know what he's capable of."

He knew. Briars had already caused one death.

He rubbed both hands over his face and roared in frustration. *Pippa! Come back to me!*

Annie hugged his back but he shook her off. Between them, the women in his life would drive him to Bedlam. "If she comes back here," he said, "do not let her out of your sight."

"I'll search the gardens for her myself," Annie assured him. She gave him a weak smile but he couldn't return it.

He rushed from the house and barked orders at his retainers to search for Pippa on every road into and out of London. They were good men, well-accustomed to receiving odd assignments from their master without asking questions.

He met his mother halfway down to the waterstairs. He didn't speak to her and she didn't acknowledge his presence. The Ashbourne barge was ready for them with six men dressed in his livery at the oars. He settled on the seat beneath the canopy alongside his mother just as the rain began. He scanned the riverbanks, hoping to see Pippa but knowing he would not.

She was gone.

She was gone.

"I didn't want you to find out this way." His mother's voice was soft and he barely heard it over the splash of oars and rain-drops and the cries of the watermen who'd ventured that far up river.

"You didn't want me to find out at all," Ash said.

"That is unfair."

"Is it? I am thirty-five. When *did* you plan on telling me?"

"When you came of age. Then when your father became ill. Then again when he died and you became the earl. And on Georgiana's death of course. I very nearly told you then."

"But you didn't. You didn't and now we are all paying for it. I could have stopped this, Mother. Do you realize that? I could have made sure that no one ever found out."

"But would you?"

He glanced at her. She was like a stranger. Her hard face was blanched white but it was softer, slacker. She was showing her true age. Fine lines creased her brow and feathered her lips, but she still had the same determined glint in her eyes and straight back. Years of training would not allow her to completely give up.

"Of course," he snapped. "Why wouldn't I?"

"Because you never seemed to particularly care for the earldom."

"Of course I cared! I'm the bloody earl aren't I?"

"Don't shout," she whispered.

"I'll shout if I damn well want to," he said, quieter. "Mother, I might not always like some of the traditions that came with being the earl but I take my duty very seriously."

"Your duty is to this family," she said. "To further its interests in England, to provide the best for its members, current and future."

"I have! I am doing just that!"

"Are you? Your first responsibility should have been to wed and have an heir, yet—"

"I'm marrying Pippa," he ground out.

"Until recently, you have refused to marry," she amended. "And you have not forced your sister to accept any of the offers that have come her way. If you had, we wouldn't be in this situation."

"What!" he raged. "I would never force my sister to marry anyone. My duty to Annie is to ensure she is happy. My duty to my family's future is to ensure I am wed to the *right* woman. A woman I am happy to spend my life with." A woman he loved with every aching piece of him.

*Come back to me, Pippa.*

"You never liked your posts on the Continent," she said with a defiant tilt of her chin. "And all the Savoy men have been involved in ambassadorial roles before they inherited the earldom."

"I did my duty in that regard."

"Grudgingly. And not always with good results."

He stretched out his leg and rubbed his thigh. It seemed to ache more than ever today. The rain splashed off his boot and dampened his silk nether hose. He didn't care. "True enough. I made a better spy than ambassador. And if you'd left me be, I could have continued in that way instead of being stuck at my desk, buried in paperwork."

"You were needed here."

"So you convinced Walsingham to bring me back. Because of what happened in Spain."

"You nearly died in Spain."

"Ah. Motherly concern. How kind of you."

There was a long pause before she said, "I may not have given birth to you but I have loved you as any mother would love her son for these last thirty-five years."

"Really." He looked out to the river bank and tried to see through the rain for a figure he knew so well. She wasn't there.

"If you dislike me using my influence with the queen to do what is best for you—"

"What is best for me!" He swung round to face her. "You do not know what is best for me, *Mother*. What was best for me was to sort out my own problems in Spain instead of being whisked back here like some lackey of yours and the queen's. What is best for me now is that I find Pippa and marry her. You're right, I don't care about the earldom except that it is the only thing that can keep her safe. Does that shock you?"

Tears sprang to her eyes and she looked down at her hands. "Shock me, yes. Surprise me, no. I have long suspected you didn't care much for the title and everything that came with it."

"I care," he said, regretting his outburst because it wasn't entirely true. "Just not as much as you do." He settled back against the cushions but kept his gaze on the riverbank. "I've had traitors of the noblest breeding beg me to overlook their misdeeds instead of arrest them. Have you ever seen a lord beg, Mother? Not just plead, but really beg for his life. Some cry, some pray, others want their mamas or soil themselves. It is degrading. They are reduced to being ordinary men, no better than the sailor lost at sea, or the farmer whose crops failed and cannot feed his family. A title means nothing in the end."

"I haven't heard you be so maudlin since you gave up drunkenness."

He almost laughed at that. "What I wouldn't do to be drunk right now."

The barge bumped gently against a set of waterstairs and Ash alighted, helping his mother out to the stability of land. They headed north on paved roads made slick by the light rain. Rivulets of muddy water trickled between the stones, winding their way towards the river. The countess, holding Ash's arm, set a brisk pace.

"How do you propose to make Briars hand over the letter?" she asked from beneath her fur-fringed hood.

"By using my formidable charms."

She sighed. "Oh dear."

# CHAPTER 18

*P*utting on boys' clothes again was like sinking into a comfortable bed. No tight stomacher, no padded skirts to tangle about her legs, no threat of pins unsticking at an inopportune moment. Best of all, Pippa could go about unnoticed. She could also run faster.

She'd taken a risk in returning to Ash's rooms to find her forgotten disguise folded neatly in the chest at the foot of her old bed. But Ash hadn't gone looking for her there. At one point, she'd heard shouting coming from a distant part of the house. It sounded like the countess, but that was impossible. The old matriarch was too composed to raise her voice.

Pippa left Ashbourne House through the servant's entrance near the kitchen. She pulled her hat down and walked with a purposeful stride. She'd found people were generally left alone when they appeared to be performing an important task.

No one accosted her. Ash did not come chasing after her. The house was quiet. Too quiet, like a breathless hush had settled around it while everyone waited expectantly.

That meant the rumor must have reached the servant's ears. No wonder everyone walked on the tips of their toes. None would want to encounter the lord of the house at a time like this. She couldn't blame them. His wrath could be terrifying when he unleashed it.

She shivered in the cool, damp air and drew her cloak closer. Then everything around her suddenly burst to life, as if a wind had whipped through the house and blown everyone out. Servants rushed here and there, grooms emerged from the stables, and even the horses stamped and snorted as if sensing something was afoot.

Pippa headed towards the gate that led to The Strand but stopped. One of the servants was speaking to the gatekeeper in earnest. The gatekeeper shook his head then both men looked back at the house. Suddenly the liveried servant focused on her. He frowned and moved towards her. Pippa turned and fled back the way she had come, past the brewery and bake house. Heady scents of hops and bread gave way to the stench of the stables but soon even that smell was behind her too.

Again she had to stop when she reached the river side of the house. The countess walked across the forecourt and along a path through the formal garden, looking straight ahead, her shoulders and back straight. Pippa ducked behind a juniper hedge to avoid being seen. Fortunately the countess seemed too intent on *not* catching anyone's attention to notice her.

Then she heard Ash's booming voice shouting orders. She crouched lower and watched him stride after his mother, heading towards the waterstairs. Men scurried in his wake to the stables. They saddled mounts and spoke in low tones to each other. She caught snatches on the wind, names of roads, inns and directions.

"...find her..." one of the men said.

"...not got far," another said.

So Ash had given his men orders to hunt her down and bring her back. She gulped around the lump in her throat. But whether it was a lump of fear or of hope, she couldn't determine. Part of her wanted to be far away from Ashbourne House and its unpredictable lord. But the part that remembered the look on Ash's face when he told her he loved her wanted to stay and hold him and assure him everything would be well. She loved him too.

No. Wrong. She did *not* love him. She could not love someone who'd treated her with such little regard, someone who didn't trust her and would lock her away at the first sign of trouble.

She peered round the hedge again and watched the riders leave one by one. Ash and his mother were gone from view. A few grooms chatted near the stables, no doubt discussing the latest scandal to darken Ashbourne House's door. She could get past them and the man at the gate easily enough but would need to use her powers. She doubted her disguise would work now. But using her powers was much too dangerous in the middle of the day with so many witnesses about.

Rain dampened her face and she wished her cloak was hooded. It reminded her how ill-prepared she was for flight. In her haste she had forgotten to take extra money and clothing. She only had what she wore and a few coins in her pocket. She looked back to the stables and thought about acquiring one of Ash's horses but decided against it. The groomsmen would stop her before she could mount and she was a hopeless rider anyway. The only means of escape was via the river. She could use the coins to pay the boatmen and then try to sell the ring Ash had given her to fund her flight back to Shelton and her uncle's house.

Once there, she would confront Simon and have him retract his accusations. It was the only way she could move on with her life. If her attempt failed...well, she would deal with those consequences when and if they occurred. She had to at least try. It was the only way to stop the Witch Hunter.

She hunched into her cloak, careful to keep near the hedge enclosing the maze. The formal knot garden at the front of the house was to her right, the stables, brewery and bakehouse behind her. Only a few more steps and she would be down the embankment and out of sight of the main house.

"Stop!" Annie.

Pippa ran.

"Please, Pippa, don't go! We need you now more than ever. Ash needs you."

Pippa closed her eyes against the plea and promptly tripped over something in her path. She landed face down in the dirt. Fool!

Annie almost fell on top of Pippa as she rolled over. The young girl blinked back tears and clutched her white velvet cloak at her throat. "Please stay, Ash feels terrible, he's so sorry, Pippa." She spoke rapidly, her words running together. Her eyes and nose streamed and her hood had fallen back so that her hair was a damp, bedraggled nest. "He wanted to find you himself and make it up to you but..." She smiled through her tears but it was unconvincing. "Thank God I found you. He'll be so happy. It'll be all right now. You'll see. He'll kill Briars, come back here and—"

"Kill Briars?" Although Annie's words had shaken her to the bone, it was this last statement that had shocked her into speaking.

Annie began to sob. Pippa, still lying on her back, lifted the girl's face.

"Why is he going to kill Briars?" she said again.

"Because he killed Georgiana."

"Briars?"

Annie nodded and wiped her eyes. "He's Ash's twin brother. He wanted a share of our family's good fortune and thought to obtain it by marrying me. But when I rejected him," she choked, "he told Lady Wethinall that Ash isn't legitimate and that he can prove it with the letter."

The letter. Pippa shook her head, not allowing hope to break through even though it tapped at her rib cage. "So Ash knows I did not do it?"

Annie nodded.

"None of it?"

"Yes! That's why he's sorry and he wants to find you and tell you and everything will be all right. You can marry him."

"I'll not marry him."

"Because he won't have a title?" But Annie didn't let Pippa answer. "You must marry him! He loves you. He needs you." She pulled Pippa into a sitting position with a surprising amount of strength for a girl her size. "I'm afraid of what he'll do if you don't. He's capable of quite...dark thoughts."

"I know," said Pippa wryly. She stood and brushed the mud from her clothes as best she could. "But I cannot marry a man who would happily lock away his wife when she does something that displeases him."

Annie frowned. "He locked you up? But...how did you escape?"

"I used my...wits."

Annie stared at her. "He locked you up! Good Lord, he's gone mad already." Her face clouded. "Oh God, he might kill Briars after all! I was only joking before. I thought he would simply threaten to kill him or pay him, but now I'm not so sure."

"He won't kill anyone," Pippa said, flicking damp hair from her temple. "He knows there will be consequences."

"But in his present mood and if he thinks you have truly gone...who knows what he might do?"

A mixture of emotions battled inside Pippa. Relief that she had not caused Georgiana's death, sorrow that the lady had died at the hands of her own son, pity for Annie that she had been innocently embroiled in the scheme, and even some sympathy for the countess. But her greatest emotion was fear. Fear for Ash. He was going into the lair of a killer and the threads holding him together were already stretched thin. Could he fight when his mind and heart were engaged elsewhere?

Pippa caught Annie's shoulders. "Tell me where Briars lives."

Annie stared at her. "You can't go there! You'll be in the way. Come back inside and change. Get warm and we'll wait together."

"Wait! Wait for what? Your brother to be killed? Or to commit murder? Is that what you want? If my presence can help in any way, I would rather be there than anywhere else."

"He'll be angry that you have put yourself in danger."

"I've seen the worst of his ire and I know I can endure it."

"You have no fear, do you," Annie said in wonder.

"Not of your brother. Nor should you. He adores you."

"I know." She smiled wistfully. "I'm not afraid of him." She hugged Pippa, the top of her head only reaching Pippa's chin. "But I can't let you put yourself in danger. I like you too much."

Pippa twisted the ring Ash had given her. "Very well." She managed a smile. "I think I prefer to wait here for him though."

Annie nodded then hugged her again. "You know, you make a rather fetching youth. No wonder Gertie kissed you."

Pippa stared at her. "How did you know?"

But Annie had already turned to go back to the house. "I'll send a warmer cloak down to you. And don't worry, Ash will soon return." She waved and Pippa felt guilty for what she was about to do.

She waited until Annie was out of sight then removed the ring from her finger. She placed it in her palm and closed her fist around it. With eyes closed, she softly spoke the seeking spell. Light and dark swirled, blended then a pathway cleared. It worked. He'd gone down river, as suspected. All she needed to do was follow the way and she would find Ash.

She headed down to the waterstairs and hailed an empty wherry which must have deposited passengers further upriver and was returning to the city. Once settled into her seat, she tried not to speculate about what kind of reception she would receive from Ash but gave up. It was impossible to predict what he would say or do. Ash was not a simple man to decipher.

* * *

BRIARS ENTERED his own parlor with as much ease as a man facing an amphitheatre full of lions. He stuttered greetings, attempted polite conversation and then fell into awkward silence when Ash put his hand up for him to stop. It appealed to Ash's mood to see his opponent so disconcerted. Let the man sweat.

Unfortunately his mother ended the silence too soon. "You will desist with the rumor about my family immediately," she said. Having refused to sit, she stood with her back to the large unlit fireplace. Ash held his ground between her and Briars who remained near the door. He would have to lure the cur away from the only exit point in the event a quick escape became necessary. He glanced at his mother in her full velvet skirts. Well, as quick as possible.

"R, rumor?" Briars swallowed. "I don't know anything—"

"You're a fool if you think we believe you. Lord Ashbourne knows everything." It probably wasn't a coincidence that she used Ash's title. His mother never did or said anything without reason. "And he does not take kindly to the way you have coerced me into agreeing to your terms."

"The courts don't look kindly on someone who murders elderly women," Ash said, speaking for the first time.

"Nor does the queen," his mother said.

"I doubt she looks favorably on people who've lied to her for thirty-five years either." Briars finally appeared to take some control of the situation. They were, after all, in his house. He probably had retainers outside, armed and aware of the dangerous situation. He also possessed the letter. The man would surely think all of that added up to an advantage. Or so Ash wanted him to conclude.

Ash smiled. He almost felt sorry for Briars. His brother. Twin. He studied the other man, seeing him for the first time. He was equal in height to Ash, but larger around the middle and jowly, like their father just before he died after years of excessive feasting. He had their father's eyes too but the fair coloring of Georgiana—their mother—whereas Ash was dark. He couldn't see any other similarities to himself, but perhaps someone more discerning would notice something. Pippa would.

Pippa. *Come back to me.*

He wrenched his thoughts back to the parlor, the murderer, his mother. Adoptive mother. He needed his wits about him, and thinking about the woman he'd lost and the deep ache in his heart wouldn't help. It wasn't easy to maintain a single focus, but he tried.

"I wish to speak to your father," Ash said.

Briars' mouth opened and shut without uttering a word.

"Your father," Ash prompted. "Is he here?"

Briars brushed his peascod bellied doublet as if rubbing his stomach for good luck. "My father is dead."

It took Ash a moment to realize Briars meant his real father, the last earl. "I mean the man who adopted you," Ash said. "I believe he ails."

"He is confined to his rooms at present. He is not expected to live long." He said it with such an air of casual finality that it was hard to believe he cared about the fate of the elderly man lying somewhere in one of the upstairs bedchambers. "Why do you want to speak to him?"

Ash paced around the room, keeping his right side, his sword side, to Briars. He looked out the window and up at the gray sky stretching between the roofs on either side of the grand street. It had stopped raining but the clouds had muscled in and hunkered down for the day. This part of London was home to many wealthy merchants who'd built sizable houses but they were hardly mansions in the order of The Strand's. Few had gardens and many shared external walls in order to fit as many as possible along the street. What had he been thinking confining his high-spirited sister to this dreary place?

Ah yes, love. He'd thought she cared for Briars. What a blind fool he'd been, in so many ways.

"I want to ask your father if he knows what activities you've been pursuing recently," Ash said. "I thought he might be interested, that's all."

"This is nothing to do with that bloated whoreson!"

So Briars junior and senior had fallen out, probably over money or perhaps the father simply told his son about his real parentage. If the old man was ill, he might have revealed the truth to clear the slate before his death.

"This is to do with me!" Briars stabbed his chest with his finger. "I am the son of an earl and I *will* have what is mine. By any means." Spittle foamed at the corner of his mouth. Ash found it difficult not to stare.

"You are not a Savoy," the countess said, her steely voice cutting through Briars' words. "You may have been born a Savoy but you have not been raised as one."

"Why? Why wasn't I raised a Savoy? Why choose him over me?"

"I was obviously the better looking babe," Ash said. If he could goad him into letting his guard down...

"We could not keep both of you," his mother said. She looked surprisingly small standing in front of the enormous fireplace. Two tall silver candlesticks perched on the marble mantelpiece behind her made her seem insignificant. But there was nothing insignificant about the way she stood straight as a yew with roots buried so deeply that not even the strongest wind could sway her.

"If we'd kept you both, how would we decide which twin

was to inherit?" she said. "It would create too much rivalry, too much enmity between you." She shrugged. She would have justified this to herself many times and was perhaps reciting the words she had spoken to Georgiana and the earl thirty-five years ago. "And since Richard was the smaller of the two, he was chosen to make it appear I'd just given birth when in fact you were both five months old. It was simply because of his size."

"And here I thought size didn't matter," Ash said.

"It always matters," his mother said, following his lead. He almost smiled at her. She was a countess through and through. She knew how to handle potentially explosive situations with grace and a noblewoman's ingrained sense of superiority. She wouldn't believe she'd done wrong, not even for a second.

Ash held out his hand to Briars. "Hand over the letter and this will be forgotten."

Briars hesitated. "Even Georgiana Dale?"

"I'll deem her death to be at the hands of an intruder." Ash nearly choked on the words but he got them out somehow. He just wanted this to be over so he could find Pippa...

Briars' gaze shifted between them, distrusting. "Do you give me your word?"

"Yes," the countess said but Ash couldn't utter that simple word. He just couldn't.

"I can give you my word that I will kill you if you do not hand over the letter," he said.

Briars' hand fluttered at his middle and he glanced at Ash's sword. "You wouldn't dare. Not in my own home. Anyway, I've given orders for the letter to be handed to Lady Wethinall if I am killed."

Clever move. "You do realize your scheme has a flaw," Ash said.

"Flaw?" Briars moved into the room but kept a considerable distance between himself and Ash.

"A rather important one, actually. You see, even if you produce this letter of proof, nothing will change. Granted, Her Majesty will be angry with my mother for her duplicity. She'll revoke my title of course, she has to. But I am an influential man, with or without an earldom behind me. The queen values my opinion. She even relies on me in some matters." He indicated his mother. "She also relies on Mother as a woman of her own age she can trust. They are great friends. Ah, I see you didn't know that." Ash warmed to his theme, a rather self-indulgent one but a necessary course to take to convince his opponent. And to avoid bloodshed.

If only what he spouted were true, all would be well. But Briars was more right than he knew. If losing the title and all that went with it didn't matter, Ash wouldn't be threatening Briars in his own parlor.

"You, Her Majesty doesn't know and wouldn't want to," Ash went on. "What use are you to her? Your father has all the drive and ability to make his enterprises a success. You do not." Interesting that Briars bristled at the accusation but did not deny it. It seemed Ash's guess had hit the mark.

"She may revoke my title," he continued, "but she will doubtless make a new one for me and she will always come to me for advice. I am, after all, an innocent party in this. So tell me, *Brother*, what did you think she would do to you? Give you the earldom?"

Briars eyes narrowed but he said nothing.

"It was your hope, your dream? Or was it?" Ash enjoyed Briars' discomfort, liked seeing the fear and uncertainty deep in his eyes. "You wanted to marry Annie, perhaps kill me before I produced heirs so that your children would inherit all the Savoy properties. Is that right? Doubtless you know you wouldn't get the earldom, not through Annie, but perhaps you thought Her Majesty might look kindly on you and create a title just for you. Or reinstate the earldom for your son, if Annie bore you one. How does that fit?" He saw from Briars' startled expression that it was true. "I cannot blame you for wanting the name and wealth that is your due. So, am I right?"

Briars blinked, swallowed. "Something like that," he said hoarsely.

"But then your plans had to suddenly change. You had to make good your threat because Annie refused you." Ash shook his head. "You really haven't considered this thoroughly, have you? You see, if I allow you to live—and that is quite doubtful at this juncture—do you think the queen will welcome you to court after I make it known you're a murderer and blackmailer?"

"Shall we wait and see?" Briars puffed out his chest. "The fact you are here looking for the letter proves that you and the countess are scared of the consequences."

The shot hit the mark, straight and true. "It proves that we care about Annie," Ash said. "You and she have been linked. We would like this to end conveniently for all parties involved, including you, to avoid scandal. If you give me the letter, it might still end satisfactorily. You will be allowed to return to your normal life."

"As what?" Briars spat. "Merchant? Burying myself in piles of paperwork while you sit in the big house! No, my *lord*, this is not the life for me. *You* have my life, you conceited cock."

"I can assure you," Ash said lazily, "my cock is not conceited."

"Language, Richard," his mother said but there was tightness in her voice. She was worried. Very.

"I sympathize with you regarding the paperwork," Ash said to Briars. "But you are the conceited one to think that you could marry my sister. *Your* sister, as it turns out."

"Half," Briars said.

"I know that."

"Do you?"

"Of course. The same father, different mothers." He looked to the countess. She coughed and twisted her rings.

A terrible dread washed over him. "You are her real mother, aren't you?"

"Surely after all this," she spread her arms to indicate himself, Briars, "you realized that Annabel is not of my flesh either."

"Yes, but..." Actually, no. He'd been so swept up in his own problems that Annie's didn't even count in his thoughts. It was so obvious he could kick himself for not seeing it. The countess's inability to produce a child for so long, a sixteen year age gap between himself and his sister, the marked difference in Annie's appearance and the countess's. And yet, she did not look like the late earl either. "You said half-sister," he said to Briars. "But if Mother here is not Annabel's real mother then...Georgiana is her mother too? But our father is not hers?"

"Oh no, he was quite faithful to me after that one union with Georgiana. No, Annabel is Georgiana's daughter by Fallon."

"Fallon!"

"Yes. I decided to adopt her. I'd always wanted a girl child."

"And Georgiana allowed it?"

"Of course. Fallon wouldn't leave his wife and it was unthinkable for Georgiana to bring up a child out of wedlock. Since you were already fifteen and in no need of a nurse anymore, it was a neat arrangement to switch her duties to her own daughter."

"Quite." He stared at the woman who could speak of her deceptions so casually, as if they were insignificant. Perhaps to her, they were. She seemed to truly believe she had done the right thing by Georgiana. Perhaps she had. Who was he, a man and a privileged one at that, to determine what was right or wrong for a woman in Georgiana's situation? Still, the things he'd learned today were shocking and he needed time to fully ponder them.

He didn't have time. He didn't have enough wits about him either, not after losing Pippa. It was the only explanation he could give for his failure to react when Briars dashed towards the countess. He held her throat in the crook of his arm, a knife to her white skin above her equally white ruff.

Ash could do nothing but watch and maintain his composure. It wouldn't serve his purpose to allow his enemy to see he was rattled by the slowness of his own response.

"If you two have quite finished discussing your sordid family history," Briars snarled, "perhaps we can talk seriously."

The countess tugged at his elbow but Briars' hold was too firm and she gave up. Even so, she retained an air of unfazed serenity. She didn't shriek, didn't struggle and didn't appear to be about to expire. Trust his mother not to faint when fainting would have been the perfect solution to the problem.

Ash's fingers flexed over his sword hilt. Briars shook his head. "Do not draw or I'll slash her throat." He smiled and it was only then that Ash saw the man who had killed Georgiana in cold blood. Briars was not the stumbling fool he had portrayed these past weeks but a callous creature who could carelessly spill life in his own parlor.

"You tried to have me killed in Haverford," Ash said. The pieces were coming together now, but still he cursed himself for not working it out earlier.

"Those idiots should have slain you that night," Briars said. He shrugged and the countess winced as the knife came perilously close to piercing her skin. "But it was rash of me to hire them. When Annie told me you were going to Haverford to investigate that witch's death I panicked. I followed you and found a few desperate souls willing to shed the life of a peer of the realm." He spat. "Incompetent fools."

"But that has been the one and only attempt. Why not others?"

"You appeared no closer to finding her killer so the threat was not as imminent as I thought. Besides," again the smile of a deranged man forced out from behind his mask of respectability, "I soon realized I needed you alive. I could not blackmail the countess if you were dead. What would be the point? What would she have to lose? No, I needed you to live until after I'd married your sister—"

"I would never have let you marry her," the countess hissed. "You are beneath her and you are her brother. I was simply going along with your scheme to give me an opportunity to steal back the letter."

It seemed Annie's final refusal of Briars had been timed rather badly. Ash was probably to blame for that. He was to blame for so many things today. Like Pippa...

"You knew she was a witch," Ash said, fighting back his impatience to get this encounter over with and join his men in search for Pippa. When Briars frowned at him, he added, "Georgiana. You called her a witch just now."

"I heard some of the locals in Haverford call her that."

"She could have killed you," Ash said. "But she chose not to because you were her son."

"I told her I was. She cried." Briars snorted. "Kill me, you say? With what, her embroidery needle?"

"She has—had—powers beyond your imagination. She chose

not to kill you as she lay there dying because she loved you. You were her son," he said between clenched teeth.

Briars snorted again and spat into the hearth. "Love. You forget, *Brother*, that I am a Savoy. Love is not a commodity I believe in." His knuckles whitened around the knife handle. "I do, however, believe in revenge."

In the heartbeat that followed, the blade sank into flesh. The point drew a bloodied line across the countess's throat. Her eyes widened in surprise. She stared straight past Ash to the doorway, tried to say something.

Ash, sword drawn, charged at Briars.

Too late.

His mother crumpled to the rushes, her gloved hands clutching her throat.

Someone shouted, like a ferocious barbarian warrior. It must have been himself because Briars stood with his mouth shut, his knife aimed at Ash's chest. He would have thrown it too but one of the enormous silver candlesticks toppled off the mantelpiece and hit Briars on the back of the head.

No, not toppled. Picked up and thrown by an invisible hand.

A rush of air cooled him as a boy ran past and knelt at the countess's side. Numbly, he realized he knew the curve of the boy's back, knew the gentle hands that replaced his mother's at her gashed throat.

"Pippa," he croaked. "Pippa?" he said louder.

"She'll live."

It wasn't the answer to any question he'd been thinking and that shamed him into silence. He watched as his love saved his mother's life.

The countess, her skin the shade of moonlight, sat up and rubbed her throat. When she'd satisfied herself that she was whole and alive, she turned to Pippa. Ash had never seen her stare with such curious wonder at another human being before.

She blinked slowly. "You are..."

"Another witch." It came from Briars. He too sat up, a hand pressed to the back of his head.

Ash looked down at his twin brother. And rammed him through with his sword. Briars fell to the side, twitched then became still, sprawled in a pool of his own blood. "No witnesses." He looked at his mother in warning. "I'll not risk the Witch Hunter taking her."

He saw from the look on her face that she understood everything.

A servant entered, screamed and ran out again.

"Let's go," Ash said. He helped his mother up and took her arm, almost carrying her towards the door. He dared a glance at Pippa but she wasn't looking at him as she held the countess's other hand.

At the entrance, his mother shook them both off. "I can manage."

Pippa protested but Ash didn't. He knew it would do no good. His mother was as stubborn as...a Savoy. She may not have been born one but she certainly became one. Perhaps she was right and lineage did not determine character—it was all in the upbringing.

Two burly retainers arrived but didn't block their way. "Your master tried to kill Lady Ashbourne," Ash told them without breaking his stride. "Have the authorities visit me if they require further explanation."

He followed his mother and Pippa out of the house. He was acutely aware that Pippa had said only two words since she'd re-entered his life so dramatically.

"We came by river," he said to her as they neared the end of the street. It was an inane way to start a conversation but he had to say *something*. It wasn't the right place to apologize for his actions. Not yet. Later, if he could get her alone.

Then again, if he had to go down on his knees and beg her forgiveness in front of the entire population of London, he'd do it.

Pippa stopped and looked like she was in two minds over a choice she must make. The choice of staying or going.

"You must return with us," the countess said. "I need to thank you properly."

"I don't need thanks," Pippa said. Like the boy she was pretending to be, she crossed her arms and hunched her shoulders into the light rain that had begun to fall again. She headed away from them. Away from him.

"Pippa!" He ran after her, stopped her with a hand to her arm. But words failed him. There was so much to say...where did he start? He slid his hands up to her shoulders and searched her face for a sign that she cared for him. A flutter of eyelashes, a smile, anything!

She gave him nothing. She shook him free and began to walk off again.

Don't. Wait. Stay. "Please." He heard the desperation in his voice and didn't care.

She kept walking.

He thought he'd had a broken heart before, but now he knew that it had merely been torn. This, *this* was what it felt like to have it truly broken. The wrenching pain, the sheer heaviness of grief pressing down on him. He wanted to sink into the mud, succumb to the pain and let it succor him, fill him.

But he refused to give in. Again he ran after her. Light footsteps followed him.

"Perhaps," his mother said in her soft manner that brooked no refusal, "you will allow me to thank you properly. For me." This last she said with humility and a tone he'd not heard his mother ever use. Passion. "I *need* to thank you for saving my life, Phillippa. I cannot do that here."

Pippa stopped. Without turning to face them she lowered her head. Ash wanted to trace the elegant curve of her neck but refrained. She would not want his touch. Even he knew that.

She nodded. She was going to return to Ashbourne House with them! He would have shouted it to the world if she didn't turn and stab him with a sharp glare.

"I need some supplies anyway," she said.

Maybe one day she would allow him to touch her again.

# CHAPTER 19

The rain kept both Pippa and the countess under the canopy at one end of the barge as it eased along the Thames. Due to a lack of space, Ash had to sit elsewhere. He didn't seem to mind getting wet and Pippa was grateful for the space between them. When he was close, she always seemed to lose her head and give in to his alluring presence. That's the only explanation she could give for returning to Ashbourne House. The countess's plea had nothing to do with it.

"Wethinall House," Lady Ashbourne ordered the rowers. Immediately, the barge responded and curved to the right.

"You're going to confront her?" Ash said. "Now?"

"The sooner the better. She must be made to understand that circumstances have changed. Her cohort is dead, the evidence of your...past is destroyed, or soon will be. I think I am the perfect person to *make* her understand." The barge bumped gently against the stone landing and Ash helped his mother out before stepping out himself. "No," the countess said, removing her hand from his, "I'll do this alone."

He hesitated, looked back at Pippa. She turned away. She couldn't quite meet his gaze yet. She felt too close to unraveling, thread by thread.

"You need an escort," he persisted.

"Don't be ridiculous," the countess scoffed. "Go home. Your sister needs you."

Again the hesitation before he responded. "I'll send the barge back for you."

She nodded and looked to Pippa. "We'll talk later."

At Ash's signal, a rower used his oar to push off from the landing. Pippa watched the countess make her way to Wethinall House beyond the waterstairs, her hooded cloak protecting her against the weather. She wondered if Lady Ashbourne had designed her absence to allow them to be alone.

Alone. Pippa swallowed. She wasn't ready.

Ash sat in the seat vacated by his mother but kept as much distance between himself and Pippa as the cushioned bench allowed. Silence stretched thinly, the only sounds coming from the splish of oars in the water and the patter of rain on the canopy. No one else was out on that part of the river, even the swans had gone elsewhere. Just when she thought she couldn't stand it any longer, the silence snapped.

"There will never be enough days in my lifetime to make up for the wrongs I've done to you." He spoke so quietly she could barely hear him. "I'm so sorry, Pippa. I...I've been foolish beyond reason and I know there's no excuse for treating you so poorly." He rested a hand on the cushion only inches from her own but he didn't try to make contact.

She restrained herself from closing the gap. It wasn't easy. His pull was stronger than ever, stronger than any powers she possessed.

"I know I can never do enough to make up for all my wrongs," he said.

"You killed your brother for me." She wasn't sure why she said it but it struck her that he must be hurting. He'd almost lost his mother and he'd killed his own twin. He may not have come to terms with those facts yet but he soon would. She wished she could be there for him when the time came.

But she would be long gone.

"I couldn't let him live and be witness to your...uniqueness," Ash said. "I'll not allow anyone to harm you, Pippa." His fingers touched her fingers, tentatively at first, then his hand closed around hers, warm and solid. He squeezed and she instinctively squeezed back before she realized what she was doing. "I love you."

She closed her eyes against the sting of tears. Three words said with simple honesty and breathless desire. They cut through her like a blade, straight into her heart.

She bit her tongue to stop herself responding as she wished. *I love you too.* She tasted salty blood.

"I'm sorry," he said again when she said nothing. "I don't know what I was thinking. I...suppose I wasn't thinking at all. The thing is...I *knew* you couldn't be to blame. I knew it and yet I was quick to judge." His other hand touched her cheek in an exquisitely sweet caress. "There was a woman in Spain," he said, not sounding at all like his resonant, assured self. "I was an ambassador in the Spanish court and she was a young widow of high birth. I thought I loved her. I thought she loved me."

Pippa's heart constricted like a tight fist. He loved another?

He snorted softly. "I know now that what I felt for her was not love. This," he pressed their linked hands to his mouth, his lips soft against her knuckles, "this is love." He dropped their hands into her lap. She didn't try to break the connection. Not yet. She very much wanted to hear his story. "I was sending intelligence back to Walsingham of course. The Spaniards must have suspected. They enlisted her help to discover my methods of transmitting information. She did everything she could to find out. Everything. She told me she loved me. Foolishly, I believed her. I trusted her. I planned on bringing her home and making her the next countess. She demanded proof of my love, of my intentions—so I gave away my secrets. She betrayed me to her king. I knew immediately it was her." His grip tightened. "She was killed the next day."

"You?"

He didn't answer for a long time. "I didn't wield the sword but I didn't warn her either even though I knew in advance."

He blamed himself for her death and still struggled with the guilt. Pippa didn't need to look at him to see that. It was there in his thick voice, his tense body, his extraordinarily uncharacteristic actions of earlier. "And you thought I had betrayed you too."

"No." His thumb massaged her knuckles. He sighed. "Yes, but it doesn't justify what I did."

No, it didn't, but it was an explanation of sorts. To be angry with her was one thing but to blame her without proper reason then to lock her in...those were not the actions of the man she had fallen in love with.

He pulled her hand to his lips again and bowed his head. "I'm sorry—"

"Don't," she said bluntly. "You're forgiven." It was the truth. However, she suspected his forgiveness of himself would not come for a very long time.

He opened her hand and kissed the palm. His breath disarmed her, swept her away. She gasped as the simple gesture ignited desire. She ached to kiss him, make his pain and guilt go away. Tell him she would always love him, no matter what.

She did nothing.

"When we are wed—"

She snatched her hand away. "I'll not marry you, Ash." She sat on her hands lest they betray her. "I cannot. I'll be leaving as soon as possible."

"What? No, you can't!" He was down on his knees in front of her, his hose getting wet and muddy on the barge's deck. He blinked up at her. She looked away, eyes burning. He slid his hands up her thighs and she shuddered, soul-deep. "You said you forgave me." It was a plea, bare and fragile and heart-breaking to hear.

"I do. But I must still leave. You must see that my staying will endanger you and your family, especially now that you may lose the protection of your title."

"I won't."

"My uncle will come here looking for revenge."

"Let him come! I'll deal with him when he does. He and St. Cyr. Don't be afraid, Pippa. Together we can be strong. We can beat them."

"No."

"I am still the earl." She heard the tremor in his voice, smelled his fear. "I can keep you safe. I can keep everyone safe."

"No. It's too dangerous—"

"It's too dangerous for *you*! Pippa, you cannot run forever. Where will you go? No, you must stay," he said with finality. "There is no other solution. You'll stay and marry me and I'll keep you safe."

He was so determined, so blind to reason that she had to use the only weapon she had left, the one she'd hoped not to use. "Besides," she said with forced lightness, "I don't love you." What it cost her to say it, to see the pain her words caused!

He jerked his head back as if slapped. His face, usually so dark, became pinched and pale. A muscle pulsed high in his cheek, its rhythm erratic.

He sank back on his haunches but rose again almost immediately. "You might," he murmured. "One day."

She shook her head and bit back the torrent of sadness flooding her, drowning.

Like an old man who'd labored his entire life, he stood slowly, painfully. They had reached Ashbourne House and the barge docked at the waterstairs. Ash held onto the canopy to steady himself as he stared blankly up at the nearby trees. She couldn't see his face from where she sat but she noted the sag of his shoulders and saw his Adam's apple bob like a boat on a stormy sea.

Annie, standing on the riverbank, squealed and ran down to the barge. She helped Pippa alight and went to hug her but Pippa pushed past and headed up the stairs. Behind her, Annie said, "Oh Ash! Thank God you are both all right. Mother?"

"On an errand."

"Ash? What is it?" Annie's concern reached Pippa, already several steps ahead of brother and sister. "Are you unwell?"

"No," Ash said, his tone unreadable.

"But you're in pain! I can see it. Are you injured?"

"Mortally."

Pippa strode up to the main entrance of the house. She didn't care who saw her dressed in boys' clothes. The ruse was long overdue to be put to rest anyway. She would wait for the countess to return as promised then she would take what she needed for her journey and leave. She hadn't told Ash she was going to confront her uncle. It would only make matters worse because he would follow her. Of that she was sure. He would follow her to the edge of the earth if he could.

She stopped, one foot on the lowest step leading up to the front doors. Oh Lord, give her strength to go through on her plan. Make it work. If it did, then perhaps she and Ash could be together after all.

But she wouldn't allow herself to think that far ahead.

*　*　*

ASH BARELY HEARD a thing Annie said. He was too intent on watching Pippa disappear into the house. He wanted to run after her, convince her to stay. If only he knew the right words.

But he suspected nothing he'd say would be right. Not ever.

Just as Pippa was swallowed up by the house, Fallon was spat out.

"My lord!" the steward called, waving a hand in the air to hail his master. It was the loudest and most agitated Ash had ever seen Fallon. A bad omen.

Ash sighed. Surely nothing else could possibly go wrong today. "What is it?"

"Her Majesty..." The elderly steward pressed a hand to his chest and sucked in a deep breath. "...has requested your immediate presence."

Damnation! It seemed the queen had heard the rumor.

*　*　*

THE QUEEN WAS NOT in a good mood. Her white face paint might hide many things, but it didn't hide the lines furrowing her forehead or the small mouth turned down into a grim frown. Ash bowed extra low and added the flourish that often amused her. When he looked up, however, she was still clearly not amused.

"A rather interesting tale has reached our ears, my lord Ashbourne," she said from her cushioned settle, the only seat in the chamber long enough to fit her enormous skirts.

"A comedy or tragedy, Madam?" he said with a smile.

"A tragedy. A very grave tragedy. I summoned your mother

the countess here too." She looked at her two ladies hovering nearby as if she suspected to see her amongst them. "Where is she?"

"I'm afraid I don't know," he lied. "She doesn't always confide in me where she is going."

"You should keep tighter rein on your household, my lord." The queen's clear, sharp gaze settled on his. "For it seems much has been going on that you are not aware of."

"You majesty? May I enquire—?"

"You know perfectly well what I'm talking about, Lord Ashbourne. Do not try to hoodwink me."

Ash decided to be honest with her. She was a shrewd woman with ears and eyes in every great household in England. It was entirely possible she knew more about what went on at Ashbourne House than he did.

"Your Gracious Majesty is too clever to be hoodwinked," he said.

The corner of her mouth twitched. "A tactful sentiment for one not known for his diplomacy."

He smiled. "You have me, Your Majesty. As you say, polite sentiments do not come naturally to me."

"That is why I value them more from you than from any other. Come. Sit by me, my lord. I wish to speak with you in private."

Private? With two ladies and at least five courtiers within spitting distance? But it was not an invitation to be scoffed at. He sat on a low velvet-covered stool placed near the queen. And then, at her insistence, he told her everything he knew about his parentage. He finished with an account of Briars' death, but not Pippa's part in it.

She showed not even a flicker of surprise. No wonder his mother was such great friends with the queen, they were so much alike. "If you assure me his death was necessary to save the life of the countess, then I accept your account."

And with that, he was absolved from killing Briars. Killing his twin brother. All he had to do now was wipe it from his nightmares and he would be truly free. Pippa could help him with that.

If he could convince her to stay.

"Now, to the business of the earldom."

The room felt hot, close. The courtiers seemed to be nearer without having moved. Their quiet chatter grew softer and necks craned towards the queen and her earl. Her Majesty picked up a fan of white feathers from the small table at hand and fluttered it rapidly. She didn't look directly at Ash.

"Madam?" he said on a whisper. His thigh ached like the devil but he didn't rub the soreness away.

"We cannot ignore the rumors, my lord. We..." She glanced sharply at him then away. "We cannot. Do you not see?" She swept her fan wide to encompass the room and everything in it. "You are illegitimate. We cannot break the rules for you." Her gaze settled on him, gentle, motherly. She touched the fan to his cheek. The soft feathers caressed and then were gone. "Not even for you."

"If your gracious majesty would allow me to defend my honor and that of my family."

She nodded.

"It is rumor only," he said. "There is no evidence of my father's...indiscretion."

"A letter has been given to us."

Damnation! Lady Wethinall. She hadn't waited for Briars' death. The temptation to bring down the Savoys must have been too great.

"I think you know what it says," the queen went on.

"I do." Ash swallowed. He needed a drink. Something to obliterate his parched throat. Obliterate this God awful day. "And so?"

The queen laid the fan in her lap and sighed deeply. "It is a knife to my heart, a pain I must bear. As must you...Richard Savoy."

His name. She had never used it before. He'd always be Lord Ashbourne and sometimes just Ash "You take away the earldom?" Incredulous, he stared at her. He'd never quite believed it possible until this moment. Suddenly the room shifted, the rich colors of the tapestries and painted walls swirled about him, made him dizzy. He reached for the table edge to steady himself but it too moved, toppled over. The thump drew him back into the room with all the speed of a fish cruelly hauled out of the water by a fisherman's line.

The queen's hand rested on his shoulder. She peered into his face and said, "There is no other choice."

No. No, there wasn't. Not for her. She could do many things, but making him legitimate was beyond even her.

As if he were the elderly monarch and she his strong subject, she took his elbow and raised him up. "Go. Speak to your mother then send her to us for counsel." She steered him to the large door, her thin frame pressed as close to his side as her skirts would allow. "Do not see this as the end. You must have fortitude. For your family's sake. Perhaps," she leaned in conspiratorially, "you will one day rise again."

She let him go at the door and he numbly realized he was being ordered to leave. He bowed, as elaborately as when he'd arrived, and turned to go.

"You were to be wed, were you not?" Her Majesty said, loud enough for the courtiers to hear.

"Yes."

"And she's from gentle but plain stock?" He nodded. "Then it is unlikely she will see this change in your fortune as too much of a disappointment." With a wave of her hand, she turned. He was dismissed.

He pushed open the doors and strode through the usual crowd awaiting an audience. He registered the stares and whispers but didn't care. He kept walking until he was outside, in the palace forecourt, instinctively heading towards the stables and his horse. He couldn't think of anything else except getting back to Ashbourne House, getting back to Pippa before she left.

He accepted her departure. Knew she must go. Far away.

Because he couldn't save her now.

* * *

WAITING WAS EXCRUCIATING. Pippa had changed into woman's clothes, packed her satchel with supplies for her journey and now there was nothing to do but wait in her rooms and avoid Annie, Gertie and anyone else who wanted to see her.

Wait. Wait for the countess because Pippa had promised to hear her thanks, and wait for Ash because she couldn't leave without saying goodbye. She just couldn't. But the countess hadn't yet returned and Ash seemed to have disappeared. Since Pippa was avoiding the servants, she couldn't ask where he'd gone.

Finally there was a knock on her door. She sprang up from the seat by the window and answered it. But it was only Fallon and she almost closed the door on him again.

"My lady," he said, bowing.

"Mistress Ingleside," she corrected him.

"There is a gentleman to see you."

"Me?"

"A Simon Rowe."

She clasped a hand to her mouth but not before a gasp escaped. Her uncle—here!

"Would you like me to remove him?" Fallon said, straight-faced.

She could have hugged him for offering. Instead, she shook her head. "No. I must do this. Where is Lord Ashbourne?"

"Whitehall."

"The palace?" Well, it explained his absence at such a time. "Where is Master Rowe?"

"In the south parlor. Sir Guy de St. Cyr and three retainers are with him."

She shivered. So many. Perhaps she should wait for Ash... But then she remembered how he'd dealt with Briars, the only other witness to her witchcraft apart from her uncle. She didn't want another death. Not even Sir Guy's. She would meet the men on her own.

She followed Fallon to the south parlor but was met by Ash as he entered through the great hall. Fallon told him of the visitors before Pippa could say anything. Ash glanced at her. He looked tired and somehow flat, as if the life had been sucked out of him. The hollow eyes he turned on her were framed by dark shadows. He blinked once, twice, and his gaze wandered over her, as if he was committing her face to memory.

"What is it?" she said, breathless. "What's happened?"

"I'll explain later. Let's deal with your uncle and St. Cyr." He seemed to rally, to grow taller once more as he strode ahead. "Come. We do this together," he said. "Don't worry about my safety," he went on, addressing her greatest fear. "I am well capable of taking care of myself. St. Cyr will not find me so easy to kill this time." He sounded more like the Ash of old. Strong. Brash. Devil-be-damned

She caught up to him but had to trot to keep apace. "No-o, but combined with their men..."

"Under no circumstances should you use your powers." When she didn't answer he put a hand on her shoulder to halt her. "If you can't promise me that, then I'll not allow you to go in there."

Dutifully, she nodded. He seemed to accept it and continued walking until they reached the south parlor.

"When this meeting is over," he said, before entering, "you must go." Heavy lids hooded his eyes but she didn't need to see them to know darkness simmered within.

He would allow her to leave? What had happened to change his mind? What had the queen said to him? Ah, of course. She had revoked his title. Without the earldom and the influence that went with it, he couldn't keep her safe as he'd promised. No wonder he looked haunted. Like a ghost, all the essence of him gone. His sense of self, his place in the world, and all the responsibilities that came with the title—gone. Some of the servants would no longer be necessary. His mother's pride would be dented. His sister's marriage prospects diminished.

And he could no longer keep Pippa safe. That's why he was letting her go.

She said nothing. Couldn't. Not until the outcome of this confrontation was clear. If they failed, she would still have to leave, especially now that the security of the earldom had been taken away. Perhaps after considerable distance and time had come between them, she would one day be only a faded memory to Ash. The memory of him, however, would never dull. She would always be able to taste him, smell him, feel him everywhere she went.

Ash opened the door. She saw Sir Guy first, standing straight and formidable directly opposite near the large window. He glanced from Pippa to Ash then back to Pippa. One eyebrow raised, his mouth turned down in a frown. He looked concerned. Ash didn't appear to notice him. His glance flicked around the room, taking in the three armed, thick-browed retainers and finally settling on her uncle.

"Rowe," Ash said by way of greeting.

Simon bowed. "My lord. I've come to take my niece home."

So it was to be like that. Direct. No pleasantries between gentlemen.

"You are trespassing," Ash snarled. "Get out. You too," he said to Sir Guy. "And take your thugs with you."

"They're not mine," Sir Guy said. "And I'm afraid it's not quite that simple." He turned his attention to Pippa. "Your uncle has been in London these past two days."

"Two days!" she said.

"I had convinced him not to approach you here, that I would handle the matter."

"Seems you failed," Ash said.

Simon stretched his neck, a nervous habit which was aggravated when he wore an oversized ruff. "We are in agreement on that matter, my lord," her uncle said. "When he informed me of your marriage to my niece, I terminated his services."

Ash turned cold eyes on the Witch Hunter. "Then why are you still here?"

"I thought it necessary to be around for this...discussion," Sir Guy said.

Ash's lip curled. "So you could witness me killing him if he does not leave? How convenient."

"Not for Rowe," Sir Guy said. "but there'll be no killing today."

"Too late," Ash said.

Simon flinched as if he'd been pinked by Ash's sword. "I don't want him here any more than you do, my lord. But it seems he has taken his duties to heart in my niece's case." He shrugged. "And I'm beginning to think the presence of a justice of the peace might be of some use since you insist on abducting her."

"I am not abducting her. She is here of her own free will."

Pippa felt like an actor on stage when she stepped forward out of Ash's shadow. Everyone watched her, expectant. "Lord Ashbourne is right." She heard a breath escape him but didn't turn to look at him. Didn't dare. "I am here because I want to be here. And I will stay or go as I choose. No one can keep me where I do not want to be." She spoke to all three men in that room, but wasn't sure if any of them truly understood her words. A woman wasn't supposed to have opinions let alone be able to take care of herself in the wide world without a man's guiding hand. She'd proved, to herself at least, that she could.

"So," she went on, "I will not be returning to Shelton with you, Uncle."

"You have to! I am your guardian. Your only male relative."

"Hire a lawyer to argue your case if you wish but I'm not sure you will want everyone knowing how you treated me. How you locked me away for five years—five years!—without friend for comfort simply to get your greedy fingers on my land."

Instead of looking concerned, he seemed pleased. "I do not think we need to go through any legal channels, my dear. In fact, I'm sure you will return with me when I am through with you." Her uncle stepped toward her. Both Sir Guy and Ash moved between them. The three retainers joined in the dance, hands hovering at sword hilts, eyes gleaming at the possibility of action.

Simon held up his hands in surrender. "I see you have used your witchcraft to ensnare his lordship."

Sir Guy rolled his eyes and stepped back.

"You call her a witch again and I *will* kill you," Ash said.

Simon's gaze shifted to Ash's rapier and he must have seen the blood smeared on the blade. He swallowed. Sir Guy smiled. In that moment, Pippa almost liked him. Ash, apparently, did not.

"You find my sword amusing, St. Cyr?" he said. "Or my choice of words?"

Sir Guy didn't answer, but shrugged and stayed near the wall where he seemed to be content to be an observer. The three thugs moved away a little but stayed within striking range.

"As to your choice of words," Simon said, "I believe I didn't call anyone a witch."

Ash breathed in deeply and out slowly through his nose. "Let's get to the point, gentlemen. I'm a busy man." His hand rested on Pippa's shoulder, neither holding nor directing, simply there. She leaned into it, secure in its solidness. "I will be blunt. You believe you have seen Pippa use witchcraft, Rowe, and you're threatening to expose her so that she will return with you, enabling you to keep control of her considerable fortune."

She tensed but Ash's thumb lightly rubbed her shoulder and she relaxed a little. She had to trust him. This confrontation was what she wanted anyway, it's just that she hadn't expected to do it with Sir Guy present. A witness. An extremely dangerous one.

And now Ash couldn't protect her.

"I *know* I have seen her." Simon puffed out his chest. This was what he was waiting for, a chance to prove his point. "She set my house on fire."

"An errant spark," Pippa said quickly. "Rather a convenient one for me as it turns out. The resulting fire aided my escape."

"You used your witchcraft to knock me over!"

"You are mistaken," she said.

"I do not lie, girl," he growled. "You are a witch. Arrest her, Sir Guy. You shall have your day in court, Phillippa. You'll be tried as a witch."

Sir Guy moved then stopped and raised one eyebrow at Ash. "What say you, Savoy?"

Pippa's breath caught. 'Savoy'. Not 'Ashbourne' or 'my lord'. Somehow, Sir Guy knew. How, she couldn't speculate. Ash also noticed it. He went very still, except for his fingers which curled into fists at his sides. With that single word, Sir Guy was letting them know that he knew Ash had lost his title and all the power that went with it.

ASH HEARD Pippa gasp and desperately wanted to reassure her, tell her everything would be all right. But he couldn't. It wasn't all right.

Not yet.

It was up to him to make it so.

Suddenly he saw things very clearly. Like a path winding through a dense forest, he knew what he must do. He drew out his blade. "Do not come any closer, St. Cyr, or I will run you through."

The Witch Hunter didn't move but did look slightly amused by proceedings. That only made Ash angrier. He'd had enough. He was sick of watching everyone else direct his life—his mother, the queen, even Pippa by insisting she leave. No more. He may not be able to get his title back but damned if he was going to lose Pippa too.

Her long fingers twined around his sword arm. "Ash, put it down. Please."

"No. You're mine, Pippa, and you're not going anywhere. I'll protect you or die trying."

Her fingers tightened. Rowe shouted, "Arrest her!"

Sir Guy sighed. "Even without a blade at my heart, I could not. There simply isn't enough evidence."

A vein popped out on Rowe's forehead. "I am a witness!"

Ash stopped breathing. St. Cyr was letting her go? Simply because Rowe wasn't a strong enough witness? His blade dropped a little and St. Cyr moved forward and bowed to Pippa. "My heartfelt congratulations on your wedding, Mistress Ingleside." He looked to Ash, nodded. "Savoy."

Ash watched for any signs of dangerous movement—a grab for his sword hilt or dagger, a clenching of fists. But St. Cyr kept his hands at his back.

"Thank you," Pippa muttered.

One corner of St. Cyr's mouth lifted in a smile but it didn't reach his eyes. He cast Ash an unreadable glance. "I'm almost sorry I'll miss all the fun." He nodded again in farewell and headed for the door.

"Where are you going?" Rowe said, spitting his words out along with a glob of saliva.

St. Cyr paused. "I've neglected my estate and my duties too

long. You ended my commission, Rowe, and I see no reason to pursue my own interests in this matter since there is simply not enough evidence. I hope your men are excellent swordsmen. They'll need to be. Good day."

Ash went numb with relief. He was leaving without taking her? He didn't want to arrest her, kill her? He almost laughed out loud as he watched him go.

"But...you can't!" Simon shouted at St. Cyr's retreating back. "She is a witch!"

Ash slammed the door behind St. Cyr. "You are in my house," he said, leaving Pippa's side to stroll over to her uncle. He felt stronger, bigger, whole. The little weed and his curs didn't stand a chance. "We are both armed but I doubt you or your men have much skill with the rapier considering their swords shine. Mine, on the other hand, is well used, as you can see."

Rowe backed up into a chair and promptly sat on it. Even with his men surrounding him, he looked small and afraid, and not only of Ash. He was afraid of Pippa too. Ash glanced at her and saw her smile as she realized it too.

"There's no need to fear him now," he said to her.

"No," she said. "I am free. And I'll not let him take away my freedom again." She joined Ash in standing over her uncle. "You are my last surviving relative," she said to him, "so I'll not let you leave empty-handed. Since this has all been about property, *my* property, I'll give you one."

A spark of hope cut across Rowe's white face. He almost smiled. "Which one?"

"Ah, this is the beauty. You see, one of the properties I own is..." she smiled, "yours. You've been leasing it off me, haven't you, and pocketing the profits from it as well as the profits from my other holdings."

"B, but...that's not fair! I took you in! I cared for you, fed you, clothed you—"

"Kept me imprisoned!" Pippa wanted to strike him, just to see him flinch, to feel the power she now had over him. But she refrained. In her current mood, a simple slap might kill him. "You can keep your Shelton estate but as a lease only. I don't think you deserve it outright since I've paid you back a hundred-fold with the profits you've been stealing from me for years."

"But—" His mouth snapped shut as Ash pointed his sword in Simon's direction.

"If there is so much as a whisper against my wife's name," Ash said, "I will hunt you down and kill you very slowly and painfully."

Wife. He'd said it as if it were a certainty. It seemed he was going to claim her despite the loss of his title. He smiled at her, confident, assured.

In that moment she knew she *would* marry him. The Witch Hunter was gone and ridding them of her uncle was now a mere formality. She was safe. Ash was safe too, title or no.

"Even better," she said, feeling lighter than she had in a long time, "I will break the lease. You'll be left with nothing."

"And then I'll kill you," Ash said. He shrugged at Pippa, clearly enjoying himself. "A man has to have some fun."

She grinned. "Oh, there'll be plenty of fun once we are married."

His eyes danced with surprise then hope. "Promise?"

She heard Simon hiss then the whine of rapiers being unsheathed filled the small parlor.

Ash sighed and stepped in front of Pippa. "You interrupted a moment," he said.

"I'm sorry it has come to this, my lord," Simon said. "But you don't seem to grasp the seriousness of the situation."

"I think I grasp it. Just mind the tapestries," Ash said, withdrawing his own blade. "Or you'll have to face my mother, and I can assure you she is already in a very bad mood."

"Then perhaps we can do this outside." Simon looked pleased. "You may have three of your men join you if you prefer."

Pippa didn't trust him. Outside, Ash could call on any number of his men. So why did Simon want to go out there?

Witnesses. He was hoping to expose Pippa in a public place. He might attack her himself and with no weapon of her own, she would need to use her powers.

Going outside might mean the end of her. Remaining inside

could see the end of Ash—four armed men against one. She didn't think her uncle posed much of a threat. She'd never seen him train in the art of swordsmanship, but the other three had the ugly look of men determined to shed blood.

"We stay here," Ash said.

"No," she said. "Ash—"

"Pippa, I know I've given you few reasons to have faith in me today—"

"That's not true."

"Listen to me." He cupped her face in his left hand, the tenderness at odds with the strength she felt coursing through him. "You need to trust that I can keep you safe." His thumb brushed along her cheekbone, a feather-light caress that destroyed her fears.

She took his hand and drew it to her lips. "I trust you."

"Good. Now, go outside. I'll not have you risking—"

"No! If you're staying, so am I."

"Pippa—"

"Enough!" Simon said. "Get him!"

The three men lunged at Ash. Pippa instinctively stepped back against the wall as he swung round and slashed the nearest man across the face. The ruffian swore and clamped a hand over the bloody wound stretching from mouth to ear. The other two men quickly took his place. Ash neatly kept both occupied, his blade cutting, blocking, thrusting with expert skill.

She'd seen him fight Sir Guy of course, but here was something else. With the Witch Hunter, anger had distracted him, made him wild and reckless. Now he was all efficient movement. He remained focused, cold. Like a sleek cat, he struck over and over with calculated accuracy. The other men could only defend.

"Go, Pippa!" he shouted at her.

Simon stepped in front of the door, blocking her exit. Not that she'd been going to leave anyway. "You will stay here, my girl, for as long as he does."

"I am not your girl," she snapped. Anger surged, rippled along her skin to her fingertips. She held it in check and kept her hands to her sides. Why did he want her to remain with Ash?

"Ah," Simon said, looking past her, "Stoner has rejoined the fight. It'll be all over soon. Of course, you may wish to use your witchcraft to help your betrothed."

He was right. Ash could handle two men with ease but three was more of a challenge, especially when Stoner, even injured, appeared to have twice the amount of skill as his companions.

She closed her eyes, wanted to scream to Ash's men who must be outside. Why were none of them coming to their master's aid? Why didn't Fallon interrupt?

Her eyes flew open at the sound of a sharp cry of pain. Ash held off two men, a third sat on the ground, clutching his shoulder.

"Get up!" Simon shouted at him. "I'm not paying you to sit down!"

"Are you paying them to die?" Ash flicked one of his opponent's swords away and parried the other's thrust.

Simon snorted. "I don't think they'll be the ones dying today." Despite his bravado, a hint of uncertainty crept into his voice.

Ash ducked beneath a wild stab. "No? You think my men will let you walk out of here unharmed? No matter what happens to me, you will all be dead before you leave my land."

"They will let us go if I take a hostage." He leered at Pippa. "Unless that hostage decides to use her powers to save herself."

In front of independent witnesses. She was beginning to understand the depth of her uncle's cunning.

"I'll kill you," Ash snarled.

"Ash," Pippa warned, "you do your part and I'll do mine." She turned to Simon. She couldn't bear to watch the fight. Her nerves were strung out like tight lute strings and watching Ash only pulled them tighter. "Don't you think I would have used magic by now if I possessed any?"

"Don't take me for a fool, girl. I've *seen* you."

Behind her, steel chinked against steel, interspersed with grunts, some from Ash. She had to look around.

He stood in the center of the room, surrounded. With a coordinated move, all three men lunged at him, knocking his blade from his hand as he swiftly ducked and rolled. He swore and picked up one of the wooden, straight-backed chairs near the fireplace. The embroidered cushion flew off as he smashed the chair over one man's head. The thug staggered to his knees and Ash kicked him in the face, knocking him back onto the rushes. He didn't get up.

With a rueful smile, Ash jumped on another chair and grabbed the fire tongs. He wielded it as if it were as light as his rapier. He struck one man around the ear, sending him stumbling into Pippa. She stepped neatly aside, picked up a silver candelabra and hit him. She looked to Ash. He grinned. She grinned back, almost enjoying herself.

The third man, Stoner, seemed to hesitate now that he was on his own. He quickly rallied, however, when Simon shouted abuse and swiped his rapier at Ash's knees. Ash jumped over the blade and landed back on the floor with graceful ease. Lightning-fast, he grabbed a sword lying forgotten on the rushes and slashed at his opponent. Blood gushed from Stoner's stomach. Eyes wide with shock, he crumpled to the floor.

Pippa moved to go to Ash but blinding pain suddenly smashed through her skull. She stumbled, was caught roughly.

Simon.

She struggled but might as well have been a snowflake fighting against a blizzard.

Ash yelled. Ran across the room. But stopped when Simon produced a knife and rammed it against her throat.

Men charged into the parlor. Ash's men. They must have heard him shouting. She registered it all but couldn't think clearly, couldn't formulate a plan. She could barely stand, barely hold her aching head up.

"Ash," she murmured through the pain splitting her head open.

"Let her go," Ash snarled. He was white with rage and fear. She could see the two emotions warring inside him, see them eat at him, destroying the cold fighting machine he'd been. He swiped at the sweat beading on his brow before it dripped into his eyes. "My men will not let you leave alive if you harm her."

"And if I don't harm her?" Simon said. "If I take her with me? What will your men do then?"

Pippa blinked, warding off the tiredness threatening to cloud her mind. She would be no one's hostage, least of all his. She struggled but he held her too tightly and she was weakened by the blow.

"No," Ash said to her. "Don't do it." It was a warning not to use her powers.

If she didn't, Simon would take her. He would win. On the other hand, if she did use her witchcraft, he would still win—too many witnesses. All the thinking hurt her head. She fought against the need to close her eyes and sleep.

*Concentrate!*

Would Ash's men be reliable witnesses against her? Perhaps they would do whatever their master wanted. They seemed to like him. She hoped they loved him enough to set aside their fear of witches.

She stilled her body and heart then summoned her inner strength. She concentrated on pushing Simon away from her, getting his filthy hands off her.

Nothing happened.

She focused again, pictured her uncle being flung across the room. Again nothing. The blow must have weakened her powers. Her witchcraft had abandoned her.

No! Not now.

"Well?" It was Simon's voice in her ear. "Aren't you going to do something?"

She closed her eyes. Hopeless.

Simon's grip tightened and the blade cut into her skin. "Do it!" he hissed.

"I can't," she whispered, as much to Ash as to her uncle. Her gaze met Ash's across the room. He was so close. So very close and yet she couldn't touch him.

Ash rubbed a hand through his hair and swore loudly. He must be frustrated. He could do nothing except watch.

"I've seen you," Simon said in her ear. "Do it! Do it, damn you! Show them. Show *him*." She turned her head a little to the side and saw the Witch Hunter standing with Ash's men. He didn't move to intervene but he was watching events with interest.

"I can't," she said again. "I'm not a witch."

"No? So you won't be able to stop this?" His blade bit into her flesh.

She screamed. This wasn't supposed to happen! She wasn't supposed to find her true love then die in front of him at the hands of her greedy uncle!

The blade stopped. It had broken skin but only just. Blood trickled down her throat into the small ruff at her collar. Trickled not gushed.

"Wh, what?" Simon grunted.

It took Pippa a moment to realize he was using all his strength to push against the knife. She was holding it off with what little she had left in her. Her powers hadn't completely deserted her but they were greatly depleted. She couldn't keep even this simple task up for much longer.

She looked to Ash. No words passed between them but he seemed to know what was happening. He lunged. Her uncle was too intent on Pippa and never saw the sword coming. Ash thrust it through Simon's throat. He gurgled and fell to the floor.

"He couldn't kill his own niece," Ash said to no one in particular but Pippa knew it was aimed directly at the Witch Hunter. With luck, no one would have noticed that Pippa had used her powers to stay her uncle's knife.

She didn't get to see Sir Guy's reaction because Ash pulled her into a fierce embrace that knocked all the air out of her. He pressed her face against his chest and checked the wound at her throat. It must not have been too deep because he heaved a sigh and she felt him relax. Gratefully, she allowed him to hold her, allowed all her fear to be absorbed by his strength.

"I'll vouch that you killed him to defend your bride," Sir Guy said, sounding close.

"You will," Ash agreed. He kissed the top of Pippa's head and she snuggled into him, breathing in the scent of sweat and man. Her man. He steered her out past on-lookers who would no doubt take care of the scene. She didn't know where he was taking her until she was in her own rooms, the door closed behind them. Safe.

"Thank God," Ash murmured into her hair. His breathing

quickened, became ragged. He held her tighter as if to satisfy himself that she was solid, alive. "Pippa—"

She didn't let him finish. She just wanted to kiss him. They were both alive and nothing would come between them again. She took his face between her hands and pulled him down so she could have her fill of him.

Ash couldn't believe Pippa was kissing him. He'd nearly lost her. The agony of those moments watching Rowe's blade at her throat, praying he wouldn't twitch. He'd suspected she was weakened by the blow to her head, but had not known it would affect her powers. She must have used her last reserves to hold the knife off.

He clutched her to him, not wanting to break the kiss but wanting to reassure her. It was all over. She was his. She must be since she was kissing him with a desperation that matched his own.

He'd thought her lost to him, thought she didn't love him. He still didn't fully understand what games she'd been playing but he didn't care. She was alive and she was going to marry him, out of love not for security or convenience.

At least he thought so. He pulled back, breaking the kiss, and studied her. "Let me see if I understand this," he said, holding her shoulders so he could watch her. He wanted to be absolutely sure of her answer. "You're going to marry me now?"

She grinned. "Yes. It seems like the right thing to do since I love you and you've already ravished me twice."

He smiled back, an uncertain, one-sided smile. "You love me?"

She kissed him lightly on the lips before saying, "Yes! Isn't it obvious?"

"Er, no. You *said* you didn't—"

"Forget what I said. Actions speak louder than words."

They did? Very well. He stopped talking and kissed her again. She obliged by offering up her mouth and melting into him. It felt amazing, but it wasn't enough. He fumbled with her skirts and finally found the skin of her thigh underneath. "I think I prefer you in skirts and bodice. One can be easily pulled down and the other pushed up. Very convenient."

"Men's clothes offer interesting possibilities too," she said. "After all, I can do this." Her fingers rubbed his crotch through his breeches and he groaned into her mouth.

All too suddenly, she removed her hand and he groaned again, but with disappointment. "We shouldn't be doing this," she said.

"You're not going to make me wait until we're married, are you?"

"Perhaps I will."

He caught her hips and pulled her back against his body. "Cruel woman."

"Indeed," she said. "Now, I'm going to freshen up while you be the master of the house for a while."

He sighed. She was right. He had a duty to perform. His servants needed to be spoken to, orders given. The south parlor must be spotless before his mother's return. Then he must prepare what he'd say to them all regarding the loss of the earldom.

He lightly kissed her. "I'll have hot water sent up. Soak while you wait for me."

"Don't forget to speak to your sister," Pippa said, touching his lip with her fingertip. It was all he could do not to suck on it.

"Doubtless she already knows that someone died in the south parlor," he said.

"I mean about her parentage. I overheard what Briars told you and the countess."

He'd forgotten about that. Annie had a right to know about her own parentage. It would be a blow coming on top of everything else. Perhaps she already suspected the countess wasn't her mother but she would hardly know Fallon was her father. It was time she did, and Ash was the best person to tell her. He didn't think his mother would do a very sympathetic job.

His mother. Strange that he still thought of her as that, even after everything he'd learned. She may not have given birth to him and she certainly hadn't shown much maternal love as a child (certainly less than Georgiana) but she was still his mother. She loved him in her own way, and he had to admit he loved her. Hopefully Annie would come to the same conclusion.

"She's not going to like it," he said. "My sister thinks it's her God-given right to spend my money. She's about to find out it's not even her birth right."

"Then you need to convince her that nothing will change. The earldom may be lost to our family but she can still spend as much money as she wants. Between the two of us, we have a fortune."

*Our* family. Those were Pippa's words. He smiled and kissed her again because he simply couldn't help it. She was irresistible, even when covered in blood.

"Do you think you can put up with this simple gentleman for the rest of your life?" he said. "Even after what I did to you?"

She placed a finger over his lips. "You may be a simple gentleman now but you're all mine. Now kiss me again because it's the last time until we are wed."

Of course he had to oblige. He would never be able to deny Pippa anything.

# EPILOGUE

1 month later

*A*s Lady Ashbourne, Pippa would have been summoned to court immediately upon her marriage. However as the wife of Richard Savoy, gentleman, it was a full month before she was introduced to the queen. Accompanied by her new husband, sister and mother-in-law, she pretended she wasn't nervous when they passed the dour guards at the gatehouse. Or when they entered room upon room of furnishings so rich they hurt her eyes. Or even when the conversations suddenly stopped as courtiers turned and stared at them in the presence chamber.

No, it wasn't until the queen herself addressed her in the relative privacy of the royal privy chamber that Pippa admitted her nervousness. Her stomach had fallen into her pretty new slippers.

"You must be Mistress Savoy," the queen said, holding out a hand covered with more rings than Ash's mother wore.

Already kneeling, Pippa bowed over the rings and said something that she later couldn't recall. It must have been suitable because the queen bade them all to sit. Her six ladies hovered nearby, embroidering or staring out the window, probably pretending they couldn't hear a word.

"My dear friend," the queen said to Lady Ashbourne, "what a trial these past few weeks must have been on your poor nerves."

"My nerves are all the stronger for the trial, Madam," the countess said with a level gaze. "I thank you for your concern."

"And your daughter?" the queen asked as if Annie weren't even there. "The death of her betrothed would have been a blow to your family."

Out of the corner of her eye, Pippa saw Annie stiffen. No one had mentioned Briars in her presence since his death, and for all Pippa knew, her sister-in-law had quite forgotten him.

"Not as much as Your Grace would suggest," Lady Ashbourne said. "And certainly not as much as the loss of the earldom."

Everyone in the room drew in a collective breath except Ash, sitting beside Pippa, who let out a soft moan. It was a most presumptuous thing to say, even for a woman reported to be one of the queen's closest companions.

But then the queen threw back her head without a concern for the jewels precariously twined through its auburn threads and laughed with uproarious abandon. Not a single person joined in but she didn't seem to care.

"My dearest friend," the queen said, clutching the countess's hands in both of hers in a clash of rings, "these sordid events haven't changed you in the least. Your son may have lost the title but you haven't lost your heart of pure steel." She settled back in her chair and regarded the countess. "We are much alike, you and I, much alike." Her amusement faded and her blue-gray eyes narrowed. "That is why I can't abide to see your family suffer like this."

Suffer? Pippa had never been happier in her life. When Ash wasn't trying to couple with her in every room of the house, they took long rides or walks so she could explore her new surroundings. If he was busy then Annie introduced her to her favorite shops and friends, and made her attend as many balls as Pippa's poor feet could stand. It seemed the family's recent scandals made them highly sought-after guests.

The queen lifted a finger and her gentleman usher handed her a document. She handed it to Ash in turn. "We bestow upon you the Barony of Asheldean." She grinned and leaned forward as if to share a joke. "We simply couldn't bear to stop calling you Ash."

Ash dropped to his knees and bent low over her hand. "You do me a great honor, Your Grace. Your generosity is as boundless as your beauty."

To Pippa's immense surprise, the queen snorted. "A gallant attempt at flattery, my lord Asheldean, but I see marriage hasn't silvered that rough tongue of yours completely. Let's pray it never does as I appreciate your bluntness. Lord knows more of it is needed in these gilded halls."

Ash laughed low in his throat, and the queen waved him back into his seat.

"We'll perform the official ceremonies later," she said, "however as this charter stipulates, the estate of Asheldean is in a fertile valley in Shropshire. The manor house is in need of some care but I trust you will find it adequate."

"Madam, my wife and I are eternally grateful," Ash said.

"Then it's all settled." She held out her hand once more. "Please call upon us again Ash, Lady Asheldean." Pippa, Ash and Annie rose, bowed over the rings and backed out of the privy chamber. When the countess made to follow, the queen's hand touched her arm. "Stay, Lady Ashbourne, and regale us with news. You always seem to know more of what goes on in this realm than my most trusted advisers." Her deep laugh was cut off by the closing of the heavy doors.

Pippa didn't mind the stares of the milling courtiers as she walked with Ash and Annie through the presence chamber. Ash stopped to talk to a group of men. He introduced her and made small talk, then they continued out into the courtyard.

It wasn't until she felt the warmth of the sun on her skin that Pippa began to breathe again.

"I can't believe it!" Annie squealed. "A barony. Baron Asheldean. It's not an earldom but it'll do. And we can still call you Ash." She jumped and threw her arms around her brother's neck, momentarily hanging off him like an autumn leaf on the end of a twig.

"I think that's the first time I've seen you smile in a month," Ash said, placing her to the side.

"I'm happy," Annie said, wiping away a tear. "A barony. We're peers again."

"*I'm* a peer again," Ash corrected her. "You're a spoiled little sister of a peer who hasn't learned a thing from recent events."

Her brow crinkled. "Learn? Learn what?"

"Leave her alone, Ash," Pippa said, smiling. "She's happy."

Ash scooped an arm around Pippa's waist and pulled her into his hard contours. "What about you? Are you happy?"

Her grin widened. "Blissfully."

Annie clicked her tongue. "You two have become nauseating. So," she said, changing her tone from mock disgust to childish excitement again, "what do you suppose the house is like at Asheldean? Probably not as big as Dewbury Hall, but we can improve it."

Pippa felt Ash shake with laughter but his face didn't show anything except complete serenity. "Expect it to be in great need of improvement," he said.

"Oh?" Pippa said. "You know of it?"

"No, but Her Majesty said it needed *some* care. She hasn't got the people and the privy council eating out of her hand because she doesn't know how to sell them unpleasantness when necessary. Asheldean is probably little more than a ruined keep."

"I don't care," Pippa said, snuggling into his side. "It'll be ours. When can we go see it?"

Ash kissed the top of her head. "We can leave within the week. Two of your estates are on the way—we can check on those too if you like. Will you come, Sis?"

Annie clapped her hands. "Of course!" She stopped and Pippa would have collided into her if Ash hadn't steered her aside at the last moment. "Oh no, I promised Fallon I'd travel with him to Haverford. He wants to see where Georgiana is buried. We both do," she said quietly. "Do you mind if I join you later? I'm sure Mother won't want to come. She adores London too much. Oh, there's Susannah de Morton and her brother." She waved at a young couple walking towards them. "He does have a fine leg, don't you think Pippa?"

"Er, yes, a nicely shaped calf," Pippa said, although the legs in question were too far away to be shapely or otherwise.

Annie hurried on to meet the de Morton siblings. "I thought she'd never go," Ash said. He bent and licked Pippa's ear.

She swatted him away, giggling. "It seems your sister *has* learnt a thing or two."

"Hmmm?" he murmured into her hair.

"Fallon... Haverford..." His soft lips trailed kisses to her earlobe and she sighed. "Never mind."

"Speaking of learning something," Ash whispered, pulling away a little, "there's something I want to teach you."

"It involves me being naked, doesn't it?"

Mischief danced in his eyes. "Of course. All the best lessons occur without clothes."

"As long as you're naked as well."

One corner of his mouth lifted. "That's not entirely necessary to my plan."

"I find it very necessary to mine." She pulled his head down and kissed him firmly. "And I might remind you, resistance is futile." She wiggled her fingers at him.

He raised the eyebrow with the scar cutting through it. "Seems I'll have to submit then."

Pippa reached up to kiss him again when she heard Annie's laughter floating towards them on the breeze. "Oh dear! I just realized something."

"What?"

"Annie is Georgiana's daughter."

"So?"

"Georgiana had powers. Powers that are inherited through the female line."

"Oh no." Ash stared after his sister who was laughing at something the de Morton youth said. "As if she wasn't a handful already."

**Did you like the two Witch Born novels?**
Then you'll love the ASSASSINS GUILD. Read on for an excerpt
of THE CHARMER, the first book in the Assassins Guild series
which is now available.

# THE CHARMER: AN EXCERPT

## About THE CHARMER

He was the last man she needed, but the only one she wanted.

Orlando Holt has never assassinated a woman before. The lovely, feisty Lady Lynden will be his first. She's supposed to be a vicious murderess, but when Orlando begins to have doubts, he sets out to discover the identity of the person who hired him. What he learns will turn his world upside down, and propel him headlong into love with a woman who's immune to his charms.

Twice widowed by the age of twenty-four, Lady Susanna Lynden has had enough of charming men. Her last husband knew all the right things to say to get her to the marriage bed... then made her life miserable. Money may be scarce and her house falling down around her, but the exotic fruit from her orange trees will keep poverty away. Except someone is thwarting her at every turn. Someone who may even want her dead.

## CHAPTER 1

*Hampshire, November 1598*

Orlando Holt had never killed a woman before. He'd assassinated a bear tamer, a viscount, three French noblemen and two Spanish ones, a knight, a painter, a physician, an acrobat in Cathay, and five apothecaries. He had nothing against apothecaries, but he'd come across a disproportionate number during his three-year tenure in Lord Oxley's Assassins Guild. All the apothecaries, and every other target, had been men and thoroughly deserving of the Guild's justice.

Lady Lynden would be his first woman.

He watched her from his hiding place behind a yew bush, the only shrubbery in the walled garden with enough leaves to hide him. Aside from the dozen densely foliated trees lined up against the brick wall where Lady Lynden worked, most of the garden was bare. A few rust-red leaves clung stubbornly to the roses and other shrubs here or there, but they were rare. In contrast, the green leaves of the dozen trees seemed lush and vibrant, and quite out of place amid the autumnal landscape. Unfortunately, he was too far away to use them as cover. Thank God for the yew.

That was the problem with autumn. It was better than winter for shadowing a potential target—less chance of freezing his balls off—but the warmer months offered more places to hide. If he were really lucky, village women would shed their clothing in the summer and paddle in a nearby stream when they did the washing.

He didn't think Lady Lynden would go in search of the nearest body of water and take a dip in her underthings. She was a she-man, as his brother used to call women who wore masculine clothes or liked to do a man's work. Orlando couldn't see Lady Lynden's face from where he squatted, but he noticed the loose calf-length farmer's trousers, the woolen jerkin, and the wide-brimmed farmer's hat, all in dark colors for mourning. She'd rolled the sleeves of her shirt up to the elbows, revealing tanned forearms, and by the way she dragged around a large pail filled with what looked to be soil, he knew she was no delicate flower used to a life of embroidery.

Yet Lady Lynden was a noblewoman. According to Hughe, she was the widow of a baron who had returned home to live in the manor owned by her country gentleman father. She wasn't supposed to be this she-man doing heavy garden work. He knew it was Susanna Lynden because Hughe's client had said she'd be working in the walled garden at Stoneleigh without the aid of a gardener or other servants.

She straightened suddenly and looked around as if she could sense him watching. But he was too well hidden, despite crouching no more than a few feet from her. She sighed and removed her gardening gloves and hat.

Orlando almost overbalanced in surprise. He took it all back. Lady Lynden was no she-man. She was a beauty. Hair of the fairest gold, braided and pinned to her head, creamy skin, an oval face with delicate features, and large eyes. He couldn't see their color from where he hid, but he'd wager they were blue to go with her pale hair and skin. Where her forearms were brown, her face was as English as the queen's.

Yet a description of her individual parts didn't do her justice. She was extraordinary. Her face captivated him, rooting his feet to the muddy earth, and he couldn't stop staring. It had been a long time since he'd seen a woman as achingly beautiful as Lady Lynden, yet here she was in a Hampshire backwater dragging pails of earth around, dressed in men's clothes.

And he was supposed to kill her.

He passed a finger over his upper lip just as his target wiped the back of her hand across her forehead. She glanced around then pressed her hands to the small of her back and rubbed. So the hard work was not to her liking after all. What about the clothes? Did she dress like a man because she wanted to or because it was practical?

Orlando watched as she picked up a trowel and began digging through the dirt in the pail, turning it over. A few minutes later, while her back was turned, he crept quietly away through the ivy-clad arch and out of the walled garden.

He had never killed a woman before, and he wasn't about to start. Not without being absolutely certain she was the murderer Hughe's client claimed her to be. Hughe himself had said the job probably wouldn't be the quick in-and-out that Orlando preferred and that a thorough investigation was needed. That meant doing something Orlando had hoped to avoid, staying.

He raced to the nearby woods and retrieved his pack from the inside of a hollow log where he'd left it. He didn't need to change clothes and he wasn't hungry, having dined at the village inn before coming to Stoneleigh, so he slung the pack over his shoulder. A few minutes later, he was once more leaving the woods and heading for Stoneleigh. This time he didn't creep. He whistled. Loudly.

As expected, Lady Lynden came to the arch of the walled garden to investigate. "Lo?" she called out. "Who is it?"

"Madam, my humble apologies." He removed his hat and bowed low, sweeping the brim across the gravel path. "I didn't mean to startle you."

"You didn't startle me. I simply came to see who whistles out of tune near my garden." Her voice was like honeyed wine, sweet and thick, but with a hard, flat edge.

"Out of tune? Dear lady, you wound me."

She rolled her eyes, and he was pleased to see he'd been right. They were as blue as a bright summer sky.

"Why are you smiling at me like that?" she snapped, stamping one hand on her hip. The other was tucked behind her back.

"I can't help it. You're a vision of beauty, a balm for my travel-weary eyes."

She didn't blush or smile coyly or do any of the things ladies did when paid a compliment. She merely scowled, scrunching her pretty little nose up as if she found his words, or his presence, distasteful. "You do not put balm on eyes, young man, unless you wish to go blind."

"Young man? I suspect I am older than you." Lady Lynden was four and twenty and already a widow twice over. Orlando was four years her senior, yet he knew when he smiled his dimples gave him the appearance of youth. Those bloody dents in his cheeks were the object of much teasing ever since he'd reached manhood. The only consolation was that women of all ages seemed to take joy in them.

Lady Lynden revealed the hand previously hidden behind her back. It clutched a rather vicious-looking short-handled gardening fork. "I asked who you are," she said. "Answer me."

He held up his hands. His pack slipped down his arm and hung in the crook of his elbow. He wasn't in any danger from the shrew. She might be stronger than the average woman thanks to her gardening, but he was larger and had been trained by Hughe. Women were no match for him.

"Orlando Holt at your service." He bowed again. When he straightened, she was still scowling. It didn't make her any less beautiful. "I was hoping you could give me work, madam."

She lowered her weapon and her stance relaxed. "No, I'm sorry, Mr. Holt. There's no work available here. Try up at Sutton Hall over the fields." There was no flutter of her lashes or wistfulness in her voice when she spoke of her previous home. She had given it up and moved back to her father's neighboring house of Stoneleigh when her second husband died and Sutton Hall had passed to his heir, a cousin. That had been a year ago and she was still at Stoneleigh and still unwed. Orlando wondered when her father would find her husband number three.

"I was at Sutton Hall earlier," he said. "There's no work for me there either." He held his breath. Waited. But his lie seemed to slip by unnoticed. She merely shrugged and turned to go. "Wait!" He caught her arm but dropped it when she tried to jerk herself free with such force that he probably bruised her. He cursed under his breath. He hadn't let go when he should have. Instinct had made him hang on. Instinct and training.

Lady Lynden's eyes narrowed, and if it wasn't for the slight tremble of her hands, he would have thought her unafraid. "I told you. There's no work here."

He nodded at her garden fork. "Then why is the lady of the house doing men's work and dressed in men's clothes?"

"Who says I'm the lady of the house?"

He liked the way she tilted her pointy little chin and the way anger made her eyes grow darker, like the Mediterranean Sea in the late afternoon. He smiled again because he couldn't help himself. She was a shrew, and he enjoyed a challenge.

Pity she was a potential murderess and not a candidate for keeping him warm at night. Although there were no Guild rules stipulating the former precluded the latter, Orlando liked to think even he had enough moral conviction to stay out of her bed.

"You speak like a lady," Orlando said, hefting his pack up onto his shoulder, "walk like a lady and have the bearing of a lady. In my book, if a rose looks and smells like a rose, it probably is a rose."

One side of her mouth lifted in a sardonic smile. "In that case..." She pointed the fork at his face and scanned it down his length to his muddy boots. "You look like a vagrant..." She sniffed the air and pulled a face. "...and smell like a vagrant."

He sniffed his armpit. The stink wasn't *that* bad considering he'd been traveling for three days. "I am not a vagrant. I am, however, in need of good, honest work. Garden work," he added. "I'm a gardener."

She raised both brows. "Really?"

He nodded. "I was most recently employed at Collier Dean, a grand house in Sussex. You've probably heard of it."

"I haven't. Do you have a letter of recommendation?"

"No, alas. I didn't think to get one before I left."

"That was foolish."

"What can I say? I'm a fool." He grinned and received a frown in return.

"Why did you leave?"

"I'm traveling to Salisbury to visit my sister."

"You're from Salisbury? That explains the accent."

His accent was a London one, but she seemed to know no better and he saw no reason to enlighten her. "I thought it time I visited her, but I ran out of money. I used my last coins dining at The Plough in the village." Lie upon lie upon lie, all smoothly spoken. He was an expert at them, as were all the members of Hughe's band, past and present. It was vital for survival to be able to act in any role at any moment with no preparation.

"What type of garden work did you do at Collier Dean?"

"Digging, weeding, pruning." What else did gardeners do? There wasn't much call for it working in the Assassins Guild or at his family's London house. They had a small garden to service their kitchen, but it consisted of a few herbs and such. Certainly nothing like the exotic trees he'd seen backed up against her garden wall. He shrugged. "Whatever was required of me."

"You weren't head gardener then?"

"Head, body, hands and feet." She didn't even crack a smile, so he forged on. "I was under the direction of the lady of the house, a keen gardener like you, madam."

"Did she grow oranges?"

"What?"

"Oranges. Did she grow them?"

"Uh, no." Only a madman would try to grow oranges in England. They were a fruit more suited to warmer climes like Spain. Surely they weren't the trees he saw in her garden. Why would she want to grow them when she could have perfectly good English fruit trees like cherry or apple?

"Then you are of no use to me," she said. "Not that I need a gardener."

He thought it best to keep his mouth shut. Lady Lynden didn't look like she would appreciate him pointing out that her hands were covered in hard calluses and she had dirt smudged on her forehead, or that the pails of soil looked much too heavy for her to drag around. This last he could not admit to having witnessed anyway.

"I'm very busy. Good day, Mr. Holt." She marched off, giving him a fine view of her shapely calves. When she reached the far wall and the dark green leafy trees, she turned around. A flicker of either surprise or irritation crossed her face before she waved him off, as imperial as any queen. "Try Cowdrey Farm," she called back. "It's quite a walk to the west, but Farmer Cowdrey will have work for a strong lad like yourself."

"I'm eight and twenty, not a lad. And I'm a gardener, not a farmer, but thanks anyway."

She turned her back to him once more but not before he heard her muttering, "Beggars can't be choosers."

"I'm not a beggar either. Or a vagrant." *I'm an assassin. And a bloody good one.*

He trudged back along the gravel drive to the road leading into the village. Lady Lynden might have been the most beautiful woman Orlando had ever seen, but she was as prickly as a hawthorn. Ordinarily he would avoid shrews like her but not this time. He had to thoroughly investigate the claims against her and if she were guilty, then he would have to assassinate her.

Women who went about murdering their husbands could not be allowed to escape justice.

* * *

Susanna Lynden sat on the ground under her largest orange tree and watched the retreating back of Orlando Holt through the garden arch. It was a broad back attached to the sort of shoulders that would be useful for hoeing garden beds and for sinking one's teeth into if she felt so inclined. Which she absolutely did not. She was not ready to take a lover, and she suspected Orlando Holt would make a terrible one anyway, or terrible for *her* at least. Too handsome for his own good and certainly too charming. Men like him never stayed true to their women, and she'd had enough of straying men.

Good lord, she must have been lonelier than she thought. She'd met Holt only briefly, yet her mind had stripped him naked. Perhaps it was time she got a lover. How did a gentle-woman go about obtaining one? Nail a handbill to the post outside The Plough announcing the vacancy? She threw her head back and laughed, startling a yellow butterfly perched on a leaf.

No, there would be no lover for her, or a gardener. Not even a laborer. Pity, because Holt would have been perfect with his experience and his size. She'd be lucky if she could afford the wages of the three servants they currently kept as well as food enough to feed them, her father and herself. The little money they had needed to stretch until she'd found a city shopkeeper to stock her marmalades and succades. Finding someone was taking longer than she expected.

She drove her fork into the soft earth and pushed herself to her feet. Her head touched one of the low-hanging green oranges, and she ducked out from under the canopy. She slapped on her hat and stood back to survey her oldest and strongest tree. Its leaves were a healthy green and the fruits almost the same color. They would turn orange soon and need protecting from the winter. Already the air felt chilly even when the sun was out.

How cold would it get this year? She'd only lost one tree last winter, but the others had dropped most of their fruit. She hadn't been able to give them the full attention they needed while living up at the Hall, and her father hadn't the strength to do what was necessary to protect all of them from frost. This year she'd wanted to try a new housing technique for ensuring their safe wintering, but time was growing short along with the days, and there was still so much to be done. The temporary and somewhat flimsy shelter would have to do for now.

She picked up her pruning knife and lopped off the straggling branches to make it easier to cover the trees. It grew more and more difficult to reach the higher ones, and soon her arms and neck ached. She removed her gloves and massaged her shoulder.

"Those trousers really don't suit you, Susanna."

She ground her back teeth together then turned around with what she hoped was a genteel smile on her face for her late husband's cousin. She had to remind herself that he meant well, but it didn't make his stupidity any less, well, stupid. "I find skirts too restricting in the garden."

Jeffrey—Lord Lynden—squinted and stretched his neck. With the high collar and his chin resting on the stiff ruff, his neck appeared unnaturally long. "Is that dirt on your forehead?"

"Probably. I find I can't escape the stuff out here."

"I suppose not." He indicated the pruning knife. "What are you doing with that?"

"Pruning."

"And what's in the pails?"

"Dung from Cowdrey Farm's cows mixed with soil."

He pulled a face. "It looks like hard work."

"I can manage, and I enjoy being out here with my orange trees." It was true, she did like gardening, but she could certainly use some help. Not that she would tell Jeffrey she couldn't afford a laborer. Any mention of money, or her lack of it, would only bring up the topic of her marrying again, something she wished to avoid. With Farmer Cowdrey having asked her countless times already, she was becoming an expert in avoiding the subject altogether. And avoid it she must. Two disastrous marriages had proved to her it wasn't a state she wanted to enter into again, ever.

"I can provide one of my gardeners to help you if you like," Jeffrey said.

He'd never offered her staff before. Considering he loathed spending money on things that didn't directly improve his own estate, it was quite a generous offer. What did he want in return? "Thank you, but I can manage."

He regarded her closely, still frowning. Jeffrey was always frowning it seemed, so unlike her late husband, his older cousin. Phillip had been dark-haired and silver-tongued, a combination that meant everyone liked him, particularly women. Jeffrey was more serious, hardly ever laughing with abandon as Phillip used to do, and flirting wasn't an art he'd mastered. Most of the village women crossed the road to avoid speaking with him.

Susanna knelt down on the ground and dug through the fertile mix of dung and earth in the pail.

"That reeks," Jeffrey said. "Must you do it now?"

"I have to put it around the trees."

"This moment?"

"I can think of no better one." She stood and eyed the nearest tree several feet away. Her lower back ached just thinking about moving the pail and digging through the dung and soil. "Would you mind dragging the pail over there?"

"Me?"

She turned to look at him and almost burst out laughing. He had his wrist pressed to his nose, the white lace cuff trailing over his mouth and chin like a snowy beard. "I see no one else here."

Half his face may have been covered, but it didn't hide the disgust in his eyes. "This is why you need a man to help you."

She refrained, just, from pointing out that he was a man.

"What about your servants?" he went on. "Can't one of them help?"

"They're busy and too aged for this type of work in addition to their usual duties."

"You should replace them with more able-bodied ones." He took a step back and she sighed. It seemed Jeffrey was like his cousin in one respect. Neither liked to get their soft, white hands dirty.

"Jeffrey, why have you come here?"

"To offer you the use of one of my men for your garden."

He'd come just for that? Surely not. "No, thank you."

"You won't need to pay me."

"No."

"But you can't do this on your own! Look at you. Your knees are dirty and your skin is brown!" He sniffed. "And that smell. It's disgusting and unseemly. A woman of your station should be inside sewing, not mucking about in filth. Admit it, Susanna, you're in over your head with those orange trees. I don't know why you care about them so much. They take up all your time since you came back here. You should have left them to die after your mother's passing." He must have known he'd over-stepped because he had the decency to flush and look away. He knew how much Susanna had loved her mother. The trees were her legacy. She would not let them wither.

"Thank you for your concern," she said carefully lest the wave of emotion washing through her burst out. "But I do not want your help."

He pursed his thin lips so that they disappeared entirely. "Susanna," he finally said on a sigh. "Why do you thwart me so when all I want is to care for you? As my cousin, it's the least I can do. Allow my man to help." His gaze darted away and wandered around the garden, avoiding her. "He's new to my employ but trustworthy. And very strong, very capable. He'll do whatever you ask of him. I highly recommend him to you."

Why was he insisting? What could possibly be in it for Jeffrey? He wasn't a terrible person, but he never did anything out of the goodness of his heart. If it had been anyone else, she would have thought he was trying to woo her, but being her cousin by marriage meant a union between them was unthinkable as well as illegal. Perhaps he needed her to act as lady of Sutton Hall for some important visitors.

Like his cousin before him, Jeffrey planned on putting Sutton

Hall on the map, or at least the map used by the nobility with influence at court. Being a baron wasn't enough for Jeffrey. He wanted to be *noticed*, and that meant having the right people visit and ensuring they were entertained during their stay. Phillip had been a natural host, charming and witty, attentive but not sycophantic. Jeffrey would have a more difficult time of it. He plodded through conversations, failing to grasp subtle changes in moods or clever retorts. He needed a friend to guide him through prickly political and social situations with high ranking guests, which was why Susanna would be a terrible hostess. She'd learned from her two marriages that being the perfect gentleman's wife didn't come easily to her. She preferred her garden to the ballroom and tending the orange trees to indulging the whims of fat noblemen.

"Susanna, please, I insist. I beg of you to accept my offer to help."

Insist? Beg? Rather strong words for a simple offer. She shook her head and grabbed the edges of the pail and dragged it along the path.

"Whoa, mistress, stop," a vaguely familiar voice said from behind her. Before she could turn around, big brown hands grasped the pail and lifted it. Lifted it! She looked up, straight into the blue eyes of Orlando Holt.

"Where do you want it?" He gave her a smile and a dimple appeared in each cheek. Now that he was closer she could see that he was indeed older than she first thought. Those dimples made him look impish, as if he'd been caught stealing from a plate of sweetmeats. She had the ridiculous urge to press her smallest finger into them.

"Lady Lynden?" he prompted. His smile widened. The man knew what she was thinking. She was certain of it. Curse him.

"Over there," she said, pointing to the nearest tree. She watched as he carried the full pail to the tree. He wore only a jerkin over his shirt, like her, but where her clothes were big and loose, his jerkin stretched tautly over his shoulders and across his back.

"Who is that?" Jeffrey said, coming up beside her. "A new servant?"

"A vagrant," she said and bit back a laugh. Holt had emphatically argued with her over the point only a little while ago. She couldn't deny sparring with him had made her feel more alive than she had felt in months. Odd how such a simple exchange with a stranger could do that. She must have been more desperate than she thought for witty company. It certainly wasn't the handsome and charming male company she missed— she'd had enough of that from her two husbands to last a lifetime.

"My name is Orlando Holt," Holt said, rejoining them. A few strands of his blond hair had flopped over his forehead but otherwise he showed no signs of exertion. He nodded at Jeffrey in greeting. "I'm a servant here."

"You most certainly are not!" she snapped.

He grinned again. Good lord, did he ever *not* smile? "I am. Mr. Farley has added me to his staff."

"You spoke to my father after I told you to leave?" The insolent, devious...*vagrant*! "Go back inside and tell him you'll not accept his offer." When he didn't move, she took a step closer, but that was a mistake because it only emphasized how much bigger than her he was. She came up to the middle of his chest.

"I have offered my services and your father has agreed to my terms," he said, his eyes sparkling with humor. "He is the master of Stoneleigh, is he not?" It wasn't a question that required an answer. The slippery eel knew that. "Besides, I need the work." He held up his hand to stop her, as if he were the master and she the servant. She was so shocked she didn't know what to say. "Cowdrey Farm is too far away and I'm a gardener, not a farm hand."

"Ha!" she managed, annoyed that he'd predicted her argument.

He forked an eyebrow at her and looked like he would say something more, but Jeffrey spoke first. "You should have come to Sutton Hall. There is plenty of gardening work."

"There is?" It was her turn to lift a questioning brow. Holt kept on smiling, not in the least disturbed that he'd been caught out in his earlier lie. Had he been to Sutton Hall at all? He said nothing and she turned to Jeffrey. She could only confront one liar at a time. "Then why were you offering me one of your gardeners if there is so much to do up there?"

Jeffrey blushed to the roots of his bright hair. "Uh...I... "

"So you are the master of Sutton Hall?" Holt asked when Jeffrey failed to complete his sentence.

Jeffrey adjusted his black velvet cloak so it draped more elegantly over his left shoulder, and thrust his chin out. "I'll ask the questions, not you. But I'll have you know that I am Lord Lynden. I am also Lady Lynden's cousin."

"By marriage," she added.

"And so it should be I who provides her with a man to help in the garden. Be off." Jeffrey flicked his long fingers toward the arch. "Tell Mr. Farley you've changed your mind and cannot work here. Susanna," he said, turning to her, "do not trust this stranger. His methods are underhanded and his manner impertinent. Take my man instead. Indeed, let me speak to your father this instant."

She caught Jeffrey's arm before he could move off. "Thank you, but there's no need to drag Father into this. Since he has already employed Mr. Holt here, I must accept. Thank you for your offer, it was kindly done." And insistently. Very. She was glad to be able to refuse without qualms. She didn't want to find out what strings Jeffrey had attached to his proposal.

"You're going to accept this vagrant?" he spluttered.

"I have no choice. Father is the master of Stoneleigh."

He stared wide-eyed at her. The yellow flecks in his eyes glinted in the afternoon sun that had finally wrestled the clouds aside. "I never thought to see you give in so easily, Susanna." He made a miffed sound through his nose, bowed perfunctorily, and walked out of the walled garden. She went to the arch and was relieved to see him gather up the reins of his horse and ride down the long drive to the road.

"So," Holt said, standing with his feet apart as if he'd planted himself there, "what do you want me to do next? We have some time before sunset."

"You, Mr. Holt," she said, pointing at him, "should not get too comfortable. I'm going to see my father and insist he withdraw his offer. You lied about asking for work up at Sutton Hall, did you not?"

"No lie, m'lady. The steward shooed me away. If he lied about the lack of work because he didn't want a stranger on the premises, I cannot be held to blame."

"Well, I refuse to have someone so ... so ... presumptuous working alongside me."

"Presumptuous? I simply saw a job that needed doing and offered my services to do it."

"Mr. Holt, perhaps it isn't clear to you, but we cannot pay you." She wasn't embarrassed to admit it. One glance at the partially patched-up house and the sorry state of the outbuildings would tell him money was scarce.

"I only require food and a roof over my head," he said. "Do you have a barn?"

"The roof leaks."

"The stables?"

"There's no room." It was filled with crates of jars and equipment for making their marmalades and succades. Silver needed her space along with the small cart and tack.

"A spare closet in the big house?"

"You get above yourself, Mr. Holt," she shot back over her shoulder as she passed under the arch.

His chuckle followed her all the way to the house.

**Now Available:**
THE CHARMER
The 1st book in the Assassins Guild series.

# A MESSAGE FROM THE AUTHOR

I hope you enjoyed reading this book as much as I enjoyed writing it. As an independent author, getting the word out about my book is vital to its success, so if you liked this book please consider telling your friends and writing a review at the store where you purchased it. If you would like to be contacted when I release a new book, subscribe to my newsletter at http:// cjarcher.com/contact-cj/newsletter/. You will only be contacted when I have a new book out.

# ALSO BY C.J. ARCHER

## SERIES WITH 2 OR MORE BOOKS

After The Rift

Glass and Steele

The Ministry of Curiosities Series

The Emily Chambers Spirit Medium Trilogy

The 1st Freak House Trilogy

The 2nd Freak House Trilogy

The 3rd Freak House Trilogy

The Assassins Guild Series

Lord Hawkesbury's Players Series

Witch Born

## SINGLE TITLES NOT IN A SERIES

Courting His Countess

Surrender

Redemption

The Mercenary's Price

# ABOUT THE AUTHOR

C.J. Archer has loved history and books for as long as she can remember and feels fortunate that she found a way to combine the two. She spent her early childhood in the dramatic beauty of outback Queensland, Australia, but now lives in suburban Melbourne with her husband, two children and a mischievous black & white cat named Coco.

Subscribe to C.J.'s newsletter through her website to be notified when she releases a new book, as well as get access to exclusive content and subscriber-only giveaways. Her website also contains up to date details on all her books: http:// cjarcher.com She loves to hear from readers. You can contact her through email cj@cjarcher.com or follow her on social media to get the latest updates on her books.

facebook.com/CJArcherAuthorPage

twitter.com/cj_archer

instagram.com/authorcjarcher

bookbub.com/authors/c-j-archer

Made in the USA
Columbia, SC
01 December 2019

84145903R00195